CUMBRIAN GHOST STORIES

WEIRD TALES FROM AN OLD LAND

TONY WALKER

Copyright © 2019 by Tony Walker

All rights reserved.

No part of this book may be reproduced in any form or by any electronic or mechanical means, including information storage and retrieval systems, without written permission from the author, except for the use of brief quotations in a book review.

❦ Created with Vellum

CONTENTS

Introduction	v
1. A West Cumbrian Coal Mine	1
2. The Woman of Wasdale	12
3. The Crier of Claife	28
4. The Little Man of Carlisle	46
5. The Hitcher	62
6. The Highest Inn in England	69
7. The Bewcastle Fairies	80
8. The Croglin Vampire	92
9. The Fortuneteller's Fate	104
10. Cross Fell	131
11. An Old School Revenant	143
12. The Orphan of Cartmel	158
13. The Demon Clock of Mosedale	178
14. A Grizedale Forest Wedding	213
15. The Derwentwater Haunting	255
16. The Mallerstang Boggle	275
Also by Tony Walker	289

INTRODUCTION

This is a collection of sixteen short stories in different styles set in different time periods set in our modern county of Cumbria, though the stories acknowledge that once what is now Cumbria was Cumberland, Westmorland, Lancashire North of the Sands and parts of North Yorkshire.

Some are traditional ghost stories, and some are more horror stories of the kind I used to read in the caravan at Allonby on school holidays. These would be The Demon Clock of Mosedale, The Fortuneteller's Fate and The Highest Inn in England.

As the collection grew, I began to become interested in using old stories for inspiration. The Little Man of Carlisle, the Bewcastle Fairies and the Mallerstang Boggle are based on actual folklore, though I have made them into pieces of fiction that bear little resemblance now.

The Grizedale Forest Wedding is a longer piece which is probably inspired by Angela Carter and The Company of Wolves.

I have tried to cover most of the county, but have left out some places inevitably. I was saying to my partner that I had been to every village in Cumbria but then I went to Little Urswick and the next day to Hethersgill, which I'd never been to before, so there is always still more to explore.

The Beast of Barrow and The Devil's Visit to Kirkby Lonsdale are at the planning stage!

I suppose my influences for these stories are three: classic M R James type ghost stories, H P Lovecraft style weird tales and Folk Horror.

I hope that both local Cumbrians and visitors will enjoy the stories and be able to link them to places they know and have visited.

Tony Walker
Maryport
September 2019

1

A WEST CUMBRIAN COAL MINE

John Bragg was a coal-miner. He was a friend of my grandfather William Fell. In the early 1960s, they worked at various pits around the West Cumberland coalfield, moving from one to another as they were closed down. There was a particular pit that he worked at near a village called Siddick on the coast. They've landscaped the area now and there's no trace that there was ever a mine there.

Miners are traditionally superstitious men. Their lives hang on a thread when they are underground. There are so many ways they can die — by earth as the rock collapses on them, by fire as a spark from their picks ignites the invisible fire-damp gas, by water as the sea breaks in and floods the galleries that run miles out under the sea, and finally by air — as the dreadful sucking gas known as choke-damp steals all their oxygen.

Some men would refrain from washing their whole back as they sat in the tin baths in front of the fire when they came home from work. They said that if your whole back got washed, that was inviting it to get broken — as if the bath water would wash its strength away so you couldn't withstand the falling rock.

They were all superstitious but John Bragg had a reputation for being the worst. He always took a scrap of blue silk with him when he went down the pit. It had belonged to his fiancée — Dorothy. They were due to get married but the Asian 'Flu took Dorothy. That was years ago, but he wanted no one else. The men he worked with were hard men, and they didn't tolerate weakness in others, but they never mocked John for his bit of silk. They knew how her death had affected him and they knew that even beyond the grave, he still loved her.

There was one gallery deep down in the mine that had a reputation for being haunted: The Lady's Gallery. I suppose that during it being worked men must have died down there but oddly, the reports of the ghost, such as they were, never referred to men. It wasn't dead miners that haunted the gallery but something different. Something that shouldn't ever be down a mine at all.

People used to avoid going down there unless they had a specific job. It was off the main thoroughfare — the long tunnel that they took on their way to the coalface way out under the sea. Even though it was out of the way, the Lady's Gallery was a handy place to store things - things like wheels for the bogeys that transported the coal, or bricks for building walls or any other structures that they might need underground, and general odds and ends that kept the mine ticking.

My grand-dad said that what scared the people who went to the Lady's Gallery were the odd noises. They said that the worst was the sound of rustling silk — as if someone was rubbing the material between their fingers: always behind you and always in the dark. As if it was standing there in the shadows, just outside where the light reached. As if it was watching you.

Most of the time, people forgot the thing in the Lady's Gallery. There was a job to do — the coal had to be hewn, and the sea kept out. However, there was an upsurge in interest in the story after one miner reported hearing it when he went to the Lady's Gallery. This man had a reputation as a bit of a clown and so no one took the story seriously. They thought it was just him trying to get some attention. No one took it seriously that is apart from John Bragg. The story of The Lady's Gallery seemed to obsess him. People didn't like to ask him why he was always talking about the story, because he seemed so eager and strange about it.

One time, my grandfather did ask him. He felt he knew him well enough to pull his leg about his fixation on the place, after all they had been boys together. But when William Fell asked him why he seemed able to think of nothing else, John Bragg just smiled a strange smile and said, "I know who it is."

"Who what is?" said William.

"Who it is that rustles the silk."

My grandfather half guessed, but asked anyway. "And who is it?"

John pulled the scrap of blue silk from his pocket where he always kept it and rubbed it between his fingers. "It's her; it's my Dorothy."

William thought he was half mad and changed the subject.

Then the next day, John tried to persuade him to go to The Lady's Gallery when they had finished their shift.

William said, "When I'm finished in the pit, I'm going home. I spend too many hours in the dark as it is."

John tried to persuade him. "If we just waited there, I'm sure we'd hear it."

"If we miss the end of our shift, we might have to wait a long time for the cage to come back below. I'd hate them to forget about us down here." He tried to force some humour, despite how uneasy he felt at seeing John's frantic, eager eyes.

John said, "But she's come here for me. I can't ignore her."

"Ignore who?" said my grandfather, exasperated.

"Dorothy. She's come here to talk to me."

My grandfather looked at him in silence. Could John really believe that his dead bride had returned from grave to meet him in the inky blackness of a coal mine, away from the bustle of the work, in a place so silent itself that the only sounds were men working miles away or the dripping of water from the roof?

"You can't be serious." he said finally.

John nodded. "I know in my heart, Bill. She comes and whispers to me at night; she tells me to come and meet her down there." And then he looked embarrassed, as if he'd just disclosed a terrible personal secret. All his hope was in his eyes — the hope of a man that death had cheated of love.

William felt sorry for him. He wanted to help him, but he knew that this was insane. Later, he said the most unnerving thing about it was that John was so serious; he truly believed that some dead woman was calling to meet her in that place without light, deep underground.

William shook his head. "I'm sorry, John, but I won't do it. It's not good for you to dwell on this."

Two weeks passed and then it so happened that William's son was ill. John Bragg should have been off work that day, but he volunteered to do an extra shift to cover William so that William could take his son for medical treatment. William knew he owed John a favour after that but he was wary about what he would ask him to do. At first John asked him nothing. Then, in a few days, when they were getting ready to go underground, John said, "I still want to go to the Lady's Gallery; will you come?"

William felt like saying that if John was so sure that it was Dorothy, why didn't he go on his own? But he couldn't leave the poor sick man to do that. He knew he should go with him to make sure he was all right and to bring him back up to the light when they proved that it was just his imagination — that Dorothy was dead like everyone else who'd passed away. For if William knew anything, it was that the dead do not return.

John asked again. "Please Bill. It would mean a lot to me.' He continued quietly, 'And you do owe me a favour."

William sighed and turned back to his gear, making sure everything was working and safe. But John persisted. "Will you come with me tomorrow, Bill? After we finish?"

William felt he had no alternative. "I will," he said, "but I can't see any good coming of it."

When William went back home that night and told his wife that he would be late the next day and why, she told him that John Bragg was a fool and that he was a bigger fool for agreeing to go with him.

She said, "I know it's sad that Dorothy died, but it's not healthy that he dwells on it. And you shouldn't be encouraging him by going there with him."

William groaned. "But I owe him a favour. He swapped shifts with me."

She said, "Your sense of honour will get you in trouble one day, William Fell."

So they went to work the next day, William and John and all the other miners. John was in high spirits. People commented on it as he worked. "You'd think he'd won the Derby," said one. "Either that, or he's got a woman lined up," said another. William kept quiet. He knew why John was so happy — he thought he was going to meet his dead love.

At the end of the long shift, they hung back as the rest of the men made their way along the tunnels, walking the three miles back to the elevators that would take them up to the surface. William had a strong sense of foreboding. They walked down the tunnel. It was so low in some places they had to stoop to avoid banging their heads.

In this tunnel, there was a long electric cable tacked on the ceiling from which dangled electric light bulbs. The rooms that lay off the main tunnel, such as the Lady's Gallery, were not lit. The only light in those rooms came when the miners entered and shone the battery-powered headlamps that they fastened to their hard hats, and the batteries only had a limited life. Enough to last through a shift and then a bit more. That was another reason that William was not keen to linger too long in the Lady's Gallery; he feared his light would die and then they would be in the impossible dark, a blackness so complete it was as if someone had snuffed the world out.

They were a long way behind the others now. And as they got closer to the Lady's Gallery, even John became quiet, as if his excitement had turned to apprehension. And finally, they stopped by the dark entrance to the man-made cave. "Here," said John.

"Aye," said William, "here." William saw his lamp flicker. "We need to be mindful of the life left in these batteries," he said. "We can't be here too long."

John turned to William, as if nervous, and said, "You have to wait with me, Bill. You promised."

They entered the Lady's Gallery and William sat himself down on a box that lay in the middle of the cavern. John just stood there.

"What now?" said William.

John shrugged. "Maybe we should switch off the lights? Maybe that will encourage her? She always was shy."

"Do you have any other form of light?" asked William.

John shook his head.

William grunted. "Luckily, I brought a candle and some matches. They're in my pack."

William started to search in his pack, while John sat on a big coil of rope. He looked expectantly into the dark tunnels that led off the Gallery. William got out his candle and his matches and set them to the side. He also had a flask of water which he sipped from then handed to John. John smiled and took it. Handing it back, he said, "She will come, you know. She loves me. She told me last night."

William regarded him with a sense of pity but also of fear because the man was clearly mad; what if she, Dorothy, it — a revenant — did come? He tried to distract himself. Beside the candles he placed an old-fashioned pocket watch. Old-fashioned, but it still told the time well. William gave their enterprise one hour, and then he was going for the cage.

He felt the weariness in his muscles after his hard physical labour and although his box was not a bed, and it was far from comfortable, as the silent minutes counted themselves round the watch face, he found his concentration fading and his head drooping and his eyes closing.

Then he heard it.

Something fluttering out of sight in the dark tunnel. William snapped awake, "What was that?" But he knew it was the sound of rubbing silk. He spun round to check John was still there.

John was standing up, a look of pure joy on his face. "It's her. I knew she'd come."

"Did you make that noise?" asked William.

"No, Bill. I told you. It's Dorothy."

William looked around him. The light in his headlamp battery was fading, and it hardly illuminated the Gallery at all. There was a silence, then he heard it again. The sound was coming just out the light — from one of the darker tunnels that lay beyond the Lady's Gallery. William stood up. He shouted, "Is there anyone there? Show yourself! Give up with your silly games!"

There was no reply.

John was smiling. "I just want her to show herself. Come on, Dorothy. It's me, John. Don't be shy."

William noticed that John's light too was faint.

"I'm going to light the candle," he said. He scrabbled with the match because his hands were shaking so much. But then he succeeded and the flickering yellow flame caught and grew. "Come on, John. Let's go. This is just someone playing a trick."

"No, Bill. It's Dorothy." And John called again into the darkness, calling for his shy love to show her face.

William put his hand on John's shoulder. "John," he said. "I'm as brave as any man, but this is getting the better of me. Let's make our way back to the main tunnel and then to the cage."

John shook his hand off. The sound of rustling silk came again. This time it was distinct. It was coming from the darkness in the tunnel that led away from the main workings of the mine.

"See, she's there," said John. He was pointing down the tunnel. "I saw a shape. Something moved."

"Your eyes are tricking you. Or it's someone playing a joke on us." But William knew none of his mates would have had the patience to wait for so long in a pitch-black tunnel. It was a lot more sinister than a joke.

"No, she's down there," said John. "Maybe she's too shy to come out and see me with you here."

"I'm not leaving you on your own."

"I'll be all right Bill. It's Dorothy. She loves me."

William felt fear rise in him and he struggled to keep it down. Then John's helmet lamp flickered and died. The diminution of the light brought the shadows crowding in on them. The darkness danced and moved as the single candle flame quavered in the faint drafts.

"What if it's not Dorothy, John? What if it's something else?" said William.

John shook his head. "Of course, it's Dorothy. Who else could it be? The silk is the sign. It's her a sign that she's coming for me."

Then William's head light died, and all it left them with was the light of the candle. He had some matches to re-light it, if the draft blew it out, but not many.

The darkness came very close and as if with that weakening of light; the sound came again, this time more insistent, closer and louder. Whereas before it had come and then was quiet, this time it was a frantic rustling. It no longer sounded like a woman's dress, but like something quite different — something wicked and old.

William took John's arm. "Come on. I don't mind admitting that this is unnerving me. Let's go now."

John shook himself free, angry now - annoyed at William's attempt to keep him from meeting this dead thing that stood, just out of sight in the annihilating blackness of the tunnel.

Without warning, he turned and ran into the dark. Down into the tunnel where the sound was; where whatever it was waiting for him.

And even William's courage failed. He could barely stay where he was. Every nerve urged him to turn and run, but he couldn't leave John in the dark. He shouted down the tunnel. He shouted for John to come back but his voice echoed unanswered down the black and vacant tunnels that stretched down into the centre of the earth, perhaps all the way to hell itself.

"John, where are you? The candle's nearly gone," he yelled. But there was no reply. He looked at the stump of the candle in its pool of wax. He had maybe ten minutes left. The watch told him they'd been there nearly two hours. He couldn't afford to stay much longer or he'd get lost there in the dark himself. And with no light, it would be free to come when it wanted.

William shouted again for John. And this time he thought he

heard something. He listened hard and shouted and listened again. And then he knew he had heard it — just behind him. Not in the tunnel where it was before, but standing behind him in a direction that cut him off from the way out to the cage. There was no doubt - it was the rustling of silk.

William picked up his pickaxe, and he shouldered his bag. When it was secure on his shoulder, he took the candle with its fluttering flame, hoping that the breeze wouldn't extinguish it as he walked. He brandished the pick like a weapon. "Whatever you are," he said. "You'll not take me."

He walked, slowly, fearing that it would reach out of the surrounding dark. But he walked out of the Lady's Gallery, and if the thing was there, it let him leave.

As he got to the main tunnel, the candle flame guttered and died. But ahead — only yards — the electric lights still burned. He could see the way ahead to the Cage and he ran towards it. When he got there, panting and out of breath, he heard the machinery working as the Cage descended. When it got to the bottom, he saw that there were two electricians in it. One of them was Jack Tubman, a man nearing retirement who'd worked down the mine for forty-five years.

"Thank God," said William. "John Bragg's gone missing near the Lady's Gallery."

"The Lady's Gallery?" said Tubman. "And what possessed you to go there of all places?"

William told the story and Jack and his mate listened. A knowing look passed between them.

"You go up now, Bill. We'll speak to the foreman and go looking for him."

The mine managers organised an extensive search, but it did not find any sign of John. After searching as many of the miles of the tunnels as they could, eventually they called the search off.

And then, four days after he disappeared, they found John's body in the middle of the Lady's Gallery. As if something had put it there.

Jack Tubman came round to tell William personally. William's wife offered him tea in the small terraced house and as he sipped it, William asked him. "What did he die of?"

Jack shook his head. "No one knows. He was stone dead, but without a mark on his body."

William saw his hand was shaking. He said, "Of fear then?"

Jack shrugged. "I don't know."

William said, "The poor fool thought it was his dead fiancée."

Jack shook his head. "I doubt that," he said firmly.

"Then what was it? If not her."

"No one knows what it is. But that thing's always been there. Ever since they first sank the shaft. Whether it came down with us from above, or more likely it was there waiting for us. I don't know, but one thing's for sure — whatever he met down there, it wasn't Dorothy."

2

THE WOMAN OF WASDALE

The sun was still high in the west when we parked up the camper van in the rough gravel car park by the trees on the eastern edge of Wastwater. High summer up in the north and the daylight lasts practically forever. Most day-trippers were gone, and that left the carpark to Sally and me to be our home for the next two days.

After parking up, I stepped out of the van and dropped onto the gravel. I walked across the narrow lakeside road, onto the springy turf towards the lake itself. I glanced behind to see our camper van sheltered by a stand of larches still in full needle. Behind that, the height of Yewbarrow loomed. The larch trees stirred in the slight breeze and a blackbird sang from on high somewhere, duetting with the deep croak of a raven that flew along the cliff-line behind and above. The lake was quiet.

Wasdale is truly an awesome place. When I say it's awesome, I mean that it inspires awe, not that it's just okay. Wastwater is little visited compared with the central lakes and so much emptier and wilder. There is a small settlement with two pubs at Nether Wasdale on the seaward side and the famous Wasdale Head Inn way up at the narrow head of the valley.

Dawdling, Sally followed me over the road to the lakeside and we stood, hands on hips, craning our necks to look at the foreboding mountain on the far side with its steep, apparently unclimbable, sheet of scree plunging precipitously down into the dark water.

The lake water was indigo, almost black. Wastwater is the deepest of the lakes and the lake bed continues to plunge down into the inky depths at the same gradient the mountain wall enters the water.

Sally said, 'It's almost scary.'

I laughed. 'It was you who wanted to come here.' Sally had done the research into where in the Lake District we should visit. I just drove where she told me to go. We stood in silence for ten minutes, then Sally walked to the edge of the water. 'You can see where it gets deep.' She pointed at an abrupt change in the water's colour about twenty yards out. Turning, she said, 'I read there's this little shelf and then it drops down really deep to the bottom.'

'I wouldn't fancy swimming down there,' I said.

'You could always swim back up.'

'Not if your leg got snagged on something.'

'Like what?'

'A tree branch. Some weeds.'

She shook her head. 'I think nothing grows down there. There's no oxygen.'

'So you wouldn't rot either; you'd be preserved forever.'

She frowned. 'You're morbid today.'

I laughed. 'I'll get the barbeque on.'

So we ate our sausages and burgers and sat outside with cans of lager watching the night deepen, wrapped in our warm fleeces until it grew too cold and we retired into the van.

Sally was fine with me during the day, full of smiles and light-hearted as she'd ever been, but she never wanted to be intimate with me anymore at night. Even when I attempted to cuddle into her, she stayed rigid and unwelcoming. I'd grown used to it over the past few months, and I suppose after twenty years of marriage, things can get a little stale, but I'd always treated her well. She acknowledged that. She even used to joke that I was worth more dead to her than alive, what with the hefty life insurance policy she'd talked me into taking out. Still, it was only right. Men die before women and I needed to provide for her when I was gone. Thinking over, I tried to reach out for a cuddle again but she wasn't having it. So, I rolled over and listened to the owls in the trees outside until I fell asleep.

It was pitch dark. A sense of someone outside woke me. I couldn't say it was a sound; and I certainly saw nothing, but I just had a sense of cold — an intense chill like someone opened a freezer door.

I sat bolt upright with Sally still gently breathing beside me. I was on the window side of the bed and flicked the flimsy cotton curtain so I could see. It was pitch black outside. Clouds must have rolled in to cover the sky because it was now a dense, heavy dark. If you live in a city, you never see a night this dark. It was so murky I couldn't make out anything outside the window, but weirdly, I knew there was someone out there.

It could have been a fox, but it seemed bigger than that. I got scared because it was so weird. We were so far out in the wilds, with no one about. Maybe it was a sheep, nosing around in the dark, but it was altogether colder and darker in feel than any sheep. And I had the weirdest sensation like electricity connecting with me. Like someone had just put a buzzer to my forehead, but it didn't stop at the skin or the skull, it came right into my mind. Somewhere inside, a voice said, 'Marcus.'

My name.

I admit, I panicked, sitting up.

Sally muttered, 'What? What time is it?' but I didn't answer.

The voice said, 'Marcus.'

That was all. And then the cold was gone, and the presence vanished.

I'd felt nothing like it in my life before. I'd never heard a voice in my head before.

'What's the matter, Marcus?' Sally snapped. 'You woke me.'

'Nothing. Go back to sleep.'

'Did you have a bad dream?'

'Yeah. I'm fine. Don't worry.'

And with that, she turned over and went back to sleep.

But I didn't sleep. The cold thing, whatever it was, didn't come back, but my mind started racing about how maybe I was getting schizophrenia or something. But it felt like someone was calling me, like someone had something urgent to tell me. It felt real. And then I thought it felt real to mad people too. That was the problem: their insanity seemed like reality.

I lay there, sweating, my heart racing.

But my fear couldn't last. I was dog tired. Eventually, I settled, and I fell asleep just as dawn light seeped into the van.

Sally wakened me moving about. I became aware she was doing her make-up. She always looked good. A lot of women in their forties don't bother, but she'd kept her figure. She'd started going to the gym three months ago and was watching her diet, with the result that we'd both lost weight, which I couldn't complain about.

'What was all that about?' she asked, applying some cream or lotion to her face.

'What?'

'You jumping up in the middle of the night.'

I was groggy. 'Nothing. Just a bad dream.'

'What about?'

I knew she was squeamish about ghosts and stuff. Either that or she'd think I was a looney, so I didn't mention the thing outside. It wasn't real, anyway; I'd convinced myself of that by then. I said, 'Nothing. I can't really remember.'

'Thanks for waking me. It took me ages to get to sleep again,' she said sarcastically.

In fact, it hadn't at all. I knew because I'd heard her deep-breathing minutes afterwards.

'Sorry,' I said.

'You'd better get up. We're going up Scaw Fell today.'

'Yes, of course.'

'But I want breakfast first.'

I swung my legs out of the bed. 'Sure. I'll put the bacon on.'

'And black pudding. But first make the coffee.'

I smiled. 'Of course.'

She was grumpy with me because I'd woken her. She hated not to sleep but more than that; she was terrible before her first cup of coffee. It was in my interest for an easy life if I got coffee and breakfast sorted first.

I pulled on a t-shirt and some shorts. It was going to be a hot day. I opened the van and felt the warmth in the morning sun. I set up the barbeque and got cooking.

And then we went up Scaw Fell. It was a long hike up the mountain, further and steeper than I'd expected, but we made it, even though Sally lagged a bit and I had to wait for her trudging up after me. There was a fine view from the summit. Because the day was so clear we could see all the Lake District but also over to Galloway in Scotland; Snaefell on the Isle of Man; the mountains of North Wales and even over to the Mountains of Mourne in Ireland.

At the top, Sally's phone rang. I was sitting down with a sandwich and flask and had just handed her a cheese and tomato butty. I thought it was probably one of those phone calls saying you'd had an accident that wasn't your fault or did you want to trade on the stock market, but she immediately stepped away from me and walked several paces. She lowered her voice, and the call took a couple of minutes for her to finish, then she walked back.

'Who was that?' I asked.

'Wrong number.'

'Wrong number? You spoke to them for a bit.'

She smiled. 'I like to be polite. Not just cut them off'

And that was that.

When we got back from climbing Scaw Fell, we were dusty and tired and sunburned. We walked back via the Wasdale Head Inn and I had a pint of Jennings and a burger and chips. No barbeque for us tonight.

Outside the van, we sat again with our books. I like Science Fiction. Sally reads romances. She didn't really talk much, and I thought she seemed preoccupied. Most likely, I'd upset her again, though I wouldn't be able to figure out what I'd done unless she told me. And the fact I didn't know was also usually a cause for complaint. Tentatively, I said, 'Are you okay?'

She nodded, but didn't look up.

I waited a while then said, 'I haven't upset you, have I?'

'No. Why what do you think you've done?'

I shrugged. 'Nothing. I just don't know if I have. I never meant to.'

'No, you haven't upset me.' But she was definitely keyed up. Probably she'd tell me the next day. Then it would turn out I had done something.

The night fell. The owls called. Another beautiful day. We planned to stay at Wastwater one more night after this one. Before that, using this as our base still, the next day we were going to walk over to Ennerdale over the mountains, stay here again in Wasdale and then after that drive south to Broughton in Furness, and find somewhere to camp there at the bottom of Dunnerdale.

That night, I fell asleep quickly, due to the exercise of climbing up Scaw Fell and the beer no doubt. Again, Sally refused to cuddle into me, so I was sure I'd upset her.

In the middle of the night, I woke again and I instantly knew it was back. It was the cold. I hadn't thought about it all day, but it filled my mind. There was definitely something outside the van — something moving. I felt the same fear zap through me. I sat up.

Sally woke. 'What is it?' She didn't wait for me to speak before saying, 'Not again, Marcus, for God's sake. I need to sleep.'

I leaned and lifted the tiny curtain at the window. Tonight at least, there was a moon. I could see the car park and the trees bathed in its baleful light. But all seemed quiet.

'Marcus,' the voice came in my head. The same feeling like an electric buzzer in my brain. I slammed the heel of my hand into my forehead to shut it up. 'Jesus,' I moaned.

'What the hell is the matter with you, Marcus?' Sally was irritated, half sitting up. I'd certainly upset her now.

'Did you hear that voice?' I said and that second it came again, ringing like a glass bell in my head. 'Marcus.'

'No, there's no voice. What is wrong with you? For God's sake. You've really woken me now.'

But I wasn't listening to her. I could feel the cold radiating through the metal wall of the van. I had to see whether there was something outside. Even though I was terrified — terrified of finding something out there, but even more terrified of not, and then I would know I truly was going mad. I grabbed a kitchen knife as I went past the galley and opened the door.

It was cool outside, not cold, but cool. Nothing stirred. I stood for a second with the door open to the night air. Sally was standing behind me looking at me like I was a crazy person.

'There's somebody out there,' I said.

'No, there isn't. You're an idiot.'

'No, there is.'

'Marcus.' It said nothing but my name.

I stepped down the metal steps, the cold triangular struts cutting into the soles of my bare feet. I brandished the knife. 'Who's there?' I yelled into the dark.

There was no sound.

'See?' Sally yelled. 'You're stupid. Now come in or I'll shut the door and leave you out there.'

I wasn't ready to come in, because I felt it. I walked out from the camper van. I couldn't see it but I felt the cold. Not a physical cold, but an intensity as if something had been so cold for so long, it could never get rid of the chill.

I had the knife pointed in front of me. 'Where are you?' I cried out into the dark.

And then she appeared from nowhere. She was a woman. Normal height, but in a nightgown. And water was running off her. She was drenched; her soaked nightgown clung to her, and she looked so cold. Black hair plastered her face and her eyes were white like those of a boiled fish. Her skin shone in the moonlight like she was shaped of cold wax. I thought: what the hell has happened to her? Did she fall in the lake?

Then she said, 'Marcus,' and vanished.

I was shaking like a leaf when I went back to the camper van. True to her word, Sally had closed the door against me. I half thought she might have locked it in spite for me waking her up, but she hadn't.

I put the knife down where I got it. She was back in bed when I got back in the van.

'What the hell is the matter with you, Marcus? Was there anyone there?' She didn't wait for me to reply before spitting, 'Of course there wasn't!'

I stood, supporting myself on the sink.

'For God's sake Marcus, you're such a wimp. Scared of the dark at your age.'

I said, 'There was someone.'

Her brow furrowed. 'Who? Don't be dull. There's no one else camping near here.'

But there was something in her voice when she said that. Like she wasn't sure if it was true. She sounded worried, and I thought: at last, here's was some care for me. I said, 'A woman.'

'A woman? Are you sure? Could it be a man?'

'No, I don't think so. She vanished.'

'Vanished? You're making no sense. How could she vanish?'

'I think she was a ghost.'

She let out a long cruel laugh. 'I always knew you were a simpleton, Marcus. But you've surpassed yourself with this.'

I was wrong. She didn't care. I usually bite back on my tongue, but now I didn't. 'You may think I'm stupid, but you still like my money.'

She stopped laughing. Now she tried to be kind. 'Don't be silly, Marcus. You've given yourself a fright. Come back to bed.'

I did, but she still wouldn't let me hold her.

We went for our walk to Ennerdale the next day. It wasn't as sunny, which was actually a good thing as the climbing wasn't as hard as it had been in the heat. On coming back, I said we should go to the pub. She seemed ill at ease, on the look-out for something, scanning the lakeside as we walked along the road.

We had a meal at the Wasdale Head Inn. I got talking to the old bloke in the corner. He had a thick Cumbrian accent, so he was hard to understand at first. I guess he was a retired farmer or something.

It annoyed Sally that I was talking to him, but she ended up talking to a couple from Newcastle. Eventually, after asking about him and his life in the valley a bit, I asked if there was a ghost around the lake.

He cackled. 'You've seen her, have you?'

'Who?'

'The drowned woman.'

That was a shock. That was exactly what I had seen. I took a sip of my beer. Then I described her.

He nodded. 'Aye, that'll be her. Margaret Hogg.'

'Margaret Hogg?'

'Aye, a woman from Surrey. Her husband choked her then drove her up here and put her in the lake. That was 1976. They didn't find her until 1984 when they sent divers out looking for a French girl who went missing. Otherwise she'd still be there.'

'How did they know it was her?'

'The water's so cold and lacking in oxygen she didn't rot. Mind you, he just missed dropping her in the deepest part. He weighted her down, but she only went on the ledge — a hundred foot down. If he'd got it right, she'd have sunk right to the bottom and no one would have ever found her.'

'And have other people seen her? The ghost.'

He nodded. 'One or two. I've never seen her myself, but I knew a lad from Nether Wasdale as saw her. That was a couple of years ago now, but now and again people say they've seen her. It can be anywhere round the lake.'

I sat back. In one way, it reassured me I wasn't going mad. In another it was horrible because I'd really seen such a thing. I was trembling. The pint glass in my hand was shaking, so I put it down. I think he saw it.

'She's got you shook up, hasn't she?'

I rubbed my eyes. 'It was just so weird.'

He laughed. 'I wouldn't bother. She can't do you no harm, son. She's dead.'

I sat back. 'But what does she want?' I asked.

'What does she want?' He seemed to ponder that. Eventually he replied, 'Well, they do say she has good intentions. She comes to warn you of some terrible thing that is going to happen.'

That was worse. 'A terrible thing? Like what?'

He shrugged. 'Oh, I don't know. It's all nonsense anyway, just stupid ghost stories.'

He could see he'd scared me, but I wouldn't give up. 'What happened to the lad from wherever, Nether Wasdale was it?'

'Jimmy?'

'I don't know.'

'Yes, Jimmy.'

'Well, what terrible thing happened to him?'

He grunted. 'It's just superstition you know.'

'But what happened to him?'

It took him a long time to answer, eventually he said, 'Well, he died in a motorcycle accident.'

'How long after?'

'Not long. Days.'

'So how was that warning him?'

'She appeared twice or three times by his bike.'

'Did she speak?'

'I don't know. It's just a coincidence.'

I took a drink of beer. It didn't help. 'Maybe,' I said.

He gazed at the table. 'Don't pay it no mind. I shouldn't have said nothing.'

'No, it's okay.' But I couldn't concentrate on him anymore, I was just thinking about the drowned woman and what she was warning me about.

'Why did he kill her?' I asked suddenly.

'Who?'

'Margaret Hogg's husband.'

'I dunno. Something to do with an affair. Best forget about her now, lad. Honest, it'll do you no good going on about it.'

I didn't speak any more to him about the drowned woman, and I said nothing about it to Sally. As we walked back from the pub, it was still daylight and even as preoccupied as I was I couldn't help but see how beautiful the place was. Wild and remote, but beautiful. A light breeze ruffled the water of the lake and the waves were very dark because the lake was so deep. I shuddered when I thought about Margaret Hogg being dumped in the depths. Ghost or no ghost, that had happened to a real woman — killed by her husband.

As we walked along, there was a bloke camping by the side of the lake. It was wild camping, and he wasn't supposed to do it. He had a one-man tent, and a van parked up next to it. As we got close, Sally seemed to stiffen up. She kept walking, but it was like she was forcing herself to act normal. That was weird. I couldn't understand it. Then she started talking about the view. The bloke nipped into his tent before we got too close. It was only about a hundred yards short of our camper van. I said, 'He looked like the fella that runs the gym at home.'

She shook her head. 'No, he doesn't.'

'Did you see him?' I said. I turned as I walked to stare back but he was gone now, inside his tent.

'No, stop staring. It's rude.'

'He can't see me. He's in the tent.'

'Marcus, stop embarrassing me.'

I felt a flush of shame. It seemed I was always an embarrassment to her. 'Sorry.'

'Well, keep on walking then.'

When we got back to the van, she was nice to me. I have no idea why, but then I never do. She's not nice as much these days but even so it was welcome, whatever the cause of it.

'Do you want a drink?' she asked.

We sat on the camp chairs outside, watching the last golden light of the sun in the west. 'No, I'm okay,' I said.

'I'm having one.' She poured herself some of that Parma violet gin and a Feverfew tonic.

'Nah, I'm okay.' Truth was I was still thinking about that woman.

She came out from the van with two glasses. 'I poured you one anyway,' she smiled.

She gave me the glass, and I thought I didn't fancy it but it might relax me.

It relaxed me so much that I had another. Sally was so nice to me it was just like old times. But I'm not a spirit drinker so I had forgotten how strong gin is. After two or three of those, I was unsteady as I climbed back into the van. I didn't bother to wash or clean my teeth. I felt drunk.

Sally got into bed beside me and as I lay there, the van started spinning. At least I would sleep, I thought.

And not see her: the drowned woman.

Much later. 'Marcus.' The voice was inside my dreams now. I felt sick and cold with fear. I struggled to wake up. I felt drugged. I felt heavy. My arms and legs felt tied down.

'Marcus.' She said again. I wasn't sure if it was inside my head. I wasn't sure whether I was awake or dreaming.

But there were voices inside the van. From the depths of my sleep, it sounded like a man talking to Sally. I must be dreaming. I let myself fall back into slumber. It was easier.

'Marcus.'

I felt her cold hands on me. She was shaking me awake. But I was only dreaming. I needn't listen to the drowned woman. It was much easier to sleep.

From far away, another world, I heard a man talking to Sally.

She said, 'Do it then.'

He said, 'Here?'

'Where else?'

'I don't know. I thought we'd get him outside.'

I thought I should get up, but I honestly couldn't move and then the drowned woman started shaking me again, violently, rocking me awake. 'Marcus, Marcus, Marcus…'

'What the hell?' the man said from somewhere. 'He's awake. You said—'

'I did. I did. I gave him a double dose. That stuff you got.'

'Rohypnol. Not enough then.'

And then I sat up. The woman was saying, 'Marcus, Marcus, Marcus...' in my brain. Buzzing like an alarm.

She was summoning me out of my sleep. My head was heavy, woozy. I was still drunk. Everything was dark but the lights of the van were on. It was deep night.

'Marcus, Marcus, Marcus.' The drowned woman wanted me to go outside the van. She seemed urgent about it.

My head was so woozy. I blinked. There was a man in the van standing next to Sally. They both stood there watching me. He had a rope in his hands. A blue polypropylene rope.

'Marcus!' The drowned woman's voice was like cold water washing over me. I jerked up. They both looked shocked.

'Do it!' Sally screamed. 'Now, before he gets up.'

But I was out of bed. Still doped up, but I was moving. He snatched at me as I went past but I tugged myself out of his grip.

'Do it!' Sally yelled, but I yanked free towards the door of the van.

Then he said, 'I can't. Use the knife.'

Sally had the kitchen knife in her hand. I thought she might hesitate, remembering the years when she had loved me, but she twisted her face with hate. I was just an impediment to her now. My life stopped her getting what she wanted. She wanted both him and my money. So she yelled and lunged.

The knife stuck in the top of my arm. I felt like I'd she'd punched me but instantly blood spouted from the wound. She pulled the knife back to stab me again, this time somewhere vital, but I stumbled to the door of the van.

'Marcus,' the drowned woman said. She was standing in the van between me and Sally.

Water dripped from her. Her cold dead lips formed my name. 'Marcus.'

But Sally and her boyfriend saw her. They couldn't help it. She materialized right in front of them.

SALLY SCREAMED and dropped the knife. As the woman stood there in front of her, Sally put her hands to her face and screamed again. The man backed off, behind Sally, away from the drowned woman.

She just stood there, accusing them. Accusing them and saving me.

I grabbed the door handle, still bleeding like a pig from my arm wound. I grabbed it, turned it and leaped out. I ran. I ran and ran, sprinting up the road alongside the dark lake and didn't stop until I got to the pub. I hammered on the door and they let me in. They saw the blood and called the police.

Later that night, the police stopped Sally and her boyfriend on the A66 near Keswick. They arrested them for attempted murder. It turned out at the trial that Sally had thought she'd have him choke me and dump me in the lake. They'd dump me in the deepest part. Never to be found.

But the drowned woman warned me. I guess she'd tried to warn Jimmy at Nether Wasdale about his bike, but he hadn't understood.

The drowned woman warned me and saved my life, and I guess it was because she didn't want someone else to go the way she had.

That was nearly a year ago. I'm with another girl now. Someone who's nice to me. Someone who hasn't once mentioned life insurance.

3

THE CRIER OF CLAIFE

It was a winter evening in December 1856. The wind blew along the lake raising a welter of ripples on water turned red by a sun already descending behind the Heights of Claife.

I worked on the ferry then from the Bowness side. There had always been ferrymen to take passengers over to Claife and Sawrey, since the days of the monks. In fact, my father was one, but since the railway arrived at Windermere bringing all the tourists seeking the beauty of the Lake District business had boomed.

The night I am talking about, the light was fading. I stood with my mate Alf Mumberson on the Bowness side, taking a pipe. I'd done reasonably well that day, and was considering finishing when we heard a call from the Claife side. As Alf had taken the last passenger, I expected him to let me have this one, but instead he stirred and stepped towards his boat. Half-turning, but not meeting my eye, as if there was something he was ashamed of, he muttered, 'I'll take this one Davey. I know her.'

'Right,' I said, not wanting to cause a fuss, though she was my passenger by rights.

I say 'she', but the wind had snatched the passenger's

voice and I'd not even registered that it was a woman calling, but he had. It seemed he'd even recognised the voice.

I'm known for my easy-going ways — too easy going my sister says. Anyway, 'I'll wait for you,' I said. 'You never know, I might get another fare before the dark falls.'

He grunted. 'You don't need to wait, Davey. Get yourself home.'

I said, 'But you'll only be ten minutes, surely. Then you'll be on your way back. I'll wait.'

But he had his feet in the water, already pushing the boat off the shingle. As he stepped in, gently rocking the hull in the water, he said, 'As you wish, but don't wait on my account.'

I waved his words down. 'No, it's fine. I'll walk home with you.'

And then he was gone, rowing across the waves, heading for the far shore over Windermere. I even thought he was rowing faster than normal, as if eager to meet his passenger. As I peered over in the failing light, I only saw his passenger as a slender figure, black-clad against the shoreline and the rising tree-cloaked hills behind.

I saw him arrive on the yonder shore and greet the person, and then it appeared they were in discussion for they didn't strike immediately back. As I watched I grew bored, and the light grew dimmer by the minute, until they were mere shadows within a tangle of shadows. I'd said I'd wait, so I would. But it was cold. I pulled my coat and scarf tight around me and lit another pipe.

Night fell fully and finally, and he still hadn't returned. God alone knew what he was doing on the far shore with his woman passenger. Maybe it was some girl from Sawrey or even Hawkshead he had taken a shine to.

The cold grew and seeped into my bones. I stamped my feet and finished my pipe, tapping out the ashes on the rock. I decided there were no more passengers for me this night, so I dragged my boat up and tied it fast, shipping the oars.

Still Alf Mumberson didn't return. It was proper night now, and the skies dark with clouds so no stars nor moon shone through. The wind strengthened with the night and after another fifteen minutes, I left Alf Mumberson to his fate and walked home to Bowness.

The next morning, Alf arrived late; I'd already had three passengers. The weather was better, but in the clear morning light, Alf looked pale and tired.

'What happened to you last night?' I laughed, giving a wink.

'I told you not to wait,' he said gruffly.

'I was there about half an hour after you went. What were you up to? Have you got a woman over there?'

'None of your business.'

A few passengers came over and we were busy. Later when we had a breather, I joined him in a pipe. As we puffed, he said, 'Well, if you must know, there is a woman.'

I grinned. 'Thought so. So that's what you were up to in the dark. I hope she took you somewhere warm.'

He seemed strangely serious. 'Warm isn't important, love is what's important.'

I mocked him. 'Love is it? My my, now the lad talks of love.'

'If you'd known love, Davey, you wouldn't be so hard about it. It's the most wonderful thing in the world.'

I feared he would go off on a lyrical speech about the beauties of love, so I cut him short. 'So who is she?'

He gave a sly smile. 'You'd like to know, wouldn't you?'

I shrugged, indifferent. 'It's nothing to me, Alf. Just don't be catching your death of cold in those damp woods.'

But now I'd broached the subject, he couldn't stop talking about it. Just before we ate our bread and cheese for lunch, he said, 'Davey, she's the most wonderful woman I've ever met. Beautiful, clever and refined.'

'Then what's she doing with a rough boatman?'

He huffed. 'Maybe she sees qualities in me that others don't. Maybe she sees I've got prospects.'

'And do you?' I said, knowing he hadn't.

He snorted. 'You're not worth talking to Davey Strong.'

I laughed. He was a moody one, always had been, easy to sulk, but easy to bring round. I said, 'But you won't tell me her name?'

'Sabine. She's called Sabine.'

I raised both eyebrows. 'And what kind of a name is that? No Margaret or Joan or Ann good enough for you? You have to find a Sabine.'

'She's not local. She's not from round here.'

'Then where's she from?'

'I don't know—London, or America.'

'London or America? There's a bit of a difference.'

He shrugged wildly, irritated by my insisting on details. 'I don't know. I don't care. Just she loves me and I love her.'

'But you meet her on the lakeside. Outdoors. Does she take you to meet her family?'

'She says she will. She says she'll take me to see her father soon.'

After that, I got a passenger and then another and rowed them back and forwards between Bowness and Claife. The clouds gathered, and it began to spit with rain. Night would not be long coming on that dark winter afternoon at the close of the year.

We waited a long time with no passengers and Alf seemed lost in his thoughts. I was about to give it up and go home when again the call came from the Claife side. This time, even I could hear it was a woman's call, light and sweet and clear, calling over the water.

He stood up instantly, as eager as a pointer dog.

I raised an eyebrow. 'Sabine?' I asked.

He nodded.

Teasing him, I said, 'I should take the fare. It's my turn. Like it was last night.'

'No!' he yelled. He turned to me, his lips raised as if he was going to snarl no again, but he calmed himself and said, 'Please, Davey. You know I love her.'

'Aye, I don't doubt it.'

'And she loves me.'

I was more circumspect this time. 'If you say so.'

'What do you know, Davey Strong? You've never been loved, so how can you know?'

I'd known Alfred since we were boys at the village school, and everyone in Bowness knew everyone else's history. I wasn't married, it was true. I had been engaged, but she'd gone off with another and

I hadn't found anyone else, but I was content enough living with my mother and sister. Still, it was hard of him to say that. I gave a cold look. 'You'd better be getting to your lovely Sabine.'

He nodded. As he went to launch his boat, I said, 'So, is it tonight she's going to introduce you to her father?'

Without looking back he said, 'Maybe. I don't care. I only want her.'

Then a thought struck me. 'Where do they live even?'

He gestured as he sat and prepared to row. 'Up in the woods.'

'Claife Woods?'

He nodded, taking up his oars.

'There're no houses in Claife Woods.'

'Yes, up there.'

And then a strange presentiment came upon me. I don't believe in ghosts or anything supernatural. But Claife Woods are said to be haunted. Maybe she was a ghost?

I waited a long while, and when Alf didn't return, I walked home alone in the dark.

Alf Mumberson didn't turn up at work the next morning. Some of our regular passengers asked where he was and I said I didn't know. 'He may be ill,' they said.

'He may be,' I answered.

When Alf finally arrived it was afternoon. I saw him shuffling along the road from the village. He looked drained, and I began to think perhaps he was sick. As he came along the road to the ferry point, I called out, 'Alf, where've you been? Are you all right?'

He nodded and was about to speak when a fit of coughing overtook him. When he got up to me, I saw how pale and wan he looked. He had huge dark circles under his eyes.

'Good God, man, what the hell has happened to you?' I said.

'Nothing.'

'You look dreadful. Are you ill?'

'No.'

I shook my head. 'You look terrible.' And then I noticed dried blood on his collar. 'What's that? Did you cut yourself shaving?'

He tried to look and put his fingers to the stain. 'I must have. I don't remember doing it.'

Then I saw his stubble and realised he hadn't cut himself shaving at all. I narrowed my eyes. 'How was Sabine?' I asked. 'Did you meet her father?'

He shook his head. 'Not yet. She says soon. She says soon she'll take me to the house in the woods.'

I was growing more and more suspicious. 'So what did you do all that time I was waiting?'

He muttered. 'Just what men and women do.'

'In the cold? Outdoors?'

'You wouldn't know, Davey. If you're in love with someone, you can't be put off by cold.'

'So she takes you to the woods? That doesn't sound like a respectable girl.'

He was defensive. 'She's very respectable. Very refined.'

'Enough that she couples with you in the woods?'

'Don't be coarse, Davey. You don't know.'

I grew more suspicious. 'Has she asked you for money?'

He laughed scornfully. 'I have no money. She loves me. It's not about money.'

'Aye, maybe.' I said pensively, 'But it's about something.'

We lapsed into a brooding silence. A passenger came, a man and his wife heading to Hawkshead. They were local farmers, and I knew them well. When I rowed back to Bowness, Alf was sitting on a rock, staring over the water towards Claife. He looked worse than ever and the dark brown of the dried blood stood out against the grey-white of his collar. I knew he was waiting for dark and Sabine's call.

Without thinking, I said, 'I'm coming over with you tonight.'

'What? No, you aren't.'

I put up my hand. 'I'm worried about you, and if this Sabine's as refined as you say she is; there's nothing to bother about.'

His lip twisted. 'You're not coming to meet Sabine.'

I adopted a gentler tone. 'Alfie, look at the state of you. I don't know what she's doing, but it looks like she's sucking the life from you. I just want to make sure she isn't deceiving you.'

'She's not deceiving me.'

'Then, I'll come.'

'No, you won't.'

I cleared my throat, standing on the shingle shore of the lake. 'Do your mother and father know about her?'

He shook his head.

I continued. 'Why haven't you told them?'

He grunted. 'I'll tell them in my own time.'

I tilted my head. I asked, 'Has she told you not to tell them?'

He remained silent, and I knew it was so: Sabine had asked him not to mention her to his parents. 'What about me? Does she know I know about her?'

'Of course, not Davey. Why would I mention you?'

'So as far as she's concerned, nobody knows that you go to meet her.'

A pause, then he said, 'I suppose. What of it?'

'Hmm.' I studied him as he sat on the rock staring over the lake. 'I'm coming,' I said. 'If there's nothing to worry about, then there's nothing to worry about.'

'No, you're not.'

I said firmly, 'If I don't come, then I'll speak to your parents about her.'

He turned round in a cold fury. 'How dare you, Davey Strong? What are you to me or I to you that you should make such an imposition?'

'What am I to you, Alfie? Well, I should think I am your friend, and have been since we were boys.'

That put him back, and so, with bad grace, he agreed that I would come over the lake with him to meet his mysterious Sabine.

The light was fading as she called. He stood up instantly. He cupped his hands to his mouth and shouted, 'On my way. I'll be there soon.'

He stepped towards his boat.

I said, 'We'll both go in your boat.'

He said quietly, 'I'd rather you didn't come.'

'And, I'd rather I did.'

I got in the boat after him, sitting on the thwart that served as a seat for passengers. He didn't speak as he dipped his oars in the water. I trailed my fingers to test its temperature and felt the ice-cold of the first melted snow-water from the fells above the lake. He took slow regular strokes, not speaking, his back to the far shore where Sabine waited.

The light was gone, the sun now sunk behind the Heights of Claife. Only a faint grey glimmer in the sky to the south reminded me it had been day at all. Alf was a stooped silhouette, rowing regularly and faster than normal as if giving his last energy to this mission to see his love.

I couldn't see her standing there on the Claife shore as the bow of the boat scraped the stones. Alf jumped out, his boots and trousers underwater as he took the painter and pulled the boat up. He didn't speak to me, as if he'd forgotten I was there, but I got out after him, splashing through water until I felt rocks underfoot and dry shillies.

Alf had hardly bothered to pull the boat safely out of the water, so I did so, taking the rough rope from where he'd dropped it in the wet and dragging the hull with a scrape over the shillies. When I was certain the boat was high enough up so it wouldn't drift away, I turned to look for Alf. At first I couldn't see him, and I certainly didn't see Sabine. But I heard him talking, in tones suggesting an overflowing of love for his hidden interlocutor. I stepped towards them but, on a sudden whim, hung back. I was strangely nervous.

It was not pitch black. I saw a shape I took to be Alf, but could see no one with him. I could hear his voice clearly now—'Oh, my darling, Sabine, how I've missed you...'

And then, I thought I heard a low muttering. From his responses, there seemed nothing strange about the voice and I wondered whether it sounded like the crystal voice of his darling love, but to me it was the voice of no woman; it was low and guttural as the voice an animal would have if it could speak words. I could make out none of the words, but Alf obviously could because he was replying, 'Yes, yes, my darling, of course.'

They moved.

I wondered what she was leading him into so I shouted into the shadows where he stood. I felt again this strange reluctance to go closer to where this Sabine was standing.

It seemed he turned to me and he said loudly, 'Davey go back. Go home. I'll be all right.'

'How can I? We came in one boat. If I go then how will you get home?'

'Don't worry about me. I'll be fine. I'll be with Sabine.'

A breeze from the lake rustled the piles of autumn leaves that lay in the dark at the bottom of the wood. I could just make out the line of tree trunks that lay behind Alf and his Sabine. I thought I saw her take his hand and lead him towards the forest, but I could be mistaken; it was so dark.

They walked rapidly towards the trees.

'Alfie, where are you going? Come back!' I yelled.

But he ignored me. There were definitely two shadows there now, and I could hear his voice and her low muttering as they walked into the wood.

With mounting panic, I began to wonder what kind of creature Sabine was. From this voice and the weird darkness that hung around her, she was no ordinary woman. But he was going with her.

'Alfie!' I yelled, fear filling my veins and lungs. 'Don't go!'

He called back in a voice that sounded almost happy, 'It's all right, Davey, Sabine's taking me to see her father.'

They disappeared, but for myself, I could not move to enter the Claife Woods. A strange terror of the thing called Sabine gripped me. I stood and watched Alfie go, and cursed my cowardice, but I could take no step towards him.

I stood there for minutes, maybe longer. If Sabine was this, what then was her father? Shaking, I walked back towards where I'd beached Alfie's boat. It was fine for me to leave. I was imagining everything. He didn't want me to follow him, and how could I in the darkness? I tried to convince myself that was the reason I didn't go into the woods. I stood by the boat, my hands on the rough wood of the bow, ready to push off, then jump in before rowing back to Bowness. I could come early tomorrow morning and wait here for him on this shore with his boat. He never left Sabine before morning, anyway. And yes, tonight he would meet her father.

I heard the wind in the trees. I felt it on my cheeks, cold now. I heard the lap of the little waves around the boat. Somewhere in the dark geese honked as they flew by unseen.

BUT OF COURSE I couldn't go. I couldn't leave him. No matter how frightened I was by the woods of Claife and what they held, I couldn't leave him to her and her terrible father.

I swallowed hard. And then the clouds cleared, and the moon shone full. The pale silver light revealed the black of the trees of Claife and I stared up at the dark hill. That was where Alfie was. I knew with awful certainty that Sabine these nights had been preparing Alf to meet her father, and that it was a meeting he would never return from.

There had always been stories about the woods of Claife—of people going missing, people wandering through the woods and never returning. Of course that might be true, but I'd put that down to natural accidents in the tangled woodland over tumbled crags. Others said it was the Crier of Claife, the thing that lived in the woods. I'd paid no heed to it. I'd laughed at their superstitious nonsense — until now. Now I knew, with the ancient knowledge all humans have, that something supernatural walked here now.

But the moonlight gave me courage — fleeting and intermittent as it was while the moon danced behind clouds, now hiding in darkness, now revealing the landscape in white.

I could see the trees. I could see the hill. Alfie was in danger. I had to catch up with him and persuade him to come back from there, even if I had to pull him out of Sabine's arms. And I had to do it before they met her father.

I SIGHED HEAVILY and tried to slow my hammering heart and then I turned and by the light of the pale moon; I walked slowly towards the edge of the trees. I hesitated long there, my courage slipping through my fingers like cold water, but I tried telling myself that Alfie would get further and further ahead of me. It worked. I forced myself to enter the forest.

I FELT the trees enfold me. Their spiky branches and wiry arms all around, above and to all sides, and below my feet sinking in mulch and mud. I took a breath, there was a path of sorts that ascended zig-zag through trees and over rocks. Sometimes the way underfoot was carpeted by soft leaves, and other times, I stepped up over slick boulders, breathing heavily, hoping I would not slip as I climbed the hill. This was the way he must have come; there was no other path.

But I could see no sign of him, or his Sabine. So, I struggled on, out of breath, up the steep slope, pushing away branches that would tear at my eyes when I could see them and suffering their scratches when I could not. My breath was ragged as I climbed as fast as I could and faster than was comfortable. When the moon hid, it was dark, and I missed my step on mossy stones, slipping, and once falling on my hands that were cut by sharp rocks.

But in my panic to save him, I was climbing faster than they were. I heard a voice, undoubtedly Alf's voice, still murmuring sweet nothings to his beloved's dread ear. I stopped, suddenly silent, but they kept on walking so I hurried on. I was making a noise as I pushed my way along the narrow forest path. At least I could see my feet in the moonlight, but that meant they could see me. If they cared.

I saw Alf's silhouette on the path ahead. The path here was less steep as if it were levelling out. He was there and beside him a dark shape. It was unnaturally tall and thin. It could be a woman, I supposed, but a woman dressed all in black and over six feet tall. The shape moved strangely too, as if it were drifting. It seemed to suffer none of the trouble crossing this broken ground, but moved with an eerie grace. If grace is an appropriate word to describe such a creature.

And my heart beat faster again, not just from the exertion but from the weirdness of what I was seeing—Alfie was apparently enthralled by something he thought was a woman, but clearly was not. I waited until they turned out of sight, wondering what on earth I was going to do to tear him away from her. Perhaps both of us together could fight it off?

On impulse, I grabbed a stick that lay to the side of the path. It was wet and rough; it was far from perfect but would perhaps do as a makeshift weapon.

My delay in getting the stick, allowed them to turn the corner ahead and as they were now out of sight, I hurried forward to catch up, but round the corner of that forest trail, I saw no one. For once, it went straight ahead, but there was no sign of Alf or his companion.

I exhaled heavily in frustration, but also in relief. I admit that the thought that I had done all I could to save Alf crossed my mind—done all I could but to no avail. No one could blame me or call me a coward. It was a way out.

But Alf was gone. I stood, bemused, confused as to what I should do, and I reasoned with myself, that the only course of action now was to return to the lake and from there, row back to Bowness and home. Perhaps I could get help from there. I would tell a story of how Alf had followed this mysterious woman into the trees, and then when he returned, I would relate how I had followed him but failed to find him in the end in the thickness of the wood.

I looked around. I counted. I thought a reasonable time had gone by and I could leave, but then I saw a way to the left. The left-hand path lay just ahead. I had missed it earlier. That was the only way they could have gone and disappeared from sight so quickly round the corner in front of me.

I HELD my stick fast and my throat tightened. I felt my hands trembling and my knees shaking, but now I had no excuse. That was the way he had gone, and my conscience would force me to follow.

With a heavy breath, but gathering courage, I pushed my way through a thin screen of branches that lay just inside the path and followed the track between the trees, climbing slightly, my feet slipping in the leaf mould. I had my stick.

And then I heard a voice. It wasn't Alfie's voice; it was the low guttural voice of the thing that had brought him here. The sound of it, stopped me. I stood still in my tracks, listening. The thing spoke in a cadence of intricate sounds, as if reciting poetry or some strange ritual. The volume went up and down, rhythmically. Sometimes she whined, sometimes she yelled as if calling something.

I inched forward and saw a building, or rather the ruins of a building ahead beneath the trees. It looked like it had been a house once, but was no longer. Shattered walls were open to the sky through scraps of a long-broken roof. It was round, as if it had been a folly made to look like an ancient Roman temple. Or perhaps it was indeed an ancient temple, long lost in these thick woods.

The chanting came from inside the walls. I could see the six-foot monster as it sang ancient eldritch words. I understood nothing, but the sound of them brought memories of something old and wicked. Something that lurked here waiting to be summoned.

With every fibre of my flesh wanting to pull back, instead I pushed myself forward. Stick in hand, gripped tightly and ready to bring it down on the thing. What was this thing—this Sabine doing?

As I heard her pitter-patter; her words of blasphemous prefiguration, I knew she was calling something; something that came from a cold world, way outside our ordinary creation.

It must only be that Alfie was to be her sacrifice: some supplication to the monster she summoned.

With a roar, I ran at her, sprinting within the ruins of the tainted temple, my stick brandished in my hand. I acted bolder than I felt, because inside me my guts ran like water.

There, on a broken altar, Alfie lay, staring at the sky. His shirt was torn, his bare chest exposed to the moon. And she saw me, this Sabine. In her hand she held a dagger of silver, bone-handled with a blood-red ruby at the hilt. She wore a long cloak made of smoke: black smoke that writhed and wrapped around her tall thin form. The cloak fell open at the front and revealed her to be naked; her thin white breasts drooped like the sucked out dugs of an old crone; the hair between her legs was grey and her skin was white, run through with blue veins like fleshy marble. Her face was that of a corpse, long-dead: cadaverous and drawn close.

Grey hair straggled over her face and her teeth stuck long and yellow like those of a snake. Like a snake also were her eyes; irises golden with pupils like pulsing, flickering spots. She opened her mouth and her swollen, pale tongue lolled as she said, 'Father, come!'

With those words spoken, she raised her silver dagger and plunged it into Alfie's chest. I heard the thump of impact and his scream and a sound like air escaping a punctured leather bag. Alfie twitched and shuddered and his life blood spouted from his chest.

I dropped the stick I held and threw up.

And then whatever she had called, came. I heard it behind me appearing in the trees. Sinuous and slippery, not corporeal, it slid through the wood like a slick of black oil. I heard its gibbering cries. I heard its inhuman moan, and I knew whatever intelligence or idiocy it had was second to its hunger.

I fled. The gutless fool I was: I fled.

I had some sense of it fastening on Alf and feeding from his pierced body. Half a sight of it slitting him open with scissor like nails, but I ran.

I ran down the trail, down the path, slipping and falling, cutting myself but luckily not breaking any bones, not that I cared then, but not slowing until I reached the bottom of the hill. In the trees behind, I heard it. It had eaten Alf and now it came for me.

But I would not let it. I remembered some story of them not being able to cross running water so I ran for Alf's boat, and jumped in the water, shoving it ahead of me and then rolling in it, nearly capsizing in the water. But I got in and rowed frantically. Nothing followed, and I had got halfway across the lake, at the deepest point, where the water ran cold from December rain, and I slowed. I paused, hanging on my oars. My heart still beat. My neck and chest were drenched with cold sweat. I could hardly think from the horror I had seen. But it seemed I had escaped, even if Alfie hadn't. My mouth was sour. I spat into the lake water and turned to row again.

And then I felt a weight settle in the boat. I looked amazed as she appeared from smoke. Sabine sat there, her cloak thrown open, but instead of the old crone, now she was a young maiden; her breasts full and up-tilted. Her cloak lay open as before. The hair between her legs black and curly. Her lips were red as blood, her cheeks white as snow, apart from a high red blush at her cheekbones. Her hair was lustrous black and hung beneath her shoulders. Wicked as she was, she was the fairest woman I ever did see.

A beauty as an innocent girl, but her eyes spoke of who she really was. Her face was flushed with blushing blood, but though she was restored; her eyes were still those of a great golden snake.

'Hello, Davey,' she said, hissing, 'I am Sabine.'

I looked at the cold lake water. At least it would give me a clean death. As she watched, I leapt up and jumped clear of the boat into the lake.

I had expected to die, but the lake saved me. Frigid as it was, I swam to shore at Bowness and Sabine did not follow.

After that, I went to London, giving little reason for leaving even to my family. Sabine did not follow. From Liverpool, I took ship to Australia to be as far away from her as could be and instead of dark Westmorland winters; I had bright Australian skies above me. And still she did not follow.

But I am not rid of her. She did not follow me across the water. In my dreams, there she waits. If I ever come back to Windermere, she will be waiting for me, calling over from the Heights of Claire.

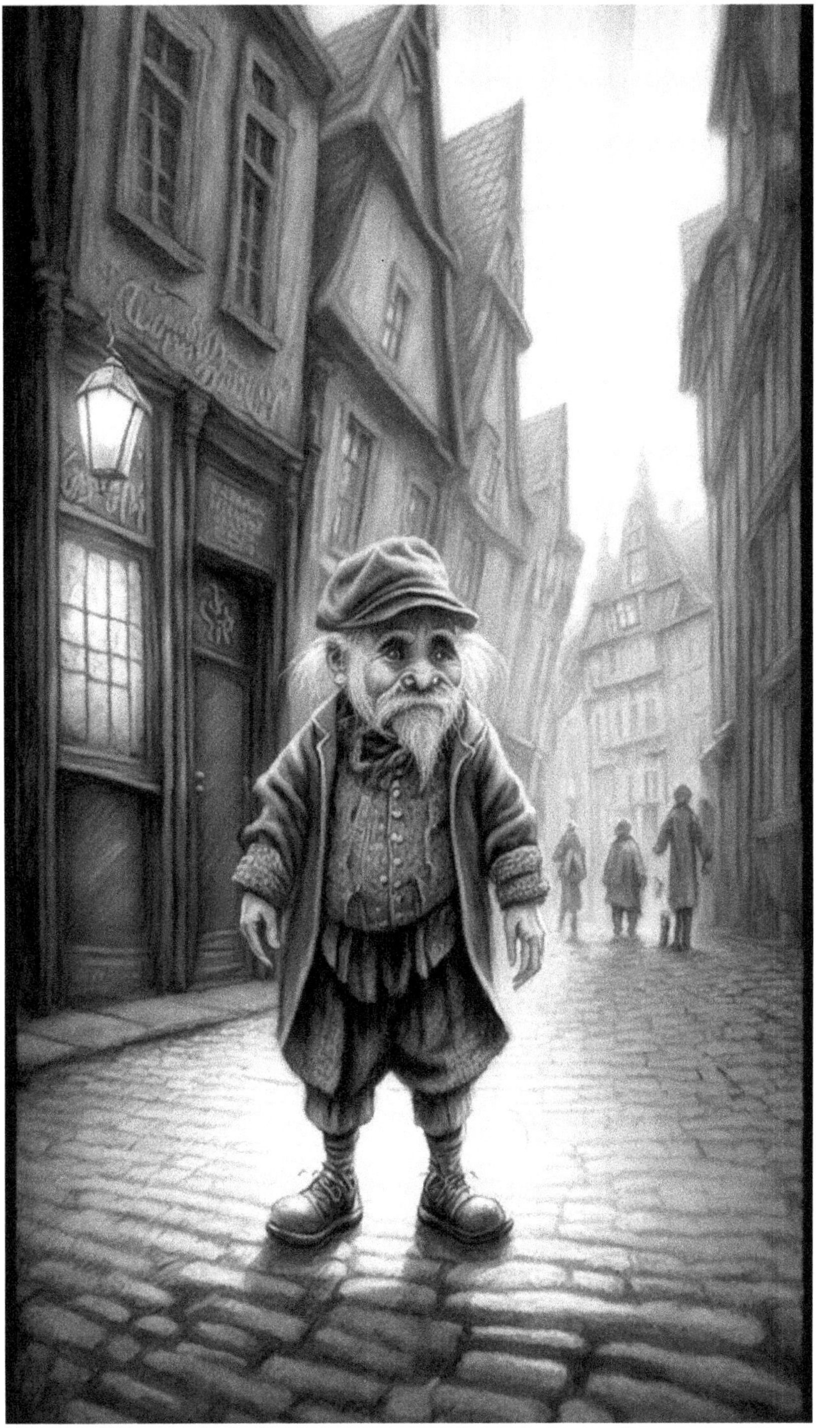

4

THE LITTLE MAN OF CARLISLE

It was 1986 when this all happened. The first time I saw him when I was coming out of the Stars and Stripes on Botchergate. I'd been to see Bob Calvert, who used to be with Hawkwind, now solo. He was fantastic — a genius. He rocked it, but there wasn't much of a crowd to be honest. Anyway, that was the night I saw the Little Man. He stood about four foot tall with a wide-brimmed brown felt hat with a flat top. He dressed like someone from the 17th Century anyway, with silver-buckled shoes.

He was across the road near the church. He could have been watching anybody, but I felt he was watching me. I ignored him.

I went for a pint in the Border Rambler on my way home. It was maybe half eleven by the time I said my goodbyes — they know me in there so there were lots of goodbyes to say — and was once again on Botchergate. He was there again, the other side of the road. Steve Leech came out behind me and I pointed and said, 'See that bloke?'

But he shook his head. 'What bloke?'

'The little one, with the silver-buckled shoes.'

'Nah, mate. I think you've been on the weed again.'

I harrumphed at that. We walked a way together then he split off to go round the Crescent, and I strolled over towards the citadel then down English Street. I normally cut through the Cathedral grounds to Abbey Street, but at that time of night the cathedral precinct gate was locked.

I live with my mam in one of the old houses on Abbey Street. It's too big for us, really. Dad died nearly fifteen years ago, leaving just us two. Downstairs in the main room is her piano. She used to be a music teacher, but she's 82 now and crippled with arthritis. The doctors say they can't do anything, just fill her full of painkillers. It breaks my heart to see the pain she's in, and how she shuffles around the house. But she puts on a brave face, always saying she can manage.

She was already in bed, so I did my best not to make a noise and went to bed myself. That night I thought about the little man with the silver buckle shoes. Maybe he was some kind of fancy-dress nutter. I don't know. I fell asleep about 2 a.m.

I didn't see the Little Man again for about a week. This time, I was walking through the cathedral grounds and there he was by the big wooden door with the iron rivets in it. Standing there. Unlike that Saturday when I'd seen him before, there weren't many people about. He was definitely looking at me. He just stared at me as I walked by. I give him a hard look and he smiled back. I would have said something, but it was raining and I wanted to get out of the wet.

To tell the truth, he was starting to weird me out and I wondered if it was the weed. It always made me paranoid, and I knew I needed to pack it in.

I didn't see the Little Man for a bit, but then I was at work in the Board. I work as a barman and anyway old Mr Jones came in. He owns the bookshop over the road. He likes a pint too, and he's usually good crack. I got him his Guinness, and he stood at the bar as he always does.

'Do you know, Malcolm,' he said as he wiped the Guinness foam from his top lip, 'There is a secret tunnel in the cellar of this pub?'

I raised an eyebrow. 'A secret tunnel?'

'Yes.'

'Where does it go?'

'All under this part of Carlisle are secret tunnels. Dug by the Druids.'

'Really?' You hear a lot of shit when you're a barman, but Old Jonesey isn't usually one of the bullshitters though. He usually gives you interesting nuggets. This might be one of them, but I was sceptical. 'I've never seen it.'

He tapped his nose. 'The owner boarded it up.'

'Who, Sam?'

He nodded. 'The very same.'

'I find it hard to believe.'

'Ask him.'

'I will. But where did it go?'

'*They*. There's more than one. To the Cathedral and the Castle and all under the old part of the city.'

I snorted. 'So you say.'

'So I do say. It's historical record.'

I had to go away to serve another customer. I didn't get a chance to speak to Jonesey much after that. By the time he wanted his next pint, he'd changed the subject and was going on about the tips for the races the next day. He liked a flutter on the horses.

I did see Sam though. I forgot about the tunnel, but then when he asked me to change the lager barrel, it reminded me. When I came up, rubbing my hands to get rid of the dirt I'd picked up moving the barrel in the old cellar, I said, 'Sam, is it true about the tunnels?'

He narrowed his eyes. 'What?'

'Mr Jones, the book shop bloke; he was telling me that there was an old tunnel that ran from the cellar of this pub.'

'Did he? Old Jonesey should keep his mouth shut.'

I was taken aback. 'Why? Is it true?'

Sam looked grim. 'It was true. I blocked it up. I put a board against it and rolled barrels against the board.'

'That old chip board?'

'Aye.'

'I wondered what that was doing there. Anyway, what's so bad about the tunnels?'

'They're bad luck. There're stories of people going into them and getting lost, and there're stories of things coming out of them.'

'Really? There's lots of them then.'

'A whole network. Under the old city. They go as far as the railway station. And the castle the other way.'

'How come I never heard of them?'

'I don't know, Malcolm. How come you didn't?'

That puzzled me. I said, 'So, you can get into them?'

He said sharply, 'No, you can't and you won't. Not from my cellar anyhow. Get back to serving beer.'

Mam was still up watching the telly when I got in. I hung my coat up and made us both a cup of tea. I sat down on the threadbare chair and said, 'Mam, is it true that there's a network of tunnels under Carlisle?'

She nodded, not taking her eyes from Last of the Summer Wine on the TV. 'Yes,' she said. 'Very old. The druids dug them. Or the Romans.'

'How come you've never told me about these before, mam?'

'I don't remember you asking.'

'Well, if I didn't know there were any...'

I eyed up the chipboard every time I went into the pub cellar after that. There were those aluminium barrels in front of it, but I started using those to change the old ones, so the pile got less and less. Then I tried the chipboard. It was nailed in place, but I could tear it off. Except, I'd probably lose my job as Sam was so against it. He didn't mention the tunnels again, and neither did I.

Then, it was the Wednesday night, and we were quiet but the bitter ran out, so I went down to change the barrel, leaving that lawyer from Scotby waiting for his pint. And as I went down, thinking about nowt much, there was the Little Man with his brown felt hat and his silver-buckled shoes.

My heart went off like a jackhammer and I froze on the bottom step. 'What the hell?' I said, though I didn't say hell. 'What the hell are you doing here?'

The Little Man raised his hand and pointed to the chipboard. Then he vanished. I swear down he vanished.

I went upstairs, pretty shook up.

Sam was there. 'Did you change that barrel?' He said, 'Cause Mr Dixon is waiting for his pint.'

Then he looked at me. 'Are you all right? You're white as a sheet.'

Mr Dixon volunteered from the other side of the bar, 'He looks like he's seen a ghost.'

I said, 'I just saw a little dwarf man down in the cellar. Then he vanished.' I said it low so Dixon couldn't hear us.

Sam whispered, 'With silver-buckled shoes?'

I nodded. 'So you've seen him too?' The fact he'd seen him made me feel better.

'Aye,' he said. 'Only once. When I was a kid. And then I saw him up Stanwix the same week. But never since.'

'What does he want?' I said.

'You be careful,' Sam said. 'Do you want the night off?' Now, that was most unlike Sam to be caring and considerate.

I shook my head. I rubbed my clammy brow. 'No, I'll be fine. But what does he want: The Little Man?'

'He wants your soul,' he said.

That didn't make me feel better.

I went home after work to find the house in darkness. Mam was sitting in the living room with only candles for light. Three or four of them flickered and guttered in saucers, pooling wax and smelling of burning wicks. She was bent over her coffee table and on it was a strange board. She had her finger on some kind of wooden thing and it was moving around the board. The board seemed to have letters on it and the word 'Yes' and 'No.'

'What are you doing?' I asked.

'Ouija Board.'

'Ouija Board. Isn't that evil?'

'No, only if you contact a demon.'

'Have you?'

'I don't think so.'

I stood above her. The little planchette moved under her fingers. 'It's spelling out words,' she said.

'What words?'

'Mostly gibberish. But I got the name Alan.'

'Who's Alan?'

'I don't know. But he's gone now. I've got another one now.'

'Do you want a cup of tea?' I said losing interest. It was hard to see in the gloom and I went to switch the light on.

'No!' she said.

'You don't want a cup of tea?'

'No! Don't switch the light on. It'll ruin the atmosphere.'

I made the tea by the light of a succession of matches, which burned my fingers because mam had all the candles. I made her a cup of tea and went back to where she was still sitting; the planchette darting around under her fingers.

'What are you doing it for, anyway?'

'To contact your dad. I think he had a secret bank account.'

'Really?'

She didn't answer. She was so wrapped up in what she was doing. I said, 'Did you?'

'What?'

'Contact dad?'

'No, just Alan. And now this new one.'

I sat down on my normal seat and wished I could put the telly on. 'Who's the new one?' I said, sipping my tea, which was too hot. I normally let it cool for a while, but normally, I've got something to do while it cools. I didn't, sitting there in the dark.

'Something Belly,' she said.

'That's a weird name.'

'maybe Bella something, but it goes on and I can't quite get the ending.'

'What does he want?'

'He keeps asking for help.'

'What for?'

'Not sure. Just keeps writing "help me".'

Then she went back to sliding her planchette around. 'Hang on,' she said.

I sipped more tea.

'That's interesting,' she said.

'What is?'

'This Belly just wrote "help me, Malcolm."'

I spluttered tea. 'Malcolm? My name.'

She stared at me, her rheumy old eyes glinting in the candlelight. 'Yes, Malcolm. Your name.'

After that, she was in a lot of pain from her arthritis. Sitting hunched up over that board hadn't helped. I got her two paracetamol and a glass of water, though I knew she wouldn't sleep.

Neither did I. My mind kept running over the Ouija Board: Help me, Malcolm. Help with what? How? More weird stuff. I wondered if I was going mad.

I was working at the Board the next night, and I dithered over which t-shirt to wear: Motorhead or Metallica. In the end, I settled for AC/DC. You can't go wrong with the Legendary Australian Heavy Rockers.

In fact, I was humming 'Dirty Deeds Done Dirt Cheap' when I arrived at work. Sam did not look himself. He was sinking a whisky, and he never normally drinks.

'What's up, boss?' I said.

He was shaking, visibly pale. 'I've seen him now.'

'Who?' I asked, but I knew who he meant: the little guy with the silver buckles.

He knew I knew too, so he just jerked a thumb. 'Down in the beer cellar. By the chipboard into the tunnel. He wants in.' He narrowed his eyes. 'By the way, did you move the barrels out of the way? 'Cause there's a lot less of them blocking the entrance than there was.'

I shook my head. 'Not me, boss.'

He looked thoughtful. 'Then it must be that little bastard who's done it. He wants into that tunnel as sure as eggs is eggs.'

'And they is,' I mused.

'What?' he snapped.

'Eggs. They are eggs,' I said by way of explanation.

The shift went as normal. As Sam had changed the barrels before I came in, I didn't need to go down into the cellar. Mr Jones the bookshop owner came in and had his usual Guinness. As he sipped the dark beverage, wiping the foam from his lips that he always got there, like a comic cream moustache, he said a propos of nothing, 'Of course, this place is full of gods.'

'Where is?'

'Carlisle.'

'Really?' I'd never seen any.

He sipped his drink. 'The Celts had lots of gods. Then the Romans brought theirs'

He could be interesting at times. Other times not so much.

He went on. 'And the saints who infested the area in the Dark Ages: they acted just like the druids before them; going from area to area performing odd little miracles.'

'Did they dig more tunnels? Like the druids did before them?'

He looked at me like I was stupid. Then he continued with a happy little smile. 'Some saints were gods, just refashioned.'

'I've never really heard of these gods. Give me some examples,' I said. It was a quiet night, and I was polishing glasses as I listened to him.

'Very well,' said Jonesey. 'Let's start with the Celts, the earliest ones; first there was the multi-skilled god Lugos, after whom Carlisle is ultimately named. He was worshipped down into Italy and across France, Belgium, Britain and Ireland.'

'Is that so?' I said, putting down a polished glass and picking up another to polish.

'There were local gods too. One of them was Belatucadros, who was an important god for the Carvetii or deer tribe of Cumberland. He was a horned god, a god of war and hunting.'

'Who did you say?'

'Eh?'

'The name.'

'Oh, Belatucadros. An odd name. It seems to mean Decorated by Death.'

That shook me. I put the glass down and squinted at him. 'But this Bela — what's his name — was local to us?'

He laughed. 'Yes, once upon a time.'

I thought of the ouija board, but Jonesey was in full flight.

'Yes, but of course over the centuries as no one worshipped them, these old gods lost their power and dwindled into being little local spirits. They maybe even adapted with the times, like the druids became saints. Old Belatucadros probably became a little local sprite before fading away completely...'

'Sprite? Like a leprechaun?'

He nodded. 'That's probably the origin of the Irish leprechaun, worn down versions of local spirits and gods.'

I remembered pictures of leprechauns from a kid's book I once had. I said, 'Why do leprechauns wear silver-buckled shoes?'

'Some wear brass buckled ones.'

'Don't split hairs.'

'Well, it's the dress of the 17th Century. Maybe they just liked the fashion of those times. Who knows?'

I muttered, 'What help would he want?'

He blinked. 'I beg your pardon?'

'What help would he want from the living?'

He stared at me strangely. 'Dear boy, I have no idea what you are talking about.'

Mam was in a lot of pain that night, but I tried to get her as comfortable as she could be and made sure she had her painkillers and a glass of water by the bed. Lying in my narrow bed, I saw all the hours in, hearing the chime of the clock outside ringing in one and two and three and four o'clock.

Mam got up in the night to make herself a cup of tea and I lay there tensely waiting for the sound of her to fall. We would need to move house. She simply couldn't manage the stairs anymore. But she wouldn't have it. Whenever, I raised the subject she snapped at me,

'I am perfectly capable of looking after myself. I am an independent woman!'

The second was true anyway. The first had been once.

That must have been about four o'clock in the morning and the city outside dark and still, just the sound of mam tinkling around in the kitchen with the teacup and the spoon. She would only drink out of bone-china and she had a set of silver spoons with the heads of the kings of England on them.

And then he appeared. The little man with his broad-brimmed hat and silver buckles that glinted appeared in my room. I could see him in the light that fell in my room through a chink in the dirty red curtains.

My heart hammered. I sweated. I tensed my fists as I lay under my blanket and sheets. I closed my eyes tight hoping he would go away, but when I opened them again, he was still there.

Clearing my throat, I said, 'Are you Bela...' I struggled to remember the odd name, 'Belatucadros?'

For the first time he smiled.

'What do you want?' I said, through half-closed eyes.

But he didn't speak. And when I summoned the courage to look at him directly, he was gone.

Nothing happened for days. Mam struggled. I served beer and listened to heavy metal and smoked dope. I smoked more than I had for months. Sam calmed down. It seemed he hadn't seen my little Bela again.

Mr Jones came in, drank his Guinness and talked about Tudors. No more Celtic gods, just Tudors and a little about the Corn Laws. I didn't ask him about my little man either.

Then, it was late. We'd been busy and Sam had left the keys to the pub with me to lock up. I'd seen the last of the customers out and wiped the tables. I'd collected and washed all the glasses and made sure all the doors were locked. I had the keys in my pocket, and I was tense as hell, all alone in there. I had to go down to check the cellar to make sure all was well, see how we were doing on the barrels and make sure the gas was okay.

I didn't want to.

But I had to.

I lifted the sneck of the wooden door at the top of the cellar stairs and peered down. I flicked on the bakelite switch that dated from the 1920s and peered down the steep flight of bare boards that made up the staircase.

I shook my head, gathered my courage and stepped down. The floor board creaked, as did the next one. For some reason, the creaking, which I never usually even noticed, made me tenser.

I reminded myself that the little man had never really harmed me. Even if he had once been a god, what kind of power did a midget in silver-buckled shoes have now?

The switch at the top of the stairs also turned on the bare bulb that hung on a fraying wire in the beer cellar. I halted about halfway on the stairs down before I could see into the cellar, because if I could see into the cellar, I would see him; I knew it.

My breathing and heart were going nuts. I was really sweaty, like a pig, and I wanted to turn back. I stood on the stairs for five minutes. I had to check the cellar.

Or did I?

I could tell Sam I'd done but really, I'd do it tomorrow, when he or Florence or some of the other bar staff were in. I didn't enjoy being on my own in the pub with the little man in the cellar.

My heart still hammered. No, I would do it. I'm not a wuss. I'm a rocker. I thought of Motorhead's song: Bomber, and that gave me courage. Okay, here goes.

I ran down the stairs. And there he was at the bottom.

He stood there by the chipboard panel. There was only one shiny beer barrel blocking it. I regretted moving all the others now. The Little Man stood there in his broad-brimmed hat, with his silver-buckled shoes shining in the electric light.

I was trembling. I didn't know what to do. Then he pointed at the brick floor and the dirt overlaying it. Someone had scraped a message with a stick. It said: Help Me.

This was truly nuts. 'Help you?' I said.

He nodded and smiled.

'How?'

He pointed at the chipboard panel.

'You want into the tunnel?'

He nodded and grinned.

'But you can't remove the panel?' He didn't say anything, and I wondered whether this once mighty god was ashamed he had so little physical power now. But then I remembered what Sam had said about him wanting my soul.

Truth be told, I'm not sure I even have a soul. I've never seen it and I've actually never felt the need for one, but I might have.

Feeling surreal, I found a metal bar in the cellar and used it to prize off the chipboard. The chipboard was damp and the nails holding it into the brick walls were rusty and came out easily with little showers of damp plaster and dirt.

I gasped, falling back as a tide of stinky ancient air poured out from the tunnel. It was dark and damp and I couldn't see into it, but the Little Man stood expectantly.

'You want me to go in first?' I said.

He said nothing. I guessed he did.

I took a step into the darkness and then remembered the torch that Sam kept in the cellar in case of power cuts. I grabbed the tin-metal torch which was reassuringly heavy in my hand like I could clobber anyone or anything I might meet down the tunnel.

I switched the torch on. The light was dim; the batteries were probably old, but even in the yellowy light I could see that the tunnel was long and dark and damp. At first, bricks walled the tunnel. Maybe Victorian, probably older. I took a few steps and glanced back. The Little Man followed me. I don't know if that was good or bad

Then I turned and said, 'I don't know why I'm doing this for you, but if you are a god, I want you to promise to do something good for me.'

I didn't know what I wanted, but I felt otherwise he was just taking advantage. The Little Man looked benignly at me. He said nothing; he didn't smile, just kept on looking back at me. I snorted.

Worthless trying to bargain with someone like him. He was probably imaginary anyway.

But the tunnel wasn't. I kept on walking. After the bricks ran out, the tunnel was walled with stones, old looking stones. They could have been Roman, who knows? or Druidic, if that's a word.

We went on until we came to a cross junction. There was the way back, a way ahead and tunnels going left and right. I looked back at the Little Man for guidance. He pointed left, so left we went. We kept on walking for about a hundred yards. The tunnel was featureless and silent. It was like being in a grave. No sound, not even rats. Rats would have been scary, but comforting because they were real.

Then we came to another junction. A way ran off to the right, while the main way ran on in front of me. He pointed right. The tunnel here was narrower and looked like it had been dug out at a different time. The slabs of stone in the walls and ceiling weren't regular like the Roman stones. They were just old bits of sandstone, heaped up. It was a wonder they hadn't collapsed. Then after about twenty yards, I came to the first collapse. Heaps of sandstone had fallen onto the ground. I could pick my way over it, but it reminded me how dangerous these tunnels were. I looked back for reassurance, but the little man just pointed ahead.

So ahead we went. The torch light was getting dimmer. I got scared, but I was committed now. He walked on behind me. He seemed to know where he was going. And then after another five minutes, the tunnel changed. It got wider, and the ceiling lifted. It was as if we had intruded on another building. The stonework in this part of the tunnel was better. I pivoted round, but he'd stopped.

'What?' I asked. 'Where to now?' There was only one way, well two. I guess we could have gone back, but what was the point in that? It felt like we'd arrived somewhere.

Instead of answering, the Little Man pointed then he jerked his chin as if I was to walk on. I did, but he didn't follow. I stopped again. 'Aren't you coming?'

He shook his head.

This was odd. He wanted me to go on, but wouldn't come himself. I grew suspicious. 'How come I have to go?'

He didn't reply in words; he just jerked his chin again. That was that way I was to go.

I glanced around. I was in some kind of underground space. It wasn't a cavern. It looked manmade, and it had been made with some skill, but a long time ago, looking at the sandstone slabs neatly laid to make up the floor, but worn as if by centuries.

'Really?' I said.

He nodded again. I shrugged, then sighed and walked on. I played the torch beam around, weak as it was, to see where I was. I was in a room now. Big. Suddenly it occurred to me that this looked like the cathedral, but it was a part I'd never visited. I was underground and I wondered if it was the crypt. I wandered on. There were no coffins or sepulchres here, but as I turned a corner, I saw past the wall on my left that there was a heap of stuff in the middle of the room. I looked back, but the Little Man was way behind. It occurred to me that as he was pagan, maybe he couldn't enter a consecrated space.

I hesitantly approached the heap. There were bits of sculpture and carvings. They looked to be of various ages. I recognised a Roman altar. I'd seen ones like it in Tullie House museum. The inscription read: Diis Manibus… which I recalled meant "to the Gods of the Dead". I do remember some things despite what they said at school.

I had a good peer at the stuff in the heap.

Then there was a stone with a carving of a bound Devil. It had Viking runes on it. There was a carved woman on a horse. And then, I found a little effigy. I reached down and picked it up. It was of local sandstone, and about the size of a big brick. It was carved in the shape of a man with horns protruding from his head. He held a round shield in one hand and a worn inscription on the bottom was hard to read. I ran my thumb along the rough stone to help my eyes read the inscription. It seemed to read: Deo Belatucadro.

It stuck me that this was what the little man wanted. The rest of the stuff was so heavy and so mixed, I wouldn't easily be able to move it, even if I wanted to. I figured this was a secret place in the Cathedral that where the priests had heaped up and locked away all the pagan stuff from here. Probably very hush-hush but it seemed to be effective because Little Belatucadros, couldn't enter.

Holding his statue, I walked back to where the Little Man waited for me. His eyes lit up when he saw what I carried, and he licked his lips. It seemed he would come forward, but he didn't. As I approached him, he reached up for the statue and I gave it to the liittle fella. The Little Man with the brown felt broad-brimmed hat and the silver-buckled shoes, hugged the effigy to him, like it was a long-lost puppy.

And then he changed.

He sort of melted into smoke and grew, so he was no longer the little man. Even his shoes changed and instead of their silver-buckled neatness, I thought I saw the feet of an animal, maybe a stag, maybe a ram, before the smoke dwindled and turned into a mist, then a vapour. I got one last look at him. He had the head of a ram, or a goat with long curly horns and slitted amber eyes. And as he vanished, he bleated. And maybe that was thank you. But maybe it wasn't.

Whatever it was, I had to make my way back along the tunnels with the failing flashlight. There were not too many turns, and luck was on my side because I saw the light of the beer cellar ahead of me just as the torch batteries died.

I followed the light at the end of the tunnel, and I have never been happier to step into that shabby, dirty beer cellar with its stink of old ale and bare electric bulb.

I locked up the pub and went home, my head full of what I had seen.

I was surprised to find all the lights blazing at home. I put my key in the door and went in. My mother was in the front room. She was dancing to an old 78 of Glenn Miller on the gramophone.

I frowned. 'What on earth has happened, mother?'

She beamed at me. 'Malcolm, Malcolm, I'm pain free! My arthritis pain has gone. Look!'

And she shimmied and shook in front of me in time to the big band swing sound. She was as lish as a twenty-year-old girl. 'Well, well, well,' I said.

She grinned. 'Yes, I was in town today and I went to that hippy shop down that alley off Devonshire Street.'

'I know it, yes.'

She was eager to continue with her story. 'So, I was asking if they had anything for arthritis and the girl said they'd just got a new product that morning. She said she couldn't speak for it, as it was so new, but I said I'd give anything a go so I said I'd take it, and she said fine that'll be £1.50. So I gave her the money, and she wrapped the tea and I took it and came home, after I'd had a look in Bulloughs, and saw Marjory, which was nice. Her Stan hasn't been so good, you know. It's his brain, they think, but they don't really know. That's doctors for you, a bunch of idiots. And then, when I got back, I made some tea, and just about half an hour ago I felt all the pain suddenly lift. It's amazing! It's a miracle!'

'Hmm,' I said. 'Show me the packet.'

So she danced her way to the kitchen, the strains of Glenn Miller still filling the house and she picked up an opened packet. I read the front. It said:

"Dr Bela's Miracle Arthritis Cure."

'You got this today?' I said.

'Yes, Malcolm, and I'm glad I did.'

I opened the packet and looked at the contents. To be honest, it looked like shredded brown felt. The sort that might be used to make a broad-brimmed hat. I said as much.

Mam said, 'I don't care if it is felt, Malcolm. You just soak it, and it works!'

Now it is possible that this is a coincidence, and it's possible that it isn't. I never saw the Little Man again, in Carlisle or anywhere else, but I like to think he helped my old mam with her pain. So, wherever he may be, on this earth or fuller's, good luck to him, I say: Good luck.

5

THE HITCHER

The snow came down like somebody emptying buckets full of frozen goose-down way up high. A glance to my left showed the sun had disappeared from the west behind the mountains and what light remained drained by the second from grey to blue to black. I'd been a fool to come this way, I knew, but it was the quickest route to get back to Keswick on Christmas Eve and I wanted to see the kids' faces before they went to bed. The quickest route normally, though now I regretted not taking the longer route by the motorway which they'd at least keep clear.

Working on a Christmas Eve is the curse of being self-employed. I'd worked previous years but this Christmas Eve was snowier than any I remembered.

The windscreen wipers flicked back and forward, struggling to clear inches of snow as I peered into the gloom. I was just coming through Grasmere. Christmas trees sparkled in the windows of the houses I passed and people had hung snowdrop style lights along their house eaves. I got glimpses of warmth and family gatherings as the atmosphere of Christmas deepened.

It deepened for them, but all that deepened for me was the snow. I knew I had to climb up to Dunmail Pass and there was a chance I would slip and slide on the ascent, or skid on the way down. I needed to be careful not to come off the road because hardly any traffic was passing now. No one was as foolish as me.

I was heading up the straight before the hill now, leaving the lights of Grasmere behind me. The twin tubes of light from my headlamps illuminated cotton wool blizzards. The strain of concentrating on the road was giving me a stiff neck and a sore head. If someone ran in front of me now, I wouldn't see them, and if I hit the brakes, I'd slide.

Then I saw a figure to the side of the road thumbing a lift. I did a double take. Was someone really out there in this? Where the heck were they going? I thought of driving past, but maybe they'd miscalculated the time and the weather just like me and wanted to get home for Christmas. Luckily I was going so slow that when I pumped the brakes, I slowed at a steady rate rather than skewing off to the left or right.

The car stopped. The indicator lights winking harshly, the engine idling. Where were they? I twisted my head and peered right. I hit the button to wind the window down and with an electric whirr the cold and the wet came in. Feathers of snow invaded the car interior - winter ghosts that vanished as soon as they arrived. Still no one.

'Hello?' I craned my head and shouted again. 'Hello? Is there anyone there?'

I was just thinking I'd mistaken a snow-shrouded gate post for a person and about to set off when there came a rap at the driver's side, not the passenger side with its open window. I felt an inexplicable jolt of panic. The snow billowed in from the left as I wound down the right window, causing a cross draft of frigid air. Someone stood outside the car. I shivered, whether from the cold or from some primitive fear of strangers on dark winter nights, I don't know.

It was a man. I think it was a man. The figure stood tall and dark with snow flurries blowing round his hooded face. 'Thanks,' he said. His voice was deep and the accent local. That reassured me. He was a mortal man after all, one of my own people.

'Where are you going?' I asked, wishing he'd either get in or leave me to my journey.

'Just up the road.'

'Further on than the pass?'

He nodded. I could hardly see the gesture with the dark and the hood of his coat up. I was getting cold and keen to be on my way. 'Get in if you're getting in.'

The dark figure walked round the front of the car, his legs lit up by each beam in turn. Then the door opened, and he sat in, bringing chill with him.

I set off, pulling the car slowly back into the main carriageway, not that you could see it now, the snow was so deep. Nothing had passed me while I sat pulled up waiting for the stranger. And it was weird too how he knocked on my window, as if he was expecting to get in and drive.

I got up to maybe twenty miles an hour. It would take me all night to get home at this speed.

'You live locally?' I asked.

'Yes. Not far away.'

'Ah.'

Then he was quiet. As we progressed slowly up to the start of the pass, he said nothing and I began to feel there was something very odd about him.

After ten minutes, when we were climbing, and the wheels had already slipped and shifted once, he said, 'Would you do me a favour?'

I hesitated, cleared my throat and said. 'Sure.' Then I laughed. 'Depends what it is.'

'Would you take a message to someone for me?'

'Well. I need to get back home, really. Sorry.'

He paused. 'You're going there, anyway.'

'What?'

Despite the intensity of my concentration on the road ahead, I twisted my head. 'What?'

He was staring straight ahead, his hood still up. 'It's just a card. A Christmas card.'

I directed my stare back to the road. I couldn't lose concentration on this high, windy road or I'd wreck the car.

'What do you mean I'll be going there, anyway? I have to get home.'

I felt him stuff the card into the pocket of my coat, uninvited with a muffled 'thank you.' Then a minute later, he said, 'When you see him, tell him I miss him.'

'See who?'

'Can you let me out here, please?'

I looked at the whirling snow and the dark outside the car. 'Here? You'll freeze to death.'

'Here please. I can't go where you're going. Sorry.'

The guy was clearly crazy. I was glad to be rid of him. I thought he was foolish, but I wasn't going to fight to stop him. How could I? He would have to bear the consequences of his action.

I started to brake. 'Okay. I don't think…'

He interrupted me. 'Thank you, stranger. I'm sorry it has to be you. You're kind.'

I really needed him out of the car now. He was starting to freak me out. He might even murder me out here if I didn't let him go. I would stop, let him out then set off again. Home for Christmas.

The door thunked shut, and he was gone, vanished into the blizzard. Maybe he'd get a lift from someone else. Maybe I should call the police? Not that I had any mobile signal among these hills. Best I just get home. That would be enough of a struggle.

And so I drove on. The snow lessened slightly, but it was dark. I saw the entrance tracks to lonely farmhouses set way back down their drives, but then even they grew less frequent as I climbed up into the truly wild country. I crested the pass top, went by the cairn I knew was there from previous journeys but couldn't see now. Then I started to descend. If anything, this was the more dangerous part of the journey. The bends looked unfamiliar and I couldn't tell where I was. Then a sudden curve in the road loomed in my headlights and I stamped on the brakes.

The car slid and swerved like a bronco as I tried to get control back. It gathered pace and fear shot through me. If I went over the edge here, it would be the end of me. The car began a lateral slide and there was an enormous bang.

The next thing I knew was silence. The engine had died, and it was cold. I must have lost consciousness briefly. I blinked and shook my head to clear it. I couldn't stay in the car; I'd freeze to death, so I struggled to get out. I unbuckled the seat belt and shoved the door. It opened easily, and that was amazing because when I stood outside, With my fingers in the dark, I felt how buckled the metal was. It was a miracle I'd survived at all. I pulled my coat in tight and turned up the collar. But weirdly, I didn't feel cold.

My plan was to walk down the road until a car came. So I walked. I walked for a long time and the night was so dark it was as if I was the only person in the world, alone in a realm of snow and shadow. And then I saw a lane leading off to the left. The sign on it needed painting, but it said, 'Greensyke Farm.' It was incredible I could see to read because there was no obvious light source.

I figured I could keep walking on the road, but to be honest, who would be out driving in this weather? Or, I could walk down this lonning to Greensyke Farm. Farmers were bound to be in. And so I left the road and walked the stony path. My feet didn't slip on the snow-covered rocks and soon I saw a lone farmhouse ahead. There was a light in the window. No Christmas decorations but a light there as if to guide travellers.

It took me a further five minutes to get to the farmhouse and once there; the snow blowing round my ears and face; I knocked on the door.

No one came. I thought maybe no one was in, despite the light. Then I reasoned that they wouldn't really be expecting visitors, so I rapped again and this time there was the sound of movement deep within the house.

The rattling of bolts and opening of latches came muffled from behind the front door, then it was thrown open, not cautiously, but as if in welcome.

An old man stood there. 'You're here. I knew he'd send someone. He always does.'

'What?' I said.

'Come in, come in,' he said. He looked and sounded like a normal farmer. They're so down to earth normally but this guy sounded as crazy as the man I'd given a lift to.

'Look,' I said, still standing at the door with the weather behind me. 'I just need to use your phone and then I'll be gone as soon as the rescue people come to tow my car.'

The farmer looked at me sadly. 'The phone won't be any use to you. But come on. The cold's getting into the house, even if it doesn't bother you.'

And he was right. The cold didn't bother me. But at his request I stepped in.

The house was old-fashioned. It looked like it came from years ago. I scanned around for the phone. I'd persuade him to let me use it. I'd pay him if I had to.

'Do you have the card?' he said.

My hand went to the pocket of my coat. I did have the card. He saw me move to it and said, 'Could I have it, please?'

Without speaking, I took the card out of my pocket and gave it to him. It said, 'dad' on the front in rough, male looking handwriting.

Fear rose through my throat and mouth and eyes like a cold flower. I heard my voice falter. 'What's going on here?'

'My son David sent you. He always knows who it will happen to. That's why he gave you the card. He's never forgotten me even after all these years.'

My mind whirled. I remembered stories about the myth of the ghostly hitchhiker. Maybe this was what this was. Except the guy hadn't vanished, he'd got out like a normal person.

I heard my voice waver. I couldn't ask this; it was too weird.

But the farmer smiled. He looked kind and at the same time sorrowful. His card was in his hand. I saw tears in his eyes. 'It's lovely,' he said. 'Was there any other message?'

I brushed back my hair with my hand, knocking the remaining snow out. I remembered what the hitcher had said. 'He said he missed you.'

The farmer nodded. 'And I miss him too. But it's just for a while. Until then he must use you and people like you to deliver messages.'

I finally worked up my courage. I had to know. I asked, 'Your son...'

The farmer kept smiling.

I cleared my throat. 'Is he...' I felt weird, but I finished my sentence. 'Is he dead?'

'No, lad.'

'What then?'

The farmer looked at me with a sad smile. 'We are.'

6

THE HIGHEST INN IN ENGLAND

It styles itself the highest pub in England - the place we went. Whether that's true I don't know, but it's certainly high. You are right among the mountains, rising ruggedly on all sides. The road is narrow, coming up passes from Patterdale one side and from Ambleside the other. Yes, England's Lake District — the most beautiful part of the country they say. It's very beautiful, of that there's no doubt.

I won't go back, though. Ever.

This all happened several years ago now. I had gone on holiday with my wife Margaret and my daughters Ellie and Hazel. We live in Manchester and I work as a project manager in the IT department of a medium-sized company.

I remember we were happy the day we arrived. The sun was shining. We'd enjoyed the drive through the beautiful scenery and then when we got to the Inn, we were impressed by its setting. Who wouldn't be?

"Man, this is beautiful," I said, stepping out of the car on that fine summer day. Down below I saw the lake glittering, while above birds of prey circled on the warm updrafts.

"I'm surprised it's not raining," said Margaret. The Lake District is famous for its rain.

"Yep, we're lucky." I grinned. 'Born lucky.'

The girls being teenagers, Ellie 14 and Hazel 16, were less than ecstatic at the grandeur of the scenery. I knew they would rather have spent time chilling with their friends back home - sitting in each other's bedrooms talking about boys and makeup. But I'd dragged them out here for their own good. That's what I thought, anyway.

As I opened the car door, I looked at Ellie, slight and fair-haired; she was the more biddable of the two. Hazel had her mother's dark colouring and her stubborn temperament, made worse by teenage hormones. Ellie hopped out, but Hazel hadn't got out of the car yet and was sitting with her earphones on - Listening to some LA rapper as if this present earth and air were less to do with her than drive-by shootings in Compton.

"What do you think, Ellie?" I said pointing around.

Standing by the car, Ellie looked up from her iPhone and smiled. "Yeah, dad. It's lovely."

Margaret nodded too. "Yep, stunning. What a view!"

I bent down to speak to Hazel through the open car door. "What do you think?" I said it loud and purposefully. She was being deliberately rude. She pretended she hadn't heard, so I repeated myself.

"What?" she said, scowling, pulling out the earphones.

"Beautiful view!" I said.

"Whatever," she said and went back to deliberately doing nothing. I felt a flash of anger. Margaret saw it and placed her hand on my arm. "I'll get her out," she said.

I walked away to where Ellie was admiring the landscape. "It's nice, but it's pretty remote. I wouldn't like to be here at night!" she said.

"You *are* going to be here at night, you doughnut." I ruffled her hair. "We're staying here!"

"Oh," she said. She paid no attention to anything I told her, but she was a lovely sweet girl.

Margaret had got Hazel out of the car and all four of us went into the dark bar. There was a low murmur from the tourists sitting round eating their Cumberland sausage and drinking their Jennings ale.

There was no official reception - the guy at the bar doubled as meeter and greeter. I said hi. "Got a room here tonight. Name's Rogers."

He got down his big handwritten book and by running his finger along the entries, found my name.

"Two rooms?" he said.

I nodded. "One for my wife and myself, and one for my daughters."

"Fine," he said. He showed us up. We creaked our way up the dark wooden stairs. The doors were all different, nothing machine made. They looked as if they'd been there for donkeys' years. The rooms were old and quirky too, with low dark beams and rugged plastered walls. The place looked ancient, but luckily there was an en-suite bathroom in both the rooms.

"Nice," said Margaret.

"Lots of character," I said.

Ellie came round the door from her bedroom just down the short uneven corridor.

"What do you think?" I asked.

She pulled a face. "I don't like it. It's spooky."

Margaret laughed. "That's just your imagination. Just because it's old."

Hazel appeared. "I don't like it either."

I groaned. "What a surprise."

"It's got no WiFi. I've got no Internet. What am I supposed to do?"

"You're not supposed to be on the Internet; you're supposed to be enjoying the natural beauty and the company of your family."

She shrugged ill-temperedly.

"Anyway, let's go out."

We got back in the car and took the precipitous, narrow road down to Ambleside - the call it The Struggle; I'd hate to go down in the ice. From there we parked beside the lake and went on a walk.

The weather had cooled, but it was still pleasant. We three walked ahead with Hazel trudging moodily behind. Then we took a rowing boat and went out on the lake. It was truly beautiful. I felt calm and relaxed - a million miles from work and my stupid boss.

We went back to the Inn and freshened up. Margaret is a very tidy woman, and she made sure we bagged our muddy boots and no dirt got on the wooden floor and its rugs. After my shower, I went down to the bar. I had a pint of Cumberland Ale and waited for my family.

The place was quieter now. There were still some tourists. The barman/manager was called Alf. I asked him how many bedrooms they had.

"Just four. We do most of our trade from meals and day tourists."

"Anyone staying here but us?"

He shook his head. "No, you're the only guests tonight. This lot will go around eleven." He gestured to the bar and its drinkers.

Then the girls and their mother came down. They had dressed for dinner and they looked nice. We decided to eat there and then. I ordered according to Alf's recommendations. I had local salmon which was fresh and good. Margaret had something with quails' eggs. Ellie had a burger. Hazel didn't eat; she just sat with her earbuds in.

"I'm going to rip those out of your ears if you don't stop being so rude," I snapped at her. Grumpily she took them out and sat with her arms crossed, not speaking.

Soon the customers began to leave. Alf came and joined us.

"Want a photo?" he said. "I'll take one so you can remember the nice time you had."

"Sure," said Margaret. She delved into her bag and pulled out her digital camera. We arranged ourselves to be photographed. Hazel didn't want to be in it but Margaret sternly told her to grow up and get over herself. That didn't go down well, but we all managed to sit in a line, three of us smiling at least.

"Say cheese!" Alf said. The camera flashed, and he handed it back to Margaret.

"Let me see," I said. Margaret passed me the photograph. It was a great one of us all. Even Hazel who looked moody but pretty with her unsmiling face.

"Oh, you could have smiled," said Margaret.

"Didn't want to. What's to smile about?" snapped Hazel.

I touched Margaret's arm. "Leave her. No point starting a fight."

Ellie looked around the bar with its stuffed foxes' heads, brass hunting horns and old pictures of hunters in red coats walking across the fells. "This is a spooky place," she said.

"It can be," Alf replied. "Especially in the winter when the fog's down and you can't see your hand in front of your face."

"Do you get snowed in much?" I asked.

"Well, I don't live here. Me and the wife have a cottage about two miles along the road. When the snow hits, I can't even get to the Inn, so we shut up."

"Does anyone live in?" asked Margaret.

"No, the chef lives in Ambleside. The bar staff are all local so they just travel. You're here on your own tonight!" he laughed.

"What if there's an emergency?" I said.

He said, "You've got my phone number? It's a landline, because mobiles don't work up here - no signal. My number is in the book in your room. I can be here in minutes."

"Ok," I said reassured. I couldn't see we'd need him, anyway.

"But I'm here by seven thirty each morning. Either me or the wife when I have a lie in on Sunday."

"Is it haunted?" asked Ellie.

"Of course!" Alf grinned.

Margaret looked up. "Don't be scaring her. She's got a vivid imagination."

He sounded apologetic. "It's all made up. Just a story. But the place is very old."

"Tell me!" said Ellie, laughing.

Margaret said, "You won't sleep. Let's talk about what we're doing tomorrow."

"No, please," she beseeched Alf. "Tell me, please!"

I shrugged. "If she has nightmares, it's her own fault."

"We're only next door, John," said Margaret.

Alf, seeing he had permission, went on. "Well, though this building is 200 or so years old. It's built on the site of an older house. It's said it was the house of Adam Scot who was a warlock. He had to live up here because he'd been driven out of the town by the folk who he terrified with his so-called magic. Apparently, he always picked on outsiders. People who felt different and were unhappy. They said he killed them and ate their livers to give him strength."

"Eew, that's gross!" said Ellie. Margaret laughed. I saw that even Hazel was listening now.

"So he lived up here with the ravens and the wolves, and worse things that came in the dark of the night to visit him. Some say demons and succubi."

"What's that?"

"A succubus? It's an evil spirit in the form of a woman," said Alf. He'd obviously told this story many times and it was further polished each time he recounted it.

"So did he kill many people?" asked Ellie.

"It is said he would prey on travellers. People out late at night, making their lonely way from Patterdale to Ambleside. There were lots of them who weren't seen again. One woman lost her little daughter and they say her ghost wanders the fells hereabouts, looking for her. What she doesn't realise is that Adam Scot took the girl."

Ellie shuddered. "I'm scared now."

Her mother put her arm round her shoulder. "It was hundreds of years ago, my lamb. Don't worry."

"And it's totally made up!" I butted in.

Alf laughed. "They do say that there's a room in this building, never discovered yet, that holds the bones of Adam Scot's victims."

"Bullshit!" I exclaimed. I was perhaps overreacting because he'd managed to send a chill up my spine and I didn't want to admit it.

Alf laughed. "Same again? Last one before I leave you."

I nodded. Alf poured the pint. "I'll be switching the electric pumps off, but if you want a whisky or a brandy, just take one from the optic and we'll settle up tomorrow."

"Very trusting," I smiled.

"You seem an honest man," he replied.

I looked over at Hazel. She was quiet, not even listening to her music. I saw her looking at her mother, as if seeking some comfort and reassurance but Margaret was busy fussing over Ellie.

Alf came with my pint. Then he began to switch things off and lock doors. When he had his coat on, he said, "Turn this light off when you go upstairs will you? I'll be back in the morning. Full English breakfasts?"

I nodded. "Not for Hazel. She's a vegetarian."

He waved and closed the door behind him. I heard it lock.

"But we can get out right?" asked Hazel.

"Of course, we've got keys," I said.

I slowly sipped my pint. Alf had put a fire guard around the log fire that was slowly dying but still giving off pleasing warmth.

"You're quiet," I said to Hazel.

"Me? No, I'm not."

I reached over and stroked her hand. She didn't pull away as she normally did these days. I said, "I miss our chats. We used to get on so well."

The ghost of a smile played across her face as she remembered. "I was a real daddy's girl. What a wuss I was."

"It's not all about being tough and grown up Haze. You've got to leave room for softness and care in your heart."

She shrugged. "I'm going to bed." Margaret got up with Ellie. "I'll go up too. Don't you be too late."

"I'll just finish this. Maybe have a whisky. I'm just enjoying the fire and the quiet."

When they'd gone I was alone in the barroom. I poured myself a whisky from the optic as he said. It felt naughty helping myself to drinks, but I would be scrupulously honest when I settled up the next day. Tumbler in hand, I sat near the fire just enjoying the peace. The only sounds were the crackling and spitting of the logs and the faint sound of the wind as it moaned around the old building.

And then I thought I saw something. Something vague and ill-defined, but man-sized, like a memory or even a premonition.

I rubbed my eyes then I stared into the corner where I was sure something had moved. But there was nothing. Just a table and some chairs. Nothing to worry about. I tapped a finger on my whisky tumbler. I laughed to myself.

But there it was again.

Not a vision this time, but a feeling that there was something or somebody there. I felt so stupid but I actually walked over to the empty corner and looked around me. But there was no Adam Scot to be seen. Reassured, I sat back down and finished my whisky.

I saw that Margaret had left her camera on the table. I picked it up and turned on the viewing screen to see that last nice picture of us four she'd snapped in the bar. Just to see if we looked like a happy family.

I'd seen the picture when she took it, but when I looked at the image again, it wasn't as I remembered it. For one thing, Hazel's face was blurry, and behind her, I could swear there was the shadow. Not an ordinary shadow. But as if there was an image behind this one, like when a painter paints over an old picture, but then time fades the covering image and reveals what used to be beneath.

The shadow was the shape of a man. I could swear it hadn't been there before. But of course that was ridiculous. It must have been there. It was obviously some fault in the camera screen, or maybe my eyes in the poor light. Shaking my head, I knocked the whisky back and retired to bed.

Margaret was reading when I got up to the room. She yawned and smiled.

I yawned. "I'm tired."

"All the fresh air."

By the time I brushed my teeth and got my pyjamas on, Margaret was asleep. Her chest lifting gently with each breath. I lay beside her warm body and then fell asleep myself.

A piercing scream wakened me.

"What the fuck was that?" I shouted, jumping out of bed. I clicked the light on. My heart was hammering. Margaret was sitting up in bed, her face white. "It came from the girls' room," she said.

I ran through and burst the door open. There was Ellie standing screaming, pressing herself against the wall, like she was terrified of something and wanted to get away from it. The thing she was terrified of was Hazel. Hazel stood there, vacant eyed in the middle of the room.

I grabbed Ellie. "It's ok; she's only sleepwalking."

"She's never sleepwalked before."

"It's a new place, a strange place. I'll put her back to bed."

"But it's not just that, dad."

I tried to comfort Ellie before going over to steer Hazel back to bed. "What, Ellie?" I said.

She was shivering. It took her ages to get the words out. Then she stammered, "There was a man in here with us."

I frowned. "Don't be silly. How could that be? I'm the only man in the place."

She was shaking. "He wasn't an ordinary man. He was dressed in black and he was hard to see. I woke to hear him bending over Hazel and whispering things to her. Then I screamed, and you came in and he's gone."

Margaret was standing at the door in her night-dress. She cuddled Ellie. "Just a dream, my love. That silly Alf's stories got you all scared."

"No, mum. I know what I saw. It was an evil warlock. It was Adam Scot."

We spoke no more about it. In the morning, I just told Alf we'd changed our plans. Something had called us home unexpectedly. He was nice about it and refunded the second night's stay.

Hazel was very sleepy that morning. Ellie told her she'd been sleepwalking, but she didn't believe it. She was quieter even than usual. When we were ready to go, I couldn't find her, so I went back into the Inn and up the stairs. She was just standing in the room.

"You ok?" I said. "I can take you to the doctor's if you're not well."

She didn't speak. I went up and put my arms around her. She seemed cold to the touch. Maybe she really was ill. I said, "Come on, Haze. Let's go home. You can go see your friends."

I went to the bedroom door, but she didn't follow. I turned. "Hazel?" I said.

There was definitely something odd about her.

She said, "I can't ever leave here."

That was bizarre. She'd never even wanted to come in the first place.

I squeezed her arm and pulled her out. She didn't resist, but she didn't actively come with me either. When we got to the Inn's door, I realised I'd left the boot of the car open and it was raining. I hurried over to shut it. Ellie and Margaret were already in the car. I turned round to see Hazel just standing at the door of the Inn. She didn't come out, just stood there. And it looked to me like she wasn't my little Hazel anymore. But it was a silly thought, so I opened the car door for her and went to get her. She felt limp and dragged her feet. It was all most odd, but I got her to the car, got her in and her sister buckled up her safety belt for her.

When we were all in the car, we headed home. I put the radio on. Margaret fed me grapes that she'd bought in the town the previous day. We drove down the motorway. The girls were quiet in the back listening to their own music but that was normal.

We got home in the early afternoon. The girls went up to their separate bedrooms, and I didn't see them for the rest of the day.

The next day, I had a day off as I'd expected still to be in the Lake District. I can't lie in bed, even when I'm off. I've got too many years of getting up for work ingrained in me. So I got up and made a cup of tea and some toast for Margaret.

As I walked into our bedroom with the tray, Ellie came down from the attic we'd converted for her. She looked ashen. She said, "Hazel's not there."

"What?" said Margaret.

I said, "Are you sure?"

Ellie nodded. "Come and check."

"She'll have gone out to see her friends," said Margaret.

"It's not even nine in the morning," I said.

And Hazel wasn't there.

You can imagine the state we were all in. We searched the house and rang all her friends, all of whom told us they hadn't seen Hazel since before we set off for the Lake District. We called the Police and reported her as a missing person.

I don't know why but I went and got the camera again. I switched it on and waited impatiently while it booted up. Then I switched on the viewfinder and looked at that photograph and it was daytime now so I couldn't blame the poor light. I couldn't blame the screen, because it worked fine. But in the picture, Hazel had gone. And in her place, a dark, shadowed being stood.

That night two police officers called at our house - a man and a woman. Margaret saw them first through the window. She could hardly control herself. We knew what they were coming to tell us.

We showed them in. They were very polite. The woman said, "Please sit dowThe

"I'm afraid I have some very bad news."

I was shaking. Margaret started to cry. "Just say it," I said.

"Ambleside Police…"

"Ambleside Police? Where we've just been?"

The woman nodded and continued. "Ambleside police have found the remains of a young female in a secret room at the Inn where you stayed."

Margaret stood up, suddenly, agitated. She muttered, "That can't be. Hazel came back with us in the car."

I stood there, a terrible realisation coming over me and I knew:

Whatever had come back with us to our house wasn't Hazel.

7

THE BEWCASTLE FAIRIES

It was Christmas 1653, not that there was a real Christmas that year since Oliver Cromwell and his Puritans had banned Christmas as a pagan festival. Instead, we were to have a 'silent contemplation' of the birth of Christ.

Silent contemplation, my arse. I needed ale. So, I set off Christmas morning leaving my good wife Jane with the plucked goose and my sons and daughters to do the work needed before I returned to eat. Myself, I got my old bay mare Jenny. The fact that the horse is called a similar name to my wife is a cause of some confusion to me at times, especially after a few pints sunk.

I clip-clopped on Jenny along the road to Bewcastle. The road is rough. You couldn't get a cart over the ruts and stones in the winter mud. But Jenny managed it just fine.

I arrived at the King's Head, a rough, tumble-down sort of place, but very close to my heart to be greeted by Ned, the landlord. 'What are you doing here today Alexander Armstrong? Shouldn't you be having a silent contemplation of our Lord's birth?' He cackled.

'I'd rather do it over a pint of your best ale. I can contemplate while I'm looking into the bubbles,' I said.

And so I drank one. I drank another one from my leather tankard, which I take with me everywhere on the off chance I may call into an alehouse. Then I sank yet another. There was no one in the pub that Christmas Day but me. At least Ned had the fire on.

'Banned Christmas, eh?' Ned said as way of conversation.

'Cromwell,' I spat.

'You a Royalist then, Alex?'

I shook my head. 'I'm an Armstrong. We Armstrongs look after each other. Not English, not Scotch, not Royalists not Parliamentarians. Just Armstrongs. We live here in the Debatable Lands and we see to ourselves. So, no Neddy. I'm no Royalist. And I don't care whether Christmas is banned. I never cared for it much, anyway.' I looked around. 'Seems it scared the rest of your customers away.'

Ned said, 'No, never had many in Christmas morning. Usually they choose to be with their families.'

He was making some point. I said, 'Maybe they have wives better favoured in the looks department than my Jane.'

He looked like he might say something more but I was a good customer so he spat into the fire instead.

After five pints, I was feeling a little unsteady.

'You having a goose?' he said.

'Aye.'

'You'd better be off, hadn't you?'

'Suppose.'

'Well, Merry Christmas,' he said, standing.

I stood too, with a little wobble. The beer had gone to my head. 'Merry Christmas, Neddy.' I gave him a big hug which took him aback rather. He showed me to the door. He held it open so I could go out. The cold wind blew in, fluttering the fire, rattling the pots and squeaking through all the holes in the wainscotting. It was snowing.

'Very Seasonal,' said Ned.

'Aye.'

'You've a bit of a ride home.'

'Aye. But Jane's a good horse.'

'You mean, Jenny,' he said. 'Jenny's your horse. Jane's your wife.'

I laughed. 'Thanks for reminding me, Ned.'

The poor old mare stood shivering, hitched outside. In Bewcastle nothing moved as I rode through the snow. It got in my face, cold and wet, and down my neck. I leaned over the saddle and trusted Jenny to take me home.

But the snow grew to be a blizzard, and we could hardly see. Jenny was struggling because the snow had grown so deep, and I was getting cold now and shivering with the wet. I wished myself home and thought of the goose waiting for me. I regretted my comments about Jane's looks. She was a dutiful wife and cooked a fine goose. If rather plain of face and fat of arse.

We came into a stand of trees. Snow clung to them and whipped across my face. I'd ridden this road a thousand times, nay, ten thousand, in my years, but this place looked strange to me. The snow was in heaps and still blowing, whipping across. Jenny's mane had snow on it. My fingers were blue with cold and numb. My hat had a crust of snow as did my shoulders and even into the turn-ups of my sleeves.

The wood went on a while, perhaps because our progress through the snow was difficult and slow. I began to think I would freeze to death before I got home.

And then behind the flitting curtain of snow, I saw a light: a golden light. It came from beyond the trees. I'd never seen a light like it before. It was like the sun rising on a beautiful summer morning, but in the middle of the snow and the trees.

We struggled through the weather and the path took us towards the light. As we got closer, the snow faltered and then vanished as if it were banished by the golden light. As if we'd crossed a curtain. And now, I could see the source of the light. It came from a hill I recognised as the one they call Skelly How. They say it is an ancient place and the old folk shun it saying it is the home of the fairies. But they are idiots.

I thought nothing of such stupidity, but the change in the weather was odd. I looked around amazed at the golden glow. It was as if the sun had suddenly chased away the snow, and we stood within an enchanted circle.

Jenny neighed and shook her head to clear the ice from her mane.

I took off my hat and shook it and then I saw a man. I didn't see how he appeared; it was as if he had just appeared.

He was the strangest-looking fellow. Tall and thin with white hair as fine and crisp as if it were made of spun sugar. His complexion was bone white too with a sharp nose and black lips. His eyes were the deepest violet with no pupils, just enormous violet irises which blocked out the whites completely. He wore a long gold brocaded coat of blue satin — hardly suited to the weather I had just been travelling through, though more fitted to this warm place I found myself in now. From his look, I wondered if he was French.

He spoke English like a gentleman from down south, not one of us country folk. 'Alexander Armstrong, is it?' he said quite pleasant.

I nodded. 'Who asks?'

'My name is Mr Spindledrift Goodfellow.'

I cleared my throat. 'I'm not familiar with that name, Mr Goodfellow. Where do you hail from?'

'Here and there.'

I peered at the strange-looking man. 'Where is that exactly?'

He laughed. 'Under dale and over hill.'

I grew suspicious. 'I'm not familiar with that place. It seems to me that you are being rather evasive, Mr Goodfellow.'

'Oh, no. Not at all, Mr Armstrong. ' He seemed to be keen to change the subject. 'To cut to the chase, Mr Armstrong, I find myself in need of someone to take a particular object off my hands. Think of it as a trade..'

'A trade?' Here it was. Typical Frenchman.

'Yes. Here it is.' He reached into his coat and pulled out a golden sphere. A soft glow emanated from it and I thought it was humming to itself, though I could be mistaken.

'What's that?' said I.

'It's an egg.'

'An egg?' and when I looked at it, it did now seem that it was egg-like. Not shaped like an egg, no it was perfectly round. But something egg-like inhered to it. 'What kind of egg?'

'A magic egg.'

I threw back my head and laughed. He was surely jesting with me for there is no such thing as a magic egg. 'And what will it give hatch to?' said I.

'Your fortune.'

I laughed. 'My fortune?'

'Riches beyond your dreams. Are you interested?'

I looked at the egg. It might even be made of gold and if he was foolish enough to trust me with something obviously valuable, then that was his loss.

I tilted my head. 'So, what's the catch?'

He looked innocent. 'No catch. Why would there be a catch?'

'Because strangers don't normally give me golden eggs for nothing in return.'

He said, 'I didn't say for nothing. But it's for almost nothing.'

'What is the cost?' said I.

'Just a tiny thing,' said he.

'A tiny thing? What tiny thing?'

'Just a drop.'

'A drop of what?' I felt he had something to hide.

He smiled a crooked smile. 'Just a tiny drop of your blood. It'll be easy enough to get. Just a scratch.'

'That's a most extraordinary request.'

'It's a most extraordinary egg.'

'And it will give me riches?' It would give me a few shillings at least if I sold it, that's for sure.

'Whatever you want.'

'And all this for a drop of blood.'

'Yes, indeed. Just a tiny drop too.'

I thought this man to be a fool. I stared at the golden egg in his outstretched palm. 'Can I feel it?' I asked.

'Certainly.' He handed me the egg. It was heavy and smooth and cool in my hand. It certainly felt heavy enough to be gold, though I'd never handled such an amount of gold before. 'It's really gold? I asked.

He nodded briskly.

'And you'll give me this in exchange for a drop of blood?'

'Yes.'

'But why do you want blood?'

'To make sure you return the egg. I want it back a year and a day from today.'

'So St Stephen's Day next year?'

'I don't like to call it that, but yes.'

I shrugged. I kept the egg in my right hand and extended my left arm. The sleeve of my coat rode up exposing my hairy forearm. 'Take your drop.'

His grin broadened. He took out a little crystal phial, fiddled with the stopper and, when he had removed the stopper, he went towards my forearm with the fingers of his left hand. For the first time I noticed his fingernails. They were long and sharp, each one extending from his finger-ends like the claws of a chicken and it struck me that there was something exceedingly birdlike about him.

He darted forward and pierced my arm with the pointed nail of his index finger. I drew my arm back with a yelp, but he said, 'Arm.'

A stream of blood ran from where he'd pricked me. It was nothing really, so I extended my arm towards him again. He took his little crystal bottle and placed it under my arm to catch the drips.

'That's more than a drop,' said I.

'What's a drop or two between friends?' said he, grinning and showing me his sharp little teeth.

And then his crystal bottle was full. He pushed the stopper back in it.

'So that's it?' I asked.

'Absolutely,' said he.

'Give me the egg.'

'Of course.' He was still smiling. It was obvious I had the better part of the deal because all he had was blood and I had a golden egg. Even if it was brass, I'd still get a shilling or so for it in Carlisle. I had no intention of returning to this spot next St Stephen's Day. None whatsoever, despite what Mr Spindledrift Goodfellow might think.

'I can leave now?' I asked.

'You can. But be back next St Stephen's Day with my egg.'

I took the egg. Slipped it in my pocket. The weight was reassuringly heavy. It might even be gold. It might even be. I smiled.

As I turned Jenny to leave Mr Goodfellow, he said, 'Think of this as an act of philanthropy, Mr Armstrong, but remember this is merely a loan. Once it has given you a year of riches.'

'Yis, yis, aye,' said I as I trotted off on Jenny.

Soon, like a curtain falling, I was back in the snow and the golden glow was a memory. In fact, it felt like a dream. So much so, that I tapped the pocket of my overcoat but found the heavy egg reassuringly present.

I got home. Got my goose, drank my ale and fell asleep by the fire while Jane and the girls cleared up. The lads had gone courting to their fancy pieces. Christmas came and went. And New Year. I had a fine New Year, made even better when my uncle Joseph from Lanercost died and left me £5.

When I heard that, I took the egg from the hidey-hole I'd found for it in a hole in the byre wall and I swivelled it round in my fingers, talking to it like it was a child. 'So did you do this, oh egg?' said I, but the egg didn't reply, just glistened in the light of my lantern. 'Did you bring me £5? If so, I thank you.'

And in January, five cattle strayed onto my land. So I kept them. Andrew Hetherington from over Gillalees turned up at my gate saying they were his, but I saw him off at the tip of my sword. They maybe were, but he couldn't prove it. Silly fool hadn't marked them.

In February, my daughter Mary got a wedding arrangement and me a generous dowry from Tom Greenhow from Triermain's father for him to take her off my hands.

I had thought of taking the egg to Carlisle to sell it. It seemed hard to believe that my good fortune was tied to this thing. But I smiled when I held the egg, turning it over and over in my fingers. Maybe it really was magic.

In March, the weather still didn't improve, but my Jane took ill and died, which was a blow, for I had no one to cook and clean for me. The children were mortally upset at the death of their mother, but they were always soft.

So, I had to hire a maidservant to do the work that Jane had done for nothing, especially with Mary going soon. The cost of it grieved me, though I did drive down the price from the ridiculous sum the girl first asked.

She was a comely one, the new maid Sarah Morton. Very comely, dark-haired and young. With a few drinks taken, one night, I grabbed her firm arse, and that was that. She agreed for me to be her husband. I am an attractive man, if I say so myself. My animal deals were going well, and I prospered. Now, I had a lithe young thing in my bed at night, and because she was to marry me, I didn't have to pay her now for the housework. So, Jane's death worked out well. After I took Sarah Morton to my bed, the children refused to speak to me, and left. Another cost removed.

In April, the weather improved, and I decided to take my trip to Carlisle. I got Jenny out and took the egg to get it valued. It took me all day to get there, but I stayed in the Crown and Mitre. Then I walked round to see John Walker, who was a jeweller and silversmith who had a shop on English Street. Walker was a Scotchman, originally from Kirkcudbright, though I didn't hold that against him.

He knew his stuff and as he sat there with his eye-glass and the egg up close. 'Where did you get this?'

'Here and there.'

He snorted.

I asked, 'Is it gold?'

He nodded and said in his Scotch brogue, 'Aye, it is. Pure too. Honestly Mr Armstrong, this is a most uncommon thing. It's worth a fortune.'

He was foolish to tell me that. 'How much would you give me for it?'

'Well,' he began to mutter. 'I knew his brain would be calculating his profit. 'Really...' He mumbled on.

I grew tired with him. 'How much Mr Walker?'

He stuttered. 'I'll give you £200 pounds for it.'

'Scotch or English?'

'Scots.'

'Make it English.'

'Very well.'

'It's worth more than that,' said I and he remained tight-lipped. It might be worth more than that, but I'd have to travel to York or London to get more. £200 was a fortune indeed. So I agreed. '£200 pounds English then. When can I have the money?'

'Tuesday.'

It was Saturday. 'Too long.' I said. 'Make it Sunday.'

'I don't trade on the Lord's Day.'

I snorted. 'You trade any day.'

'No, sir; I do not.'

Idiot that he was. 'Monday then,' I said.

He looked pained. 'Monday it is.'

'Grand'. I shook his hand. I don't think he was too pleased with me from the limpness of the grip. He said, 'Can I keep the egg, to raise money against?'

I laughed, taking the egg back from his feeble paw. 'I think not, Walker. I think not. How do I know you're an honest man?'

He looked taken aback. 'I assure you, sir. I am. A good Christian too.'

'Aye, well, you'll have the egg when I have my money. I'll see you Monday, midday sharp.'

And that was that. I extended my stay at the Crown and Mitre and enjoyed myself with chops and ale. Monday came, Walker gave me the money, and I him the egg.

My journey home was uneventful, but when I got back, Sarah Morton was gone. And before we had officially married too. Never mind, thought I, I'd had the use of her. I hired a new maid at a less wage; she was not as handsome as Sarah, but she did. I had he use of her too, but didn't marry her.

I had no more strokes of luck or windfalls, but it didn't matter as I had my £200 and that did me well.

The year went by and winter came. I lived by myself, with yet another maid; it seemed they didn't tolerate me too well, or my roving hands, but there were always more. And I liked the variety.

Christmas found me at the King's Head in Bewcastle, sinking Christmas pints with Ned. The weather was bad; rain rather than snow, but sleety cold rain. I took rather too much ale in my leather tankard and stayed overlong. Ned's wife put me up in the rude hovel they call an inn-room, and it was St Stephen's Day by the time I'd had a hair of the dog that bit me, and was ready to saddle my Jenny and make my way home.

The rain swept across the moor as I rode. I got to the trees again and saw a familiar golden glow. Mr Spindledrift Goodfellow. I'd forgotten about him and his egg since I'd sold it in Carlisle. But I didn't intend to make his acquaintance again. No, sir, I did not.

I rode through the wood, head down. The glow persisted. It was to my right. I knew a rough track. It would be a bad in this weather, but my Jenny could manage it, so I took the reins and steered her up towards the fell.

The light shifted until it was right in front of me. That was odd. I steered right, back towards the main road. And the light shifted in front of me again.

The weirdness of this unnerved me. I decided I did not want to meet Mr Spindledrift Goodfellow at all that day, so I turned right round and headed back to Bewcastle. I'd spend another night at the King's Head and come back when it was no longer St Stephen's Day.

But the light grew in front of me, some yards ahead, and then suddenly a dome of light appeared above and on all sides. The rain vanished, and I sat on horseback on what to all appearances was a mild Spring day.

Mr Spindledrift Goodfellow stood there in a blue coat, brocaded in gold. His long white hair hung down his back. His bone white skin shone with a strange pallor. His violet eyes fixed me and he licked his lips showing his tongue and rows of sharp white teeth. I was no longer sure he was French.

'Good day, Mr Armstrong,' said he. 'I hope you weren't trying to avoid me?'

I coughed. 'No, of course not.'

'You didn't forget our appointment?'

I shook my head.

'Good,' said he. 'I trust my egg brought you fortune.'

I nodded.

'Then,' said he further. 'The year is done. One year and one day, just like in the old bargains. And now I'd like my egg back.'

'I don't have it,' said I, bold as brass. That's the way to face down these mountebanks and charlatans.

He cocked his head. 'You don't have it?'

'No. And what will you do about that?'

I thought him being so thin and spindly, what could he do against a man like me in the prime of health? Gone a little to corpulence I admit, but still strong in the arm, like my name. I thought, once I put my fists up, he would bluster and bluster, and fuss and fuss like a woman, then go.

'What will I do?' he smiled. He seemed amused.

He reached into his coat and pulled out the little crystal bottle. I saw it held a filament of red. He took off the top, turned the bottle upside down and dabbed it on his index finger. Then he licked it. He grinned. 'Very tasty, I think I'll have some more.'

Still with the bottle in hand, he said, 'And don't worry about the egg. Mr Walker sold it to me for £300. It's more your lack of honesty that is of interest to me.'

I swallowed hard. My throat was dry. 'Of interest to you?'

He laughed again; his tiny sharp teeth were wet with spit and stained with my blood. 'Of interest,' said he. 'Because I can't touch an honest man. Luckily, you're not.'

'I don't know what you're talking about.' I decided not to turn to fisticuffs. I'd just go home. I turned Jenny and began to trot off, but every way I went, the dome of golden light followed me, imprisoning me. And he was always there. He neither went further away, nor did he come closer.

I went this way and that and he followed me, laughing as if my panic was a jest. I had to get away and clicked and spurred Jenny, kicking her with my heels. But I couldn't get away from that infernal Mr Spindledrift Goodfellow.

After half an hour, my heart was in my throat. My blood pulsed in my ears, both Jenny and I were lathered with sweat.

He grinned. 'Try as you might, Mr Armstrong, you can't escape your fate.'

'My fate! My fate! I'll have nowt to do with you.' But I stopped. There must be some other way. He stood in front of me now.

And then I was on the soft tussocky turf, lying on my back. Jenny stood over me, then started grazing. It was as if she was glad to have me off her back, and didn't care I was laid low, the callous, faithless animal.

And Spindledrift Goodfellow had my head cradled on his lap, stroking my jugular vein with his sharp fingernail. I felt my artery bound under his firm touch. He tapped the blood vessel, as if testing its pressure.

'Who are you?' I said hoarsely.

'Mr Spindledrift Goodfellow.'

'But who is that?'

'They call me many names: The Light Bringer, the Prince of the Air.'

'You confuse me, sir. Indeed you do.'

He whispered more names. 'The Adversary, the Lord of the Flies and the Serpent.'

It's long since I've read the Bible or gone to church, but I was beginning to realise into whose arms I'd fallen.

And Spindlethrift Goodfellow continued in a sing-song voice, light as thistledown. 'Or Old Nick,' he laughed. 'They sometimes call me that.'

He gazed down with violet eyes, his needle-like nail on the pulse of my neck. 'But you can call me the Devil.'

8

THE CROGLIN VAMPIRE

To find Croglin Low Hall, go through Croglin and take the first left. When you come to the crossroads turn left again. You will pass by the farmhouse known as Croglin High Hall to your left. Croglin Low Hall lies a little further on, to the right. Croglin Low Hall is where we are going. There is no public right of access to Croglin Low Hall and tourists are not encouraged to visit. No one is. Not any more.

The area is wild now, but in the 17th Century, it was almost inaccessible. It's strange then that a family should come from the South of England to farm here when there were much more fertile farms to be had much closer to where they came from. They arrived in Croglin just after the English Civil War, when the country was devastated and hardly recovering from the ravages of conflict. The Fishers, whose family owned Croglin Low Hall had moved out for reasons of their own quite a while before. The Fishers weren't the first inhabitants of Croglin Low Hall. The Hall was originally owned by the Howards, who also owned Greystoke, Corby and Naworth castles and were Dukes of Norfolk and Earls of Carlisle at various times.

The circumstances of why the Howards gave the hall up are obscure and lost in the mists of time.

The Howards renovated the original medieval hall and built a chapel, but by the 17th Century the chapel was tumbledown and disused. It is said there was a crypt in the chapel, but more of that later.

Somehow the Fishers obtained Croglin from the Howards. Apparently, they got it at a good price, but they only stayed a while there. They moved to a smaller farm some miles away at Cumrew. The living was harder on the new farm, because it took in more fell land, but still they wouldn't move back to Croglin. There was a story in the locality that the Fishers left Croglin because they were frightened. What they were frightened of nobody said, or if folk said, they weren't believed, because the story sounded too outlandish.

Whatever the truth of it, Croglin Low Hall remained empty for years. Old Augustus Fisher died and his son Joseph inherited, but he wouldn't move back either. It was a chance conversation with his solicitor in Carlisle about another matter entirely that led to the suggestion of renting out the empty Croglin Hall.

They could get no local people to take the lease and so, Fisher took to advertising the lease further afield and somehow it got to the attention of the Cranswell family. The Cranswells originated from Suffolk and were two brothers and a sister. They had been orphaned, though the circumstances of how that happened, are no longer clear. They were also Catholic, which meant the good protestant folk of the Eden Valley shunned them and were suspicious of their loyalties.

Why the Cranswells fled so far from Suffolk to Cumberland is lost, but there must have been some reason to travel so far over such poor roads. They travelled at the end of August by stage-coach, first from London to York, then from York to Carlisle and then they came by horse to the wilds of Croglin.

August that year was very rainy, with only a few days of sun here and there. The Cranswells were gentry rather than farmers and sub-let the land to local farmers. They had independent means and intended to spend the time in leisure, reading, writing and walking the countryside.

The year turned, the harvest was brought in and Autumn turned the trees golden-brown and the leaves fell in damp heaps around

Croglin Hall. Though Cromwell and his Parliamentarians discouraged it, the local folk kept the customs of Harvest, All-Hallows and Christmas much as their ancestors had. The Cranswells kept themselves to themselves and let local life go on around them without joining in.

What they got up to on their lonely farm was a mystery to their neighbours. Though they spoke and greeted those they came across, they were rarely seen out and about. The flickering of candles was seen through the mullioned windows, though they did seem to go away and for weeks at a time, Croglin Low Hall was shuttered up, until they returned from wherever they had been; London, Suffolk or even further afield.

Spring came, with Snowdrops then Daffodils. Bluebells filled the woods in April and sweet yellow and white blossom like foam coated the hedgerows in May, filling warm evenings with heady scents. June was warm, July hotter and cloudless days extended from week to week.

Dorothy was the youngest. Her two brothers John and Jacob had always looked after her since the death of their parents. She had always been a sickly girl with an overactive imagination. She spent her days at Croglin in embroidery and reading and conversation and looking out of the window at the shadows of clouds drifting along the high green fells to the east.

One particular airless summer night at the beginning of August, John and Jacob sat with Dorothy watching the moon rise. After a time, the candles burned low and the white moths batting around the flames grew fewer. The temperature dropped a little, but not much. Dorothy stretched and said, 'I think it's time to go to bed. I'm yawning my head off here.'

She retired and her brothers remained in low conversation. Her bedroom was on the ground floor, along the corridor. She entered her familiar room and locked the door as was her habit from sleeping in so many inns as they roamed around the countryside in England and abroad. Then she undressed, washed from the jug and ewer and got into her bed, but she couldn't sleep. It was hot, almost unbearably so.

Dorothy lay in her bed, the bedclothes cast off because of the heat. She had closed her window to stop the moths getting in, but had not fastened the shutters. She gazed out of her window, propped up on her pillows as the long summer day faded out and night took its place. A huge ivory moon rose, and she lay there, watching it through the diamond-cut window panes.

An owl hooted in the darkness outside, a curlew called from far away, and Dorothy grew tired. Her head grew heavy and her eyelids closed. She was almost asleep when some sixth sense shocked her awake. She sat up in bed and looked out of the unshuttered windows.

There were lights outside where there should be none. Two lights flashing red like the eyes of a fox caught in a lantern light. But she knew they were not the eyes of a fox, because they were too high off the ground. And then she started back, frightened that they were of a man — a stranger intruding onto their grounds late at night. But they did not seem to be the eyes of a man, because of their colour: they were a glimmering blood red.

Dorothy thought of calling out to her brothers but told herself she was being foolish. No man's eyes gleamed red like these, almost as if they had their own strange luminescence. And what would a man be doing here? They had no livestock to poach, and it was not on the way from anywhere to anywhere, so no one would use their grounds as a shortcut.

It must be some animal, and there were no wolves or bears hereabouts, much less lions or tigers so she told herself not to fret or vex herself about these eyes in the dark.

But still she watched, fascinated and frightened. It seemed the lights came from where she knew the ruined chapel was. It was a place she hardly ventured into. She had gone to it a number of times, thinking to look over the historical and romantic ruin, but had always hesitated because there was something about the old ruin that unsettled her.

The lights like eyes moved outside her window. Dorothy lay in bed and followed them with horrified fascination. The cold moon cast a silver radiance over the lawn and path to the Hall. At first the lights stood in the inky shadow, but now they approached closer and that meant they would soon cross into the moonlight and she would truly see what manner of thing they were.

As the shadow separated out from the deeper shadows surrounding it, Dorothy started as she made out the shape of a man. Those red lights were indeed his eyes.. She could not understand how a natural man's eyes gleamed in such an eerie fashion. And then with a flash of fear, she thought perhaps it was not a natural man at all.

Normally, she would not give such a thought an instant's consideration. She was not a woman given to superstitious dread, and she laughed at the country folk for their beliefs in elfs and trolls and all manner of dobbies and boggles. But now, a terrible horror seized her as the shape slithered and shuffled across the gravel path outside.

The thing fully emerged into the moonlight, but still somehow she could not clearly see it. It was man-shaped, but thinner and more spindly. The lights were indeed its eyes and below the eyes she got a sense of a mouth. It seemed that whatever it was; it was coming to her window.

Dorothy thought of getting up and running out of her room, but to go to the door would have meant she had to go right by the window. Besides, she had locked the door from the inside and so would have to stand there and unlock it — with her shaking hands all the while visible in the spill of moonlight. She hoped it would pass by her window, so she lay still and shook with fear in her bed.

Dorothy stared at the shape but at the last minute, when she was certain it was coming to look in the window, it half turned and started to move around the house.

Seizing her opportunity, Dorothy jumped up and ran towards the door. Her hands were trembling so much that she found it hard to turn the key. And then her heart nearly stopped. Behind her, she heard a scratching as if of long nails on the glass of the window. Whatever it was, was outside. Just feet away.

Dorothy stood petrified with fear still not daring to turn her head and look round to see it. Her fear destroyed her concentration, and she fumbled the key in the lock and could not stop her hand shaking enough to turn it so she could escape.

Then she heard it unpicking the lead which held the glass in place. She forced herself to look and saw that one pane of the mullioned glass had come away and a long bony hand stretched in and turned the window catch to let itself in. In a panic, she ran at the window, determined to pull closed the wooden shutters and stop it gaining entry.

But she was not quick enough. She got to the window, got her hand on the shutters, but it was in, pulling itself into the room.

Whatever it was, it came in through the window with a rush and grabbed her — its fingers in her hair, its mouth at her throat. It stunk of death and graves and its wiry strength was inhuman. It thrust her back. She flailed at it with her arms but to no avail. She felt it bite her neck as it forced her onto the ground. Blood ran from a wound on her neck and she screamed and screamed.

From along the corridor, Dorothy's brothers heard the noise and came and battered at the locked door. The creature looked up and as the door was smashed open, it turned and fled out of the open window, leaving her lying on the floor, bleeding profusely from a wound at her neck.

One brother, John, clambered out of the window and went after it. He ran into the darkness to where he thought it had gone. But it was fast and before he could catch it — and perhaps it was lucky for him that he didn't — it disappeared into the pitch blackness around the ruined chapel.

It was a great shock to her — to them all. They had felt so safe there at Croglin, so far away from their political enemies. They thought they had escaped all danger, but it was not so.

John and Jacob had not seen the thing as clearly as Dorothy and when she told them about its leathery skin and foul odour, they said it must be a vagrant — a madman loose in the countryside.

And because Dorothy always wanted to believe the rational explanation, she herself eventually came to tell herself that it was indeed true: the creature that had seemed so supernatural at first must merely have been a dangerous lunatic. And it was not just merely because she had been terrified for her life.

Her nerves were shredded. She said they could stay at Croglin, but seeing how fearful she had become of the tiniest thing, they felt it would be best to leave the area for a while. They had a standing invitation to visit friends in France, and so they took it up and John and Jacob took Dorothy away from Croglin to recover — over to the Continent.

They did not give up the tenancy though. Though they stayed away for a while moving from friend to friend, spending time among those who plotted and conspired to return a Catholic king to England, eventually, as autumn turned to winter, it was Dorothy who urged them to return to Croglin. She argued that they had paid for the tenancy, and besides, she joked, it would be very bad luck to come across two escaped lunatics in the same place.

So indeed, they returned to Croglin as the first snow fell and coated the eastern fells, and then the moors, woods and bogland around Croglin Hall grew thick with white drifts and travel around the locality became impossible. They got in fuel and food and spent the winter there. Dorothy had the same room, but always closed the wooden shutters. John and Jacob took to carrying loaded pistols with them around the house. But nothing happened until one night in March.

Dorothy was lying in bed in a deep sleep, when into her dreams intruded a terribly familiar scratching at the window. She struggled to get fully awake, gasping for breath as terror constricted her chest. With shaking hands, she scrabbled for a candle and a flint and steel to spark it with. When she got a flame, cradled behind her trembling hand, she saw that the shutters were opened. Staring in at her was a brown shrivelled face, and she saw its long bony hands picking at the lead of the windows. Its glowing eyes fixed on her and it opened its dried mouth, showing receded gums and long yellow teeth like those of an old dog.

This time she screamed immediately. Her brothers ran down the corridor with their pistols. The door was left unlocked now and as they burst in; she pointed to the window, but the creature had gone.

The brothers ran to the front door and round the side to where Dorothy's window was.

"There!" John yelled.

Jacob looked where his brother pointed and saw the thing moving across the lawn towards the ruined chapel. He fired his pistol, and it seemed he hit it in the leg. It stumbled but did not go down, and it scrambled away into the darkness and they lost it.

THE NEXT DAY the brothers summoned their neighbours to the inn at Croglin. As they sat with their ale, John and Jacob explained what their sister had seen, and what they had shot at. Dorothy was with the women in the next room, but the door was opened and there was much clucking and nodding through at her.

John Penrice, the farmer at Croglin High Hall said, "My youngest Nelly, had bite wounds at the throat. We put it down to rats."

Another neighbour, Adam Bell, said, "Aye, but that chapel has always been a place best avoided. Ever since the Howards left."

There was much nodding and agreeing.

"So will you come with us?" John Cranswell asked the men in the inn.

"Are you afeared to go yourselves?" William Graham, the man who spoke, was well-known for his ill-temper and pleasure at others' misfortunes. John and Jacob ignored him and then John Penrice said, "Aye, I'll come with you."

Adam Bell was the next to join. After that all the men agreed to come until there was around ten of them all told, lads and men; sons, brothers and fathers of the village and surrounding farms.

Fortified by ale, the walked from Croglin village. Adam Bell looked at the sky. "We were talking too long. It won't be long until it's dark. We should have set off sooner."

John Penrice laughed. "Keep your courage, Adam. I've brought lanterns," and he nodded to his son Edward who held up two brass lanterns.

Another said, "Still, it would be best if we got there and did what we need to do before nightfall."

"I reckon we have an hour, if that." Adam Bell said. He sounded less bold now than he had when he had a leather tankard of Croglin ale in his fist.

"It will be enough."

"And what are we do do once we get there?" William Graham asked with his usual mischief.

John Cranswell said sourly, "Put an end to the thing that hurt my sister."

The sun had not set by the time the men got to Croglin Low Hall. Dorothy with the village women came along behind, but the mood of everyone grew sombre as the clouds gathered, darkening the day, and the ancient stone walls of the chapel, stood there, the dark red sandstone tumbled in places but still standing high enough to hide whatever was lurking below.

They stood in front of the chapel and John Penrice said, "Are we ready then?"

John Cranswell nodded. "There's nothing much above ground. Just the ruined chapel with the roof in and the walls fallen. I am guessing whatever it is, lies downstairs in the crypt."

Jacob Cranswell, by way of explanation said, "We've never ventured down there. At least I haven't."

John nodded. "Nor me. Why would we? I had no wish to disturb the dead in their vault."

John Penrice said, "Aye, well. It's time to disturb them now. Or perhaps disturb those which have never died."

A humourless laugh rippled round the gathered men. Adam Bell, showing courage for the first time, went to the ruin. "There's stairs down," he said.

"Yes," John Cranswell said. "That's down to the crypt."

Adam Bell said, "We'll need lanterns. The steps down are dark, in the shadow of the walls and trees." He looked up over his shoulder. "I reckon we have ten minutes until the sun is down."

"Best get to it," John Penrice said. Some of the other men, including William Graham, produced torches and used flints and steels and shavings of kindling from their tinder box to light them until they burned, fluttering in the breeze.

Still they hesitated.

"Come on, you Jessies. Time to man up," John Penrice proved the bravest, and with him at their head, the small knot of men advanced to the top of the stairs, and stood there.

Then John and Jacob Cranswell forced their way forward from where they had been talking to their sister. The local men parted for them. It was the brothers task to avenge their sister's injury and fear.

They held up lanterns and descended.

Jacob looked to John. "This door has been newly opened." He pointed to a scrape in the dirt that showed the door had been pushed open recently.

"Yes, but it's locked now," said John, trying the handle.

"What manner of dead man locks the door after him?" said Adam Bell, his voice shaking.

There was silence then. John Cranswell knocked the locked, old door in with his heavy boot.

The damp rotten smell of the crypt assailed their nostrils: the odour was a mix of moulded wood, old rain, beetles but something sourer too. Shelves lined the walls of the crypt and on them, decayed coffins. Some completely in, yellowed bones showing through the broken panels in the lights of the lanterns. But the lanterns cast shadows as much as they did light and the shifting shade gave the impression of things moving in the crypt.

The men crowded the door; the ones behind braver than the ones in front. 'What's there? What do you see?" called the ones behind.

"Just coffins. Old coffins," called back John Penrice.

"And what's in them?" yelled the voice of William Graham, who made sure he was the hindmost.

"Old bones, just old bones," said John Cranswell, his voice low and fixed as he looked among the ruined coffins.

His brother stepped forward to get a better view, the shadows flickering and shifting over his shoulders. He shook his head. "They're of different ages."

Jacob pointed. "That one. It is least decayed."

And it was true, there was a coffin there of newer design and less rotted than the others, as if it had come from elsewhere and was ensconced here among the local caskets.

"There's no name on it," said Jacob. "Here, help me with the lid."

His brother came, and others and they soon removed the lid.

"It wasn't nailed," Jacob said.

They shifted the full coffin and beheld the manner of thing that occupied it. It was naked and withered. The shape of a man, but taller and thinner and spindled. Its fingernails were like curled brown talons and its thin brown lips drew back to show fangs like those of an animal. Dried on its chin was blood as if it had recently fed on something living.

"Call Dorothy," John said.

Dorothy was outside at the top of the stairs with the women. "I don't want to come, brother," she called down.

"But only you can say if this was the thing that attacked you," John said.

"Still, I will not come. Say that it is. I don't need to see it again," Dorothy said.

John Penrice nodded. He stood with the Cranswells looking at the thing in its coffin. "Let's burn it, anyway."

Adam Bell was behind, not daring to come closer. "There's only minutes left before the sun goes down. What if it's true that these things stir once the sun is gone."

Jacob pointed at the thing's leg. "A pistol ball. Look."

And there in the dried flesh of the dead thing was the ball of a pistol such as that fired by the Cranswell brothers. Such as the shot they hit it with as it stumbled back to its foul lair after attacking their sister.

"That's good enough for me," Jacob Cranswell said. "Bring tallow and shavings and we'll set this vile thing afire."

Tallow and candles were produced. They packed them in the coffin alongside the monster along with the driest of wood they found inside or outside the crypt. Then as they stood back at the door, Jacob Cranswell set light to the coffin with the thing inside and watched it burn.

The coffin burned well with clouds of foul smelling smoke and the crowd fell back choking and coughing, retreating into the night outside while smoke poured from the crypt. They stood there, gaining courage from their numbers, until the smoke ceased. Jacob Cranswell went down and confirmed there were only ashes and cinders left. After that, the people drifted away in dribs and drabs going to their own farms and cottages across the wild winter countryside around Croglin, some from as far as Cumrew or Renwick.

The Cranswells didn't stay in Croglin. They went back to France or Suffolk or London. No one knew. And the Fishers never returned either, selling Croglin Low Hall eventually to strangers.

Nearly a year later, Adam Bell sat drinking with John Penrice in the alehouse at Croglin. He drained his tankard and looked to John to get him another. "So that was that," he said. "The thing was burned and all trouble ended."

John Penrice was quiet, then he spoke. "Except it didn't. I hear there has been trouble at Scarrowmanwick. Some such stories as we had round here: rats biting the necks of children while they sleep. Women on their way back from Penrith waylaid and gone missing. Strange shadows haunting the roadsides and graveyards."

Adam Bell shook his head. "But how can that be, John? We burned the thing. I saw the blaze good and proper with my own eyes."

John Penrice shrugged and said quietly. "Aye, Adam, we did see it burn. But what if there was more than one of them?"

9

THE FORTUNETELLER'S FATE

The dowdy woman scuttled down the pavement of the bare Wigton street. A wind blew down the road, almost shoving her along. In the gardens of the houses were plastic bottles and in the gutter a sodden magazine about cars. In front of one house was a damp, ripped leather sofa, in front of another a broken fridge. Two youths with hoods up pushed by her, going the other way, but the woman seemed intent on her destination. She got to a rusty gate that had been originally painted cream. She prodded it open and darted the few steps up the short path to knock on the stained plastic door of a house that had seen better days. The woman stood there until the door was answered by another woman of a similar age, short blonde hair, clean and tidy, and the first woman stepped in quickly, as if she didn't want to be seen entering.

Once inside the blonde woman said, "Can I hang up your coat?" and smiled. "I'm Amy by the way."

The visitor took off her coat, smiled back, and handed it to Amy. "Thank you," she said in a quiet but self-possessed voice. Amy showed her through to her parlour. A brochure on the table said, "Tea and Tarot". Amy saw the woman looking. "I've just had them printed. What do you think?"

The woman picked up a brochure and flipped it over. "Very nice."

"Sit down, please," Amy said. "Mrs Smith, was it?"

The woman nodded, "Yes, but please call me Joan." She sat.

"So," Amy said, "Joan." She smiled. She gave the woman her professional concerned look. A lot of these people came with immense emotional burdens and she wanted to show she cared. They were suckers though: easy money from those hurt by bereavement, relationship breakdown and other minor tragedies. She laughed all the way to the bank. Amy's face grew soft. "I offer Tarot, or tea-leaves? Which would you like?"

Joan said, "Do I get a cup of tea too, if I go for tea-leaves?"

Amy nodded and gave a broad grin. They were going to get along fine. "Of course! You get tea anyway."

"I think I'll go for the tea-leaves then."

"Well, I'll sort that out first." Amy stood and went to make a cup of tea in the kitchen, while Joan sat in the armchair, hands folded over her lap. When Amy came back, she hadn't moved. What? Was she stupid or something? Anyway, she was paying, so Amy didn't actually care.

"Lovely cup of tea," Joan said, sipping at the bone china teacup.

"Ooh, that's a nice necklace," Amy said, suddenly leaning forward despite herself. That was worth a bob or two. Amy wondered if she could get the woman to give it to her as a gift.

"Thank you," Joan said, clapping her hand over it. Amy noted that Joan wore a brown dress, unfashionable, but clean. Details and accessories could tell you a lot about people. Amy thought that the accessories actually were what gave you hints about how the customer saw her real self. She reached out to stroke the silver necklace. Joan seemed reticent about it at first, but let her. It was in the shape of a spider, with a dark red stone making up its body, the eight thin legs extending out to catch the conceit of a silver web. "Is that a ruby?" Amy said. It looked valuable.

Joan shook her head. "A garnet."

"Oh, that's nice. Is it silver?"

"Platinum actually. I got the necklace in Brazil. My husband has a gold mine."

"Oh, that's grand." Amy imagined dollar signs and grinned. This could really work out well, if she milked it. Amy added, "In Brazil too? I've never been there. Never been further than Preston, myself," Joan giggled. "I'm sure Brazil's very exotic."

"It's different to here, of course," Joan said.

"Is that a Brazilian accent? Do I hear a hint of an accent?" Amy asked.

Joan shook her head.

Amy let the platinum spider fall away. "Anyway, back to this reading. Is there anyone in particular you want to contact?"

Joan's face clouded. "My son."

"Oh, I'm sorry." Amy gave her concerned look again. She tried her best to sound authentic. She had to sound like she cared at least, or they wouldn't buy in. She fluttered her eyelashes while she waited for an answer.

Joan looked down at her hands. Her fingernails weren't painted. The spider necklace lay over the throat of her brown dress. "Thank you," she said.

Amy could hear the heavy sadness in her voice.

Joan said, "I wasn't sure you could help. I miss him so much."

Amy's face grew tender with concern. She reached out and touched the back of Joan's hand. Joan turned her palm up and took Amy's fingers. Cold hands, warm heart. Time to turn it up.

Amy paused. "I'm already feeling him."

Joan fixed her with all her attention. "Is he here?"

Amy half closed her eyes. Her eyelids fluttered. She nodded slightly. "John is it? That's the name I'm getting."

"James," Joan said.

"Yes, James. I knew it was a J- name."

"What does he say?" Joan sat forward.

"He says he's happy." Amy smiled sadly, but she hoped, reassuringly.

Joan nodded. "I'm so glad." She raised her hand to wipe her eyes.

Amy saw that mascara stained her fingers where they'd brushed her tears. She said, "He says for you not to worry. He's at peace."

There was a pause, Amy looked into space and frowned. "He died in an accident?"

Joan didn't answer at first. It was obviously still raw.

"It was sudden?" Amy asked.

Joan smiled slightly then nodded. "Yes."

"He says he looks after you. From Heaven."

"Good," Joan said. "I always know when he's near. He was my beloved boy."

"He says he watches in the morning when you sit at your dressing table, getting ready for work."

"I'm so pleased," Joan said.

Amy's eyes suddenly flicked open as she returned to normal mode, as she called it. She smiled and said, "Have you finished your tea?"

Joan made to gulp it down, but Amy put her hand on hers to stop her. "No rush. You take your time."

Joan looked around. Amy saw her glancing out of the window. The window looked over the back garden. "The garden's a mess," Amy said. "I never get round to it."

The house dated from the 1950s - post war austerity style. The furniture was old and the ornaments cheap.

Joan finished her tea. Amy took the cup and swilled round the dregs, pouring them out to reveal wet tea leaves remaindered in the shapes of stars and seashells. Amy gazed into the cup and frowned. She had a sense of something acrid, like a bad taste. That was unusual. She mostly had to put things on but this was real. Amy did have a talent once. Her grandmother said it was a God given talent to help suffering people. Grandma was dead though and helping people didn't pay the bills.

"What is it? What do you see? Something bad?" Joan looked worried.

Amy smiled. She shook her head. "No, no," but she looked again, her brow furrowing deeper.

"What is it? You've got me anxious now."

"No, nothing." Amy smiled. "Nothing. I think you've got money coming," she said finally.

Joan sat back. Her hands gripped each other tightly. She had no rings. "You had me worried. I thought my end was come."

Amy put her friendly, but concerned look on. "No, there's fulfilment. I get the feeling of great satisfaction."

"That's good," Joan said. Then she asked. "Isn't that good?"

"Of course." Amy reached and took Joan's hand. She squeezed it. "Don't worry. You're going to get everything you want."

And when Joan had gone, Amy said out loud, "And so might I, if I play my cards right."

Amy sat with her friend Jill in the Muffin Break in the run down town centre. They both had cappuccinos. Jill was an older woman, middle-aged, gone to fat, badly dyed blonde hair with a hard face, but Amy knew she had a heart of gold. Silly cow.

"Here, have my cake," Jill said to Amy, pushing her plate across the table. "I'm supposed to be on a diet."

"You're not fat, Jill," Amy said, lying, and took the cake anyway. Jill had paid. As always.

"Oh, I am. You should see me in a full-length mirror! Jeff keeps telling me to diet, but he's no Adonis himself."

"I remember the wedding. What a lovely couple you were!"

Jill said, "That was a long time ago. How's business, love, anyway? Haven't seen you for ages."

"So-so," Amy said. "You?" She never admitted when she was doing well. It was always so-so.

"All right actually. I'm doing that new Angel reading thing. It brings them in."

"You're still offering the psychic medium work though?"

Jill nodded. "Yes, but I find you have to offer the punters something new all the time. Otherwise they get bored and go to those that will."

Amy said, "Yep, you've got to get your marketing right. It's a business. Some of them in our line forget that when they're bleating all that crap about helping suffering souls." She grimaced. "Makes me baulk."

Jill winced. "It's not crap, Amy. I do want to help people."

Amy patted her hand. "Of course, love. I didn't mean you."

Jill shook her head. "I only tell them what I really get coming through. I don't make stuff up."

Amy raised a sceptical eyebrow. "So, you never exaggerate?"

Jill shook her head.

"Come on! You must milk it a bit at times," Amy said. She was grinning.

They both laughed. Jill said, "A little bit, sometimes. I mean you've got to. Just a bit." Her face went serious. "But I really like to be straight with my clients."

Amy groaned internally. What a dope. It was a good job Jill always paid for the coffee and cakes or Amy wouldn't waste her time with such a milksop. Losing patience, Amy said, "Just tell them what they want to hear. That's what they come to you for."

"I won't lie," Amy said. She shook her head vigorously like a little girl.

"I'm not asking you to lie, hun. I'm just saying — ham it up at times. They love it. That's what they really want."

They both laughed again. Amy ate more cake. Jill said, "I wish you could still smoke in here. It's raining outside and I don't want to get wet."

"Well, we're nearly finished," Amy said. Then she added quickly, "You're paying? Just I'm a bit short."

Jill smiled. "Of course. I'll get this."

Amy finished her cake and Jill's. She licked her lips and then picked up a paper napkin to wipe them delicately.

Jill said, "You coming to the Halloween gig next week?"

"No. I didn't know there was one."

"Didn't you get the email from the spiritual development circle?"

Amy shook her head. "I think Iris has taken me off the mailing list." That was because she called Iris a silly cow to her face.

"Well, I'm inviting you. It's £50 a table for the night, but you should make more than that."

"£50? Where is it?"

"Caldbeck Tower."

Amy was impressed. "Caldbeck Tower? That's a spooky place." Amy had never been inside but she knew the look of the place and its age would really bring the punters in. She said, "How did you manage to book that venue?" She sometimes worried Jill had better contacts than she did.

"Ah, that would be telling," Jill said. She tapped her nose, looked pleased with herself, then said, "One of my clients owns it — Mrs Jones."

"Mrs Jones? Seriously?" Amy snorted. "Sounds like a false name."

"Well, I don't care what she calls herself. She's a lovely woman and she's letting us book her castle for Halloween." She shuffled. "Anyway, I need to go." Jill stood. Amy got up and followed her to the till, where Jill paid.

On their way out, Amy said, "Thanks again for the coffee, Jill."

Jill put her arm round Amy's shoulder and hugged her protectively. "No problem. I know you'll pay me back when you make your millions."

Amy thought of Joan Smith. That necklace wasn't cheap. It was stylish. She had money. She could get it off her, if she was smart.

They left Muffin Break and stepped out onto the dismal street, dodging the drizzle. Amy turned up the collar of her coat and fiddled with her umbrella. Jill was in a hurry to get away. Amy said, "So I can come on Halloween, to Caldbeck Tower?"

Jill tapped Amy on the back of her hand. "Of course you can. There'll be a few of us there and Iris is advertising it so we should get a good crowd. I'll make sure you get a good table."

"Thanks so much."

Amy kissed Jill on her cheek and said, "So, remember - ham it up and charge double!"

. . .

It was afternoon and getting gloomy when Joan Smith arrived at Amy's house for her reading. She was early. Amy took that as a good sign; it meant the woman was keen. She made a big effort to exude positive energy as she showed Joan Smith in, helped her off with her coat and led her through to the parlour. They sat down almost simultaneously. Amy's face grew serious, but kind. "On the phone I mentioned about the price increase?"

Joan nodded.

"I hope you don't mind. My outgoings have gone up. I hope you think I'm worth it."

Without hesitation, Joan smiled. "Of course, I do. You're worth it. You tell me such wonderful things."

Amy's eyelids flicked closed and fluttered like butterflies. She had learned to do this ages ago and clients really loved it. Her voice softened and she said, "Joan, I wanted to tell you that John... That was his name wasn't it?"

Joan smiled and said, "Yes, John." Her spider necklace gleamed in the light of Amy's front room lamp.

"Well, John came to me the other night."

"Really? Which night? Last night?"

"No, not last night. The night before."

"Ah, I see." Joan looked thoughtful.

Amy continued. "Well, he came to me and he said for me to tell you not to worry. He's over his pain now."

"I'm so pleased."

"He says your mother is with him. She's looking after him. He loved his grandma, didn't he?"

"Oh, he did. My mother loved him too."

Amy opened her eyes and smiled broadly. "Well, that was a lovely message to get. A cup of tea?"

"That would be lovely."

"And afterwards you can tell me about your husband's business. A diamond mine wasn't it?" She grinned. "I bet you've got loads of lovely jewellery from him."

Joan smiled. "Oh, yes, I have. He's been very kind to me."

That made Amy feel warm inside.

Amy left Joan and made a pot of tea in her lovely china teapot that she had got from a second-hand shop. She laid out some biscuits too. Not the expensive ones. She'd got a multi-pack from the Value Bargains Store. When she walked back through to the living room, Joan was sitting with her hands folded over her lap looking into space. Amy said, "Here we are. You look like you were lost in thought then, Joan."

Joan smiled. "I was. I was thinking about my son."

Amy sat down. "And you know he thinks about you too." She reached and put her hand comfortingly on top of Joan's.

"You have such a lovely energy, Amy," Joan said. "Delicious."

Amy tilted her head. "That's very kind of you to say, Joan." She gazed at her, for what she thought was a reasonable amount of time, then said, "Tell me, Joan. Have you ever thought of doing this yourself?"

Joan smiled faintly. "Mediumship?"

"Clairvoyance, yes. It's just you seem to have a talent."

"Do I?"

"Well, what you said about my energy..."

Joan said, "You have a distinct energy. It's what drew me to you in the first place."

"Thank you so much." Amy sat back and sipped her tea. She put down the teacup in the saucer and said, "Did you see my advert in the local paper? I never did ask you."

"Yes, that's it. In the local paper. But I was drawn to you because of your energy. It's very full."

"Full? That's a strange thing to say."

"It's a strange business."

Amy giggled. "Yes, I suppose it is! Anyway, back to your reading. Is there anything in particular you want to know?"

Joan regarded her with her dark brown eyes. She touched the spider necklace and twisted it round and round in her fingers. She paused then said, "I'm just interested if you can sense anything about me?"

"What do you mean?" Amy was puzzled.

"Any impressions you get about me."

Amy sat back. She steepled her hands and rested her chin on them. "Well, you're a very nice lady, I can tell that. You have a very warm energy."

"Thank you," Joan said.

"And..." Amy narrowed her eyes in concentration. "I think you've suffered some tragedies in your life. You're from Brazil aren't you?"

"Yes, that's right."

Amy smiled. This was going well. She said, "And I sense a darkness about you."

"Darkness?"

Amy reached out and stroked Joan's forearm to reassure her. "Not from you — about you — in the past, I mean."

"Ah."

"Maybe a sadness. I sense suffering. Can you take that?"

Joan nodded and smiled sadly. "That makes sense."

Amy sucked her lip. "You're a very mysterious lady. I get that."

Joan's face was expressionless.

Amy said, "But I think you are going to have a very pleasant surprise. No, not a surprise - a gift. Maybe even a reward. Does that make sense?"

Joan smiled. "It would be nice to get a reward."

Amy grinned again. "Of course it would. Now have you finished your tea? I'll take a look at those tea-leaves."

For the next half an hour, Amy told Joan things of little consequence that tripped off her tongue while her mind went round what she usually said to clients to make them feel good about themselves, and her, of course. Especially her. She wanted them to leave thinking that she was a lovely person who'd really helped them, and who deserved a little something by way of a thank you.

Joan smiled and accepted everything she told her. Then Amy said, "Well, Joan. I have another client in ten minutes."

"So that's it?"

Amy patted Joan's hand. "Sorry to disappoint - no lottery win! But we've had a good session, haven't we?"

"Oh, yes. Splendid."

Both women stood. Joan smoothed down her plain brown dress.

"So that'll be £40." Amy grimaced. "Sorry!" She smiled apologetically. "But I did mention the price increase, didn't I?"

Joan nodded. "That's fine." She opened her purse and pulled out two crisp blue £20 notes. Amy took them with a smile. She wished she'd asked for more. "Thank you so much!" She cocked her head to one side while she took the notes and then she put them on her little telephone table in the hall. She got Joan's plain fawn mackintosh and helped her put it on. Then she looked out for the other client through the little window in the door. For some reason, she didn't like her clients to bump into each other. It was the idea of them conversing somehow. As Joan was about to leave, Amy caught her elbow. Joan didn't pull away.

"Oh, I nearly forgot," Amy said. "Are you going to come to our Psychic Fair at Caldbeck Tower on Halloween?"

Joan looked like she hadn't known about it. She processed the news then said, "Of course. I'd love to."

"Do you know where Caldbeck Tower is? I know you're new to the area." She gave a laugh.

Joan nodded. "I know where it is."

"Great then. See you there on Halloween!" She delivered the final word with a spooky flourish. Joan smiled indulgently in response. Amy grinned, and then gave a rapid little bird wave of her hand and, with a trill, said, "Bye!"

Joan left and walked away down the dismal street without turning back. Amy grinned. Under her breath, she said, "I'll soon have her eating out of my hand. Then she can give me that nice necklace. For starters, anyway," and closed the door.

JILL PICKED Amy up in her gleaming black Audi. Amy tottered out on her heels gripping her black sequined clutch bag that contained her

Tarot cards. She was dressed in a black satin dress. She'd thought it appropriate for the occasion — suitably mystical. She lowered herself into the passenger seat.

Jill said, "You look nice."

"You too!" She didn't mean it. Jill was also dressed in black. However, Jill's dress was new and designer, unlike Amy's purchased from the charity shop on the High Street. Still, she was a fat cow and Amy wasn't.

"You excited?" Jill said, pulling the Audi onto the road.

She thought she'd better put it on so Amy clapped her hands in girlish delight. "Oh yes! *So* looking forward to it." She paused. "Let me get it straight how it works, though; the punters just come round the tables and pick the person they want to do the reading?"

"Yes, we're setting up in the Baronial Hall. Honestly, hun, it's fantastic. It has little snugs with settles. I guess the aristocrats in the old days used to sit and read in them but they're perfect for doing a reading with a client. Though we've got tables, obviously."

Amy grinned from ear to ear. "Sounds fantastic!" The money would be fantastic anyway. Just to add a flourish, she stamped her little feet in a girlish tap-dance of joy on the Audi floor.

"Careful of the car!" Jill said. "It cost a lot."

"Oh, sorry." Amy blushed. Like I give a shit, she thought.

"Only joking."

But maybe she'd offended Jill, and she needed future favours so she puckered up her face. "Thanks for picking me up by the way. I know it's out of your way."

"Not a problem. I'll give you a lift back too."

"I hope so, or I'd be pretty stuck!" Cheaper than a taxi anyway.

IT TOOK around ten minutes to drive to Caldbeck Tower. It was on a road out of the village, at the beginning of wilder country. It was said that the site had been a Roman signal tower originally, but the oldest part still standing was the Norman keep. Bits had been added on in Tudor, Stuart and then in Victorian times. It had been sold by the aristocratic family in the 1920s to a man who made his fortune in cattle feed. Then it had been a girls' school briefly in between the wars; commandeered by the Army in the Second World War, then lain empty for years until bought and renovated in the 1990s. Amy did not know the current owners. She asked Jill if she did.

Jill said, "Yes, I know Mrs Jones. She's from abroad. I wondered whether she was a Lesbian because she kept talking about her "friend", who's obviously female."

"Why does that make her a Lesbian? I've got a friend who's a woman - you!".

Jill said, "I never criticise people's life choices, hun. Walk a mile in my moccasins, I say."

"What?" Amy frowned.

"Never mind."

Jill turned off the country road and the Audi's wheels crunched over the Hall's gravel drive. The headlights illuminated trees on either side. There was a white shape in a tree, which flew off.

"An owl!" Amy said. "I bet there are bats too."

Jill said, "Oh, don't say that. I'm scared of bats."

"They can't hurt you."

"Vampire bats can."

"We don't have them in this country. They come from South America."

Jill said, "I think Mrs Jones is from South America."

Amy looked out of the window. Jill's prattle really got on her nerves.

The car pulled up in the car park. There were already several cars parked but none as nice as Jill's. And what had the cow done to deserve that except marry someone with a good job? Life was unfair, Amy thought, but I'll get what I deserve in the end.

There was a light on a pole where they parked but it didn't do much to illuminate the car park on that dark night. As Amy got out, she saw the mist from the river curling through the trees. She smelled its damp. The Tower loomed up in front of them, built in massive blocks of dark red sandstone. There was a heavy wooden door, banded in iron, which looked hundreds of years old. It was thrown open and yellow electric light spilled onto the forecourt. On either side of the doorway were pumpkin lanterns, their faces cut in scary eyes and jagged, horrific mouths. "Halloween!" Jill said with a grin. Amy rolled her eyes.

As they walked towards the door, Amy glanced up at the sombre tower and the dark slates of the roof, damp and shining dully from the moisture in the air. Her feet crunched over the gravel. She shivered this time from cold. She wished she'd brought her coat and hoped it wouldn't be too chilly inside the Tower.

"Iris!" Jill saw the lady who had organised the event. She went up and gave her a hug. Iris then hugged Amy and gave her a little kiss on the cheek. "I'm glad you could come, Amy. We'll have a good turnout tonight. It'll help your bank balance. I know things have been a little lean for you recently."

Amy tilted her head to one side. "Thank you Iris, so much." Patronising cow.

Iris patted Jill on the shoulder. "Thank this lady for putting us in touch with her Mrs Jones. What a great venue it is! Come and I'll show you both the Baronial Hall.

They walked from the entrance hallway across a floral carpet then down a short corridor, past dark antique cupboards and dressers until they came to the double door of the Baronial Hall. The Hall was lit by black iron chandeliers suspended from the ceiling with frosted electric bulbs shaped to look like candles. It was a good sixty feet long by about twenty feet wide.

There were mullioned windows with black lead separating the small diamond panes. The glass in the panes was old and thick and it distorted the light shone on it. There was a gallery running around the top of the hall where people could sit, though there was no one there now. The floor was made of old oak floorboards and the walls were panelled in some dark wood. Hanging there were heraldic coats of arms alternating with the antlers of deer and other unfortunate creatures. Jill made a little sad noise when she saw them.

Pumpkin lanterns were set in nooks and crannies, and on the

floor around the walls. Their pumpkin eyes fluttered as the candles inside flickered in an unfelt draught.

"It's so atmospheric!" gasped Jill.

"Can't you just feel the spirits?" Iris said.

Amy laughed to herself. They actually believed this crap.

"Your table's over there, Amy," Iris said, pointing. There were around eight tables spaced around the hall, with two chairs each on opposite sides of the table. The tables had cloths of different coloured silks. "My idea," Jill said. "I borrowed them from that woman in the Market Hall."

The cloth on Amy's table was black. She went over and sat down. The other mediums busied and clucked around their tables getting things ready, setting out their crystal balls and skulls and amethyst angels in preparation for the guests coming in.

Amy got her Tarot cards from her clutch bag and drew the pack from the case she kept them in. She laid the cards on the black silk cloth. As she turned them over, she caressed them with her finger ends and whispered the names of the cards out loud like an incantation: The Empress, Nine of Swords, The Tower Struck Down and Death. Then she grinned. She was glad that reading wasn't for her! She closed her eyes and slowed down her breathing. She liked to pretend to spend a few minutes in meditation before starting. It was all about playing the part.

At first, her attention was drawn by the chatting of the other mediums. She heard odd words and snatches of talk. She knew all the women and she smiled to hear them. They talked such rubbish. They were such airheads with their crystals and their energies.

But then, she got a feeling like she used to get when she first started on this business, when she thought it was all true. It startled her. This wasn't how things had been for many years now. She'd buried her talents beneath years of bitterness and greed.

Unnervingly, she felt the energies of the surrounding women. To her once, peoples' energy was always coloured, deep reds, ochres, yellows, greens even. And here it was again. Colours like a lost innocence. Iris was a pure blue. Jill was orange.

But there were other energies in this place. The Hall was so old. So many souls had lived and died here over two thousand years. She sensed their coming and going. Their happiness and sadness - weddings, fights, funerals, lovemaking, the birth of children. Dogs too. She felt dogs. And there had once been a bear here. A long time back - a dancing bear, perhaps in the Middle Ages?

But there was something else. It flitted out of her sensing. It was as if it knew she could sense it and was trying to hide. What was it? She frowned. She couldn't get hold of it. And then she caught a feeling of cold. It stopped her dead. Something cold and dark and inhuman. It didn't have the energy of an animal - not a dog or bear. Not even a bat. It was something older than that, more primitive - drier somehow. She shook her head and opened her eyes.

That was odd: to be sensing things like she used to. She didn't like it. It reminded her of who she used to be when she was young and soft.

"Are you all right, dear?" It was Jill, reaching out a sisterly hand. "You look dazed."

Amy smiled. "Just getting the vibrations. It's a funny old place, this."

"It's that indeed," Jill smiled. "Great for Halloween!"

Iris clapped her hands. "Ready everyone! The first guests are arriving!"

Amy tried to smile, but she felt sick. She sensed whatever it was moving again. And it was hungry.

The evening went well. Amy forgot about her sensations and started making things up again. The punters loved it, like they always did. The pumpkin lanterns burned and Amy smelled their sooty, waxy odour and felt the heat generated by the people and candles in the room. She also smelled the mix of scents from the mediums and their mostly female guests. She had a good night. She gave reading after reading and folded the cash into her little black clutch bag.

Then Iris clapped her hands again. "Attention, people!" she said. "It's nearly the witching hour. The witching hour on Halloween!"

The mediums and the visitors all made long "Oooo!" noises and laughed.

"So," continued Iris. "We come to the highlight of our evening." She turned to Jill who was by the door out of the Baronial Hall. "Can you dim the lights, Jill, please?"

Jill nodded, and the lights turned down on their dimmer switches, the mock candles in the chandeliers going from bright to dull to worm-like orange filaments to no light at all. The Hall was lit now only by the flickering, and in some cases guttering, candles in the pumpkin lanterns. Their sharp eyes and jagged mouths looked sinister. The light from them moved and shifted and shadows were cast against the dark wood of the panelled walls, making people look large and strange. Amy glanced up to the gallery that ran above her head. She imagined faces in the gloom; the faces of all the people who'd died here, staring down at her. She shuddered.

It was quiet in the Hall. Someone squeaked a floorboard. Someone else giggled nervously.

Iris said, "So ladies... and gentlemen," she smiled at the two or three men who were in the room. "Can we all come together and hold hands for Halloween?"

People got up. There was a ripple of chatter, nervous and quiet, but excited. Amy stood and the women at the tables near her stood too. Self-consciously they made their way to the middle of the hall. Their faces looked strange in the shifting yellow of the candles.

"Hold hands now," Iris said.

Knowing she had to, Amy reached out to either side and her hands were taken by the women next to her. Iris began to intone. "And now, at the time of the year when the veil between this world and the next is thinnest, we reach out. At this join between summer and winter, we seek the doorway between the worlds. Let that which is hidden come forth. Let the spirits of this place come and speak to us."

Amy felt a shiver run up her spine. Spirits and lies were her business, but something here made her uneasy.

"Oh, no!" a woman on the other side of the circle said.

Amy jumped.

"What is it, dear?" Iris asked the woman.

"There's something here," the woman said.

"Well, that's good." Iris raised her head to look into the darkness that clustered above them. "Spirit, make yourself known."

Amy's skin crawled. She didn't like it. An oppressive weight entered the room.

"Spirit, if you are here — I offer you my voice to speak," Iris said.

There was silence. Tension crawled into the Hall like something coming up from cellars or down from attics. Something that lurked here all the nights of the year now had license to show itself.

Amy was getting more and more uncomfortable. She felt hot. The woman to her right shifted her feet. Someone coughed.

Then Iris spoke again. Her voice was now guttural. She spoke rapidly in a torrent of clickings, consonants and rough breathings. It was no language Amy had ever heard before. It didn't even sound human. It was deep and awful, like an old man stumbling down a corridor to his death, the tapping of his stick, the rasping of his breath, his faltering heart. Iris's voice was getting louder and more insistent but still the noises made no sense.

Amy's hands were clammy holding those of the women on either side. Her head spun as she thought that it didn't sound like a person's voice at all; it's more like the sound an insect would make — some fat, greedy insect.

And then the chandeliers blazed. Jill stood by the door. She had flicked on the light. She had a wide, false smile on her face. "Well, I think we all agree that was spooky enough for Halloween!"

Amy glanced at Iris. The older woman was pale and looked unwell. She was being comforted by two of the mediums. What was this rubbish?

There was a ragged ripple of applause that petered out. Jill said, "It's past midnight now and the owner who has kindly allowed us to be here tonight, wants her house back!"

Some of them laughed half-heartedly. Others were throwing each other glances and raising their eyebrows. People started to thread their way out of the hall. Amy heard good nights being said. Jill came up to her. "Well, what the hell was that all about?"

"Was she putting it on?" Amy said.

Jill said, "I don't know, but it wasn't appropriate. It scared the wits out of some of them. We've spent years disassociating psychic mediumship from devil worship and now she does this."

"She frightened me," Amy said. She heard herself saying it like she was some stupid girl. But it was true.

Jill sighed. "Go and pack up your table. Then go to the toilet and I'll give you a lift home."

Amy went and packed her Tarot cards into their box. She put it in her bag and then looked around for Jill. Many of the group, including Iris, had gone. She saw Jill standing with a woman in a brown dress. The woman had her back to her. She went up to Jill and said, "I'm nearly ready. Just need the 'loo."

The woman turned round and Amy's eyes widened. It was Joan Smith, her client.

"Ah, Amy," Jill said, "Let me introduce Mrs Jones, the owner of the Hall."

Joan Smith smiled at Amy.

Amy frowned. "But you're Mrs Smith. You come to me."

The woman nodded. "I do."

Amy's brow furrowed deeper. "But how come you are Mrs Jones? How come you own this Hall?"

Jill said, "Amy, get to the toilet and come back. I can't be hanging around here forever."

Amy, still frowning, walked towards the Hall door. She had already been to the toilet once in the evening and knew where it was. At the door, she paused and turned round. Joan Smith was staring at her.

Amy hurried to the toilet. She dilly dallied over washing her hands and adjusting her hair. She hoped that when she got back, Mrs Smith, or Mrs Jones, or whatever she was really called, would have gone and she could just go home with Jill.

Finally, she pushed open the toilet door and stepped out into the corridor. She tapped her bag where her takings were. At least that was real enough — some benefit from a thoroughly strange night.

When she got back to the Baronial Hall, it was empty. That was odd — where had Jill gone? She went out of the Hall, back to the main doorway. She thought maybe Jill was waiting for her in the car outside, but when she got to the door, it was closed. She reached for the black iron handle and tugged at it. The door was locked. A slight panic began in her belly.

Then she sensed someone behind her. She spun round and saw Joan Smith standing there. Amy gave a little gasp then said, "Where's Jill?"

"Jill?" Joan said.

"My friend. She's giving me a lift."

"Oh, Jill." Joan smiled. "Yes, she had to leave."

"Leave? Without me? She wouldn't do that." Amy shook her head vigorously as if to persuade herself what she said was true.

Joan Smith shrugged. "Yes, she's gone. I'm sorry."

"Well, how am I going to get home?"

"I can give you a lift if you like."

Amy felt relief, but also suspicion. She just wanted to get out of there, but she would do whatever it took to get the woman to open the door. She knew how clever she could be. If she had to be sweet, she would be. If she had to threaten to call the police, she'd do that too. Then she remembered she had no phone signal. She frowned. The walls of the place were so thick she could make no calls from there. So she had to be polite. She said, "Thank you, Joan. Are you still Joan?"

The woman said. "I can be Joan, if you like."

Amy said petulantly, "It's not what I like. It's what you're really called." Amy knew she needed to be calm. She forced herself to smile. "It's just I need to get home, you see?"

"I know you don't have anyone waiting for you at home though, Amy."

"No. But I'm tired. I need my sleep."

"Of course. We'll go soon. But first would you like a proper look around my home?"

"I've seen it," Amy said. "I've been here all evening."

Joan smiled. "You've only been in the Hall. There are other floors and other rooms."

"I could come back another time."

Joan laughed lightly. "Come and look now."

Amy paused. She was getting sick of this. But if that's what it took. She sighed. "Okay, but then you'll take me home?"

Joan nodded. "Of course. But first, come this way."

She half turned and stepped towards the hallway that led back to the Baronial Hall. Amy didn't follow at first. Joan looked at her as if she were a stubborn child and said, "Please, Amy. Come."

Amy followed but lagged behind as Joan walked through to the Hall. The place felt echoey and empty now everyone had left. Some of the candles in the pumpkin lanterns had gone out. Amy smelled their smoky smell. Joan's shoes clattered on the wooden floor.

"Do you live here alone?" Amy said, still behind her.

"No," Joan said. She started to mount a staircase.

Amy followed. "Who do you live with?"

Joan ignored the question. She paused on the half landing. There were some paintings of cavaliers and roundheads on the wall. "There's supposed to be the ghost of a little girl here," Joan said. "But I suppose you can feel her."

Amy hadn't attempted to feel anything. The memory she had of when she had opened up was of a dry, scuttling thing, and she didn't want to feel that anymore.

"Where are we going?" she blurted.

"Just to the first floor. I wanted to show you the bedrooms."

"I'm really tired. Can't you just give me a lift?"

"Soon. Soon. Let me show you the bedrooms."

Amy sighed and followed her. Joan flicked the lights on as she went. They walked along long corridors with locked doors on either side. Always Amy held back. Joan saw her glancing suspiciously at the locked doors. "I don't need all the rooms. I never go in them."

"Is there anything in them?"

Joan ignored her again. They walked on a little further then Amy stopped. "I'm not going any further," she said. "Just open the front door. You needn't give me a lift. I'll walk."

"Don't be silly, Amy. It's very damp outside. The fog's down. You'll catch your death."

"I don't mind. Just let me go."

Joan shook her head. "Indulge me. Just come and see the bedrooms."

Amy sighed again. Then, feeling she had no other option, walked on.

Eventually they got to the end of the corridor. Joan opened the door and put on the light. "This is my bedroom." There was a magnificent four-poster bed with drapes. Pretty pink silk sheets were thrown back as if Joan had only recently got up.

"You live here with your husband?" Amy said.

"No. I'm not married."

Amy was puzzled. "Don't you have a husband who owns a gold mine in Brazil? Or did I imagine that?"

Joan shook her head. "I've never been to Brazil."

"But you told me you got your necklace there."

"Did I?"

"Yes." She frowned more deeply. "But if you're not married, how come you had a son - John."

"James, I said. But I lied. He wasn't my son."

"Why would you lie about that? That's awful." Amy crossed her arms across her chest, as if to protect herself. Her hand went to her throat. She was very nervous now.

"I wanted to test your powers, Amy."

"My powers? Why?"

Joan said, "I sensed you had a delicious energy. I said that, didn't I?"

Amy nodded.

"And I meant it," Joan said. "Delicious."

"So who do you live here with?" There was a tremor in Amy's

voice.

"Come. I'll show you the tower."

"I don't want to go to the tower."

"There's a wonderful view."

"Tonight? It's dark. And foggy."

Joan laughed. Her laugh was a sweet tinkle that echoed in the hollow silence of the place. "True, true. But it's very special. Come."

She walked off. Amy followed. Joan walked more quickly than she did and Amy struggled to keep up. "Please let me out of the front door. Please."

"Soon. Soon," Joan said. She began to mount a spiral stone staircase. The sandstone was worn as if by a thousand feet and hands over a thousand years. They went up. The air was becoming colder and Amy could see her breath. Her heart beat faster. They passed by a door in the wall. There must be a room behind it, Amy thought, and it made her nervous. Then they got to the tower's top. There was a bolt across the door. Joan drew it back. She said to Amy, "Do you believe in monsters?"

Amy shook her head vigorously. "Monsters? No." She rubbed her forehead. "No. I don't believe any of that stuff."

Joan arched an elegant eyebrow. "Really? Are you a fraud then? Are you deceiving people?"

Amy stared at her and said coldly. "Give me a lift, as you promised." Then a shudder came over. Against her will, she said, "What kind of monsters?"

Joan threw open the door with a flourish and the cold damp night air flooded in. Amy could see the roof of the tower but not much further because of the fog. She guessed it had been a battlement in medieval times. She said again, "What kind of monsters?"

"Don't you want to go out on the roof?"

Amy said, "No. I want to go home."

Joan shrugged. "Very well." She pulled the door closed.

"What kind of monsters?" Amy repeated.

"If I told you there were things that ate energy, would you believe me?"

"But you said monsters. You and me both know this is bullshit. I don't know what you're trying to do. If you think you're scaring me. You're wrong. I eat idiots like you for breakfast."

Joan smiled. "You're a little fraud, Amy. You're a deceiver and a liar. And what's worse is that you had talent once. You could have been honest."

"Please. Shut up. I'm not interested."

"Do you know what spiders eat?"

"What?"

"You heard me."

"You're insane."

"No. I'm not. I'm like a policeman if you like." Joan laughed at her own joke.

"Police? What are you talking about?"

"We police people who lie and cheat and prey on the sadness of vulnerable people."

"I'm going to leave."

Joan ignored her. "Now, I want to show you the cellars."

"I don't want to see the cellars."

"You said that about the roof and you quite enjoyed it, didn't you?"

"No, I didn't enjoy it. Let me go home."

"After we see the cellars."

"No. Let. Me. Go. Now." Amy snarled. She wished she hadn't worn her heels. She couldn't run.

"Don't struggle like that, Amy. We need to go to the cellars."

Sudden fear struck her. Amy frowned. "That's a funny word to use - struggle. What do you mean? Makes me sound like I'm tied up in something."

Joan ignored her again. "Come on. All the way down."

Joan made her way down the stairs. Amy thought about not following. She thought maybe she could go on the roof and climb down the wall. But it was dark and wet. She would surely fall to her death. She had no other choice, so she followed after Joan. On her way down the spiral staircase, she passed by the door she'd seen before. She was just going by it when she heard a noise from beyond it. There was something or someone in there. Her heart hammered. She ran down the stairs, almost tripping. Joan was waiting. "Down further," she said.

"Who do you live with, anyway?" Amy said.

"My friend," Joan said, without looking round.

"And who's your friend?"

"My special friend. We're nearly there now."

At the bottom of the stairs, Joan switched on the electric light. There was one dim bulb for the whole place. It illuminated a damp cellar with sandstone walls. The cellar looked like it had been there since the Middle Ages but there were rusted Victorian pipes running through it and in a corner an old newspaper and a broken chair.

There was an opening in the far wall that led to another cellar. It looked like there was a further cellar beyond that. The place smelled cold and musty.

Suddenly, Amy sensed it again. The dry, scuttling thing was near. She moaned with fear.

"What's that?" Joan said, turning, smiling.

"There's something here."

"Oh yes, I know."

Amy felt the sweat on her lip and she shivered. Her fingers felt numb and tingly with anxiety and her throat pulsed as her heartbeat became rapid. Her mouth was dry, but she said, "You were talking about monsters. What kind of monsters?"

Joan said, "From under the ground."

"From Brazil? From mines in Brazil?"

Joan smiled. "No, from here. They're not thousands of miles away. They're here, under your feet. They always have been."

"What are they? These monsters."

Joan grinned. She played with her silver necklace. "Don't you know? Can't you sense them?"

Amy began to cry. "I want to go now. Please let me go." She put her head down. "Please," she said, "Please just let me go."

"Come on. I want to show you the room at the end."

"I don't want to see it."

"But Jill's there."

Amy felt like someone was choking her. Panic filled her. She said, "She's not. You said she'd gone home."

"I lied again, Amy. I always lie — just like you."

Joan walked off down the centre of the cellar towards the doorway that led to the room beyond. Amy stood. She thought of turning and running, but she knew she was lost. She would never find her way out through the corridors and halls. She glanced at the disappearing Joan and then back at the door that led to the stairs.

And then she heard it. She felt its awful presence and in her mind heard the dry scuttling of its many legs. She jerked round. She sensed it behind her. She saw that the cellar went back into gloom and there was another door. It was there. The door hung open and she couldn't see into the darkness, but she knew it was there; she felt its hunger. She felt it start to move.

Joan grabbed her arm with fingers like a steel vice. She dragged her forward, then stopped and turned. She said, "Here you are. Jill will be so pleased you're here."

"Jill's not in there. She can't be."

Joan shook her head. "My friend said her energy was very good. But I'm sure it won't be as tasty as yours."

"Please, let me go." Amy tugged at Joan's arm.

"Oh, no, Amy. I can't do that."

"Why not? Why can't you?"

"Because my friend is hungry. And I made her a promise."

Joan walked forward again, dragging Amy. As much as Amy struggled, she couldn't get free. Amy's heart was hammering. Jill couldn't really be here. "Where's Jill?" she said suddenly. "You said she was here, but I can't see her."

Joan stopped and pointed ahead. "Through that door."

Amy stared where she pointed. A dirty black wooden door stood at the far end of the furthest cellar. There was an iron bolt on it but it was drawn back. The door was open.

Amy said, "But it's dark in there. There's no light."

Joan said, "Jill doesn't need light. She can't see any more."

The door opened. The room had been a coal cellar originally, but the coal was all gone. Instead, on the floor, Amy saw an untidy shape. It looked like a bunch of rags at first with something in it, and then in the poor light she recognised Jill's expensive black dress. But now the dress was wrapped with something grey and pale. From the door, Amy peered forward. Jill was wrapped in cobwebs. She had been wound tight in spider silk.

And then Amy saw things were moving all over Jill. She looked harder and saw that where Jill's throat should be, and in the hollows of her eyes, were holes. Little black things were scurrying and moving all over her, going inside her body, into the moist darkness.

Joan was at her shoulder. She said, "My friend is a lady. She wanted Jill for her babies."

Thousands, maybe tens of thousands of spiders were burrowing into Jill's corpse, going about their business, eating her from inside out.

Amy gasped in horror. "Oh, no!" she said. She turned. Joan was between her and the entrance. Something horrible and dark was scuttling across the cellar behind, coming for Amy.

"She wanted Jill for her babies," Joan said, "But she wanted your liar's skin and meat for herself."

10

CROSS FELL

Looking out of the window, the wind was the worst, though the rain — slanting in, fine and raw — would not be much fun either. George warned me not to go: over breakfast at his charming little pub in Garrigill, he said this was no weather to be climbing up Cross Fell, especially alone, especially at the end of December, especially in this weather.

As I ate my full English breakfast with Alston Sausages, local bacon, black pudding and free-range eggs from the farm in the village, he tried to talk me out of my very last journey of the year.

'Listen, man, you must be crazy,' He said, as he brought more brown toast with luscious local butter that already lay, yellow and tempting. The white china plate holding my breakfast was sat on the scarred wood table in front of me. He had the lights on. It was early in the day but dim. I knew there was so little light on these days between Christmas and New Year, especially with the grey clouds sitting low and blanketing out the sun like wet wool, as they had done week after week since October.

'Have you seen the rain outside?' George said, thumbs in waistcoat pockets now he'd put the toast down in front of me. He nodded to the window. The curtains were drawn back, but it was so gloomy out that you couldn't see anything other than the streaming rain on the dirty glass pane. A wire of Christmas lights still flashed around the window frame but their cheer didn't distract from the heaviness outside.

I shrugged, biting my freshly buttered toast. 'It's my last one. I'm doing Cross Fell but then I should have enough time to drop into the Eden Valley to stay tonight. I've got a B&B booked at Dufton. That's what I'm planning.' Except I wasn't but he didn't need to know that.

George rubbed his stubbly chin. 'It's a hell of a slog up there, even in good weather.' I looked at his belly. It would be for him on the freshest day. Then he narrowed his eyes. 'You know why they call it Cross Fell?'

I smiled. I'd read something about this somewhere, details now forgotten. I ventured, 'Because it's got a cross on the top?'

He wagged a finger. 'Yes, but why did they put the cross on the top?' Before I could answer, he said, 'They put the cross on the top to drive off the Devil. He used to live up there.'

'You say "used to". Must have worked then.'

He frowned. 'Well, they say it drove him away, but I reckon it's an omen for you not to go.'

'What's an omen?'

'The cross.'

'They put it up centuries ago, but it's *still* an omen for me?'

He was irritated. 'Yes. Look at the weather, man.'

I continued with my breakfast. 'I don't believe in the Devil. Besides, I already told you, it's my last fell in Cumbria over two thousand feet. I've climbed all the rest.'

He still kept trying to put me off. 'Honestly, It's a dismal climb,' he said. 'A long slow trudge over bog and moor.'

'It's the height that counts. The cross is right at the top?'

He nodded. 'Yes. More coffee?'

It seemed a suitable marker: the cross. I nodded for the coffee.

Bringing the pot to fill my cup, he said, 'So why this time of year? Don't get me wrong, I'm always glad of the business, but really it's the end of December, not even New Year.'

I grimaced. 'Family trouble. Had to get away.'

'Sorry to hear that. You seem a nice bloke; hope it's nothing too traumatic.'

I nodded. 'Thanks for that George. Not sure everyone agrees I'm a nice bloke though.'

His brow furrowed. 'Does anyone know you're here?'

I shook my head. 'Nope. I left in a hurry.'

He looked as if he would say something, but then didn't and instead left me to finish my breakfast in peace.

THEN IT WAS time to leave. I fetched my pack and outdoor clothes from the quaint bedroom with its ancient, uneven black painted floorboards and door that didn't fit properly. On the way out, I saw the guest book and penned a good review. George appeared.

I said, 'There's a column here for my address. You don't need my address do you, really?'

He shook his head. Not really.

Then it hit me. How unfortunate, but I'd been in such a weird mental state when I left home, and then booked this place from the travel lodge. I can't have been thinking straight when I gave him my address. Maybe I gave a false one? It didn't matter now, anyway. I shrugged and prepared to leave.

He tried to stop me one last time as we stood at the door by the Christmas Tree. The lights blinked golden among the tinsel draped branches. There was even a fairy on the top. 'Just get the bus to Penrith from Alston. I'll give you a lift to Alston. Then you can get a bus to your B&B for tonight from Penrith.'

I shook my head. 'I'm walking. I'm determined.'

He sighed. 'Some folk are pig-headed. Don't say I didn't warn you when you have to call the mountain rescue out.'

I slung my pack on my shoulders. 'I won't be calling the Mountain Rescue out.'

I opened the pub door and almost changed my mind as the rain instantly drenched me with a runoff from the gutter. Almost, but there was never really any danger I would change my mind. I peered out. It was cold and wet and dim, but I had good gear and it truly was my last fell to walk.

George said, 'See? The weather's evil.'

I merely grinned. 'Weather can't be evil. Just bad.'

As I stepped out into the elements, George said, 'Watch out for the Devil.'

I laughed. 'Like I said, I don't believe in the Devil, George. By the way — great breakfast.'

He waved ruefully, stood looking from the open door, and then when the cold and the rain were too much for him, closed it and got on with clearing up my breakfast dishes.

Then I was alone with the elements. The first part of my journey was along a narrow lane. It was technically fit for vehicles but heavily rutted with grass growing in the middle. I didn't see any vehicles for the hour I was walking along it, head down, trying to shield my face from the rain by angling my hood away from it. I didn't see any people either. Determined, I climbed slowly up into the moors.

They call this place England's last wilderness and they are right. The Lake District can be hostile in poor weather but at least it's got its softer side. Here in the Pennines, it was just moorland and bog, sedge, rush and the constant whining wind. The only marks of man were the ancient, lichen covered limestone walls that lined the lane and the rusty barbed wire that topped them. Sheep wool was snagged here and there on the wire. But there weren't even any sheep.

Grey and cold and wet, the morning went on, and I climbed with it, higher and higher.

With nothing external to draw my attention, my mind turned inward. It was true that Cross Fell was the last of the high fells in Cumbria on my list, and it was also true that I had wanted to finish them all before the end of the year. But now, it was like tidying up my affairs.

I had more or less given up on climbing Cross Fell, or at least putting it off to a more clement time of year. Then Jess revealed she had cheated on me. She told me on Christmas Eve just as I was putting the kids' presents in the stockings to hang on the end of their beds as they slept.

'I'm really sorry, Steve, but I just don't love you any more,' she'd said.

To give her her due, she was crying though I don't know whether that was because she felt sorry for me or herself.

The story was as tawdry as I imagine they normally are. A new bloke had started at work. That was in the Spring. Then as Summer came, they'd got on better and better. I bet he made her laugh. I bet he flattered her. He was managerial. Thinking back, I remembered a work away weekend for team building. They'd stayed at an Outward Bound Centre in the Forest of Bowland. I bet that's when they got to know each other really well. Really well.

I had no evidence that anything happened then, but looking back, she'd seemed different after she came back — nicer to me if anything.

Greg, that was his name, had even given her a lift home one night in September when she'd had to work late. He'd been sitting in the car as I opened the door to her. I think he even waved at me. There's a name for people like that. Brass-necked. But I could think of a worse one too.

I realise I must have been stupid not to think any ill, but we'd been together since we were sixteen: childhood sweethearts. A match made in heaven.

And now I was in hell. The wind howled. The rain drove against my hood and got in my face. I was even climbing a mountain that was home to the Devil. So they say.

As I walked, measuring my thoughts by the tread of my boots, I glanced out through the screen of rain. The road now was a rocky track. At this altitude, piles of snow lay at the road edge, melting away in the rain. At least it wasn't snowing, that would be worse, but maybe if it had been snowing, I would have chickened out. I wouldn't have ventured out from the pub. I would have taken George's advice and sat there all day sipping Cumberland Ale by the Christmas Tree. But that wouldn't have solved anything.

Drops of ice mingled with the rain. A few hundred feet and it would be snow.

The weather really was hellish. I wasn't actually cold yet because of my various clothing layers, but it was pretty miserable walking through this. I was climbing and now as the altitude increased, I could see almost nothing. The low cloud and the rain obscured vision at about fifty feet. At least I could see the rocky path underneath my feet. It was a good path. The only good thing about the day.

I trudged on. No, I wouldn't be calling out the mountain rescue team. I guess I saw the cold and rain and bleak, endless moorland as a fitting way to end. When your wife goes off with another man, fitter, stronger, better-looking and better-paid, you question everything. You feel a failure. You start to catastrophize until life has no options, but one. I planned on getting to the summit at least. Do it by the cross.

Jess said that after Christmas, she would move in with Greg and she would take the girls with her — my two daughters. That broke my heart. I said I'd fight it and that I'd keep the kids with me, but she said I would need a lawyer, and they were all shut for Christmas. I'd tried. I'd rung all the local solicitors, but they were closed for Christmas, the season of joy and good-will to all men.

And then I'd left to come to Cumbria. I hated conflict and confrontation, so I'd let her go without a fight and let her take my daughters with her. I hated that I'd abandoned them. What a gutless bastard. Running away up a mountain. At least it was a beast of a mountain.

I walked on. To my right, a tumble-down ruin emerged from the low cloud. It must have been a shepherd's hut at one time, or God forbid a house, but who would have wanted to live up here where the weather is hostile eight months of the year? Looking at the stones, then at the sleet, I wondered whether the inhabitants died of exposure.

In the pub last night with old George and his bacon and sausages and the Christmas Tree, and the pint of real ale , I'd had something to distract me, to warm me, to give some comfort. Now, my thoughts dragged me down. The weather was sapping me. If anything, the weather got worse. The rain was definitely sleet now and as I climbed on higher, there was more and more snow in it. But I had to get to the top. Only the top counted somehow. Here would be no good.

I saw no one else. But who else would be stupid enough to come out here except me?

Higher and higher I went.

Then I thought I heard someone's voice in the wind.

It was weird; it wasn't someone calling for help. It didn't sound like a cry of pain. It sounded like someone shouting a name. I even stopped and turned round.

I listened. There was definitely something in the wind. As I listened to the keening notes that played between the wind's whine, it didn't even sound human. It probably wasn't. It was most likely the wind through some stones somewhere out of sight in the billowing mist. I looked down there was snow around my boots, just a line of it, but it spoke of things to come.

It was gloomy. Today would be very short. A very short interlude of grey day between the deepest black of night and night.

The sound came again. If I listened, I could almost hear words.

I was high now. Not that there was any view, just fog and moorland on every side. I could believe they thought this place had been the haunt of demons. Up here on my own, hardly able to see in front of me, it was easy to believe in monsters.

Onward, onward, onward. The rhythm of my feet increasingly inaudible against the rising wind. The reeds and rushes either side of the path were catching snowflakes on their stems. It was cold. I had good gloves and my hood was up. My boots were waterproof and my feet were dry, but where the wind hit my face, it was cold enough to cut skin, and snow blew into my mouth as I breathed.

Still that voice in the wind. I must have left whatever group of stones that might have been making the sound behind, but still the shrill edge of unseen singing kept on with its unearthly words. Words that if I listened, made the sounds of my name. It unnerved me.

I thought I saw a shadow behind, but with the visibility being so poor; it was hard to be sure.

Then I became convinced that someone was following me.

I came to a big band of boulders. The path went between them, but the boulders stretched out on both sides of it like a runway. I had a guidebook to the walk. I remembered reading it last night. The book said there was a band of big boulders in a circle around the summit of Cross Fell. It said that until that point the path was relatively good, after that it said the summit was a 'trackless waste of bleak bog'.

I passed through the circle of boulders, as if entering a magical realm, but not Narnia or Tolkien's pleasant Middle Earth, the place I'd entered was a realm of dark magic, a realm of cold and snow like the hell of the Northmen who'd once colonised this land.

Almost immediately the path failed. I tried to pick my way along a sheep trail between clumps of bog and reed. My boots sank in ankle deep and I pulled them out with a squelch. I had to be careful, though this was the most promising looking path, sheep weren't interested in going down mountains and this sheep trail could be a dead end. I just wanted to reach the summit.

Then I heard the voice again calling me.

It was just the wind. I had to focus. I was still climbing. I would keep on picking my way uphill through the snow. More snow loomed out of the fog. Freezing fog with a pitter-patter of snowflakes. I couldn't see the path at all now. No sheep hoofmarks either. They'd been smarter than me and had found shelter somewhere.

I heard the voice call, 'Steve, Steve, Steve.' It was like someone was wailing after me — some banshee spirit of fog and cold that lived up here.

The snow wasn't massively deep, but it covered the bog and I sank into the soft mud again, each effort of dragging my feet out weakening me further.

"Steve, Steve, Steve..." the voice called. I ignored it, focusing on putting one foot after another. I needed to reach the summit.

I got the weird idea that this voice knew what I'd done. I

stopped, fighting down panic. I really couldn't see anything. I got a fleeting idea that it would be sensible to turn back, admit I was wrong and find George's fire and ale, and then just wait for them. Stop running.

But it was too late for that. The wind howled. The snow battered me. The die was cast.

I turned into the wind and got a faceful of snow, cold, clinging and freezing me. My breath billowed out. I took out my compass. I judged the fell top was southwest of me. I took out the map. Peering, I saw the circle of boulders. I saw the path marked where it crossed them and then in a red dashed line; the path was supposed to continue on, broad and clear. Except the path didn't exist now. Not that I could find.

I looked up from the map, looked back where my footprints marked where I'd been and then round to the southwest. I must be near the summit now. Maybe I would see the cross, if it still existed, or at least some cairn to show the summit.

Fog wreathed the place and snow fell within it. The fog boiled and moved driven by the wind, but the wind never blew it away, there was fog forever, and snow and snow and snow. My heart hammered.

Then I saw him.

There was a man behind me in the fog. I couldn't make out anything but his size and shape at the edge of visibility. I called out, 'Hello! Who's there?' But the figure didn't answer. Instead, my name on the wind insinuated itself into my ears again.

"Hello!" I called again. "Is that somebody?"

It was somebody. A person. But he didn't answer. I stepped out, feet crunching into new layers of snow.

Maybe it was a standing stone in the mist. I wanted to get away. He might try to save me, and I didn't deserve to be saved.

But as I walked, the shape walked too. He was behind me now, following me up the slope towards the summit. Once I got there, I would hide. I would sit behind a rock and just wait until I was covered with snow. Nobody would find me. They said hypothermia it was a sweet death — a sweet cold death.

I walked, and he followed, not getting closer, but not falling further behind either.

The spectre followed me through the fog, as I stumbled over stones, feet sticking in sucking mud, hardly able to see anything. I needed the summit. Then I could rest. I fell once, full length, but picked myself up, gloves covered in mud and ice. He was still visible, as if he was waiting for me to go on.

He was about thirty yards away, as he walked on, far more sure-footed than he should have been across this terrain and in this weather. We walked, or rather he walked and I stumbled and then when I stopped, he stopped. I called out again but again he didn't answer. The howling on the wind had stopped too. No more names. Just the shape stood behind me.

It was as if he was waiting in judgement.

Then from the mist the shape of a broken stone cross of immeasurable age unpicked itself. I had reached the summit. He stood there behind me. It was clearly a man wearing a black coat. I could see now. His clothes were totally unsuited for this place. When I studied his face it was at first hard to focus on, as if made from the mist itself. Then my heart jolted.

'This can't be right,' I yelled. 'It just can't.'

It was Greg.

But it couldn't be Greg. It simply couldn't. My mind reeled. I filled my lungs to scream at him, but the frigid air froze them and set me to coughing.

I didn't see how Greg could be standing up here in his everyday clothes. In fact, I knew he couldn't be.

I thought of what I'd done, what I was doing. Greg stood mocking me. I'd been stupid. I'd been a fool. I'd abandoned my daughters. I didn't care about Jess now. She'd made her decisions, but my innocent girls? They needed their dad.

But my wish to die was strong. I didn't believe in an after life, I thought it would just be like being switched off. Like some old TV, I'd go dark. No more pain. Nothing.

I'd done what I'd done. But instead of facing up to it and taking my punishment, I'd run up here to die on this beastly mountain.

And I hadn't even had the bottle to kill myself, I was going to let the mountain and the weather do it for me. What a failure.

Greg watched me silently, only the whining wind and the cruel snow kept us company.

I bowed my head.

It wasn't even about him beating me. It wasn't even finally about him at all, or Jess. It was about my daughters and being there for them. Not putting my selfish despair first, not seeking a bolt hole in death. Not abandoning life, whatever pain it held.

The devil looked at me across the snowy waste. He was hungry for my weakness.

Here on Cross Fell, I had a choice. I could die, or I could live. I could run from life, or I could take my punishment.

The wind howled. The snow blew. The devil watched. And in that snow, I wept.

I threw back my head and howled. The devil wouldn't take me. I would descend from white hell to green earth. I would descend. I would take my punishment.

Greg, or whoever he really was, watched as I left the cross and walked away.

I DON'T REMEMBER the long trudge down the fell. Eventually, it must have been hours, but the snow stopped, and I dropped below the cloud line. The wet, drab December green of the Eden Valley spread out before and below me. Eventually, I descended the open fell and came to small fields and stands of trees. The village of Dufton with its ancient buildings and welcoming inn was before me.

In front of the inn were three police vans. I just kept walking to the inn. When they saw me, officers got out of the vans, wearing high-visibility jackets and carrying batons. One even had a Taser as if they were expecting trouble. I would give no trouble. At first, I didn't know how they'd found me then I remembered saying I was coming to Dufton. I'd booked that room over the phone, using a false address, but in my stupidity, I'd booked old George's place online and left my address and phone number. I guessed that George, worried for my safety had called the rescue and the police. And the police had been looking for me.

An officer came up to me. 'Steven Jones, I am arresting you for the murder of Greg Williamson on 26th December this year.' He said something more, but I wasn't listening.

I'd spend time in prison. I'd pay for my crime. But I wouldn't die.

11

AN OLD SCHOOL REVENANT

My dad burst into the room of our house at Troutbeck, and I could tell he was mad at me. "You can stop that right now," he said.

I was like: "What?"

"I'm not a fool Holly," he said. "I know the smell of cannabis."

But we weren't smoking weed. We had a couple of bottles of Blue WKD, and Rachel had smuggled in a half bottle of vodka, to help with the pre-sesh, but we were *not* smoking anything, never mind weed.

I took the opportunity to be righteously indignant in front of my friends. "Dad, it's the smell of a joss stick." He thinks he's so cool, but he's as far away from the drugs scene as you could possibly be. I think he maybe took a drag of someone's spliff when he was 19 at Uni, but that was it. My mum's worse: a sniff of advocaat at Christmas gets her all giggly and wanting to play charades.

He was wrong-footed. He could see the joss stick burning in the little fat Buddha thing he got me when he went to Hong Kong with work. "Oh," he said. But then as he couldn't back down, he said, "And you can pack that in right away." He was pointing to the Ouija Board.

I bet my friends thought he was a total tool, but I love him really, dumb as he can be for a smart man.

"It's just a game, dad. You don't really believe in all that do you?"

He blustered. "Of course not. It's just they're dangerous."

"If you don't believe in ghosts, then how can they be dangerous?"

"Don't argue with me Holly," he said, in the tone I know means that he realises he's losing the argument. "Anyway," he said. "It's not ghosts. It's evil spirits."

I put my hand to my mouth to stifle a laugh. "Evil spirits? Come on dad. This isn't Paranormal Activity III."

"You always have an answer, Holly," he said. He loves me really. "Anyway, I thought you were going out?"

"We are, but not till about ten. Drinks are too expensive, so we *pre-sesh* here first."

"Holly never buys a drink anyway," said Nev, being mischievous. "The boys always fall over each other to get her one first."

"Shut it, Nev!" I snapped at her. There are lots of things my dad shouldn't know. And that's the beginning of the start of them.

He sighed wearily and closed the door.

"Ok, let's get back to this," said Talya. She was the one who'd brought the Ouija Board, and the one most into it.

"Yeah, but we've got to finish getting changed soon," I said. There was me, Nev, Talya and Rachel in my bedroom.

Nev switched off the overhead light, and we just had the bedside lamp. It was her who'd lit the joss stick too - to give it a 'mystic' atmosphere.

We all joined hands and placed them on the little planchette thing that moves around the board - going from letter to letter to spell out words. Rachel was writing the letters down on a piece of paper.

"So," Talya said. "Is there anybody there?"

There was a round of nervous giggles. A pause. Then Rachel said, "I guess not."

"No, wait," I said. "It's moving."

And sure enough the planchette with all our fingers placed on it began to move across the board.

"You're moving it!" said Rachel.

"Really, I'm not," I said.

Talya and Nev said, "Me neither," both at the same time.

"This is freaky," said Rachel.

"Just go with it," said Talya.

"It's moving to the 'yes'."

On Ouija Boards the letters are all set out, but there is also *Yes* and *No* in the top corners of the board. That's how it gets its name — from the French and German for 'yes' run together - so Oui and Ja.

"So there is somebody there," said Talya.

"Are you living or dead?" I asked.

"You've done this before," said Nev.

I shook my head. "I saw it on *Supernatural*."

And the planchette moved again. This time it went to the 'd'.

"Dead," said Talya. "It's going to spell out 'dead'".

"Just let it go," I said. And it spelled out dead.

"You must be pushing this, one of you," said Rachel.

I knew I wasn't, but I didn't totally trust the others. I said, "Do you have a message for any of us?"

And the planchette moved towards 'yes'.

"Which one? Can you spell out her name?"

The planchette moved to the 't'.

"It's for Talya!" Nev shouted.

"Is it for Talya?" I said, and the planchette moved to 'yes'.

She shuddered.

I said, "Ok, what is the message?"

Then the planchette began to move quickly, sliding across the board. As it paused at each letter, Rachel wrote them down with her free hand. It spelled out:

Talya - you are going to...

"Going to what?" said Nev.

"It's still moving," said Rachel.

With a horrible, sense of not being able to stop what was happening, we watched as the planchette moved to 'd' then 'i' then 'e'.

"This is stupid," said Talya. "If any of you thinks this is funny, they can just fuck off."

She was about to pull her hand away but Rachel stopped her. "You can't just take your hand away. They curse you if you do. We have to thank the spirit and bid it farewell."

"This is such bullshit," said Talya. I could tell she was nearly crying. I reached up and put my free hand on her shoulder to comfort her. Then on an impulse I said, "What is your name, spirit?"

The planchette began to move again, quickly spelling the letters of a woman's name. It spelled out 'Janet'.

"Oh," gasped Talya. "Janet was my Nana. She passed away last year."

We all knew how close Talya had been to Janet. She'd more or less been brought up by her, and her death had hit Talya very hard.

I said, "Do you want to protect Talya?"

And the planchette went to the 'yes'.

"See," said Nev, who had a kind heart. "It's all good. She wants to protect you."

"But it says I'm going to die!" said Talya.

"Can you protect her from dying?" I spoke to the room, to the Ouija Board, and to the invisible spirit of Janet.

The planchette moved again and this time it spelled out the message "If she listens to me, she will be safe. I will protect her from it."

"It?" I said.

"The fate? The event?" said Rachel.

"Sounds like it was a thing, not just a happening, — to me anyway," said Nev.

"Shut the fuck up, Nev. You're scaring me to death," said Talya.

"It's just silly Tal," I said. "It's just a stupid parlour game. It's not real. I bet Nev was pushing the planchette."

Talya looked relieved. Nev looked hurt. "I was not!" she said.

And then a knock came at the door. It made us all jump. It was just my dad. He said, "Ok, are you ready for your lift? I'll drive you to Windermere but I'm not coming to fetch you. You'll have to get a taxi from town."

As we went downstairs, mum was watching the TV with our dog Hector by her feet.

"Ok loves. Have a nice night, but be careful and don't drink too much," she said.

"Mum, you remember that Talya and Rachel and Nev are coming back here to stay tonight?" Even though I lived three miles out of town, it was the most convenient of all our houses, and it was like one of the sleepovers we used to have when we were little. But instead of wearing comfy pyjamas and watching *101 Dalmatians,* now we talked about boys and clothes and the bitches at school we didn't like.

We were 18 and soon we'd all leave each other — our childhood would be gone and we'd go off to universities and jobs, but this was a honeymoon period with adulthood; we had the pleasures of being an adult but none of the responsibilities. We were determined to enjoy ourselves.

We went round town and then got into the local nightclub. Windermere is a small town, but it does have a nightclub! It was the usual night - we all got a bit tipsy. Rachel fell on the street as she couldn't walk in her 5 inch heels. Nev started crying because the boy she fancied - James Bliss - was kissing another girl. Talya was quiet.

I said, "Penny for them."

"Eh?"

"Your thoughts."

"Oh, just can't get that stupid Ouija Board out of my head."

I put my arm round her. "Don't worry. It's just silly. I'm still sure it was Nev and Rachel playing tricks."

"You're probably right."

"Want a drink?"

She nodded. "Cheeky Vimto please."

"You shouldn't drink that stuff. It'll kill ya," I said.

She shrugged and smiled. "Apparently I haven't got long left, anyway." She was joking, but I didn't like her talking like that so I punched her arm gently and said, "Come with me to the bar?"

We lost Rachel for a while but found her in a dark corner with a man in his 30s. Despite her protestations, we pulled her off him and went outside to wait for the taxi. Nev had got over her upset - James had kissed her too and promised her he would take her out to Nando's at Kendal - so all was well.

The taxi took us an odd way back to my house.

I leaned forward from the back seat and said, "Why are we going this way?"

The taxi driver shrugged and said, "Isn't this the best way?"

I said, "Well, it's a way, but not the best."

I guessed he was taking us the long way round, so the meter ran up a higher price.

"I'm only paying you what we normally pay though," I added.

"We're going past the old school," said Rachel, pointing out the window.

"Ooh creepy," said Nev.

Greengill School had been for special kids - kids with learning disabilities. The County Council owned it, but a man called Andrew Hayes ran it for years. Then it turned out he had been abusing the kids — tying them to chairs and toilets and hitting them with bamboo canes. One of them died after he chained him to a radiator and then he'd got found out and gone to prison. While he was there another of the in-mates stabbed him to death with a piece of metal. They said they did it because he was a child killer.

As we drove past, the old school stood there in darkness. Part of the roof was shattered, and it looked like a broken tooth. The night was heavily overcast with the rain gently pattering down. The iron gates were chained up but you could get in through a hole in the wall. The school had closed down when I was about ten and we used to sneak in. Though the front door was locked, the back door had been kicked in and tramps used to stay there and kids from the town would light fires and vandalise anything that wasn't already broken.

"They say he used to drink the kids' blood, you know," said Rachel.

"Who?"

"The old headmaster - Andrew Hayes. They say he was in league with the devil."

"You'll believe anything, Rachel," I said. "He wasn't a vampire or a demon; he was just a criminal."

"It's said that he comes hunting at night and kidnaps children and drinks their blood."

"For God's sake Rachel, give it a rest," snapped Talya, who I'd thought was asleep.

WE WERE at my house about a few minutes after that because the old school is just down the hill. It's not the way we normally go into town, but maybe that driver had found a shortcut. I don't know. I paid him and off he went muttering because he didn't get a tip.

My mum and dad were asleep as I let us in. "be quiet now," I said.

To be fair, the girls were quiet. They left their heels at the door and padded upstairs in stockinged feet. Hector heard us though and began to bark. "Shut up Hector!" I hissed under my breath.

My mum put her head round the door and hissed, "Be quiet! Your dad's not well. He went to bed early."

"Okay, mum. Sorry," I hoped he was okay. He has high blood pressure so sometimes he does feel unwell. He's usually okay in the morning.

We got to my room and took turns in the bathroom. It was late, about 1 am and I just wanted to sleep. I was top-to-tailing with Nev, who was the tallest. Rachel and Talya had brought sleeping bags and were going to sleep on the floor.

With the effects of the alcohol and the lateness of the hour, I soon fell into a heavy sleep. I woke - I don't know when - but it was still the middle of the night. I could hear Nev snoring gently from the bottom of the bed but I was suddenly aware of a light.

It was Talya. She was using the light on her phone to do something on the floor. I lifted my head up and saw that she was using the Ouija Board.

"Oh my God, Talya, what are you doing?" I whispered.

"Go to sleep," she said.

"No, I won't. You shouldn't be doing that now."

"I'm asking my Nana if she will protect me."

"Of course she will. But stop it."

"I can't get through to her. The board feels different."

I watched as her hand with the planchette shot in a crazy movement across the board.

"It feels stronger," she said. "It feels like a man's hand moving it."

"Don't be silly. Just stop it."

"It's moving, look how fast it's going."

And it was true, her hand could hardly keep up with the planchette. I felt a horrible sense of evil fill the room. Nev muttered in her sleep as if she too were disturbed by the sinister atmosphere that was coming from the Ouija Board.

Suddenly Rachel woke up. "What you talking for?" she said sleepily. Then she saw Talya as she struggled to keep up with the ragged movements of the planchette. "What you doing that for Talya. Stop it."

And then the movements slowed, and it began deliberately to spell words.

"What's it saying Tal?" I asked.

When it had finished the sentence, she looked up and said, "It says I've got to go to the Old School."

"It's just your subconscious," I said. "It's just because we drove past the Old School, that's why you're thinking of it."

She shook her head.

Rachel agreed with me, but Talya looked terrified. "No," she said. "It's a message from my Nana. She wants me to go there to protect me. Something's going to happen in this house if I don't go. Something will come into this house for me."

I got out of bed, waking Nev, who just turned over again.

I got down on the floor with Talya. At least she'd stopped playing with the Ouija Board. I put my arm round her. "Just try to get some sleep. It'll all feel different in the morning."

But I too could feel the atmosphere in the room. It was as if it had dropped in temperature. There was a sense of foreboding - the awful feeling you get before a funeral.

I stroked her back. "Honest."

But she shook her head again. "No, my nana loved me. She wants to protect me. Can't you feel that there's something in this house? Something wicked? It wasn't here before."

"We've summoned it with the Ouija Board," said Rachel suddenly.

"Rachel, you're not being very helpful," I said. I shook Nev awake. She could be counted on to be very down to earth and sensible at times. I hoped she'd back me up. She wasn't happy at being woken up.

"What time is it?"

"About three." I checked on my phone. "Yeah, it's just after three."

"I want to sleep," said Nev.

Talya was shivering. "I need to go to the Old School."

"No," I said. "It's crazy. Certainly, not now. Maybe in the morning." I hoped that when the morning came she'd have forgotten about all of this.

"I need to go now," she said. "I'm going to die here if we don't go." She was shaking with fear.

"Yeah, let's go," said Rachel.

"What?" I said, incredulously.

"It'll be a laugh," she said.

"Come with me?" said Talya suddenly.

"Ok," said Rachel.

"What are you talking about? Why would your grandmother want you to go to that old ruin?"

Talya suddenly said, "She used to work there. She was a cleaner there for years."

"I didn't know that, but still."

"Maybe her spirit's there in some way," she said.

Rachel had started to pull on her jeans and pullover.

"Rachel, please," I said. "All this thumping around will wake up my dad and mum."

"I'll be quiet."

Talya too was pulling on her jeans and the clothes she'd come in before we changed to go out.

"This is insane," I said.

"Look," said Nev. "We know that it's all nonsense, so let's just go with her to the School. It's not far. It'll put her mind at rest, and then we can get some sleep. Is it still raining?"

I looked up at the skylight window in my attic room. "No, it's stopped. The moon's come out."

"So let's go," said Nev.

"It'll be good crack," said Rachel.

"No!" I said firmly. "If you go, you're not coming back in this house."

At that they all stopped. They could see that I meant it. "We'll go in the morning, Talya. I promise." I put my arm round her shoulder. She seemed very scared.

And the atmosphere was still thick in the room, as if her using the ouija board had tainted it. The bright sickly moonlight that came in through the window made it worse. I could see their faces, pale and tired looking.

"Ok, so sleep," I said.

It seemed they were all settling down. Nev lay back down and pulled the covers over her. Rachel got back in her sleeping bag, still clothed. Talya was the last to move. "I'll just go to the bathroom," she said.

I was suspicious. "You know where it is?"

She nodded. "Yeah."

"Don't go out of the house Talya. Please."

"I won't."

She opened the door and stepped out. I heard the click of the cord pull as she put on the light. I heard water running. I even thought she was talking to someone. I relaxed a little. I was pretty tired. I started to doze then sleep. I woke with a start. I knew I'd been asleep for a little while. Talya hadn't come back.

"Oh damn it," I said. I shook Nev awake.

"What now?" she snapped.

"Talya, hasn't come back."

Nev sat up. "Ok, we'll have to go after her." She got out of bed and kicked the slumbering Rachel.

"Eh?"

"Get up. Talya's gone."

"I thought we weren't going."

"We weren't, but she has."

"Oh well. I wanted to go anyway."

I got up and pulled on my clothes. My heart was beating fast. Anything could happen to her out there. She could fall in the beck, she could trip over a rock in the dark. That ruined school was dangerous. The floorboards were rotten. Also, there could be anyone there — tramps seeking shelter. She was only a teenage girl.

The three of us went downstairs as quietly as possible. Even Hector the dog didn't wake. I tip-toed into the kitchen and went into the drawer where I knew there was a torch. I flicked it on to test that the batteries weren't dead and a powerful white beam shot out. It was one my dad had sent off for - 1 Million Candlelight.

We gathered by the door and I put on my rain jacket. Nev took my sister Kate's who was off at University, and Rachel borrowed my mum's.

The moonlight made everything bright. We made our way through the puddles to the field where the footpath was that led past the school.

"Is this the way she would have come?" asked Nev.

"Dunno. I don't know if she knows it. If not, we'll get there quicker than her."

We made our way over the fields. We disturbed a sleeping herd of cows that mooed unhappily. One of them coughed.

"Cow coughs sound like people's coughs," said Rachel.

We ignored her. She was getting on my nerves, anyway. If she hadn't encouraged Talya we'd probably be all still asleep in our warm beds.

We went down the hill and there in the distance we could see the silhouette of the Old School. The path went past the back hedge of the school garden, but we managed to scramble over.

"It's really muddy," said Nev.

Then we were in the back garden of the school. I could see the broken door hanging off its hinges with a black mark where someone had tried to burn it.

"I can't hear anything," said Nev. "Want to shout?"

"No." I lowered my voice. "Who knows who's in here? Could be any old freak whose taken shelter from the rain."

"So how will we find her?"

"Let's go round the front," I said. "We'll maybe see her coming on the road."

So we made our way quietly round to the front of the old school. The gates were chained together, but one of the gateposts had sagged so you could squeeze round it.

We stood there looking up the narrow country road that led to my house. The light wasn't bad but we could see no sign of Talya.

Then Nev said, "Maybe she went into the school?"

I really didn't want to go in there but it looked like there was no choice. Reluctantly I turned. Even Rachel was quiet as we faced the evil old place. I couldn't get the thought of Andrew Hayes out of my head.

"Shout?" said Nev.

"Ok." And so we shouted, hesitantly at first, but then raising our voices. "Talya! Talya! Are you in there?"

"Did you see that?" said Nev. She was pointing at a window on the first floor.

I shook my head.

"No," said Rachel.

"Something moved in the window."

"Think it was an owl," I said.

"No," she said. "It looked like a woman."

"A woman?"

"Like Talya's Nana?" said Rachel.

I turned on her. "How could that be?"

She visibly cowered back. "I don't know. Just saying."

"Let's look," said Nev.

And so the three of us went round the back and up to the door. Hesitantly, I went in. I shone the torch around. Broken, rotten wood; an old newspaper. The marks of someone having a fire on the floor. This looked like it was the old kitchen. I shouted out again for Talya. No reply.

"Well, if she's here, she must have heard that," I said.

Nev and Rachel agreed.

"She's hiding from us," said Rachel.

"Or she's not here at all," I said.

"Let's just go a bit further in," said Nev.

And so we made our way from the kitchen into the corridor that led, with its peeling wallpaper, towards the downstairs rooms of the house. Then we came to the bottom of the staircase. A lot of the stairs were broken.

"She could have gone up there," said Nev, pointing.

"It looks unsafe. Why would she?" I said.

And then there was a noise behind us.

"What was that?" shouted Rachel. Her fear made me almost jump out of my skin. What was it — a rat? A tramp? Or nothing at all.

"There is something there," said Nev, peering into the dark.

"Where?"

"In the corridor we came through."

"That's the way out," said Rachel. "If there's something there, it's blocking us in."

"Something? Don't be daft. What?" I scoffed.

"What about getting out the front door?" Nev asked.

"Chained up," I said.

I took a step towards the corridor, shining the bright torch down it. Down at the far end there was a shape. It stood in the shadows.

"Jeez!" I jumped back.

"It's definitely a woman," Nev said. Her voice shook.

"Hello!" I shouted. "Hey!"

"What's a woman doing here at this time of night?" said Rachel.

"Let's go and see," said Nev.

My hand was shaking holding the torch. I saw that Rachel had picked up a big bit of wood out of the broken banister. We advanced slowly down the corridor.

Then the shape moved.

Nev ran after it and me and Rachel after her, as much scared of being left behind as facing this woman.

Nev was ahead of me. When I turned into the kitchen she was standing there, breathing heavily. She said. "It vanished."

I said, "Vanished?"

She nodded. "But I'll tell you one thing." She looked terrified.

"What?"

"It was Talya's grandmother. I knew her and it was definitely her."

"Let's get out of here," Rachel said. "It's giving me the creeps now."

"You're the one who wanted to come. You said it'd be good crack," I said.

"Well, I've changed my mind. Talya isn't here anyway."

She was right. There had been no sign of Talya. She probably hadn't been here at all; it was just me jumping to conclusions. I was pretty eager to get out of the place too. I didn't like the idea of some freaky woman tramp hanging around here.

"Let's go," I said.

We trudged up the road to my house. It was nearly 5 am by now. I used my key to unlock the door. The house was again quiet.

"But what about Talya?" asked Rachel.

"We'll just have to wait until daylight then I'll tell my dad and we can go out and look for her. I'm sure she'll be ok. She may even come back before then."

We mounted the stairs wearily. I was exhausted. I went to the bathroom to wash the mud off my hands before I went back to bed.

It was then I noticed that the airing cupboard was open. It's big enough to walk into, but not much more. It stands beside the bathroom and my mum keeps all the sheets and things in there. It's normally closed.

Curious, but with a sense of dread, I slowly pulled open the door. Half lying against a heap of sheets was Talya.

"Talya!" I said, but I knew something was dreadfully strange. As I reached out to touch her, I felt her temperature was wrong. She wasn't warm like a living person, but she wasn't cold either. She didn't resist me but felt heavy. When I turned her, I saw there were bruises around her throat. Her eyes were open and bloodshot, her tongue was black. She'd been strangled.

Then I heard someone standing behind me. I turned round. "Hi," I said. "I'm sorry if we woke you. I didn't mean to make so much noise."

His face was the face I've known all my life, but his eyes weren't right. It was like somebody else looking through them. Somebody evil.

My dad said, "I'm Andrew Hayes."

THE POLICE ARRESTED dad for Talya's murder. In his defence he said he was possessed by the spirit of the old headmaster, Andrew Hayes.

Of course he went to a psychiatric hospital and will be there until he dies. No one believed his story.

Except me. I tried to tell them but they told me to be quiet. They didn't want to believe it. Nobody does. By using the Ouija Board, we'd opened a gate somehow, and that had allowed the child-murderer Andrew Hayes to come back from hell and kill again.

12

THE ORPHAN OF CARTMEL

It was 1950. The war was over but the country was grey and dismal, hardly recovered from conflict and heaviness and loss sat on the land. The weather too was dismal as the train from Preston pulled into Cark. I wore my gaberdine and carried a small brown leather suitcase, just large enough to hold the change of clothes I'd need for my brief stay in Cartmel. I didn't anticipate being here for very long — just long enough to find out what I needed to find out, then I'd be back at this station and back home to London.

As I left the country platform, a fine rain slanted down and even though I angled my head so my hat brim protected me a little, my face still got wet.

'Bus is that way,' a small boy pointed, recognising me as a stranger in need of help. My hand went to my pocket for some change, but when I offered him the angular bronze threepenny bit, he shook his head. It was a simple act of kindness. I smiled at him and walked on.

The bus was small, red and cream and crammed with passengers from the train. Their breath steamed the window, and I used my gloved hand to wipe away a half-moon of moisture better to see the bedraggled winter foliage of the lane we rumbled down.

It wasn't far, but it took ten minutes to get to Cartmel, what with the local stops, where headscarfed women and boys in caps and duffel-coats disembarked. It seemed the driver just knew where they were going before they told him, but then they'd probably got off there a hundred times, or maybe a thousand. Looking out of the wet clear space on the window to my left, I saw the ghosts of hills in the mist. Hills and trees and more hills. It seemed time lay heavy on this land; as if nothing ever changed.

I got off the bus in the picturesque village square outside the King's Arms. I'd booked to stay in the Cavendish Arms, which couldn't be far away. Cartmel was tiny, but even in the rain there was something about the place; an ancient energy humming in the grey-stone buildings. But maybe that was just me fooling myself as I knew I had connections here.

I asked an old man the way as he went from the hardware store to the greengrocer's. As I'd thought, it was just round the corner.

The Cavendish Arms was suitably ancient. The saloon bar had a huge medieval looking fireplace in which was set an iron grate, piled with smoking coals and wooden logs, not quite caught by the flames.

The barman saw me looking. 'Just put it on.' His northern accent was strange to my ears, but here I was in Lancashire. The land of my fathers. At least, I presumed it was the land of my fathers.

'Booking in?' he asked with a pleasant smile.

I nodded.

'You got a bit wet, by the look of it.'

Truth was I'd only been out in the rain for minutes, but it was coming down heavily. I felt uneasy. It was strange to be here after so long, after all my historical ponderings on Cartmel once I'd learned it was where I came from.

Lost in thought, I hadn't responded to his comment about the weather and he shrugged, probably finding me rude so I forced a smile.

Truth was, I just wanted to get to my room. It had been a long journey from London and I needed the time to settle myself and plan what I would do first.

The barman got my key and took my bag despite a feeble protestation. His Lancashire good-humour recovered as he made conversation again all the way up the narrow, rickety stairs.

'You've missed the races,' he said.

'I'm not here for the races.'

'You're staying a week though?'

I nodded.

'Fell-walking is it? That's popular with city folk now. Can't see why myself.'

'No, research.'

'Ah,' he said. I suppose he didn't have much to say to that.

I was alone in my room. It was small. The bed had a cast-iron frame. The mattress sagged in the middle as did the pillows but the sheets were fresh. Faded Lake District scenes in cheap gilt-effect frames hung on the lumpy walls. The floorboards creaked as I went to hang up my damp coat in the sombre dark wooden wardrobe. I had to put my hat on a chair as there was no hat-stand. Sitting on the bed, and sinking in, I regarded the room. Like the rest of the inn, the place was ancient. I'd read that this hotel was set up by the Priors in the Middle-Ages for visitors from afar who came on business to the Priory. That's why I'd chosen it. Because I was here on business too. My own business.

I ate a passable beef pie with onion gravy, boiled potato and carrots with a pint of Hartley's Pale Ale, brewed not far away in Ulverston. I was the only guest. It was February after all. After eating, I sat by the fire with my book, but I could not settle. So I went to bed.

After London's lights burning bright all and every night, confusing birds and brightening even a winter sky to dull orange, the dark of Cartmel was absolute and instant. It was quite unnerving. I switched off the small electric lamp about ten. The night rendered me blind, as if all I knew and all the foundations upon which I'd built my life so far were swept away.

Eventually I slept. I dreamed of trains and missing trains and railways and stations and signals and lines winding across England and being forever lost and confused. Then something woke me.

It was a woman. She came with a glow. A pale glow like that

which comes from dead wood. And she smelled of rivers and rain and streams running fast with winter downpours, threatening to carry me off and drown me in deep water.

The woman did not speak at first. She stood, incongruous against the cheap wardrobe. I knew she was a ghost because I could see through her. I almost laughed. I wasn't frightened. This was the sort of place one would surely see a ghost, though I'd never seen one before.

And then a scent of flowers, faint woodland flowers, well out of season now. Perhaps from her perfume: Parma violet, and underneath it the smell of dark winter water.

She raised a finger and at that, my mood altered. A sudden fear seized me, rising from my heart to my throat.

Her raised finger was a warning. But a smile too, a faint, strange smile. I heard a voice as if from a million miles away: I'm glad you've come, it said: I'm glad you've come.

Then she vanished. I tried to sleep again, telling myself I was stupid, but my heart was unsettled and my nerves in shreds.

I woke with a start and saw grey light trying to find a way in through the drawn curtains. I got out of bed in my pyjamas and pulled open the checked curtains showing a blustery day with spots of rain. The window looked down on the back of the inn where there was a van and some other general untidiness. I pulled on my trousers and vest and went with a small towel to do my ablutions and shave.

Breakfast was good and the waitress, a pleasant north-country girl asked how me how I'd slept. I lied to her for politeness sake, and ordered bacon and eggs.

I had an appointment with a Deacon at the Priory at ten so I took time over my breakfast, taking toast and tea to the ticking of the clock that sat above the dining room fireplace. I'd written to the Priory, explaining my mission. They'd been strangely unwelcoming. I hadn't expected that. I thought they'd want to help.

I was early for the appointment and stood outside the gate to the Priory. The ancient stone church must have been an impressive building in its heyday, though much diminished now. Checking the time was exact by my watch, I stepped inside the huge doors and into the cool, echoing space. It was quiet, but I could hear the wind worrying and fretting outside. Near the altar, a middle-aged woman arranged flowers. I looked and saw no one else and was about to approach her to ask where Dean Lovegrove was, when he appeared at my elbow.

He laughed. 'Did I give you a start?'

He seemed an unaccountably jolly man, out of place in that house of sombre stone. I smiled, unable to think of a ready answer. I was ashamed how jumpy I was, but my anxiety had grown all morning, not helped by seeing that thing in my room the previous night. I nodded and introduced myself.

'I guessed it must be you,' Lovegrove said. 'The time, the place. And...' he paused and looked around theatrically, 'we don't get many visitors.'

He was bright-eyed, active and thin. He reminded me of a starling.

'Yes, I've come to talk about Reverend Kirkby.' I glanced away. 'Would it be possible to talk somewhere more private?'

The Deacon's office was Dickensian. Filled with old books, candlesticks, a bundle of new candles tied with string, an inkwell and two dipping pens. I noticed Reverend Lovegrove's hands were stained with blue ink. He beckoned me to sit on one of three ancient seats of old wood upholstered in cracked leather. There was hardly room for three chairs and his desk in the narrow room. The ceiling was high though and looked to have been partitioned off from the main church in the middling past.

He reached for a big leather-bound book. 'Reverend Kirkby wasn't it? He's the one you're interested in?'

I nodded. I felt myself flush.

Lovegrove turned some pages then stabbed with his inky finger. 'Here he is. I never met him. He was vicar here until 1900.'

My heart thumped. I leaned forward. 'May I see?' As if just seeing his name would somehow make him more real, and that would make me real too.

Lovegrove was watching me curiously. I supposed my emotion must be showing. I tried to compose myself, show a stiff upper lip, giving a brief nod. 'Yes, that's him.'

Lovegrove cut through all my acting. 'What was he to you? He seems to mean something to you?'

I hadn't intended to say anything, or if forced, to give a brief lie about researching someone's family history for a solicitor tracing beneficiaries of a will, but Lovegrove stared at me bright as a bird.

'He was my father.' I blurted it out.

He tilted his head, questions forming but searching for the delicate way to put them, but I spoke before he could ask me.

'Yes, my name is Starkey. I was adopted.'

And that said it all. Adoption of a healthy child was only ever for one reason — the terrible crime of illegitimacy. I had no complaints; the Starkeys brought me up well. My adopted parents were my real parents in every detail but blood, but now they were both dead, it had freed me to go looking for who I really was.

'I see,' Lovegrove said. 'Like I mentioned, I never knew him. There may be others on the staff here at the Priory who would remember him. I'm from Lancaster myself — a stranger to Cartmel. I've only been here ten years.'

I ran my finger over his name. It felt strange. There he was, a real person. I read once that illegitimate children always doubt their right to exist, as if their lack of legality denies them the right to be a person at all.

I frowned. 'Where did he live?'

Lovegrove pondered. 'The Rectory, I suppose.'

'You mentioned staff?' I said. 'Long-serving staff. Is there anyone there who would have known him?'

'Oh, I don't know.' He looked distinctly uneasy then laughed, going back to his empty-headed starling routine with bright blinking eyes. 'There's Mrs Thwaites, the cook. She's been there forever.'

I returned to the subject of my father. "Is there a gravestone?" I asked.

He folded his arms. "Not that I've seen."

Usually, the Church of England puts up a plaque in the church for any vicar who dies. And then it struck me, he might not even be dead. That was a shock, and in a sense that made it worse. If he were dead, then that was his excuse for never wanting to find me.

The atmosphere grew uneasy, and I went to the door. As I opened it, Lovegrove said, 'Just one thing, old chap.'

I stopped. 'Yes?'

He cleared his throat. 'It's a lovely place, this. And old. The people are very friendly.'

I wondered what he was driving at. I stood and waited for him to continue.

'But,' and he grinned as if embarrassed, 'they don't like you poking about.'

I cleared my throat. 'I'm sorry? You think I'm poking about?'

He raised his hand to placate me. 'No, no. It's just they have their secrets.'

I said, 'I'm not interested in uncovering their secrets.' And then I thought: only mine.

I decided to go to the Rectory to see if Mrs Thwaites remembered my father. Or in fact anyone who could tell me what kind of man he was. But on my way over, my nerves failed me. I was passing by the tea-shop. A squall of wind brought sudden rain. There were no birds in the air, no cats on walls nor dogs on the streets, and no people visible. I stood indecisively then went put my hand on the door-handle.

But then, movement to my right made me stop and turn, even in the rain. A woman stood, huddled back into a narrow alley between two grey houses. It was the woman from my room. She stared at me like I was the only person in the world that mattered. She wore no coat. I stopped and looked. Thin, sad, and with eyes full of regret, she lingered and said, "I'm glad you've come.' Then she vanished, as if she were snuffed out.

I had the strange sense that despite the words, she was telling me to be careful.

The bell above the door of the Bluebell Teashop rang as I pushed my way in and dripped rain onto their lacklustre carpet.

'My , you're wet,' a woman said. Middle aged, thick-waisted with brown horn-rimmed glasses and fashionably turned hair. I stood dazed.

'Take a seat and I'll come for your order.'

Without speaking I went to a round wooden table, covered by a lace tablecloth. A bowl of sugar-cubes stood with a silver spoon, and a small Willow pattern jug of milk. The designs of the bowl and jug did not match; they were not a set. The silver spoon was jammed among the sugar cubes, not lying uniform aside on the table.

'What would you like?' she asked, notepad and pencil in her hands.

'Just tea, please.'

'Would you like one of our fruit scones with jam and cream? Locally baked and the cream's from Harrison's at Blenkett.'

I shook my head without looking.

She looked disapprovingly at the drips of water. 'You can hang your coat and hat up on the stand.'

I did what she told me, then she brought me tea.

The door bell tinkled again and an old country type came in.

The woman said, 'Hello, Joe. Goodness me, man, you're soaked.'

The old man laughed, revealing yellow teeth. 'It's nowt, lass. It'll soon blow over.'

She smiled. 'You've seen plenty worse I suppose, all those years in the graveyard.'

He sat down at what I took to be his usual table. He had the air of a regular customer.

'Tea?'

He grinned. 'Scone too.'

'Coming right up.'

He looked straight at me. 'Ow do?'

I nodded. 'Well thanks. Yourself?'

'Mustn't grumble. No point anyway—nobody cares if you do.'

I managed a laugh at that. He seemed quite a character and I needed something to pull me away from my ruminations on the woman I'd seen in the doorway.

'Aye,' the man continued. 'Seen much worse than this. I was sexton here for fifty years. When you dig graves in the rain, they fill up with water. So we rarely did it in bad weather. But then if someone needs buried, they need buried, and if you get a week's rain, you've just got to dig, whether the hole be flooded or not.'

And then I thought perhaps his line in conversation wasn't what I needed after all and I went back to my tea.

I trudged down the long path to the Rectory between the rose-less rose bushes, leaves up, sheened with rain. I had my collar raised and hat down as the drizzle sleeted in sideways. I stood at the door and pulled the bell and then after minutes and me thinking no one would come, a stout woman in a pinafore yanked open the door. 'The rector's not in. He's away at Lancaster.'

I forced a smile, the rain dripping from the brim of my hat. 'Mrs Thwaites, is it?'

She looked suspicious. 'Aye. Who are you?'

My voice wavered. 'You don't know me.'

'You're right. I don't.'

'It's just I wondered if I could talk to you for a few minutes?'

'What about?'

'It's a bit awkward.'

She didn't let me out of my misery, just stared hard with bright blue eyes.

I continued. 'It's just that I think you might have known a relative of mine.'

'Really? Where from?'

'Reverend Kirkby. From here.'

And then her face softened. 'The Reverend Kirby, as was Rector here?'

I nodded.

She said, 'He's been dead forty odd years.' But her previous hard expression had gone.

So he was dead then. I nodded. 'Yes. I mean I didn't know that, but yes, I suppose.'

'You didn't know, but you say he's your relative?'

I grimaced. 'Sorry.'

She shook her head. 'How did you not know that?' But before I could answer she went on. 'What was he to you?'

The quietness of my voice was a surprise to me. I said it like a small boy. 'He was my father.'

She tilted her head as if she hadn't heard right. 'Your father?'

'Yes. I believe so. My adopted father told me — just before he died himself.'

She stepped back as if some great revelation hit her. 'So you never knew Reverend Kirby?'

'No.'

Suddenly softened, she pulled the door wider. 'You'd better come in.'

As I stepped through the door, she indicated the hat stand. 'Hang up your coat and hat. I don't want you dripping all over the floor. And you'd better take off your shoes too. They're soaked.'

She said it in a stern voice but I sensed kindness underneath. I looked around. There were open doors to a neat, soul-less lounge and a tidy, empty-looking dining room.

'Come through to the kitchen,' she said.

The kitchen was more homely and there was a fire burning in the grate. A black cat, sleeping on the mat in front of the fire, looked up when I entered, then looked down again as if I was of no interest.

'Tea?' Mrs Thwaites asked.

I'd just had one, but I didn't want to offend her by refusing. 'Thank you.'

'Milk and sugar?'

'Yes. Two, please.'

And so she made me a cup of tea and I gratefully dried my dampness by the fire. She offered me cake too, and I took a slice of homemade Madeira Cake.

When she sat down finally, she said, 'I knew there was a child of course. Yes, and I think I knew it was a boy. Went for adoption.'

'Yes. That's me.'

'Have you been happy?' she asked, tilting her head.

I thought. Yes, I had been happy. My adoptive parents had been good to me. I nodded.

'Good.' She said, and I thought she meant I wouldn't have been happy if I'd been brought up with my real father and mother.

She said, 'Of course, they couldn't keep you.'

'Who?'

'Reverend Kirkby and your mother. I'm sorry to say it was a scandal.'

I sat back. A scandal. I was a scandal.

'I don't mean to be unkind, but your mother was only nineteen and your father in his thirties.'

'They weren't married?' I asked.

She looked at me hard, but not unkindly. 'What do you think?'

'I suppose not.'

She shook her head. 'But still it was terrible. A terrible thing hereabouts,' and then more quietly, she said, 'I still see her sometimes.'

'Who? My mother?'

'Yes. I don't normally mention it, not working for the Church and all, but my mother and grandmother were Wise Women. Folk used to come to them for charms and to have their fortunes told. I've got it too.' She sipped her tea. 'She hung herself in this house, you know?'

And I felt like I'd been punched. My mother hung herself?

Mrs Thwaites realised what she'd said and from my face how hard it had hit me. 'I'm sorry,' she said. 'That was blunt of me.'

She reached out and touched my hand. Just a touch of kindness then she pulled back and picked up her tea cup.

Hesitantly, I said, 'Can you tell me about them? My father and mother?'

Mrs Thwaites looked as if she were considering whether telling me more was wise, but correctly concluded that the damage was now done, so she spoke. 'Your mother, Lisa—Lisa Benn, was under-maid here when they had more staff. It was before the Great War. Your father came here, he was only here under a year and, I suppose you'd say they fell in love.'

She tutted. 'Well, it wasn't done for a village girl and the Rector to go courting, so they kept it secret. And then…' She wouldn't meet my eyes. 'Things took their natural course, as they shouldn't have. And she got in the family way. He never denied it was his, which is what he should have done to save his position. He told the Bishop, and all hell broke loose.'

'And then what happened?' My voice was quiet.

'They tried to keep it quiet, but this is Cartmel. And it wasn't going to be kept quiet. It was a disgrace. She carried the child.' She eyed me. She meant me.

'And she was a thin thing, so the bump showed to the world. They sent Reverend Kirkby—your father—away. To Barrow, I think. And when she gave birth at home, they came and took you away for adoption. The Church did.'

I said, 'But she hung herself?'

Mrs Thwaites nodded sadly. 'When they took you away, she didn't eat. Her old mother and father were worried sick, and they got the doctor, but he couldn't help. Her heart was broken, you see. She'd lost her son and the man she loved.'

I didn't know what I felt. Emotion rose in me like a huge black tide. It filled my heart and rose to my mouth, but I could not speak with the image of my mother's sadness.

Mrs Thwaites went on. 'And she let herself into the house. The Bishop and the new Rector had treated her most coldly after she gave the child up for adoption. Everyone said so, and in her anger and sorrow she came in here, went up to the attic where she used to sleep, and hung herself from a beam with an old rope she brought with her.'

She looked at me, reaching out once again to give my hand a brief touch. 'I'm sorry, Mr…'

'Starkey. John Starkey.' I said. It was all I could do to mutter my own familiar name. But what was? Kirkby? Benn?

'Can I fill up your cup?' she said.

The brown china teapot had a hand-knitted woollen cosy warming it. Before I said anything she filled up my tea and put my milk and sugar in too, stirring the cup with a tarnished silver spoon. I watched the brown liquid swirl round and round.

Finally, I looked up. 'But you see her, you said?'

She nodded gravely. 'Not often. But she's here.'

'What does she look like?'

'A thin girl with long brown hair, wearing a brown frock. She doesn't speak. She doesn't give messages like some of them do.'

It was her. I suddenly stood. 'I should go now.'

She looked concerned. 'As long as you'll be all right.'

I nodded, but as I went for my coat, I said, 'Do I have any relatives? Cousins?'

Mrs Thwaites said, 'No. Old Mrs and Mrs Benn didn't have any family, just themselves. I think Lisa was a shock to them, coming late in life when they probably didn't expect it. But they loved her. They never recovered from her death. They're buried out there.'

She lifted a hand to point toward the Piory graveyard.

'What about my mother?'

Mrs Thwaites shook her head as if I was ignorant. 'She couldn't be buried in consecrated ground. Not a suicide.'

Suicide. That word hurt me. Suicide. Bastard. Lots of nasty words. I said, 'Where is she buried then?'

'They took her away. I heard they cremated her and put her ashes somewhere. Not in Cartmel though. I don't know. Your grandparents would have known, but they've been dead a long time now.'

'And my father? Did he never come back?'

She frowned and fiddled with the handle of her teacup. 'Well, yes, he did. But I didn't know if I should tell you all of that.'

'Tell me.'

She sighed. 'He heard about your mother and he came back. It was against the strict orders of the Bishop and the new Rector, Reverend Keen wouldn't let him in the house. There was a terrible row on the doorstep. Even though he was a clergyman, he cursed Reverend Keen saying how cruel he'd been to Lisa and how he'd driven her to take her own life. I was much younger then. I was standing, cowering in the house at the kitchen door, but I could hear it all and see it. There were tears streaming down your father's face.'

As if trying to comfort me she said, 'There was no doubt that he loved your mother. It was just that the times wouldn't allow it.'

'What happened?' I asked.

'But Reverend Keen wouldn't budge. He kept telling your father to pull himself together and going on about discipline and how she was only a servant.'

'And when he said that, your father punched him. It didn't look like he was much used to punching people and Reverend Keen was more shocked than hurt, but he wiped the blood off his mouth and asked us to fetch the police.'

'It was terrible weather. Much like we have now and the mist rolled down from the fells and hung in patches in the village. Rather than wait for the police, your father left. He didn't know what to do. He probably didn't care.'

'And what happened then?'

'Well they say, he fled into the hills, not knowing where he was going, up the steep slopes, plashing through the becks.'

'But they found him?'

She shook her head. 'No, they did not. We presumed he was lost in some bog. But he was never found.'

'Never found?'

'No.'

I pushed my hand through my still damp hair. No trace of my mother or my father left on this earth. It took away my foundations. I didn't belong anywhere. I had no roots. I nodded. 'Thank you, Mrs Thwaites. Thank you for telling me this.'

She stood. 'I fear I have upset you. That was never my intention, but I have a reputation as a plain-speaking woman.'

She showed me to the door. I took my sodden coat and put on my shoes. My hat was still wet too. She was kind now. 'I'm sorry for your trouble, Mr Starkey.'

'Thank you.' And at the door, I paused at a thought. 'But at least you see her. At least there's something of her left.'

'Aye, even if it's a ghost.'

But what was she warning me about?

I went back to the Cavendish Arms, pushing through the door, drenched. It was just before lunchtime. The fire was on because of the cold and the barman stood waiting for my order. Though it was early to be drinking, I ordered a beer.

He pulled the pump and filled the dimpled pint glass with local brown ale and handed it to me. I pushed bronze pennies towards him and grunted my thanks, then went to sit, slumped at a scarred wooden table in the corner. I sank half my pint in one gulp as a terrible thirst possessed me. The rest took only two more swigs and then I went back to the bar. 'Another pint, please,' I said as I thrust the foam-stained glass across the counter.

The barman didn't say anything as he filled up the glass with beer, but I could tell he was judging me. This pint went down more slowly as I sank into the beer and into my ruminations. I went into a daze, my fist folded around the dimpled glass, still partly full.

A man was sitting at the table in the corner. I hadn't seen him come in. He was tall and thin with brown hair that looked like my own. He wasn't wet though. The corner was dark and it was difficult to see him clearly. Then I saw he wore a clerical collar. As he drank, I noticed he had a distinctive gold signet ring on the little finger of his left hand. Perhaps he was one of the clergy at the Priory, I wondered what his excuse was that he was drinking so early, but then I saw he had no glass.

I stared at him, but he was half in shadow. I went to the toilet, half thinking of talking to him to ask if he'd known my father, but he was far too young. When I returned, he was gone.

The fire crackled and then the door opened, letting in more wind and rain. I turned bad temperedly to see who was disturbing my moody reverie. It was the man from the café. He must just wander the village with nothing to do, wasting his time on tea and ale. He didn't seem to notice me but went up to the bar. 'Ow do, John? Areet?'

'Champion. Usual?'

'Aye, pint o't good stuff.' This man, Joe, stole a glance at me but I turned away back to my beer, thinking of getting my third pint, the alcohol making my head swim already.

I needed another drink. I stood, steadying myself and stepped the few paces to the counter. The barman gave me a small smile.

'Another pint, please,' I said.

He nodded and took my glass from where I'd placed it, then lined it up with the pump and pulled back on the handle to fill the glass with more ale.

The dishevelled man, Joe, said, 'I like a man who likes a drink.'

I grunted, but he persisted in his conversation. 'Didn't I see you in the Bluebell Café earlier?'

I nodded. The barman handed me my pint, and I paid. I made ready to walk away but Joe said, 'Mind if I join you?'

I shrugged. I didn't want to talk to anyone, but he followed me anyway and sat down.

He took a sip of his beer and wiped the foam from his top lip with the back of his hand, then pushed back to make himself comfortable. 'They say you're here looking into family history,' he said.

I nodded. 'I suppose. How do you know?'

He laughed. 'This is Cartmel. Everybody knows everything. Strangers at this time of year aren't common— especially since the War.'

'I see.'

There was a long pause. The sound of more rain on the window. The sound of the fire stirring as it burned.

'Just, I knew your father,' he said. 'I was sexton, see.'

He pronounced father with a short-a—the way North Country people do.

I shot him a glance. 'You knew him?'

He nodded. 'I was just a young man, but he was always civil to me.' He sipped his beer. 'Terrible what happened to him.'

'In what way terrible?'

He narrowed his eyes as if sizing me up and wondering what I knew and whether he would upset me. 'Running him out. The new Rector was cruel to him. Always was, a cold man for a man of God that one. Not like your dad. He was decent. He was a good-looking man too. Always dressed nice.' He smiled. 'I remember his ring. I remarked on it. An antique signet ring with a bloodstone in it. He said it had come down to him through his family.'

I said, 'Did you know my mother?'

He nodded. 'Lisa. Aye, I was at school with her—here in the village. Pretty lass, clever too.'

'She killed herself,' I said coldly.

He took a sip of beer. 'Aye, I know.'

I said, 'Because of me.'

He shook his head. 'Hardly. You were gone. Don't be blaming yourself for things like that. It was the new Rector who was to blame, if anyone.'

I grunted. 'Feels like it was my fault.'

'It's not.'

The beer loosened my tongue. I spoke more emotionally than I had if I was sober. I felt the sadness flood me. 'I always knew there was something wrong with me. Like there was something missing. I've lived my life like there's been a hole running right through me. Like I didn't have a right to be here on this earth, or to breathe even.'

'Don't be talking like that, lad. That's daft.'

I sat back. I'd already drunk half of my third pint. 'I'm just being stupid. Pay me no heed.'

He sat looking quietly, his compassionate eyes a contrast with how he looked as a tough countryman.'

With a hollow laugh, I said, 'I found my mother and father and lost them in the same day.'

'You never lost them. They're always with you.'

I wasn't listening, I said, 'If I just had something of theirs. Something tangible. Something that would root me. But my mother's ashes are scattered who knows where and no one knew where my father went.'

Joe nodded. 'He was up on Cartmel Fell.'

'You know?'

'Almost certain. I saw him leave the village. That's where he was headed.'

'Which direction is Cartmel Fell?'

'North of the village, but you don't want to be going up there in this weather. You'll come to no good.'

I remained silent. I didn't care. I'd come to Cartmel looking for myself and now I found I was nothing at all.

Then he stood, embarrassed by my emotions. 'Thank you for your company,' he said. 'Have a safe trip home.'

Joe left, leaving the pub and that left me alone. I stood and went for another pint.

THE DAY WAS DARK. The night came early in the winter and the heavy curtain of clouds of rain brought it earlier. The barman had put the lights on even though it was hardly one o'clock.

THE BARMAN SAID, 'Are you sure, sir? This is your fourth, and it's only early afternoon.'

'I don't care,' I said. 'Get me another drink.'

He shrugged and poured the beer.

I lingered over this beer. I'd come to try and root myself somehow by learning about my family, but there were no roots to be found. My parents were dead and had left no trace. One burned and scattered to the winds, the other sunk without a trace in the sucking bogland of the Lake District.

I don't know how or when the thought first came to me, but before I'd finished that fourth drink. I had resolved to kill myself.

The rain hit me as I stepped out of the pub door. The cloud was low, draped like a curtain holding me back from heaven, dropped like a sentence from a hanging judge. I had no clear idea of where I was going, just that I had to get out of Cartmel. That part was easy, after a few rows of houses the village gave way to wet fields, damp hedges ragged with briars and last years dead musk roses. Blackthorn,

Hawthorn and Elder blocked my way as I pushed through a disused field opening. The land sloped up, and the mist was thicker as I climbed, out of breath, feet sodden in the tussocky grass. I surprised a sheep that started away, unused to anyone out in such weather. My breath was ragged now as I pushed up the hillside, through a stand of trees, squelching into bog marked by bulrushes.

I just wanted to die. A man without rights. No right to be here. No heritage, no history. This would be my death, just like my father, to stumble in the fog from a ledge, to drown in a sucking pool, thick with weed. The cold would do for me, leaching my warmth, cooling my blood until I lay glassy-eyed, a curiosity for sheep until a raven plucked out my eyes.

I saw her by the rocky outcrop, half hidden by mist — made of mist maybe but nothing solid. She tried to catch my eye, but I knew she was dead. Just a ghost of imagination. I watched my feet, not her, and walked on, planting my feet, one by one on the rough ground. I was climbing. I don't know how far I had walked.

And there she was again, as if wanting my attention. I lifted my head and was about to speak; but what would I say to this girl—my mother far younger than I was now.

I paused, but she did not speak and neither did I.

But she wanted me to pay attention.

I shook my head. This was to be my end. There was no comfort. It was me who had caused their trouble. I could make it good in no other way than by ending myself here.

The mist swirled around. Crows called from obscured trees. Waiting.

Tears burned my cold cheeks, and she was still there as I breathed in and out, labouring to climb a rough rocky path. And there she appeared, right in front of me, as a barrier. She didn't want me to go on; I knew that. She didn't want me to kill myself. But what mother would want the death of her son; even if she had never really met him.

She looked so kind and young. But it was a vision. A regret only. And with that thought she vanished.

I stepped on and climbed up. I went higher. At times, I was on my hands and knees as I scrambled over the slippery rock, grabbing handfuls of rough grass to tug myself up. That went on until sensing something, I stopped. I stood on a hard broken ledge and felt the void in front of me. I couldn't see it but I felt emptiness. There was a drop just in front of me, hidden by fog. I inched forward until my toes were on the edge of the drop.

So this was it. Some intuition told me my father had taken the same path. That he had fallen to his death from this rock, on a day such as today, wreathed in rain, weighed down with despair.

And so would I.

She appeared by my side.

I knew she was there, but I didn't look; I only stared ahead into the mist. Into the mirage of solidity that would not bear my weight, but would give way and I would fall to break on the rocks below.

She turned to face me, still not speaking.

And then she took my hand. Like she was my mother, a thing she had done at my birth, taken my little hand in hers. And her hand was warm, not cold. Not the chill of death but the warmth of life.

She said, 'I love you, my son.'

But it was too late. I had already stepped out.

Joe found me. He thought he knew where I'd gone and he found me in the mist. As I lay in the boggy ground, I knew I'd broken my leg, but I was alive. And there by my outstretched hand, was a glint of gold. My falling into the bog had disturbed the mud and moss and brought this thing to light, its gold untarnished by the years it had lain there.

'My goodness,' Joe said, reaching over for it. 'That's your father's ring.'

He placed it in my hand and I gazed at it while we waited for rescue. 'My father's ring?' I said, amazed.

He nodded.

It had come down the generations. My father and mother had never forgotten me. Even beyond life, there is love.

13

THE DEMON CLOCK OF MOSEDALE

John inherited the clock from his Uncle Max. Max wasn't a person people warmed to, and the old man died little mourned and John was his only family. The funeral was dismal. They held it in the Masonic Lodge, up on Meeting House Lane, if it was a masonic lodge. Perhaps it was something weirder. John didn't know or care.

The clock was all John got — the men in creased suits and glasses from Max's little club got the house and all its contents — the dog-eared books and his broken, mildewed furniture. They were welcome to them all, John thought. The house had always given him the creeps — that old brooding grey house that sits above Penrith on Beacon Edge.

After the funeral, the shabby grey men from the Lodge invited the few mourners to the house for tea and tongue sandwiches. They ate them in the living room, looking out at the rain-smeared roofs of Penrith through the dirty windows of old Max's house.

"Your uncle's friends aren't very friendly," said Sarah as she looked at, then discarded, the tongue sandwich with its cheap white bread and basic supermarket spread.

"I didn't know he had any friends to be honest," said John, sipping his tea from the surprisingly un-chipped bone china cup.

"UHT milk," she said. "Tastes nasty. Don't drink it. I'm glad we left Jess at home."

"Anyway, there's our new possession," said John, pointing towards the clock where it stood in the corner of the dreary, uncarpeted room.

"It isn't going," said Sarah.

John murmured. "Hmm. You're right, but I'm sure it can be fixed. It's probably valuable you know." He leaned forward and read the maker's name from the dial. "Nathaniel Pilkington of Appleby, 1805"

WHEN THE CLOCK arrived at the lovely converted farmhouse in Mosedale, it was still early in the day. Dr John Eliot was getting ready to go to work. His wife opened the door of their country farmhouse and watched while the workmen moved the clock into the hall and carefully set it up. John was upstairs shaving. As John had suspected, they could fix it. The men were specialists in antiques and they arranged the weights and pulleys and made sure it kept good time. John looked in on his way to toast and coffee in the breakfast room, but Sarah had it all under control. By the time the family had finished their breakfast, the men had installed the clock and left.

Sarah told him she didn't like it.

"Oh, I don't know," he said. "It gives the house gravitas. We can always sell it if you really don't like it. Give it a chance though; you may learn to love it."

"I don't like its ticking," she said.

"That's totally irrational."

Their daughter Jessica was standing at her mother's knee. She said, "It smells funny — like old rags." Then she pointed at the cat, "and Timmy doesn't like it either; he's scared." John looked at the tabby which was sitting grooming itself on the stairs. It didn't seem particularly bothered by the clock. Jessica was projecting her fears onto her pet, but then he was prone to seeing things that way — it came from his training as a psychiatrist.

His wife Sarah, beautiful, blonde, 42, with a mind that liked cryptic crosswords and was good at jurisprudence, leaned in and gave him a kiss on his way out to the hospital. "You go now or you'll be late for work; just because we've got the day off, doesn't mean you can linger."

John took the kiss. He stroked her hair. "But I like to linger. It's not fair! Anyway, what are you up to today?"

"I'm taking Jessica and her friend Rachel to the petting farm."

"You get on with Rachel's mum, don't you?"

"Yeah, Sally will meet us for lunch. We have a day of leisure while you go off and heal crazy people."

John picked up his coat and went out of the door. His C-Class Mercedes was parked on the gravel drive outside. They'd lived in that house among the mountains for about two years and he loved it — they all did. John worked at the local secure psychiatric unit about twenty miles away. Sarah worried it was a dangerous job, but John didn't take any risks; there were protocols and safety measures to protect the staff. It was true that he worked with people who had committed shocking, violent crimes, but it paid the bills and gave him a certain power and prestige, which, though he didn't like to admit it to others, made him feel he'd done well for himself — and for his family. His old dad would have been proud of him — had he lived — and, who knows, John felt maybe he even helped some people.

WHEN JOHN GOT HOME that night, Jessica was tired after her trip to see the animals. They ate chicken parmigiana and John and Sarah had a glass of Italian white wine - a Gavi - while Jess had guava juice. Her parents put her to bed after dinner and they sat watching TV. All was well until around 8 pm, Jessica came down, carrying her blanket.

"Daddy," she said, "There's a nasty smell in my room."

John got up. He was used to his daughter's tricks to avoid going to bed. He gathered Jessica in his arms. "Come on, pumpkin, time for you to sleep."

Jessica smiled as he picked her up, but then she corrected her expression and gave a sulky frown. "It's true. There is a smell."

"Well, I'll come up and see," he said.

As they walked out of the living room, he heard the slow metallic ticks of the grandfather clock from where it now stood in the hallway. Something about it drew his attention. He saw Jessica look too.

"Nice old clock, isn't it?" he said, but she just scowled. He carried her upstairs. Her room was on the third floor. The staircase was made of oak, and the house was centrally heated so it was never cold.

The nearest other house was about half a mile away and the nearest pub and public telephone about four. The valley was quiet at night - all the sounds of civilization absent; all they heard was the rushing water in the rain-fed beck and the occasional caws of ravens.

Around the house, high up on three sides out of four, glowered the dark fells. John loved the quiet and the sense of place he found since moving there. This was the valley his family were originally from — the home of his people since the Ice Age. He had wanted to get back there for years and so he snapped the farmhouse up when it came on the market.

The stairs creaked as they mounted them.

"Can I stay down with you and mummy?"

"No, it's time for bed."

"I don't have school till next week; we're on holiday."

"I don't care; you're only little. You need your sleep."

And then they arrived in Jessica's room. There were her toys strewn all over the bed and her doll collection sitting on the chest of drawers watching them.

Jessica wrinkled her nose. "Pooh," she said.

"It's just your imagination."

"Sniff!" she commanded.

He drew in the air. There was a strange smell. He'd never noticed it before. It wasn't damp - it was a musty smell of decay, but with something else - some acrid after-smell, like vinegar or burning.

Jess was watching him. "See! You can smell it too!"

He put her down on her bed and pulled the covers over her.

"Can't you?" she said. "I saw you wrinkle your nose."

He smiled. "Yes, there is a faint smell. But it's not too bad. It won't stop you sleeping."

She crossed her arms in defiance, but he bent down and kissed her head. "Night night my lamb," he said, and he stepped over to the door. He was about to turn off the light when she said, "Can I keep the light on?"

He ruffled her hair. "You're not scared of the dark are you? You didn't used to be."

"Yes, I am," she said.

"Since when?"

"Since the clock came."

"That's just an excuse."

"No, it's not."

"You won't sleep with this big light on," he said. "How about I switch on your star globe?"

Jess loved the star globe. It always soothed her to sleep. It sat on the table by her bed and slowly rotated while casting stars on the ceiling and walls.

"Ok," Jess said. "But you'll be just downstairs, won't you daddy? You and mummy?"

He smiled. "Of course we will you sausage. Where do you think we're going to go?"

"If I call out, will you come?"

"Enough of this now, Jessica. You're just trying to avoid going to sleep."

He turned on the star globe and it started its pretty circuit, slowly turning and projecting the constellations around the room. He switched off the main light and stood for a while, watching its magic stars track around the walls and ceiling. "Now, sleep!" he said.

When he went downstairs, Sarah poured him another glass of wine. "What's got into her?" he said as he sat down and picked up the wine.

"She's just that age," said Sarah. "Night fears and suchlike; she'll grow out of it."

"I guess. What's on?"

Sarah had the TV controller. "Want to watch this drama documentary about the start of the First World War?" she said.

"Sure," he nodded. "Beats those bloody cash in your attic antique programmes that are always on."

When their programmes finished, Sarah went up to bed before him and he finished the bottle of wine, sitting in the living room listening to the rain that beat on the window. They'd drawn the heavy satin curtains to keep the night out, but he could still hear the wind moving down the valley and the rain hitting the stones outside. It sounded wild.

Once he'd finished his wine, John stood but before he went to bed; he admired the clock in the hallway. The clock kept good time now with its steady tick-tock. There was a painting of a man who looked like a farmer on the left-hand side of the clock face and a woman on the right-hand side who was probably his wife. Below the main dial, there was a little circle that had the sun on one half and a starlit sky on the other. John guessed that this circle had originally turned to show night and day, but it had long since got stuck.

Once in bed, John slept heavily, Sarah cuddled in beside him. They were both deeply asleep when there was a scream that rent the silence. Instantly awake, John jumped up, Sarah woke suddenly beside him and, in her fear, grabbed his arm and held him back.

"It's upstairs," he said and pulled free of her before she could answer. He ran out of the room and rushed up the stairs to his daughter's room, driven by a primal instinct to protect. He could feel the adrenaline rushing through him; feel his muscles harden and dark aggression pool in his heart and belly, ready to fight, to kill and to destroy anything that threatened his daughter. He quickly pushed at the half-open bedroom door. The little globe still cast its plaintive stars across the room, and there, where he had expected to see her sobbing in fear, Jess was asleep. She woke as he entered and sat up.

"Daddy?" she said sleepily. "What's the matter?"

He could feel himself shaking, even though she was safe. He scooped her up and brushed her tousled hair out of her eyes.

"Daddy!" she said, getting worried. "You look scared."

"I just heard a noise. I thought it was you."

Sarah had come up behind him and was peering into the room,

half holding back as if she too had expected something terrible in the room.

"Hello, mummy," said Jessica.

Sarah came over. "Back to bed now, baby," she said.

The girl yawned. "I was asleep, daddy. I was dreaming I was in a forest and there was somebody there. I couldn't see them, but I knew they were there in the trees, but Timmy was with me and I was okay."

He hugged her to him. "I'm just glad you're okay my darling."

Jessica continued to talk about her dream. "I don't think it was a person, though. It was something else."

John ignored her sleepy chatter as he put her back to bed. She fell asleep almost as soon as her head touched the pillow. John went out of the door and Sarah held him so he couldn't walk. "I was so scared," she said. He could feel her heart thumping against his chest as she spoke.

"She's fine," he said and hugged her back.

"But what was that noise — that scream?"

"Could we have dreamed it?" he said.

"Both of us?"

He shrugged. "There's no one in the house but us."

"Could the cat have screamed like that?"

"I doubt it. Where is he anyway? He usually sleeps up here with Jess."

There was no sign of Timmy. They walked down the stairs. Sarah said, "He must be out. Will you make sure he's okay?"

John nodded. "You stay here."

They were at the door to their own bedroom. "I'll come with you," she offered.

He smiled. "Don't need to. I'm sure Timmy's fine. I'll just go downstairs and double check we're locked up. Maybe a burglar tripped over a wire or something and that was him screaming."

She punched him lightly. "Don't make jokes about it. I was scared."

He crossed the room and picked up a cricket bat that stood propped up against the wardrobe. "Just to reassure you," he said. He kept the bat there in case of intruders though he knew it wouldn't do much against a man with a knife or a gun. He hefted the bat in his hand and turned and smiled at Sarah. "Be right back."

He stood on the bottom stair and listened in the dark before flicking on the light switch. He heard the house shift slightly as the wind outside moved down the valley. He heard the water in the stream outside. Then he heard something in the hall in front of him. His muscles tensed and he shifted his grip on the handle of the bat. He stepped down onto the hall floor carpet, shifted his stance and switched on the light.

And there in front of him; his back arched, tail bristled and fangs bared, was Timmy the cat. But he wasn't facing John, he was hissing and spitting at the grandfather clock. John put his hand up to his nose. "Jeez, what's that stink?" he said.

The foul odour of rot filled the hall; like something dead in the grass on a hot summer's day. The cat stood its ground as if the clock was a person or a creature.

"What are you doing you crazy animal?" he said. "Have you shit somewhere?" He bent down to scoop up the cat, but it turned on him, yowling and raking him with its claws — struggling frantically to be free. It ran up the stairs out of sight.

He dabbed the bleeding scratches, still carrying the cricket bat in his right hand. The smell was strong, but he couldn't tell where it was coming from. It tainted the whole area. John checked the doors, but they were all locked. The cat was just spooked by the new clock and its ticking, mistaking it for a real creature, something that was a threat to its cat-ness.

He walked back upstairs. Sarah was sitting up in bed looking at him anxiously as he came in the door. He put the cricket bat in its place.

"So?" said Sarah. "Mystery solved?"

"I think the cat's shit down there, or dragged something dead in. I'll sort it in the morning. Couldn't find the source of the stink in the dark."

"What about the noise?"

He shrugged. "Must have dreamt the noise. It's all secure down there — no maimed burglars or anything."

"But I heard it too."

"You sure though? You sure my waking didn't just scare you and then when I said I heard a noise, you thought you heard it too in some kind of somnolent state?"

"Don't try to psychiatrize me, John. I heard the scream."

He preferred to believe his version, but it was too late to fight so he said, "Ok, sure. Let's sleep."

Then she saw his arm. "What did you do?" she said. "It's bleeding."

"It was the cat."

"Timmy?"

"The clock spooked him and he was standing spitting at it. When I tried to pick him up, he went for me."

She leaned over and got a tissue from the box on her bedside table. She dabbed John's arm with it. "I still don't like that clock," she said. "There's a nasty feeling to it."

"Just because it came from my nasty uncle. Maybe some of his nastiness rubbed off on it?" joked John.

"You never take anything seriously, John. Sometimes you should consider feelings or hunches."

He lay down with his head on the pillow and pulled up the covers. "No," he said. "Feelings aren't facts. That's where people go wrong. Don't trust your feelings, especially your fears. Look for evidence."

She put out the light. "Good night, Mr Scientist," she said and leaned over and kissed him on his cheek.

JOHN WAS DOZING when he felt a weight jump on his chest and heard the soft purring of the cat. It rubbed itself against his face and he reached out to stroke it. "So we're friends again are we, Timmy?"

In response, the cat just purred louder. It struck him that the cat was usually aloof and independent — never this needy of comfort. "Calm down, bud," he said. "I need to sleep." The cat found the space between him and Sarah and settled itself down to doze.

SARAH WAS up before he woke properly. She brought him a cup of tea. It was just light outside. He checked the clock. "Damn, I've slept in."

"Not much," she said. "Drink your tea and I'll get Jessica up. We're going to the aquarium this morning with her little friends."

John got out of bed and went to switch on the shower. He had just got into the bathroom when he heard a scream. This time it was clearly Sarah's. He ran upstairs.

Sarah was standing at the door of Jessica's room, holding the little girl in her arms. Jessica looked fine.

"What?" he said urgently.

Sarah gestured to Jessica's bed. A red flood of blood soaked the pillow. He touched it. It was dry, as if it had bled during the night. "Nosebleed?" he said.

"There's no blood on her," said Sarah.

"Baby, did you have a nosebleed?" he said to Jessica.

She shook her head. "I don't think so, daddy."

"But where's all this blood on your pillow come from?"

She shrugged and smiled. "I don't know. But maybe from the thing in the forest."

John was baffled. "What forest?"

"I told you!" she said in her little girl voice. "I was having a dream and me and Timmy were in the woods and there was a thing there. It was watching us and it was all covered in blood. Timmy was brave, and he went to fight it."

Sarah looked searchingly at him.

"Another mystery," he said. "Come on, let's get moving. I need to get going."

He went to his room and finished dressing. When he came downstairs, Sarah was in her nightdress covered in a dressing gown serving Jessica Oatibix.

"Smell's gone," he said. "Did you find whatever Timmy killed last night? It smelled like an old dead bird."

"There wasn't a smell when I came down."

John didn't have time to talk it through. He looked at his watch. "Going to be late for ward round," he said.

Sarah walked him to the door. He was expecting his usual goodbye kiss, but she hesitated. She looked worried. She said, "I've read about young girls being the centre of occult phenomena."

"Sarah," he said firmly. "There are no such things as occult phenomena."

"But what about the scream and the blood and the smell?"

"All perfectly explainable; just coincidences that our mind strings together and thinks it sees a pattern. Don't worry, I won't let the monsters get my girls." He teased her, but she wasn't laughing. He stroked her face. "Really, don't worry. Have a nice time at the aquarium. See you when I get home."

THE WARD ROUND was a long one. In the room was John as Consultant Psychiatrist in charge. Also, there was his student Melissa - CT1 Doctor in Psychiatry. Then there was Sofia the Clinical Psychologist - originally from Athens. There were various nurses - Billy the Charge Nurse, who looked as tough as he was; Maureen who talked about nothing except how long she had to go to retirement; a pretty student nurse called Frances. The Social Worker, Sue, sat next to Melissa and the pharmacist Ned Brown — as boring as he was knowledgeable — on the far side of her.

The patients came in one by one — some with their families. There was a bit of argy-bargy with each of them about what meds they would accept and whether John could lift their Sections. Hardly any of them thought they were ill. In reality, most of them were psychotic and somebody at some point had judged them dangerous.

John's job was to recommend transfer to open wards for those who were responding to treatment and whose delusions were diminishing. Unfortunately, some of them were treatment resistant, and even the dangerous drug clozapine — the last line of defence — didn't touch them.

They had seen six patients and John was in need of a coffee. He suggested as much but Billy said, "Just one more boss? Then we can go for lunch."

"Who is it?"

"Robert."

John raised his eyebrows. Robert had delusions that he was a black magician and usually spent ten minutes shouting at John that he would drain his soul and eat his heart. John sighed. "Robert? I think I need a coffee before I can take the abuse."

Billy shook his head. "No, he's loads better this week. Frances has been spending a lot of time with him." John looked at Frances, young and fresh faced — probably only about twenty. He remembered being that keen once. He knew that the student nurses had more time to spend face to face with patients because they were not burdened with paperwork like the qualified ones. The patients enjoyed the simple human contact.

"Ok," he said. "Bring him in."

Robert came in wearing his black t-shirt and black jeans. If allowed he would don a black cloak too, but the staff didn't think it helped his mental state and wouldn't let him wear it to ward rounds.

Robert sat down, looking suspiciously all around him at the smiling professionals. He began to chant something that John vaguely recognised as lines from the Book of Revelations — something about the Beast.

"And how are you this week, Robert?" said John.

Melissa sat ready, pen in hand, to record Robert's response.

Robert stared hard at John. "Hello, Dr Eliot," he said. Then he began to smile as if at some private joke.

"What's so funny?" smiled John back. "Is my hair sticking up again?" The assembled professionals laughed quietly at their boss's joke, but Robert shook his head; he glared at John. "Little Brother, you have been meddling with the Goetia," he said.

Everyone smiled — polite but puzzled. But Robert didn't give up. He said, "I mean you doctor. It's a quote about Aleister Crowley."

"Well, Robert. I don't know what it is, so I don't know if I've been meddling with it."

Melissa leaned in. "Aleister Crowley was an occultist at the beginning of the…"

John turned to her. "I know who Aleister Crowley was."

Robert peered at John as if examining him — almost sniffing. Then he said, "Rather, the Goetia has been meddling with you; I think that would be more correct."

"Still don't know what that is. Could you explain?"

But Robert ignored him. "I smell a stink and see red blood," he said.

John sat up and frowned. He felt a flash of alarm but hid it. The talk of blood was just a coincidence. No one else looked ruffled. This all just sounded like Robert's normal religious ramblings.

John attempted to change the subject. "How've you found the medication this week, Robert?"

"Fine, doctor - just fine." Robert was still smiling to himself.

"Good, I'm glad, because I remember you said it was making you feel sick. I hoped that would settle down. A lot of these side effects do."

John looked over at Billy. "Did we send his bloods off?"

Billy nodded. "Of course."

"Good." He turned back to Robert. "Anything else you'd like to ask, Robert?"

Robert shook his head. Then he sat forward. "I see something's moved into your house."

John felt a chill between his shoulders. "What?" he said.

"Not that it's really a he or a she."

"Come on Rob," said Billy. "Time for lunch," and he and Frances got up to take Robert from the room.

. . .

When John got home, Sarah had prepared his dinner, and they sat round the table with Jessica. Jessica did not like Boeuf Bourguignon so she had spaghetti. She chattered about the fish she'd seen and the bath toys that her mother had bought her.

"Where's Timmy?" asked John.

"Haven't seen him," said Sarah.

"He's scared of the thing," said Jessica. "He's hiding."

"Don't be silly, Jessica," said her mother. "There is nothing. You'll be giving yourself bad dreams."

After dinner, Jessica enjoyed her bath time and then about 7pm went to bed. It was John's turn to read her a story from the *Magic Faraway Tree*. He tucked her into bed and told her tales of Moon-face and Silky and then, when her eyes grew heavy, he kissed her and retreated quietly, switching the light off as he left.

Sarah had poured wine again.

"We need to be careful with the wine, Sarah," he said. "It could get to be a habit."

She came and sat next to him on the sofa and cuddled into him as they watched TV. She said, à propos of nothing, "I'm scared of this house now."

Though it irritated him, he ignored her irrationality. He said, "I love the house. I thought you did too."

She sighed heavily and laid back, head on his lap, looking at the ceiling. "I did," she said. "I do. Just the scream, then the blood…"

"Those occult phenomena?" he said.

"Don't mock me, John," she said. "They were pretty weird."

"We're just stressed and tired."

"What have we got to be stressed about?"

"Well, you've given up your job." She had loved her job as a solicitor, but she had given it up so she could spend more time with Jessica while she was little. He knew that she missed the company of adults and the feeling of usefulness that work gives.

She said, "You said we could afford it."

"It's not about money. Of course we can. It's about priorities. It's about life choices."

She looked as if she was about to argue, but, suddenly, the door to the living room burst open as if someone had kicked it.

They both jumped up, terrified. She gripped onto his arm so tight her nails drew blood. John knew Jessica was the only other person in the house and she didn't have the strength to open the door so violently.

Sarah said, "What was that?"

Warily, he walked up to the door. He felt a slight draft from the hall. He heard the clock ticking; otherwise nothing. "There's no one there," he said. 'Must be the wind.'

'There is no wind.'

And it was true. The night was eerily still.

Sarah was wide-eyed. "What's happening in this house?"

He turned round, trying to reassure her. "Don't worry."

"There's something awful here," she said.

"Nothing like this has ever happened."

"Maybe it's just awoken?"

"Awoken?" he snapped. "What could possibly have awoken?" His own anxiety made him irritable, and he felt instantly sorry.

She looked at him like he'd punched her. "I know you're very clever John, but don't talk down to me."

He stepped over and sat to hold her gently. "Sorry. It's freaking me out too, but there are no such things as ghosts. You must remember that. Maybe it's a change in air pressure?" He knew how unconvincing he sounded.

"It was a hell of a change in air pressure."

And then there was a slam from upstairs.

John was instantly alert.

"Jessica's up there on her own," said Sarah.

John ran out of the living room into the hall, Sarah behind him. "Ugh, there's that smell again," he said.

Sarah said, "It smells like rot."

John said, "It smells just like gangrene. I remember it from my days as a junior doctor. I'm going up."

He mounted the stairs two at a time. Above, the door slammed again. This time, he knew it was their bedroom door, not Jessica's. Sarah's fear was forgotten as she got scared for her daughter. She ran to her. As she did so, there was a gust of warm air from below them — an air that had the smell of sulphur — like matches struck then snuffed out. He stopped on the stairs and turned. Was there something down there behind them?

Sarah was ahead of him out of sight. She screamed. She sounded hysterical. He yelled to her, but she didn't answer. His own panic mounting, he ran to Jessica's room, but his daughter wasn't there.

"She's gone," screamed Sarah. She was frantic.

"What? How can she have gone? Where?"

She was sobbing and gasping. "I don't know. She's gone!"

He grabbed her shoulders and spun her to face him. "Sarah, what's going on?" For an instant the only explanation seemed to be that Sarah and Jess were playing some sick joke on him. But he saw from her face it wasn't a joke; Sarah broke free from his grasp and looked around the room — in the cupboards, under the bed. She was shrieking — beside herself and incoherent.

John grabbed her. "Maybe she went into our room?"

"That's where the door banged," said Sarah.

They both ran through. Their room was in disarray — shelves pulled out and the contents dumped. The bedclothes were ripped up. Helen's walk-in wardrobe was standing open, her dresses pulled and tangled over the floor.

"My God, what's been in here?" she said.

He didn't answer. He ran quickly around the room, looking for Jess. All he found was the cat, Timmy, pressing himself into a corner, terrified.

"Come on boy," he said. "It's ok." He took Timmy, unwilling to leave even the cat in the room where this had happened. Timmy allowed John to pick him up.

Sarah was weeping openly, pulling at her hair. "Where's my daughter? Where's my little girl?"

"Maybe she went downstairs?" John's voice was shaking. The cat didn't try to get free — as if too was frightened and wanted some kind of safety from his grip.

Sarah's face twisted with fear. "How could she? We were on the stairs?"

They went down again. There in the hall, everything seemed normal. Everything was now quiet in the house except the loud ticking of the grandfather clock. Then Sarah stood back in horror.

"What?" said John.

She pointed. "The clock's running backwards."

As they watched, John saw the second hand was winding backwards, faster than sixty seconds a minute. The weirdness of it built a terrible sense of dread. He tried to challenge the irrationality. He held onto Sarah's arm to comfort her. The cat struggled to get away from him. He let it go. His mind was screaming for him to find Jessica. And then he heard her. He heard her little girl's sobbing.

Sarah heard her too. "That's her crying. I can hear her crying," she shouted.

"Where?"

"Somewhere near."

And then John realised where she was. He ran over to the clock and pulled open the cabinet door where the pendulums and their chains were suspended. In there, huddled in the bottom like a heap of rags was Jessica. He took her out, gently.

Sarah tried to take her from him. Her voice was coming in gasps. She said, "How did she get in there?"

"She must have got in herself," he said.

Jessica clung to him. "Baby, what are you doing in there?" he said, trying to sound comforting and calm.

Jessica wailed. "He put me there."

Sarah stammered. "Who? Who's *he* my darling?"

"The thing from the forest. He's like a bat, but he has man's legs and a head like a horse."

"This is some kind of nightmare," said Sarah.

"A nightmare couldn't put her in the clock," said John. "And how does the clock keep ticking when she was stopping the weights working? It's working now, and they're not moving at all."

"It's moving backwards. Backwards means evil," said Sarah.

John sighed. "Please, you're not helping."

"Is that supposed to be there?" asked Sarah, pointing at a small copper seal that was screwed into the inside of the clock's cabinet. It was engraved with lines and circles and looked odd.

"I don't know," said John. "Maybe something to do with the clock's maker."

"It looks more recent than that," said Sarah.

Just then, as if to mock him the doors upstairs began opening and shutting, first one, then two, then it sounded like all of them were banging in a hellish cacophony. The smell came — stronger this time: a smell of sulphur and gangrene.

"We've got to leave," said Sarah. "Please, John."

"This is crazy," said John. "I'm not being chased out of my own house by some mumbo-jumbo trickery. I don't know how this is being done, but I will find out."

"Jess and I are leaving. It's not safe here. I want you to come with us; you can't stay here on your own," said Sarah.

Without waiting for his answer, she went to get her coat and pulled Jessica's coat on over her pyjamas. She took the car keys. "We'll stay at the Mill in the village," she said. "John, please come."

John listened to the doors banging on their own. "This can't really be happening," he said.

And then they heard the boards creak from the floor above their heads, as if something heavy was walking over them.

"It's him!" cried Jessica.

Sarah grabbed at John's arm, dragging him towards the door. He allowed her to pull him. But he still looked up the stairs, as if waiting for what was up there to descend.

He put on his coat. He took the car keys from Sarah. They went out of the door, all the time he was cursing himself; there had to be some rational explanation for this, though he could think of none. And if he dared admit it, he was frightened himself.

John opened the car door. Above them the sky was overcast and dark. It was hard to see until the car cabin light flicked on. Sarah put Jessica in her seat and fastened the strap, then John said, "Timmy."

"Oh God, where is he?" said Sarah.

"He's in the house with the thing with the horse's head," said Jessica.

"Leave him. Let's go," said Sarah.

John shook his head. "I'm not leaving my cat. I'll just be a minute."

Sarah pleaded for him not to go, but he went back inside the house. He tried to turn on the light switch, but something had happened to the electricity and it wouldn't work. He thought the fuses must have blown. He had no idea why they would but at least the doors had stopped slamming.

All was quiet apart from the infernal ticking of the clock.

From the front door, he shouted. "Timmy! Come here, you stupid cat."

But Timmy did not come. John used the flashlight on his phone to light the way into the living room. He caught Timmy's startled eyes in the beam and the cat skittered past him in a blind panic, going upstairs. "For God's sake, Timmy," he hissed.

John looked upstairs. The lights didn't work. The cat had vanished. And maybe something else was up there too; something with the wings of a bat and the head of a horse. But how could that be? John knew it couldn't. And with the strength of his fundamental belief in science and rationality, he began to mount the stairs.

The filthy reek filled his nostrils when he was only two steps up. Something heavy moved in the darkness above him; it sounded man sized or bigger — no cat. His heart began to thump.

"Timmy," he called. He heard a yelp and then a scream. The animal was in pain. He jumped up the stairs, desperate to save his cat. And then Timmy appeared from the darkness, terrified, his eyes wide. He looked as if something had ripped half the fur from him. Timmy ran with adrenaline of an animal that doesn't know it's already dead. John had seen a cat hit by a car ricochet around like a pinball, alive but so broken that it would be dead within ten minutes.

The cat flew past him and tumbled down the stairs. Then John heard the thing in the dark in front of him. He peered forward. Something was there — but what? His rational mind struggled and came with the only answer it could — it must be a robber; some kind of sick sadist who had hurt his cat and who had put his daughter in the clock. What was more absurd, a story like that, or the truth he could not assimilate with what he knew of the world?

It had to be a man. He shouted, "Who the hell are you? Come down here!"

Then in the shadows, he saw the shape of something he knew was inhuman. It was too big; the shape was wrong, and he saw its yellow eyes without pupils. It started to move towards him, fast as an insect, flowing like an eel.

It was too much. John turned. He half fell down the stairs. Timmy was already dead at the bottom. He fell over him and barged forward into the wall in his hurry. The knock winded him. He thought he'd done something to his shoulder; his pain shrieked but his fear wouldn't let him stay there. The thing of darkness was there already — the thing with the head of a horse came down the stairs for him.

John picked himself up and threw himself at the front door. In his terror and pain, he could hardly open it. And then pictures started forming in his mind — pictures that that did not belong in his head; things put there by the thing on the stairs. They were images of fire and burning sulphur — pictures of creatures cobbled together from all manner of broken beasts, feelings of dread and memories of cruelty; broken jaws; hanging eyes and forked tongues.

He vomited as he wrenched the door open, falling out into the soft rain, but doubled over and retching as he stumbled to the car.

Sarah screamed in terror as he snatched at the door. "The car won't start. The motor won't turn over," she said.

He fell into the driver's seat and she turned the key. The engine didn't even cough. He turned to Sarah, and she held him, shivering and shaking. Then they sat bolt upright as the car was lifted by some inhuman force - lifted, then dropped, jolting them in their seats.

She said, "What's happening?"

He said, "I don't know."

Sarah started praying. *"Yea, though I walk through the valley of the shadow of death, I will fear no evil, for thou art with me..."*

Jessica was in the seat behind. He heard her say something. But it wasn't Jessica's voice; it was the rough guttural voice of a thing, not even a man. He turned aghast. Her eyes rolled up showing their whites, and she drooled. She spoke in a language he didn't know and the words coming out of the mouth of his five-year-old daughter were old and evil.

Sarah prayed fervently. John reached back and grabbed Jessica. With both his hands on her small shoulders, she grinned lopsidedly and in her evil old voice she said, "Submit to me or I will hurt her."

Sarah turned and seeing her daughter with her twisted face, screamed. Her mother's despair shocked Jessica out of her trance, and for a second she looked dazed, more like her normal self. John grabbed her again, half to protect, half to shake out whatever had possessed her. He snarled. "Whatever you are, leave my daughter, now!"

The thing looked at him again through Jess's eyes, then it snarled "Submit to me or I will take her."

As he held her, Jess' body slumped. She fell into a deep, sudden slumber. It had gone. At least for now. Sarah reached back and unstrapped Jess. She moved to the passenger seat and John swapped to the driver's seat. Sarah said, "Go, go. Please John, let's go."

John tried the car again, power had returned. The engine coughed and German engineering kicked in as it started.

Though the night had felt eternal, it was not late. It was only 10pm by the time they got to the Mill. John explained to the landlord that there had been a flood in the house — something about a burst pipe, and that they would need the room for two nights. He couldn't think any further ahead than that.

They went to bed; John and Sarah in the Inn's best bedroom with

Jessica between them. Jess was in her nightdress anyway and Sarah was sleeping in her underwear. John lay awake, and he knew Sarah was wakeful too, but Jessica slept as if nothing had happened. Finally, when he could tell from their breathing that both his wife and his daughter were asleep, he got up and went downstairs. The landlord was just cleaning the final glasses up before he switched off the light in the bar.

"Can I get a drink?" John asked, surprising the man.

He turned. "Of course. You can drink all night as you're a resident," the landlord laughed. "But I hope you won't 'cause I need my sleep!"

Somehow the ordinariness of the man and the setting reassured him. He ordered a pint of bitter and sat down beside the dying fire in the bar and looked up addresses on his phone. As he did so, he realised that if anyone had told him that morning he would be doing this he would have laughed at them. Not only laughed at them, but mocked them for their soft minded credulity.

The fire hissed and time passed by. John grew tired.

The landlord came back through. "Want another drink?" he said.

John shook his head. "Time for bed, I think. It's been a hell of an evening."

"Yes, sorry about the flood. I hope your insurance can sort it out for you. Full breakfast in the morning?"

"Yes," said John. "Not sure if my wife or daughter will manage to get up; they're exhausted."

He made his way up the old wooden stairs of the inn with its irregular whitewashed walls with old prints of country scenes. He opened the door to their room quietly so as not to wake the girls. He didn't switch on the light. As he entered the room, he heard Sarah's regular breathing. He looked at the bed and realised something was amiss. He stopped and looked harder; where was Jess?

In rising panic, he switched on the light. Jessica was not there. "Sarah!" he shouted, and she woke, sitting up groggily. She instantly realised that Jess was gone. She jumped out of bed. She rushed through into the en-suite bathroom.

"Where is she?"

A dreadful intuition formed in his heart. "I'm going back to the house," he said.

"What?" said Sarah. "She must be here. How could she have walked to the house?"

"She didn't walk. She didn't come past me downstairs while I was in the bar."

"What are you saying?"

"You know what I'm saying; you stay here. I'll go to the house."

"I'm not letting you go on your own. What if she's just wandered out of the room? What if she's in this inn somewhere?"

John said, "You stay. I'll go."

Sarah said, "No, I'm coming with you."

She was already pulling on her clothes. As they hurried out to the car, John could feel his heart thumping.

John started the engine. Sarah was quiet. He put his hand on her knee. "I won't let anything harm her," he said.

"I'm scared you might not stop it; look what it did to Timmy."

"That doesn't help us Sarah. We need to have hope."

And they drove - faster than was safe. Their headlights devoured the dark countryside. Illuminating the rain that fell on their windscreen, the wipers struggling to keep their view clear. They were at the house within five minutes. John parked some way away from the dark building.

"Why don't you go closer?" asked Sarah.

"Because it can cut the power in the car if we go closer."

"I hope she's not in there. I hope she's just got up and wandered round the inn and has come back to find us not there."

"You know that's not true, Sarah," he said.

John walked up to the door, the rain beating down on him. It was dark, but he had pulled an electric torch from the glove compartment of the car and he shone that on the door.

Sarah was by his side. "God, I'm so scared," she said.

He turned the handle of the door and pushed it open. The house was again quiet apart from the iron ticking of the clock. He listened for Jess — to see if he could hear her crying as he had before, but there was no sound.

He stepped into the house. He could hear his heartbeat. Sarah was still outside, coming through the door behind him. He turned to speak to her and the door closed suddenly, with enormous force. He tried the handle, but it was as if something had nailed up the door. He pulled it, but it wouldn't budge. And then he felt something behind him. He whirled round, striking out with the rubber torch, but he met only air.

"What are you?" he snarled. "Where's my daughter?"

And he felt a malevolent mirth in the heavy darkness around him; a darkness heavier than a mere absence of light; a darkness filled with a presence that used it like a cloak. He sensed its wickedness. In the dark, he tried to move and stumbled. He felt the corpse of the cat under his foot. He shone his light on it; Timmy lay there glassy eyed in death, his ragged red flesh looking gnawed and chewed.

John heard Sarah hammering on the door behind him. He shouted back that he was all right.

As he approached the clock, he could feel its ticking filling his head, loud, rhythmic, almost hypnotic, wanting him to open his mind to it.

He tried to steel himself against its influence, but it whispered to him without words. It tried to lay eggs in his soul like some parasitic worm wanting to infest him with larvae. He shook his head clear, but it was hard not to succumb. He pulled open the cabinet door of the clock where he had seen Jess before, but she was not there.

The strange copper seal was still in place. He was about to touch it when he felt something behind him and he spun round. There was Jess standing there in her nightdress. Her chin was covered in blood as if she'd been feasting on something raw and newly dead. Her eyes were white like those of boiled fish. Her jaw chattered, the teeth clattering together. As he stood there horrified, she spoke in the voice of something not used to talking with a human mouth.

"Submit to me," it said.

He said, "In the name of God and all his angels, leave my daughter."

And Jess's mouth laughed a cruel laugh. "You don't believe in those ideas, John. They won't protect you."

Jessica slumped to the floor and her mother went to grab her. Then, when they were all in the house, the door slammed again. Sarah went to open it. John said, "It's no use."

John turned and saw in the darkest corner a shape lurking - a shape that looked like it was drawn from the twisted imagination of a sickly child. It had the head of a horse and folded at its back seemed to be the leather wings of a bat. Its bottom half was that of a man. There, between its legs were a huge penis and testicles.

"What are you?" shouted John.

It didn't answer. Instead, the thing came out from its corner and it wrapped itself around Sarah and Jessica, who struggled as if they were being bound with whips and wrapped in a rotting funeral shroud.

John ran at it, but it knocked him back with its power and it held him, helpless as a child.

"What do you want?" he sobbed. "Let them go."

The thing said, "Submit to me."

"I don't know how to submit to you. I don't know what you are."

As he watched, the blackness around Sarah and Jess thickened. The thing sucked them into the clock body.

And then the front door blasted open behind jo,. An unholy wind began to blow, and it pushed John towards the door. The thing said, "When you will let me enter you and open you for he who comes after me, I will let your wife and child go."

"I'll never give in to you," yelled John.

The demon shoved John and the priest out of the door and the door closed in John's face. He hammered on it, but he could not open it.

John punched the closed front door. With Sarah and Jess inside, he was alone and desperate. The door was locked against him with demonic force. He couldn't get in.

After half an hour, he realised the futility of getting soaked in the rain. He sat in his own car and he watched the house again; the car window wound down.

Around three in the morning, John decided he couldn't wait for anyone else. His wife and daughter were in the clutches of that evil thing in the house, somehow sucked into the clock.

The only place he could think of going was his Uncle Max's house in Penrith.

NOBODY WAS MOVING on the rain-drenched streets when he arrived. He parked up on Beacon Edge and remembered stories his grandmother told him of how Beacon Edge was an unlucky place, where in olden times women would leave unwanted children to die. Forest clad Beacon Hill above the town was also the site of weird occurrences. He wondered whether that was why Uncle Max had wanted to live here.

He got out of the car and walked over to the house. A cat ran across the street further down and rain slanted in pools of yellow street light. He pushed open the rusty iron gate and stepped onto the stone flagstones that were fighting a losing battle against the encroachment of weeds.

He didn't have a key.

The front door was locked, so he walked round the overgrown garden to the back. He walked through the rank grass. There was half an old plastic coffee cup in the grass and a broken child's doll near it; blue plastic eyes and torn cotton dress. The back door was locked too. There was no time to mess about. He booted it open. It took two blows then broke inwards. He stepped round it, into the dark house.

It smelled damp. A pigeon flapped in alarm somewhere within.

John flicked on the light switch and the bare bulb hanging from a wire lit up.

He walked through the hall and stood in the kitchen. There was a dirty plate in the sink that looked like it had been there months. A stained newspaper lay on the floor. There was ill-matched furniture in the room — a table, two chairs, one broken.

He didn't know where to start. He didn't know what he was looking for, but this is where the clock came from. It was something to do with Max and if there wasn't something here that could help, John didn't know where it would be.

He mounted the stairs in the empty house, stepping upwards on flight after flight, until he came to the attic. The door was locked again but opened easily. There were skylights, but they were covered in bird shit and cobwebs. The light worked here too. The place smelled of old creosote and damp. John scanned the room. There was something weird on the floor. The floorboards were black and a circle with words in Hebrew and Greek was inscribed around it. Near it was a triangle which had different but similar words along its side. John felt his skin crawl.

There was also a bookshelf. On the shelf were a series of books:
The Book of the Goetia by Aleister Crowley was the first. His heart jumped. This was only the second time he'd ever heard the word. His patient at the hospital told him that the Goetia had been messing around with him when he said that something had moved into his house. The second was *The Lesser Key of Solomon,* and like the first seemed to be concerned with magical rites for summoning demons. There was another *The Tree of the Qlipoth* and yet more, but none of the titles made sense to John.

He picked up the *Book of the Goetia* and tried to speed read it. It said there were seventy-two demons imprisoned by King Solomon in this brass vessel. Each had a seal and a name. Crowley's book had little illustrations of them all. They were grotesque things with heads and feet of different animals. All the demons had different powers, and the magician summoned them to help him with little tasks and witcheries.

As he read through, by the light of dirty electrical bulb, he read that Bael teaches all languages and tongues instantly. He can also cause earthquakes. Amon causes feuds, Barbatos helps the magician understand the language of birds. He looked at the little picture beside each one, and he couldn't help but be reminded of the description his daughter had given him of the thing in the clock: like a bat, but he has man's legs and a head like a horse."

Somehow Max had put one of these demons in the clock. But why would Max put a demon in a clock then give it to him?

John heard movement in the house below. Someone was moving about. His heart suddenly hammered. He grabbed the book and walked to the door. Suddenly there was a crack and the sound of glass exploding. One of the skylights had burst, though there was no sign of anything hitting it from either inside or out. John felt a sliver of glass had cut his cheek, blood ran from it and he wiped it away with the back of his hand. There was nothing else in the room. If he was going to find the key to this mystery, it wasn't here.

Expecting to run into something, some other demon, John made his way down the stairs to the landing of the first floor. John could see dirty, half-empty bedrooms behind half-open doors.

He descended the stairs and then there was an enormous bang behind followed by a loud cracking noise. John jumped down three steps at a time as the staircase collapsed under his feet; wood and brick fell away. John stumbled forward onto the relative safety of the ground floor and stood there breathing heavily.

The living room opened off onto the right; another parlour to the left. The windows were boarded up. A ratty old armchair sat in the corner of the parlour beside a bookcase empty apart from half a pile of yellowed magazines.

The sound came again. Somebody was below. John thought of running out the door. He had the book, and he was sure that the demon in the clock was one of those mentioned in it. But by itself that wouldn't help him. He needed something more. Something was here. Some key item.

There was moving and shuffling below. From the basement.

Like a lightning bolt, he knew the house. He'd never been here before as far as he remembered, but he knew his way around it.

He took some steps down, but on the top, he felt dizzy, then he remembered being about 11. It all came back. His mum and dad had left him in the care of Uncle Max for a night while they went away. John hadn't remembered it ever happening until right now; as if the memory had been sealed off, unlocked only when he almost stood before the door to the basement. He knew about dissociation; he saw it so often in his patients when memories were too terrible to remember; the mind locked them away. John doubled over with nausea.

He remembered the basement. He remembered Max and his friends. In the basement, Max cut his hair and cut his fingernails.

Why the hell would he do that?

John stood by the front door, not going down yet. Whatever was downstairs was quiet, waiting for him. He flicked through the index of the book he held. He found a reference to fingernails.

On page ninety-seven he read "cut nail and hairs were offerings to the Roman goddess Proserpine."

Proserpine was The Goddess of Death. It seemed witches and warlocks used the hair and nails of a victim to create a magic link or bond.

More memories flooded him. Max made him wear a white cotton shift, like a shroud. He felt sick, trembling at the memory. He remembered Max wore a black robe. He wore a mask like one of those old doctors from the plague with a huge beak. He didn't understand.

But he had to go down. He had to search the house to find something to save his family. Movement again. He needed to arm himself.

He looked around the room. By the burned out ashes of the fire was an old iron poker. He grabbed it. It was the closet thing to a weapon he could find.

John stepped down the stairs, book in one hand, poker in the other. The stairs creaked unnervingly under his tread as he descended. As he entered the basement, John felt a stronger wave of nausea flow over him. He felt himself back there as a boy, wearing that white cotton shift, while his uncle cut his fingernails and other men watched from the shadows.

In memory, he heard the chanting of the men in the corners from years ago when he'd been a helpless boy.

He tried the switch, but the light in the basement didn't work.

Someone was waiting in the dark for him. John used his phone as a torch. He swept the beam around the damp cellar. There was no one there. Then he stopped. On the wall opposite, John could see that the brickwork looked fresh - the pointing was more recent than that of the surrounding bricks.

He walked over, and touched the wall. The bricks were loose. They'd been put in place inexpertly. When he touched them, the bricks simply fell inwards. The bricks fell with dull thumps onto the wet clay of the room behind. John looked through and by the light of his phone, he saw a coffin. It was clearly new - as if it had just come from the showroom - brass handles and polished wood. And a realisation struck him. The bricks had not been cemented in place, not by accident, but so that whatever was in the coffin could get out.

Only the fact the bricks were still in place when he entered the cellar was a reassurance. It meant that what was in the coffin had not moved yet. But what then had been moving below?

Then the man who had been hiding, rushed him. John swung wildly with the poker and connected. There was a scream of pain. He hit him again and felt whoever it was raise their arms to protect themselves from the blows of the poker. The man tried to escape, struggling towards the stairs. John let him go, shining the light on the escaping man to see he looked like one of the men from the funeral: one of those who had been members of Max's congregation at the weird Lodge in town and who'd come to the funeral tea. He had been some kind of guard here, guarding the coffin.

After getting his breath back from the exertion, John stepped through the hole towards the coffin. The room was floored with clay rather than the stone flags of the basement.

He could hardly breathe and his head was full of memories. Memories of him as a frightened boy; memories of his father shouting at Max and telling him he would never let him look after John again.

The memories threatened to tear him away from the present. He heard the men chanting. He heard the snip-snip of the scissors; he saw his uncle's black beak mask above him.

John shook his head to clear it so he could focus. He leaned over the coffin and with a grunt, moved the lid sideways.

The dead face of his Uncle Max looked up at him, rouged and preserved by the embalmer's art.

Round Max's neck was some kind of medallion on its chain. It was engraved with lines and circles in an obscure pattern. Then he recognised it.

It was identical with the seal in the grandfather clock. John grabbed at it and the chain snapped. He half expected the corpse of Uncle Max to move but it didn't. With the snatched medallion tight in his hand, John retreated. He climbed the stairs, staring at the seal. The fact that the seal was identical with the one in the clock must be significant.

In the hall, just by the front door, now hanging open because of the fleeing guard, John read more the Goetia book of demons. He knew he had little time before more of the weird cultists came now they knew he was here, defiling their saviour's corpse. He found a drawing of the seal identical to the one he held.

The seal was, as he'd believed, one of the Demons of the Goetia. He read that the magician, in this case Uncle Max, would use it to command a demon to do his will. The demons had to be forced to help the magician, so the magician tortured the seal to hurt the demon. Very often they would burn the seals to cause the demons pain.

This seal was that of Duke Jahal - who had thirty legions of devils under his command. He appeared with the head of a horse and the wings of a bat.

John read that Jahal's particular talent allowed the magician to possess other mortals and take over their bodies. With Jahal's help they could enter into another's body and possess it and live in it as if it was their own. This worked best if the victim was a blood relative of the magician who wanted to possess him.

But John had the seal. Now he knew what this seal was, maybe he could force the Demon Jahal to leave his wife and child alone.

John jumped in his car and started the engine, breaking the speed limit along the A66, thundering down the country roads from Penrith to Mungrisdale.

As he drove, he tried to think things through. It seemed Max gave John the clock to put the demon close to him.

John pulled up to a halt in the gravel parking space outside Thorgill Farm. He stepped out of the car, pulling on his coat. A cold wind blew out from the valley, the high hills. The house itself stood sullen and dark. John went up to the window and banged on it, shouting "Sarah! Sarah!"

He tried the door and it wouldn't open. Then he lifted the seal and said, "Jahal, I command you open the door!"

Now when he tried the handle, it turned, and he shoved it open.

The first thing that John noticed was the ticking of the clock and, as he looked over at it, he saw the hands running backwards as they had before. His wife and daughter were somehow in that. John's breath blew out in clouds in front of him. He saw the clock. In front of it, was the smoky image of a creature with a horse's head and the flickering wings of a bat.

Jahal was aware of him.

"Let them go!" John yelled.

There was a peal of wicked laughter, then a blast of terrible energy knocked John flying across the hall. He slammed into the wall. It seemed just having the seal wasn't enough. John picked himself from where he had fallen against the wall. He had landed on a wooden side table and had knocked off the Tiffany Lamp which had shattered beneath him. His hand was cut and bleeding. The blood smeared on the tablecloth and onto the wall. It was running down his arm onto his fingers.

The broken light bulb sparked and fizzed in the dim light where it had fallen. The power was still connected and some infernal electricity pulsed through the house.

A voice came from nowhere. "Submit to me and let me enter into you. Let me open you for him who has commanded me to enter in."

John gritted his teeth. He raised up the seal. "Jahal, let my family go."

But the demon just laughed. "You aren't hurting me Dr Eliot. Not like he hurt me."

John's cut hand was bleeding more than it should, it was dribbling onto the floor. The blood ran down his hand and was taken up by an unnatural wind. John's ears filled with a hideous howling. As he watched blood and smoke formed a mist and the mist became a dark fog and the fog became a black shape.

The carpet by the broken lamp caught fire. If unchecked, it would burn the house down. John panicked. Jessica and Sarah were trapped in the clock. They would burn if the house burned.

The black shape thickened like smoke from burning oil. But the source of the smoke wasn't oil, it was the blood dripping from John's cut hand. He heard a voice, keening on the wind. He felt his dead uncle near him.

The soul of Uncle Max was feeding from John's blood, using it to manifest a spirit shape. Max created the bond years ago with hair and blood as he prepared the way for his eventual death and reanimation in the body of his nephew.

The face made of smoke spoke. Its words wreathed round John's face, trying to find a way into him. John felt Max's power force him to the ground. He tried to stand, but Max's mind was stronger than a steel vice. Tendrils of Max's thoughts began to reach inside his skull as he lay on the floor. Max's words found their way in through his ears and up through his nose and behind the orbits of his eyes. He was trying to take John over.

Jahal stood watching, indifferent. Soon his job would be over and Jess and Sarah would be closed up in the clock forever. He couldn't care less.

John knew he had to hurt Jahal to make him stop Max.

Max was in his mind. He felt the cold cruelty of the old man. John was terrified Max would win, and enter into him.

The carpet caught further and a lick of yellow fire spread over the floor. John needed to get his family out of the clock. The clock where Jahal locked them.

Then John gripped the demon's seal that he held in his hand. He thrust his hand into the fire on the carpet. The flames burned his hand, but it burned the seal. The demon screamed in pain. This was hurting it. John's hand burned; he shifted to dangle the seal in the heart of the fire. The demon roared.

"Jahal you are free to take revenge on Max who bound you."

The demon stood up tall and seething in its anger. "I Jahal, Duke of Hell, am bound no longer," it roared. "And I will have vengeance on those who have dared to hold me to this place." Its voice echoed and roared; it cracked like a flow of lava and its rage radiated like a hate-filled fire.

Then with an enormous blast of psychic energy it smashed the smoke form of Max away from John.

Realising now that the demon was free, Max turned to face Jahal. John rolled over out of the way, his head splitting with pain as the tendrils of Max's will were withdrawn.

The demon roared and stood up. Jahal conjured a huge whip of smoke and fire.

Jahal whipped Max and the fibres of the whip wrapped round the half solid form and pulled it towards him. John saw Max's manifested body burst into flame where the whip held it. It screamed as it burned.

Jahal pulled the whip closer. When it had Max close enough, it bent down with its horse's head and it bit into the smoking form. Max screamed as he was consigned to the eternal fires.

As the demon feasted on the Black Magician, the grandfather clock exploded. Out of the shadow realm, where he had hidden them, Sarah and Jess rushed to John. He had his hand out of the fire, was lying on the floor as the flames caught the room around him. Sarah pulled him to his feet. His lungs were full of smoke and he coughed. Jess wailed with terror. Sarah dragged him. "We need to get out of here."

Behind a wall of fire, Jahal ate the soul of Uncle Max.

They got to the door, pushed their way out into the night air. Standing there coughing, John saw his beloved house go up in flames, the mighty mountains behind just watching.

"My house!" John said.

"At least we're safe. We're all out of there," Sarah said.

The house burned. John knew he should ring the fire service but he was afraid that if they saved the house something of Max or Jahal might remain.

Sarah pulled him close. "I never liked that house anyway," she said.

14

A GRIZEDALE FOREST WEDDING

"If you run off with Gowan Fell, you'll never be welcome back here," her mother said, stony-faced. Rebecca looked at both her mother and her father who stood there at the door of the slate-roofed cottage at Grizedale, the only home she'd ever known

"But I love him," she said.

Her mother twisted her face in a grimace. "You're a foolish, eighteen-year-old girl. What do you know about love?"

"I know what my heart tells me, mother," Rebecca said.

Her father sighed and her mother glowered. Rebecca set her own face as if she didn't care what they thought, turned and walked down the path that led to the forest. It was summer. She walked down the rows of her father's sweet peas and blue lupins, the heat of the sun beating on her bonnet. She had her few possessions in a pack on her back. She stole a glance to see her mother turn and step back into the house. She could feel the older woman's dark anger even from here. Her father stood at the door and looked like he would cry; he was always the soft one. Her mother had been the disciplinarian.

Rebecca walked on, pushing open the garden gate, which was stiff as if it didn't want her to go either. Then she was walking along the grass verged path that led to the forest. Around them the fells rose - high and craggy across the lake to the west where the mountain called The Old Man stood like a brooding god above the water and softer, heavily wooded hills to the east. She hadn't reached the forest when her father caught up with her. She heard him but didn't look round, for she too was angry and stubborn. Then she felt his hand on her shoulder. She let it lie but kept walking until it fell away.

"Rebecca," he said, coming after her, slightly out of breath.

She softened. She loved her father. Other fathers would have beaten such a wilful and disobedient daughter until they obeyed, but that was never father's way. He would usually persuade, cajole, and make her laugh until she came round. Usually, but not now because *love is the higher law*. She'd read that in a story of knights and ladies. Fate set who your true love would be and then you had to be with him, come hell or high water.

"Rebecca," her father said again, and she came to a stop and turned to face him. Her back was to the forest that closed in around the path like a secret.

Her father was in his mid-fifties, grey at the temples, his face tanned and lined by his lifetime of working outside. "Do you have to go, lass? Your mother thinks you'll soon regret it and be back."

"I have to go, father. You always taught me I should do what's right - what my conscience tells me to do." Her face was pained. She hated to upset him; her mother less so, but her father certainly. She took his hand.

He said, "But is it right? Have you thought of the shame it'll bring upon us?"

She scowled. "I care not for shame, father. Shame is the way the priests and lords keep us in our place. Shame shall not stop me."

He stroked her shoulder. "Then not shame, but think of me. It will break my heart to lose you."

She shook her head. "You'll not lose me, father. I shall visit." She took his hand from her shoulder and held it. "Gowan is my true love, and one must follow where one's heart leads."

Her father's brow darkened, and he looked down at his big

gnarled hand in her soft white fingers. "Gowan Fell is not a good man," he said.

She snorted. "And I've heard that one too. Because he lives a free life in the forest and pays no respect to the great and the self professed good, they call him a bad man." She shook her head. "They call him a bad man because he doesn't do what they say, not because he is one."

Her father fixed her with his brown eyes. "I see your mind is set. But if he hurts you..."

She squeezed his hand. In a soft tone she said, "He won't hurt me, father. He loves me. He is my true love and I am his; he told me so."

"Many men say such things, Rebecca."

She dropped his hand. "I thought you better than this, father. You shouldn't try to poison my mind against my love, just to get me to obey you."

He sighed. "I've never been one to force you to obey. Your mother calls me soft. Maybe I am. But I trust that your love for us, your parents, will remain and you will recognise how much we love you. Even your mother, because beneath her disapproval, she loves you too."

Tears filled his eyes. She did not like to see her father like this; he was soft and gentle, yet always strong. But her mind was made up. She wouldn't abandon her family. She wanted to come back and see her little sister and she knew that she could outlast her mother's disapproval. In the end, they would come round and see she was doing the right thing. Her sister had given her a keepsake, one of her dollies. It was a badly made thing and cheap, but little Kirsten loved it, and it had been given with tears in the small girl's eyes to 'keep you safe in the wood.'

"I must go now, father. The way is long and I want to be there before dark."

"Do you have enough food?"

She nodded. "Mother gave me bread and cheese and some apples." Rebecca smiled. "She hated doing it, but she did."

"She wouldn't see you go hungry, no matter what she thinks."

Rebecca stepped away, backwards.

"They say..." her father began.

"They say what?" She frowned - this was another ploy of his to keep her.

He shrugged. "I don't believe in such things but..."

"Spit it out, father. You've begun some wild story, best finish it. Some story about Gowan no doubt."

He didn't speak.

"They say he's a womaniser? Is that it?"

He shook his head.

"That he's a wife beater?"

"No. I've not heard that. It's what his father was."

"His father?" She was incredulous. "A story about his father to put me off Gowan?" She shook her head more in pity than anger. "Father, you have to let me grow up."

Then, seeing her mind was made to leave, he reached into his belt and gave her his knife. Good steel was rare in those days among ordinary folk and she knew he prized his knife.

"I couldn't, father."

He nodded. "You can. You'll need a knife for all sorts of things. I have another." He had but not as good.

She took it.

"Visit us soon, my lovely daughter," he said.

She smiled at him. "I shall. May the gods be with you, father."

"Remember to pray. Don't forget your faith in God."

She laughed. "I shall. But mine is the god of the woods and flowers, of the mountains and wild beasts."

"Shush girl, don't let the priests hear you say that."

And she turned and walked off, leaving her father standing on the track at the edge of the Old Forest.

And he never did tell her the worst thing he'd heard about Gowan Fell's father.

. . .

Gowan Fell's house was hard to find if you were uninvited, but for those he made welcome, the way was easy. And Rebecca was very welcome. She knew the route — walk down to the small stream where the brown trout lurk, then over the old packhorse bridge dressed in moss. After two hundred yards on the narrow path, look for the lightning split oak and then strike out through the deep wood following the deer path until you find it. The house itself was a pile of turf walls amid fern and brier and the roof was of rough slate. "I shall make a pretty garden here," she smiled to herself as she stepped into the clearing before the house.

Gowan Fell appeared from her right, silent as a beast of the wood. He put his hand to her blonde hair, and she jumped.

"You scared the wits out of me, Gowan," she said in a mock scolding voice, but her smile was wide as he enfolded her into his chest.

His arms were muscled from his work in the forest and his skin smelled of wood smoke and the wild wood. He held her tight, and she melted into an embrace she could not break free from, even should she have wanted. His kiss was fierce, his lips parted and his mouth was hungry and passionate. His hand was to the back of her head and then his teeth were at her neck, kissing and biting. She almost swooned from the pleasure of it, but she said, "No, Gowan," because that was seemly and even though she'd run away from her parents; they'd taught her what was right and what was wrong. She knew she shouldn't give herself so easily. But she wanted to.

He took her hand and led her towards his cottage. When she dallied, thinking that she would only give him her mouth and her breasts this time, he tugged her with him. She put her hand on the doorframe to pull back; he was going too fast. But impatiently he turned and looked at her with his dark eyes — like glowing islands amid his black hair and his black beard. "Come," he said, and she yielded and went with him into the dark cottage.

The cottage smelled of him; a musky odour that she did not find unpleasant. There were two rooms, the further one unused except for storage of his tools. She saw saws, axes, and other implements she didn't recognise. This one room had his bed, a low thing of bracken and sheepskin. She glanced around. There was a cooking pot, blackened above a dead fire. Then he took her chin in his fingers, and smiling, with his other hand, began to unbutton her bodice.

"No, Gowan," she said, putting no hand up to stop him.

He halted, as if listening to her objection. He raised a dark eyebrow and smiled to show his white teeth. "Very well," he said, dropping his hand to his side. She went over to the bed and dropped the dolly her sister Kirsten had given to her to keep her safe in the wood. The thing's cloth eyes stared at the ceiling and on an afterthought, Rebecca took off her cloak and placed it over the doll's face so it wouldn't see what was about to happen.

Gowan stood near the fire, the yellow light flickering on his handsome face. "Are you sure you don't need a lie down?" he smiled.

Then she felt a smile growing on her own face in return. "Well, perhaps a little one," she said.

The woodsman needed no further invitation. He undid her bodice and tugged at her blouse until her small breasts with their pale rose nipples were exposed. He took her to the ground, kissed her, kneaded her, suckled, and played with her breasts with the tips of his tongue. She was not a virgin; something her family did not know. For once, in the woods, he had come upon her while she picked bluebells and even then; she knew he was the one for her; her own true love, just like it said in the books.

Whenever she spoke of romance, her mother told her that love was for ladies, not ordinary folk, but Rebecca knew she was special. Not for her a life among the common people following their petty rules and hand-me-down beliefs, told what they could and could not do by priests and squires; she would choose freedom and to be her own woman.

And this was her choice. Gowan was her choice. It was her choice that he made love to her. Gowan began to remove her skirts and then her petticoats. She smelled him. She felt his weight. She sensed the strength in those arms. He was a real man — not like her father, kind as he was, but powerless. Gowan took what he wanted, and what he wanted was her.

The silken hair between her legs opened to his fingers, and she bit her lip and groaned involuntarily as he found her. And then in his impatience, he shifted on top of her. He took her by virtue of his strength and desire but it was her will to give in. Though truly she could not have resisted his strength.

Later, he dozed in her arms and she stroked his head. She felt his sweet breath on her chest. Gowan Fell, she thought; you are mine and I am yours. We shall be free here; we shall live a wild free life and the only laws we shall obey are those of nature and of love.

It was early summer when Rebecca moved in with Gowan Fell. He was charming and attentive. He brought her rabbits and pigeons to cook with wild garlic and the leaves of the forest. All summer long the bees buzzed, and the flies droned. Overhead, the doves cooed from the branches and the jackdaws argued as they went to roost on the warm nights. Rebecca and Gowan made love every night and in the day when Gowan was away working, Rebecca cooked and mended his clothes and set to work planting her little garden.

She went back to her parents' house to visit and her father was glad to see her. Her mother was glad too but hid her gladness behind a look of disapproval. "No good will come of this Gowan Fell," she said.

"I love him mother, and that's that."

Her father gave her seed potatoes, and she planted carrots and onions in her patch. He also gave her sweet peas and stocks to scent the evening air around the cottage.

Gowan made love to Rebecca fiercely and the animals and birds heard her cries of pleasure but paid no mind, because they knew well the sounds of love and death and could tell them apart. She liked to be taken as if she was a mare and he a stallion, or he a dog and she a bitch.

And so the weeks passed, and she was content with her life. She felt the spirits of the wildwood and when he was away burning charcoal in the deep forest, she would say her prayers to Brother Wolf and to Sister Moon. She washed his clothes in the beck to clean them of the grime and soot. Then one day she found blood on his shirt. She scrubbed it as best she could, but the stain was stubborn as guilt and could not be wholly cleansed.

She brought it to him as they sat around their rough table after they had finished rabbit stew, seasoned with her onions and thickened with potatoes and the barley her father gave her.

"Husband, (she had taken to calling him that because in the eyes of the Forest they were married, if not in the eyes of the Church) how did so much blood get on your shirt. I've tried to clean it but as you see—"

With a sudden snarl, he struck her with the back of his hand. She fell back, putting her hand to her lip and feeling the beading blood warm against her skin and tasting salt and iron in her mouth. He had never hit her before and she was dumbfounded.

"Gowan!" she said.

"Don't ask me my business, woman," he said, glowering at her, his dark brows a straight line and his brown eyes intense and full of fury.

"I only wondered if you'd been hurt," she said "It was a lot of blood and I was worried."

"My blood is my blood, not yours."

And later, Rebecca wondered whether it was his blood at all, because she had seen him naked and he had no cut nor injury. That night he was rough with her and she did not like it. She called out for him to be gentle but he took his pleasure and when he was finished, rolled over to sleep. Rebecca watched him as he slept, as thoughtless as a beast, and her heart felt as if it had been pierced by the black thorn of anguish, as when someone we love takes their affection away from us.

THE NEXT DAY she visited her mother. The older lady was softening and gave her cake and China tea that Rebecca knew was expensive and her mother's way of showing affection because she could never say "I love you" in words.

Rebecca considered sharing her heartbreak with her mother. Her brow furrowed, and she went silent. Her mother said, "What is it, child?" in as soft a voice as Rebecca ever remembered her using. In the end, Rebecca could not face the "I told you so" that would surely come, so she smiled and said, "This cake is delicious, mother. You must give me the recipe."

Her mother's face twisted, and she said, "And how will you bake a cake in the forest, daughter, with no proper kitchen and so far away from civilised folk?"

Rebecca frowned. Her mother would never change and Rebecca would never admit she was wrong, not to her mother. So she smiled thinly and said nothing.

At the end of the visit she kissed her mother dutifully and sent her love to her father. Then she made her way along the deep green roads of the Old Forest, back to Gowan Fell's cottage.

HE DID NOT COME BACK that night. And when he returned the next day he hardly spoke. He sat eating roast pigeon and licking the grease from his fingers by the fire. She went to him for love, but he brushed her off and later snored as he lay beside her. It was then she noticed a smell on him; one she recognised - the smell of another woman's sex.

The next morning, he dressed in his fine fair clothes, though he said he was going to the forest as usual. When he set off to work at his charcoal burning, she decided to follow him. She crept a hundred yards behind him. She wore her brown dress with her cloak of forest green. If he had been paying attention, he could have noticed her because she was not skilled in the ways of hunting as he was, but his head was clearly full of something else and he whistled as he went.

When he came to a fork in the road, instead of going right to where his fires were, he turned left towards the hamlet of Hawkshead. She kept back and to the side of the path so she was close to the undergrowth of hazel and whitethorn and could duck in if he turned. Once he stopped to piss, the thick jet raising steam as he held his penis with the self-satisfied look of a man who is going to get what he wants.

Hawkshead was a poor place - near the great lake with the forest behind it. Rebecca wondered how she was going to observe him now he was in the village. She came to the outskirts, stepping tentatively. It filled her heart with anxiety at what she might see and she clutched the folds of her kirtle tightly in her right hand, the left to her throat as she watched him enter between the first houses.

She didn't have long to wait before her suspicions were proved correct. A bonny dark-haired girl of her own age ran to greet Gowan Fell, throwing her slim arms around him. Gowan pulled the girl to him and kissed her deeply there and then.

Rebecca's heart broke. Hot tears flooded down her cheeks as she turned and ran back into the forest. The ice of abandonment and the fire of jealousy chilled then scalded her chest. She wept as she ran. What was she to do now? She had cut herself off from her family, because of the faithless Gowan Fell. Her mother and father had been right all along. She could run all the way back to them, but how could she face her mother's crowing victory and her father's sad eyes? We told you so, her mother would say. Her father would hold her, and they would take her back, but her pride wouldn't let her go.

Instead, she decided to wait and see what solution the morning would bring.

She did not sleep until late in the night. She heard the badgers snuffling outside her cottage and the bark of the fox deep in the wood. A shaft of sunlight woke her, that and the sound of someone knocking on the rough wooden door. At first she thought it was Gowan returned and her heart hammered, but then she realised he would not knock. A woman's voice said, "Is there anyone home?"

It sounded like an old woman. Rebecca was in no mood to talk to anyone and she lay there while the woman knocked again. Irritation fuelled by heartbreak, made her finally sit up and shout, "What?"

"Ah, there is someone home," the voice said. "Do you want to buy ribbons? Lovely silk and satin ribbons in all colours."

Rebecca exhaled. Her natural demeanour began to surface, breaking the vinegar bitterness that had soaked through her. When she'd gone to bed, she had hated the world — men for their faithlessness and women for being their willing accomplices, betrayers of sisterhood.

"A minute," Rebecca said. She stood hurriedly and pulled on her green kirtle, covering her underslip. Then she went to the door and opened it.

The woman was black-haired with strands of grey. Her face was lined and brown as if from years walking from town to town with her wares. She had a pack on her back and was already unloosening it and unpacking brightly coloured ribbons.

She took them in her hands and offered them to Rebecca. The girl shook her head and made to pull away, but she had never seen such fine ribbons. The colours were names she hardly knew.

The woman said, "Cerulean silk, and here carmine satin." She gave them to the girl who wound them round her fingers and in-between, feeling their silky texture. "And here viridian, and here amaranthine. This is smaragdine, and this one is heliotrope, while this is icterine and this one, fuliginous black."

Rebecca put her hand to her mouth and laughed. "Are these really words?"

The older woman laughed too. "Words made to charm a buyer."

Then Rebecca smiled sadly and said, "But lady, I am no buyer. I have no money."

"If not money, then food?"

"Poor fare that." Rebecca pointed at the small cauldron by the fire that had the remains of the last stew she made.

"But better than none for a hungry belly. May I come in?"

Rebecca nodded. "What is your name?"

"My name is Blodeuwedd," said the woman.

Rebecca said, "That is in the old tongue. What does it mean?"

The woman smiled. "I was Christened something else long ago.

But long ago I began to follow the ways of the woods and changed my Christian name to something that was more meaningful. Blodeuwedd means flower face, and the owl was called that one time."

Rebecca nodded. My great-grandmother spoke some of the old language, but she is dead now and none of us learned it."

Blodeuwedd said, "The old language grew here in this forest. It made us what we are. When we lose it, we lose our essence. But your name, girl. What is it?"

Rebecca told her. "I believe mine is a Christian name, or Jewish."

She looked at her. "But I see nothing of that in you. I smell the woods on you. The deep woods and water call you more than any holy book."

Rebecca nodded. "Wait while I heat the stew. And would you like tea? Please sit." She gestured to the rough chair that belonged to Gowan Fell.

Blodeuwedd sat down. "This is a man's chair," she said. "A man lives here, but he is not here now?" The intonation of the words was as if they were a question.

Rebecca frowned and said nothing.

Blodeuwedd did not persist, but waited until Rebecca had warmed the meal.

She ate it with gusto. "What meat is this?" she asked.

Rebecca looked to her feet and said, "Crow. It's the best we have right now."

"No matter," Blodeuwedd said. "Black feathers like your heart made black with sadness."

Rebecca was taken aback. "How do you know I am sad?"

"I see it," Blodeuwedd said. "I know you. And I know the man who lives here."

"Gowan Fell?"

"Aye and I know his people. I know their kind."

Rebecca wanted to ask more, but she did not. Perhaps from fear of what she might find out.

Then Blodeuwedd rose and thanked the girl. "Here is a ribbon as thanks," she said at the door.

"What colour is it?" smiled Rebecca.

"It's only red."

"Not incarnadine?" she laughed.

The woman shook her head. "Merely red. Red as blood." Blodeuwedd paused on her way out as if something weighed heavily on her mind. She made a noise as if to speak, but finally said nothing.

"Will you be back this way again?" Rebecca asked the older woman as she left.

"Perhaps." Blodeuwedd said, and then, as if an afterthought, she reached into her bag, took out a green ribbon, and gave it to Rebecca. "And this is green as life. There is a place in the forest you might find if you ever need to. At a join of the two streams, where the oaks give way to the ash and aspen, there is a white stone there that sparkles, half out of the water."

The girl nodded. "I know it. It is a pretty spot."

"It is my spot," the woman said. "Remember me there."

And with that, she turned and left.

Rebecca watched her until she disappeared into the trees of the Grizedale Forest and then closed the door and waited for the return of Gowan Fell.

When Gowan came back, he said little other than give a growl for his supper. He was not in his fair clothes but had changed to his normal working garb. He was covered with charcoal grime so Rebecca didn't doubt that he had been working as he said he had. Underneath the smell of burning, that animal smell of his had grown much less pleasant to her nose than it once had been when she desired him.

After supper, he took her. She told him no, but he took her anyway. And while Gowan Fell violated her, she hoped her father would come in with his woodman's axe and kill the beast, but no one came; she was too far away from those who loved her and so she suffered his vileness and prayed instead to her gods of the woods and the forest to send deliverance.

As they lay there, she said, "Gowan, do you love me still?"

He laughed a bitter, dry laugh. "I love your cleaning and cooking and mending my clothes."

"Nothing more?"

"And I love burying myself in you when I can not get better."

She felt quick tears, but they were drowned by shame. What a fool she was. But she would not let him hear her cry, so she clasped her hands tight so her nails almost pierced her palms, and she lay there until dawn.

Gowan was up early the next morning. She heard the small birds of the wood in full throat outside as they sang their morning chorus and orisons to the rising sun. She lay there while he pulled on his clothes, not his work clothes but the better ones that she had mended and stitched. She knew he was going hunting again. And she wondered from the blood on his clothes, whether he merely seduced the girls, or maybe did worse.

She had been charmed by the beast he was, as foolish girls will be, and as the pretty ones of the Hawkshead village would be. But a beast was a beast, and a girl was not a lover to Gowan Fell, but only prey.

And so once he was gone, she dressed quickly, and she followed him. In the pocket of her dress were the red and green ribbons given her by Blodeuwedd. She gripped them as she ran. She followed him to warn the girl he snared so she could avoid the grisly fate that Rebecca suspected Gowan would enact.

She ran quietly down the deer path that led away from their rough dwelling and to the main road through this part of the forest.

Instead of going to the village, Gowan took another path and went a way that Rebecca did not know. She watched him two hundred yards ahead, walking with an assured step, even whistling as he went, unconcerned and confident. After about two miles, the way grew broader and better trodden. Rebecca guessed they were approaching a village. Still Gowan did not suspect she was behind him. He had never looked behind at all, so secure was he.

Gowan went among the first low houses, thatched with sticks from the forest and bracken, walls made of rough stone whitewashed, flowers around their wooden shutters - lupins and red-hot pokers. The shutters were thrown open to let in the air of noon and Rebecca saw various good-men of the village greet Gowan warily, as if they knew him, but did not trust him.

She saw Gowan make his way to the tavern. And so, she thought, he had money, though he chose to give her none. Her use to him was housemaid and whore, no better than a slave.

How stupid she'd been to fall in love with him. She felt scalding tears on her cheek then she chided herself for a fool; tears would make nothing better, so she wiped them away and sat, near a cottage, within sight of the tavern door, so she would know when he came out. She pulled the hood of her cloak over her head. Gowan Fell would not suspect she was there, and even if he saw her, he would look past her hooded form.

And then after two hours, when the sun was still high, but flitting behind light clouds and not warm, he emerged. Again the village men nodded at him, but heads down, not meeting his eyes. And the girls and women, scattered out of his way like so many hens. All except one, a blonde girl who looked haughty and proud. She engaged Gowan Fell in talk and Rebecca felt a sting of jealousy in her breast. They tarried, and the flirting became more obvious. From where she stood half in the shadow of a wall, Rebecca saw a middle-aged village wife shake her head in reproach, but the girl was too taken up with the handsome Gowan Fell.

Rebecca saw Gowan reach inside his waistcoat and pull out a leather bottle. He offered it to the girl who with some little hesitation, as if pretending to obey the laws of propriety, eventually took it and swigged at it. Then grimaced and wiped the hot spirit from her lips. Rebecca saw the girl flush and laugh. Gowan laughed with her. He was a comely man, and Rebecca remembered the intoxication of his attention and how it brought a shiver to her breast and warmth to her loins, when she had first been enamoured of Gowan Fell.

And then, as surely as all such things are enkindled, the girl took his hand, and he led her down the path from the village. Again, Rebecca felt the sharp stab of jealousy. How she wanted to slap this girl and drive her away from Gowan Fell, but how now she also felt fear for the lass, foolish and vain as she surely was.

Rebecca followed them down through the beech woods as they went hand in hand, laughing and joking, towards the river. There they sat and Gowan Fell waited, as patient as a fisherman, for this blonde-haired fish to bite. It was she who moved in closer to him first, snuggling her side to his. And then, with the art of a master, Gowan Fell lifted his hand to caress the girl's shoulder. She leant her head into his and together they watched the silver water drift by. Rebecca remembered and recognised so well Gowan's artistry, his leisurely entrapping, so that a girl didn't know if it was love or lust he was after and persuaded herself that Gowan was set on love and it was her own lust that drove things to their disrobing.

And then, Gowan stood. Rebecca did not hear clearly but it was evident that he wanted to piss. Pretending to be a gentleman, he did not do it there, but rather stepped away.

They had been there long, and the light was turning golden as evening came. Up in the sky above hung the pale moon, barely lambent with the sun only just going. But Rebecca remembered how it had blazed white these past few nights as it made its way to the full moon it would achieve tonight.

And so Rebecca took her chance. While Gowan went, she ran lightly across the ground. The girl almost cried out but Rebecca signed for her to be quiet. If she'd been a man it would be different, but the girl saw no threat in another young woman.

Rebecca stood there before the girl and the girl stared back at her amazed until she said, "What do you want?"

"You must leave. Don't wait for Gowan Fell."

The girl scowled and said, "And who are you?"

"I am the wife who lives in the wildwood with Gowan Fell."

The girl shook her head. "Gowan has no wife for he has told me he is a single man, and besides neither he nor you wear a ring."

Rebecca frowned. "We are married by the ways of the forest, not the Church."

"Then," the girl said, "You are not married at all."

Rebecca reached out to touch the girl. "For your own sake, leave now."

The girl slapped her hand away. "I will not leave on the request of a jealous shrew. Gowan is with me now, so go."

The girl got up and her eyes were angry and Rebecca thought she might strike her.

"He will rape you," Rebecca said.

"It's only rape if I don't want him to. And that's what's bothering you." At this she reached down for a stone and went to throw it at Rebecca. Rebecca also saw the shape of Gowan Fell returning from further down the river.

Rebecca felt fear. If he found her here, he would surely hurt her. She turned to run. She broke through a screen of branches and crashed through the undergrowth as a rock came thudding after her. She heard Gowan Fell's voice scream, "Rebecca, I'll kill you for this!"

DARKNESS HAD FALLEN on the forest before Rebecca got back to the hut. She arrived at their rough cottage when the tawny owls were calling from tree to tree above her head. Her way was lit by bright mother Moon, but her breath was ragged as she ran then walked then ran. The briars and thorns cut her along the way and lines of red marked her legs and arms like the bloody striations of self-flagellation.

And when she was home, she lit a rush dipped in tallow and waited in the smoky yellow light for Gowan Fell.

But he did not return, at least not immediately. And as she waited, she shivered, not with cold but with fear. The smell of beast was heavy on their hovel. If she had not minded it before the odour now almost choked her. It was his smell. The smell of a man, but the smell of something else too.

When he did not return after many hours, she ventured outside, her fear now replaced by a sense of resentment and growing courage.

She would go back to her mother and father. They would tell her how foolish she'd been and that would hurt her young pride. How she'd seen herself as a spring flower, or a young fox finding its way in the woods and fields. But now she knew she'd been a fool, taken in by a lout and woman beater. And worse, a rapist. She wept bitter hot tears, gathered her few things, and stepped out of the hut.

The moon was bright outside as she walked down the deer track, her heart beating fast in case she ran into Gowan Fell. But he was not there. The nightjar called, and she heard beasts snuffling in the undergrowth, but they meant her no harm.

And then she came to the wider path. She walked down the rough way, avoiding the puddles from an earlier shower of rain, stepping on the lush grass that grew in a line down the centre. This path took her some way back towards the village she'd fled from earlier, before splitting and leading her back to her parent's house. She was lost in her thoughts of heartbreak and self-blame when she sensed someone up ahead.

She stopped. She listened and heard nothing. She listened harder, straining every fibre to catch what she'd hearkened to before, the subliminal warning that had made her halt. There was something on the breeze, but she couldn't comprehend it. And then she realised part of what had stopped her was the silence, the unnatural silence of the wood, where before there had been owls and the flitting of bats, now there was nothing, as if the whole wood was holding its breath.

There were shapes down the path. They were the size of men and walked on their hind legs, but they were not men. As the breeze shifted, she caught their scent. It was the scent of Gowan Fell, but this time mixed with something more animal — something doglike or worse. He was with another of the same kind. Rebecca stood frozen with fear. And then the breeze shifted. She saw one of them raise his snout to the air, blackness silhouetted against the dark violet of the sky behind. He appeared to be sniffing. He had scented her out.

Rebecca turned and ran. She fled in the direction of her father's house. She ran until her legs burned and her lungs were on fire and she didn't stop running until she crossed the stone bridge dressed in moss and was at the edge of the forest near to where her father and mother lived. And there she stood, hands on thighs, gasping for breath. Gasping for breath, but at the same time looking back into the forest in case she was pursued. In case, Gowan Fell had followed her to her parents' house.

She saw no sign of him, but when she had her breath back, she ran again. She stumbled and half fell through the pretty gate of her family house and along the path between the vegetables up to the door. It was deep night, and the moon rode high with her company of stars. Rebecca hammered at the door. It was her mother who answered. "Rebecca, what are you doing here? At this hour!"

Little Kirsten was beside her mother seeing who it was, then she rushed out and hugged her sister.

"Rebecca, answer me!" her mother said, tugging at Rebecca's sleeve.

Rebecca's face was wet with tears. Her chest heaved with sorrow and if felt like there was ice where her heart should be. She feared her mother would send her away again, back to Gowan Fell, that she would say, *"You've made your bed, now lie in it."*

But then her father came to the door. He kissed her cheek and said, "Welcome home, my daughter. Come in and I'll keep you safe."

"You're thin as a rake, girl," her mother said. "I'll get you some broth," and she scuttled through to the kitchen to get food for her daughter. Rebecca was crying tears of relief to be back in the safety of her family. Her father and little Kirsten crowded round as she sat by the fire. They were burning cherry wood that gave off a sweet smell. The interior walls of the cottage were whitewashed, and the furniture was made by her father, sturdy and carved with the spirals and knots beloved of the northern people. He had his hand on her shoulder.

"What happened?" he said.

At first, she couldn't speak. A mixture of shame and jealousy held her words back. Kirsten stroked her knee and gazed at her with concern. Then Rebecca looked up at the ceiling and without making eye contact she said, "Gowan went with another woman."

Her father sucked his teeth. Then he said, "Well, that's no surprise."

Kirsten looked bemused, she was about to ask a question. Their father said, "Kirsten, go to your bed."

"But father," the girl said, "it's only early!"

Just then, their mother returned, the broth steaming and with it a chunk of her homemade bread and butter from the family cow. She said, "Kirsten, do as your father says — bed!"

The little girl pouted and stomped her foot but she turned and did as she was bid. Not like me, thought Rebecca, watching her go. At the door of the living room, Kirsten turned and said, "Rebecca, did you bring my dolly?"

Rebecca's eyes widened. Her hand went to her throat. She had a flash of panic almost as if she had left a living thing to the mercies of Gowan Fell in that hovel in the woods.

Kirsten looked sad, but shook her head and smiled. "Don't worry; we can get it another time."

Rebecca reached into her pocket and pulled out the red and green ribbons given to her by Blodeuwedd. "Here have these. A kind lady gave them to me."

The little girl's eyes widened. She ran over and took the ribbons. "These are lovely!" she said. She leaned up and gave her big sister a kiss on the cheek, then she turned and left.

Her mother's eyes narrowed. "You got those from the pedlar woman?"

Rebecca nodded. "She was kind."

Her mother said, "I hope you didn't invite her, or worse still, give her food and rest."

"I did, mother. It was only hospitable."

Her mother spat. "That one, that calls herself "Flower Face" is a witch. She was trying to grab your soul."

Rebecca shook her head. "No, she was just a kind old lady."

"Mary-Hannah," Rebecca's father said to her mother. "You demean yourself by repeating old wives' tales. There is no truth in witches."

Mary-Hannah said, "There are strange things in the forest."

Ignoring her mother, Rebecca turned to her father and said, "I left Kirsten's dolly! I must go back."

Her father's brow furrowed. "I think not. Let it be. I would rather you never saw Gowan Fell again."

"But it was Kirsten's favourite. She gave it to me. I can't leave it with him."

"You're talking silliness, girl. You're tired. It's only a rag-doll."

Then her mother spoke. "No, you should go and get it. He should have nothing of ours, that Gowan Fell." She spat his name.

"I will go and get it, father." Rebecca went to rise from her chair, but her father stopped her down with a gentle hand. "No, you won't!"

"Not tonight, anyway," her mother said. "Eat your broth. Then sleep. You can fetch it in the morning."

And her father rose. "Mary-Hannah, Rebecca will not go to that cottage. She will never see Gowan Fell again. That is my word, and that's final."

Her mother was taken aback, for it was rare her husband spoke with such authority. "Then *you* will go," she finally said to her husband.

Rebecca's father nodded. "Yes, I will go. First thing in the morning."

Rebecca felt sudden fear. She remembered the wolf thing she had seen on the path in the moonlight. She remembered the blood on Gowan Fell's shirt. She reached out and clutched her father's hand. "Don't go, father. He is a wicked man, and younger and stronger than you."

Her father smiled and held her hand tight. "Don't worry, 'Becca. I will not get into a fight. Anyway, I don't believe the stories about the Fell family."

Her mother sat silent.

He said, "Pagan nonsense is all they are."

Rebecca looked at them both. "You never told me what you had heard about Gowan Fell's father."

Mary-Hannah frowned deeper, but Rebecca's father laughed. "That." He grinned at her. "They say he was one of the Folk."

"The Folk?"

"They don't exist. How could they?" He said.

"Who are the Folk, mother?" She turned to Mary-Hannah as her father wouldn't give her a sensible answer.

Her mother shrugged. "The Folk. Country people believe in them. Those that have no education and who have never been to Church."

"But what are they?"

Her mother said, "Man wolves. Men who turn into wolves at the full of the moon and who walk on their hind legs."

"Nonsense," said her father. "Go to bed, my darling. I'll get the doll tomorrow. You need never see that scoundrel again."

She gripped his arm tight. "Please, don't go, father. At least get some village men to go along with you."

He leaned over and kissed her forehead. "Don't worry, Rebecca. I'll be fine."

The birds were in the roof space, flitting and cheeping. Outside owls and bats flew. Rebecca shared a room with her sister who stirred and muttered in her sleep. As she lay, head on the goose down pillow, she smelled the night-scented stocks from her father's flower garden and she lay there thinking of Gowan Fell. Eventually, towards dawn, she fell into a heavy sleep. When she awoke, the sun was streaming in through the willow lattices in the window that served instead of the glass they couldn't afford.

She got up and went through in her night shift. Kirsten was outside in the garden playing with the dog. Her mother was in the kitchen, and when she saw Rebecca, she brought her a bowl of porridge. She handed the steaming bowl to her daughter and bade her sit at the wooden table.

Rebecca began to eat the porridge. She had forgotten how good normal food was, not the findings of the forest, but proper food farmed and grown by people. After she had finished the bowl and then run her finger around it out of her mother's sight, she said, "Where's father?"

Her mother said, without turning from where she was preparing a rabbit, "He went early to get your doll."

Kirsten had come in and was threading Rebecca's hair through her fingers. "It needs washed," she said. Then her thoughts flitting like a child's will, she said, "Daddy's gone to get my dolly." She gave Rebecca's hair a tug, "That you left!"

"Ow!" Rebecca said, grabbing her hair back. But her heart was full of fear. Gowan Fell was not a reasonable man and her father was old now. Her father might want to avoid a fight, but Gowan might not let him.

She stood. "I'm going back."

Her mother shook her head. "Your father said for you to wait here. He'll be back by afternoon."

"No, mother," she stood and went to the bedroom to dress.

She heard her mother say, "You never do what I say, anyway." Then she turned to Kirsten and said, "When you grow, be a good girl, Kirsten, and always obey your parents."

The little girl said solemnly, "I will, mammy."

But Rebecca had thrown on her clothes, her kirtle and cloak still dirty with mud and leaf mould from the forest. She ran out of the door, shouting, "I'll be back soon, don't worry. I just need to help father."

She entered the Old Forest, and went along the forest road through the ragged avenues of oaks and ash, beech and willow, until she came at last to the packhorse bridge. She crossed that and then within an hour was at the deer path that led to the hovel she had shared with Gowan Fell. She felt her stomach churn and anxiety danced its electric dance from her throat to her fingertips. She was breathing more quickly, not filling her lungs, but instead panting lightly as she came to the clearing. Smoke curled through the rough roof, telling her that Gowan was inside.

She did not knock. Gowan was lying on his bed, their bed as had been. His eyes flickered open. His bare chest was covered in scratches and smeared blood, now dry.

She grew afraid. "Is my father here?"

Gowan raised his head. "Ah Rebecca, you're home."

"Is my father here?" she said more stridently.

He shook his head. "Your father?"

"Don't pretend to be stupid, Gowan Fell. He came to get Kirsten's doll."

Gowan reached out his long, hairy leg and with the toes kicked the rag-doll from the bottom of the bed. "This?"

Rebecca ran over and snatched it. She held it to her chest as if she had rescued a living thing from him.

Gowan sat up. He was naked. She could see better now that the blood that matted the dark hair on his chest came from scratch wounds, five of them, as if someone had drawn a claw across him. The claw of a woman's hand in anger it seemed to her. He stood, arrogant in his nakedness. His penis hung long from the dark curling hair of his loins.

He reached and picked up his shirt. He threw it at her. It was covered in dried blood. "I need my washing done, Rebecca. It's timely you are home."

"I'm not staying. Where's my father?"

Gowan Fell, picked at his teeth with his fingernail. Then he shook his head. "The old fool called before. I don't know what he wanted. I sent him away."

"What have you done with him!" she screamed. Her fear for her father rose in her chest and up to her throat. Her head buzzed with terror and anger.

Gowan Fell smiled and shrugged.

She ran at him, fists flailing, but he easily threw her down. He stood over her, still naked, then he squatted and brought his face near to hers, the curly dark hair of his beard near her soft face. She smelled meat on his breath. Then he kissed her softly. "I've missed you," he said, standing.

He turned and began to search for clothes from the heap by his bed. She scrabbled to her feet and looked around the hovel. Her eyes darted this way and that and then she saw it. On the poor wooden table they had used, was her father's knife, which he'd given her to bring here. She had used it for skinning squirrels and rabbit. She watched Gowan. He had fastened his shirt and was pulling on his deerskin trousers. He still had his back to her. She darted over to the table, grabbed the knife, gripped it facing him and said, "Gowan, what have you done to my father?"

Gowan Fell turned, apparently unconcerned. He saw the knife. Her hand was trembling. He smiled. "Put that down, Rebecca, you might hurt yourself."

"Not as much as you hurt that girl."

He raised an eyebrow. "What girl?" Then he laughed. "Ah, the girl from the village. I hadn't realised you were so jealous."

"The blood on the shirt. It's hers?" Rebecca's voice was shaking because she feared it might be her father's. But the blood was mostly dry and if it was her father's it would not be dry at all.

"Blood, blood. The world is full of blood. Things kill things, Rebecca. You eat the meat of things I've killed. Don't be so squeamish."

"The girl. Is she alive?"

He shook his head. "Try to free yourself from your jealous imaginings. Come, I will show you where your father is."

Her hand trembled as she gripped the knife.

"Come," he said, most reasonably. "Round the back."

Rebecca knew that whoever had lived there before Gowan had a pen at the back for dogs. But there had been no dogs there since Gowan moved in. Dogs would not tolerate him. They slunk off with their tail between their legs, whining whenever they saw him.

"You go first."

"I have the knife." She brandished it at him. Her voice shook.

He grinned. "You won't hurt me, Rebecca. You haven't the courage. And besides you love me too much."

A ball of fiery anger burst inside her chest and she almost ran at him, but he met her stare and his eyes were quiet and cold. He smiled again, but without warmth. "Go," he said.

She went first. Gowan was behind her. They walked out of the front door and round to the left. The bracken was broken down as if someone had been that way recently. Her heart hammered and there was cold sweat between her shoulder blades and on her throat.

She stopped. She didn't want to see. "What have you done with him?" she sobbed.

"Go and look," Gowan Fell said.

She shook her head.

"Go and look," he said again. But this time he prodded her back.

She gripped the knife harder. If he touched her again, she would stab him. She exhaled, then she stepped forward. She saw the pen made from stout wood and rope. It was dark in the shade of the hovel with the trees clustering round. She couldn't make anything out. The door stood half-open. She walked up to it. "Daddy?" she said.

There was no answer. She heard her breath. She stepped closer. "Daddy?" she said again.

Then Gowan Fell lunged forward and shoved her into the pen. Before she could react, he had pulled the door closed and fastened the rope lock.

Rebecca screamed. Her father was not there. She shook with rage and fear and took the knife and slashed at the wood and rope.

Gowan Fell said, "I need a maid, Rebecca, and you will be her, willingly or no."

"I have a knife. I will cut my way out."

Gowan Fell gave a low laugh. "You will stay here and work, or I will kill your entire family."

She looked in his evil wolf eyes and she dropped her father's knife. It fell to the earth with a thud.

Gowan let Rebecca out of her cage so that she could cook for him and clean his clothes when she had finished cooking. For the first few days he did not leave the hut, nor her. He watched her even when she was working and then on the second day he let her sleep on the floor of the hut. The pen at the back was becoming cold as summer fled.

At first Rebecca wondered whether he had some care for her still then she guessed it was because he did not want his servant to die of exposure.

Around four days after she first came back looking for her father, he left her to go into the woods. She thought then of running home, but she knew if he missed her on his return that he would come looking for her and she did not doubt that he would kill all her family. She hoped that her father was back at home and she longed to see him. She imagined an argument with her father wisely realising that Gowan Fell was younger and stronger and so would win any fight, after all it was only over a dolly.

She sat outside the hovel in the sunshine. The birds still flitted around her feet, but the sun now had the colour of old gold and the first leaves lay on the woodland paths. She detected a turn from green to brown in the trees and knew they would soon be yellow and red. She knew of an apple tree, not the sour crab apples but good eating apples that must have been planted long ago. She guessed it was too soon for them to be ripe but she thought she would go and look to see how long before she could pick them.

So she set off away from the hovel, down the deer path and instead of striking on the main forest road, rough as it was, she turned left and followed the stream. The water ran over smooth round stones beside her, clear and cold, not long down from the mountains. As she went, she was possessed by a great despair. She did not know how she would ever be free of Gowan Fell.

And then she smelled the stink of death.

Something was lying dead nearby. Perhaps an old badger or a dead crow. Her nose wrinkled, and she put her sleeve to cover her mouth and walked on. But as she continued on the path, she was walking towards the smell. And then she saw that the hazel bushes to the right were disturbed as if a large creature had stumbled that way. Or perhaps two creatures quarrelling and this was the end result. She had heard of stags fighting to the death, but it was too early in the season for that.

Her curiosity getting the better of her distaste, she stepped to the side of the path, moved some branches and saw the source of the gagging smell. A decayed corpse lay face down. She recognised the clothes instantly. It was her father. His face was pushed in the muddy grass and his back was ripped open. She saw that he had been partly eaten, as if a creature had begun to consume him but got bored and slunk away. She turned and was violently sick. Then she wailed, spinning around, shrieking her distress to the woods and the sky. She fell to her knees, banging her head with her fists. Tears ran down her cheeks and she cried, "Daddy, oh my daddy." And she knew Gowan Fell had killed her father. Either as man or as beast, he had killed him.

She stood and immediately wanted to go and find a shovel to dig her father a grave. There was one at the hovel. She ran to get it, but soon, after only a few yards, her head whirling, she realised that she was lost. Her grief overcame her, and she fell to her knees and sobbed while above her, crows called and the wind shifted in the tall trees. She remained there, her knees damp as the wet sods of grass soaked her dress. All she knew was the pain in her heart, and all for a doll, and all because she had gone with Gowan Fell because she had wanted to be free. Grief ripped her heart.

A cold rage possessed her. She stood. She was lost in the wildwood. She did not care that she was lost or if she would ever be found, but she had two tasks to complete. First, she had to bury her father, then she had to kill Gowan Fell.

She wandered, disorientated, until she came to the stream. She followed it down as it ran carelessly on. She was still in the oak wood but soon the ground underfoot became damper and the oaks gave way to other trees. There were ash trees and willow and aspen. Green rushes interspersed the soft grass and her feet sunk deeper. Then she came to a place where her small stream ran into another bigger one. The rocks that stuck out of the ground were granite and the micro crystals shone as the sun struck them. The water glittered and fish moved in the deep places of the confluence. And there in the middle of the water, like a boat cresting an endless wave, a rock of quartz stood. It was fissured and cracked, cloudy in places but the sun illuminated it and it gave back light like some sacred, magic thing.

And Rebecca remembered the goodwife, the flower face pedlar who had come calling and tried to sell her ribbons. This was the place she had mentioned: *'At the join of two streams; where the oaks give way to the ash and the aspen.'*

Rebecca stood by the bank and watched the rock sparkle in the light, then, without knowing why she did so, she hitched up her skirt and waded through the water. The water was cold, even in summer, because it was mountain water. It came to her knees and the rocks underfoot were slippery with weed and moved as she put her feet on them. Nevertheless, she made it across to the shining stone. There she hugged it as if it were a person and a rescuer. She felt it smooth under her hands and warm to the touch from the sunlight. She peered into it and saw in a million fractures and imperfections, a whole other universe. Her eyes tricked her into thinking she saw the form of Flower Face deep inside. And she prayed to her: "Mother of the Forests, give me my revenge on Gowan Fell."

But nothing happened. The water rushed by. The breeze moved across her cheek. Above the clouds shifted, and the sun shone. Swallows swooped low across the water, catching flies. And she laughed bitterly. There were no gods of the wood, no brother wolf, no sister moon, just objects - a dead universe peopled by foolish imagination. How had she thought a stone could help her? It wasn't even that the stone didn't care, or the trees or the birds. They were just things without mind or soul. And so another of her dreams left her.

Rebecca swallowed. She felt the lump still in her throat and the pain of grief in her chest, but her blood ran hot. One thing she vowed; she would have her revenge on Gowan Fell whether there were gods or not.

She picked her way across the stream's bed onto the bank and she let her wet skirts drop. From here, she knew her way back to the hut she shared with Gowan Fell. She walked slowly and listened to the singing of the birds but knew it was without meaning. And on her way, she came across a bank where honeysuckle and musk rose grew among white thorn and black. She stopped the smell the roses; beautiful even though they were meaningless. She plucked them; the thorns pricking her fingers. And she grasped a twine of honeysuckle and inhaled the sweet heady scent. She took a sprig of that too. As she walked, she held the two flowers in her hand. She no longer believed in love nor in the benign gods of water and wood. There is no one as empty as an idealist who has lost her belief. But instead of belief she now had hate. And it was hate that drove her now.

When she came home Gowan Fell was at the door, wearing his good clothes. His collar was loose and his waistcoat unfastened. "I thought I was going to have to come after you," he said with a wicked smile.

Rebecca stood, the rose and honeysuckle drooping in her hands. She couldn't meet his eye lest he see the hate in there and guess what she planned.

"Come in. It's time for you to cook." He stood aside from the door, the bright wicked eyes in his dark, bearded face, watching her every move. She breathed heavily and said, "I'm going to plant these first."

"Those dead flowers? They won't grow."

She nodded. "I will plant them first." And then, she thought, I will kill you.

He took a step towards her and grabbed her round the wrist. He squeezed until her fingers went white. She gritted her teeth to stop the cry of pain, but he was too strong, and she dropped the flowers.

He heeled the rose and the honeysuckle into the dirt with his boot. "You cook when I tell you to cook." He let go of her hand and then, as if an afterthought, he struck her across her face. "You do what I tell you when I tell you, bitch."

Rebecca felt the pressure of tears, but she would not let them come. She put her hand to her cheek to feel the heat of his blow and the throbbing of the pain. She bowed her head. Then he lifted his foot and with it, shoved her into the hovel.

By the area she used for cooking was fresh meat. It didn't look like the usual crow or rabbit that he managed to catch.

"What's this?" she asked.

"Pork." He was grinning smugly.

"Where did you get the money for this?" she said.

"I didn't need money. I got it from the butcher's wife. Meat for meat." He threw back his head and laughed.

Rebecca felt her stomach turn. She saw her father's knife that she had brought back into the kitchen days before. She wouldn't make the same mistake this time. She would wait until he was sleeping.

She saw there were also fresh vegetables and a bottle of foreign wine. Gowan had brought them all back from the fair at Hawkshead.

"More gifts?" she said. Her voice was cold.

He guffawed. Then he said, "So many ladies. So many things they want to give me."

"And did you kill them?"

His eyes narrowed. "No, not kill them. Sent them back to their husbands bruised and torn, but I didn't kill them."

Her voice was icy. "How do you decide whether to rape or kill?"

"Rape is a nasty word, Rebecca," he whispered. He came closer. "But be honest, you always preferred it when I was rough."

She tasted bile in her mouth. He ran a finger across the cheek he had recently struck. He was smiling.

She turned. "I'll cook," she said.

He grunted. "Pour me wine." Then he went to sit on his chair outside, as the afternoon became evening.

She fried the pork with vegetables. She was tempted to oversalt it but he would notice that. Instead, she spat in it though it gave her no satisfaction. Revenge for her father would need deeper injury than that.

She brought him the food as he sat outside, boots kicked off, shirt open to the sun that filtered through the yellowing leaves. Crows called from the branches of the oak behind the hovel. The rooks prepared to go to roost.

"Sit with me, Rebecca," he said, motioning a tree stump near where he sat on the sheepskin-covered chair.

She shook her head.

"Sit," he snarled.

"I have work to do in the garden; I need to weed the onions and garlic."

He snorted. "Go, weed the onions. Wash the dishes and then get in my bed to make it warm for when I come to you."

Without answering, Rebecca turned and went towards the small vegetable plot that she had so lovingly tended for him. As she passed, she stooped and picked up the wilting honeysuckle and the broken rose in a quick movement so he should not tell her to drop them and throw them away. She went out of his sight to where the garden was. There with her hands she scooped two holes in the damp earth and placed the plants in them. She stood them so they propped each other up, but they were sad and drooping and she knew they would die. It was the act itself. She had not thought to do it, some unconscious impulse had caused her to pluck them and carry them and plant them here.

Somehow, it seemed like something she should do to give herself hope. And when she had scooped the soil back into the holes to support the plants as best it could, she bowed her head. She prayed, "Mother of the Forest, though I no longer even believe in you, help me in my need. If you are there, help me in the way you know best. Deliver me from the power of Gowan Fell."

And then she heard a sound, opened her eyes and turned and there he was standing behind her, a look of cruel mockery on his face. "Praying to your silly wood spirits are you? I will never release you from my power until you are dead. And when you die, it will be because I have a better maid, and I will kill you with my own hands."

He grabbed her long blonde hair, and he yanked her to her feet backwards, stumbling. Then he kicked her forward and when she fell, he grabbed her upper arm to drag her into the hovel. Once in the hovel he said, "Wash my plates. And when you're done, take off your clothes."

He went over to the bed and stood by it, pulling off his trousers. She washed his plate but kept an eye on him and when he pulled his shirt over his head and could not see; she took the knife and put it in the pocket in her woollen dress.

He stood there naked. "Done?" he said.

She nodded.

"Here," he said pointing to his feet. She walked towards him.

"Take off your dress," he ordered.

She quietly disrobed, but dropped the dress and the knife it concealed close enough to the bed so she could grab it without stretching.

She stood there bare in front of him. He looked her up and down. She moved to cover her breasts and her pubis but he pushed her arms away.

"You are mine to look at." Then he snorted. "Not bad. I can see why I chose you."

He gestured to the bed. "Get in."

She knelt and then got into the bed. Before he got in with her she said, "Gowan, did you ever love me?"

"I only love myself," he said.

"But you said that I was special, that I was the one." Her voice sounded weak.

He laughed and said, "Girls should never believe what men tell them."

Then he lay on her. Her forced her knees apart. She put her arm between her teeth and bit so she would not cry. She knew she would have to endure this. Then, when he slept, she would kill him.

When he had sated himself and was snoring, his arm drooping out of the bed, Rebecca lay awake. She monitored the sound of his breathing to make sure he slumbered. Then she inched her hand towards the dress and the knife within it. She moved it an inch, and he stirred. So she waited. Then when his breathing deepened, she moved again, her fingers crawling over the cool hard clay floor like a spider. She found the rough edge of the woollen dress and pulled it towards her with her finger ends. Then he turned and muttered. She stopped and his breathing grew heavy again. This time she dragged the dress and when it was close enough, she felt for the opening of the pocket. She reached in and felt the wooden handle of the kitchen knife. The wood was smooth. Her heart became electric with fear and hope. Her breathing grew more rapid.

She closed her finger ends on the knife haft, and then without warning he struck her heavily on the forehead. "Sleep bitch," he said. Her vision flashed yellow and blue from the blow. She withdrew her hand, bit her lip and waited.

Outside the sky was dark. No moon rode the clouds yet. Later it would rise, but no longer full. He breathed heavily. And she waited. He turned over and his arm flopped. She waited still. Then his chest rose in a regular rhythm and his snores came repeatedly. Her hand drifted towards the knife, and she clasped the hilt. She brought it to her chest and still she didn't move. She lay there with the knife in her hand staring at the dark ceiling. If any help was coming from the gods, then this was the time — some miracle to stop her from having to kill. But she realised that was just cowardice.

She wanted him dead; she wanted revenge — she was just too scared to do it herself. She waited still as if divine intervention was on its way. She heard the wind in the trees outside. She held her breath and then turned on her left side; the knife clasped in her right hand. Her hand was sweaty on the grip. She held it so tight her fingers started to go numb and then quietly she raised it. She would stab him in the throat.

She saw his dark shape beside her. He was on his back. She could see his nose and beard silhouetted. She took the knife high and brought it down with all her strength. But before it struck, she held it back. She gasped. She was no killer. But he was. He woke out of sleep instantly and smashed her hand away, sending the blade spinning into the dark room.

Then he heaved her out of bed, lifting her with both hands and throwing her across the room. She smashed into the table and she knew she was injured. He covered the ground in an instant. He picked her up with both hands and raised her to slam her against the turf wall of the cottage. He held her there while he drew his head back and butted her - breaking her nose. The pain flashed through her and blood ran down the back of her mouth and from her nostrils, making it hard for her to breathe. She threshed her head this way and that but he had her by the throat.

"You whore," he snarled. "That's what I get for trusting you."

Then he dropped her. She fell heavily to the ground. "You're lucky I need someone to clean for me. But from now on you'll be wearing a rope round your ankle to stop you getting up to any mischief." He took her and bundled her naked out of the door, back to the dog pen. "And this is where you'll always sleep." He shook his head, as if in regret. "To think I let you share my bed," he said. He threw her into the pen and roped the door shut. "I'm just too good natured," he said. Then he spat. "You won't take advantage of me again that way," and he turned and walked away.

The pain in Rebecca's nose was like someone digging a hole in her face with an axe. She couldn't sleep because of it and she saw the dawn crawl up through the trees to the east. Inside, Gowan Fell slept on. She heard him snore. She gripped tight onto the wooden poles that made up her cage. Half-congealed clots of blood came out of her mouth and she gingerly wiped them away to avoid jolting the broken bone. Her own dried blood smeared her chest. She bowed her head against them. Gowan Fell had won and her father would lie their rotting in the wood with no one to revenge him.

HE OPENED the door of her pen around mid-day. "Cook," he said.

"I have nothing to cook with." Her voice sounded strange because he had broken her nose.

Seeing the mess, he said, "Wash your hands before you touch my food." He prodded her to the door of the hut. Inside, there was a ewer of stream water that she herself had carried. She would have to fetch more for him later. While she washed her hands and tried to clean her face, he made a rough loop of rope and pulled it tight around her right ankle. He tied the other end to the cruck that held up the hovel, bedded deep in the ground. She couldn't move it.

He threw her a dead rabbit. "Skin that."

"The knife…" she said.

He stooped and picked it up from the floor where it had landed when he knocked it out of her hand. "You should know by now Rebecca, there is no weapon that will allow you to best me. If you try to misuse the knife again, I will break your fingers one by one and then I will snap your wrist. Do you understand?"

She nodded. Her nose was agony.

"Can I put my dress on?" She asked.

He shook his head. "It suits me to watch you naked."

So she skinned the rabbit. She said, "I need onions, from the garden."

He grunted, displeased, but then untied the rope. He watched her as she went into the garden and followed her as she went to the vegetable patch. There, to her amazement, the honeysuckle and the rose were growing. They had rooted overnight in some miracle and grew twisted around each other. She gasped.

"What?" he said.

"I stepped on a stone. It hurt."

"Weakling." He laughed, but he accepted the explanation. She gathered some onions from the dirt and brought them back to the hovel under his watchful eye. Just as she turned the corner, she glanced back at the rose and honeysuckle, unable to believe they were growing where she'd planted them.

She made him food, and he ate it greedily. He offered her none.

She asked, "What about me? I must eat if I am to work."

He shook his head. "Not yet. You're not hungry enough yet," and he sent her naked back to her pen.

THE PAIN in her nose was still there but had lessened so she got some sleep. The next few days were the same until it was time for him to put on his fair clothes and go back to Hawkshead hunting for women.

He made her cook him porridge for breakfast, sweetened with honey she had collected from a bees' nest in the tree near the little hill before he imprisoned her. He was there in his finery and she still naked, covered in dirt with the remains of her smeared blood on her face and chest. He let her scrape out the porridge bowl and sneered as she gobbled it hungrily.

It was then that there was a knock at the rough door of the cottage.

"Who's there?" snarled Gowan Fell.

A woman's voice answered. "I am looking for the charcoal burner." Rebecca saw the interest in Gowan's face when he heard a female voice, though she knew he had no time for women he considered unattractive and would treat them badly.

"I am the charcoal burner, Gowan Fell," he said, and he opened the door.

A young woman with orange red hair and green eyes stood there. She was of medium height but slim. Rebecca saw Gowan's eyes measure up her figure. He smiled. He must like what he saw, she thought. The woman wore a white gown. Rebecca wondered how it was not covered with mud and moss from being in the wood. The woman looked first at Gowan and smiled. then she glanced around the room and met Rebecca's eyes. Rebecca put her hands to cover herself and she looked down. What must this beauty think of her standing, naked, dirty and bloodied, with black eyes and a livid purple bruise across her face? But the woman said nothing.

Gowan stepped outside and half closed the door. Rebecca couldn't see them now but she could hear. He said, "And what does a lady in her fine clothes want with a charcoal burner?"

"My father sent me with an errand. He owns a smokery in the village and has contracts with Lowthers to provide them smoked meat. But our usual supplier let us down so he sent me here to find you."

"He sent a pretty thing like you into the forest on her own?" Gowan flirted with her. "He was risking something valuable."

Rebecca heard the woman laugh. "I'm not frightened of the forest, Gowan Fell. I was born here. It cares for me."

"It's not the Forest, you should be frightened of," said Gowan Fell.

"Then what?"

"Me."

She laughed again. "And what harm would you do me, Gowan Fell?"

He said, "Only what you secretly want me to do."

The woman laughed again, but lower. "So you are interested in my father's contract?"

"I'm more interested in his daughter."

"You'll have to woo me," she said.

"I can do that. I have what all women want."

"We shall see about that. Can you sing me a song?"

He laughed. "I'm no bard. I'm a real man not a song maker."

"Can you make things with your hands from wood?"

"No, but I can break them easily enough."

"In the village they say you have a secret," she said.

"Oh?" Rebecca could hear the self-love in his voice. He would think it was a compliment.

"Yes," the woman said, "They say you are one of the Folk."

Gowan paused but did not deny it, then said, "And you would like that - to be taken by a wolf?"

She said, "Come for a walk with me."

"Where?"

"There is a place where the two streams meet, where the oak gives way to the ash. There is a stone shot with crystal that stands in the water."

"I know it. But I won't go there. That place is full of witchery."

"Walk some way into the woods with me then. There is a place before that one, where we can lie down."

"I like the sound of that. Let's go."

Rebecca heard the eagerness in his voice.

"But the girl," the woman said, "The one you keep naked in your hut. Will she be safe?"

"Safer without me than with me," he said. "Besides, she is just a maid. If anything happened to her, you could take her place."

Rebecca didn't hear the woman's reply, but she heard Gowan Fell's laughter as he followed her into the forest.

EVEN WITH THEM GONE, Rebecca was still stuck - tied by her ankle. She couldn't untie the knot because he'd made it fast with his beast strength. But then she remembered her father's knife. In his eagerness to be with the woman, Gowan had forgotten it was there.

The rope was long enough to get to the table where the knife lay. She cut the rope with the knife, found her dress, and put it on. She took Kirsten's dolly from where it lay in the dirt and she stuffed it in her pocket. She gazed at her dead father's knife in her hand. She'd been a fool to trust her own strength and cleverness when she'd try to kill him. She knew now she couldn't beat him on her own. She thought of running home. There she would get men of the hamlet where her mother and sister were and she would tell them that Gowan Fell was a wolf and that he murdered women and he had killed her own dear father. Then they would return with fire and strong as he was, he couldn't beat all of them.

But then she thought of the poor woman. She might just be another foolish girl, but she was not safe in the woods with Gowan Fell, no matter how clever or strong she thought she was. He was a beast and his strength would overcome her. Rebecca couldn't leave her to suffer as he'd made her suffer. She began to run to her own hamlet to get help. But she had not gone far before she realised that she could not get to the hamlet and get back with help before Gowan would have done what he wanted to the woman. So when she got to where the paths split, instead of running home, she went into the woods. The knife was in her hand. Rebecca knew she had to try to save the girl, even if she died in the attempt.

So she ran as quietly as she could along the woodland path towards the crystal stone and the confluence of the two streams. And then she heard laughter, both a man's and a woman's. She slowed down and went quietly. She shifted the knife into a downward grip, the better to stab him with, but her hand was shaking and she doubted she could do it. She thought of just grabbing the girl and pulling her after her to safety. But he was fast. He ran with a wolf's speed. She feared he would catch them, but she could not let another innocent suffer at his hand.

She was close to them now. They were through a screen of brushwood; hazel and ground elder blocked the way, and the path went round to the right. If she went right, he would see her but if she didn't go right, she wouldn't be able to help the girl.

So she went right, slowly to the edge of the bush. She peered ahead. The girl was lying down. She had taken off her robe and was naked. Rebecca saw the copper red hair on her pubis and the milk white of her bare skin. Her orange mane lay around her head like a shower of fire. Gowan Fell was taking off his deerskin shirt.

The girl caught her eye. But she didn't cry out. There was a message in the look. A message not to approach. Rebecca stood stock-still.

Then Gowan turned and saw her.

He snarled. "Rebecca, and with her father's trusty knife too. You've tried twice before to kill me with that old blade. You won't succeed now and then, as I promised, I will break each finger and then snap your wrist. I will bend your neck round until you die, because I have a new maid now."

Rebecca said, "I'm not frightened of you, Gowan Fell," but her voice stammered. She held the knife in front of her but her hand shook.

He turned and picked up a rock. Then he advanced toward her. With a scream, she ran at him, slashing wildly. He easily grabbed her wrist with his left hand and then, with his right, he punched her stomach hard, knocking the wind out of her. He twisted her hand until she dropped the knife on the mossy floor. Then he put his powerful grip to her throat. She looked into his dark eyes as he began to choke the life out of her.

Over his shoulder, as her sight began to dim, she saw the woman stand. Gowan choked tighter and Rebecca heard her own breath gurgle. She feared she was dying.

But over Gowan's shoulder, Rebecca saw the woman's legs grow into roots and reached into the ground, anchoring her there. And then her arms became tendrils like the tendrils of honeysuckle, and her face became the bloom of a rose, surrounded by thorny briars. The tendrils spread across the floor, like a living forest and began to run and twine around Gowan Fell's legs. He turned, shouted and let go of Rebecca's throat. She fell back, gasping, stars bursting in her eyes.

Rebecca watched as the flower woman grew around Gowan Fell. He began to yell in terror as the tendrils ran up his legs past his knees. He struggled, but he was stuck fast now. And the briars covered with leaves and sweet roses reached around his shoulders and began to wrap around his neck and up to his face. He screamed.

And then the tendrils began to grow into him, puncturing his clothes and his body, running their plant life into the spaces of his bowels. The rose briar grew into his mouth and into his nose and the honeysuckle wrapped him round like a lover. The thorns ripped his skin and his blood ran red over the fresh green tendrils of the plant. And then the embrace of the flower woman trapped him, and she was kissing him with her honeysuckle and her fresh red roses, squeezing the life from his lungs.

And the flower faced woman kissed Gowan Fell to death, her green life entering into his skull and wrapping around his brain. Gowan Fell shrieked as the last life left him and he hung like a sacrifice in the arms of the flowers.

Rebecca saw his death. Saw the wolf slain by the rose. Revenge for her dead father, and the revenge of plant over animal.

Rebecca stood, afraid that the flower woman would take her too, for was she not an animal too? But the tree grew no more. The glade was filled with the scent of honeysuckle and roses and bees came to buzz around the flowers that took their nourishment from Gowan Fell.

Rebecca heard the voice of the flower woman. A voice she had prayed to hear but had thought was only silence, or a sound as meaningless as the noise of the river and the rain or the breeze through the trees. But these noises have their own meaning. The voice of the wildwood spoke to her on the rustle of the wind and in the drone of the bees and it seemed to say that strength was beaten not by strength, but by beauty.

And Rebecca left the glade and went to bury her father. Then she returned home to her mother and sister, and they lived at peace, because the evil of Gowan Fell was done for good.

15

THE DERWENTWATER HAUNTING

I made a lot of money and retired early. After leaving London we went up to live in the English Lake District - my wife Annie was from there. We drove the three hundred miles there one day in February, me and Annie and Benjamin in the back. Benjamin, my son, is five and the apple of my eye. Also in the car with us was Spot the dog and a mournful Cap'n Flint, the parrot, in his cage with a cover over it.

The rest of our possessions came up with professional house movers. Our maid Manuelita was following us in another car. Though she was tremendously superstitious and highly strung she was also the best maid I'd ever had. She was bringing her niece Victoria over from Madrid to be our cook for the year.

Twenty-five years of foreign exchange trading had burned me out. I'd set up my own company, made it a success and then sold it for a killing. I was looking forward to the clean air and the beautiful scenery and a chance to rest. I also planned to write my memoirs. Annie was looking forward to being closer to her parents, and I knew they would enjoy seeing more of Benji.

When I saw the house, I loved it. Annie said I was being extravagant but I could afford it so why not? It was a house on an island in the middle of Derwentwater lake, near Keswick. There was a stunning view looking down from the front of the house, past the lake and into the rocky jaws of the valley behind. The art critic Ruskin called it the third most beautiful view in Europe.

A trust owned the house, so we couldn't buy it, only rent it. It was over £1 million a year but it was worth it to me, and I figured that we could get a regular house after one blissful year in the mansion on the island.

Everything arrived from London, as well as some extras I'd had to buy both there and locally. The day came, and we moved in. A generator housed in a hut behind the house supplied our electricity and I arranged with a local firm that they would come as required and maintain that as well as do any repairs and odd-jobs.

When we first got off the boat onto the island, the dog started behaving stupidly. Old Spot wouldn't go in the house at first; he just stood at the door growling.

"What's up with him?" I said.

Annie laughed. "I bet a big nasty dog used to live here and he can smell it."

With much tugging, we dragged him in but he started whimpering. In the end I arranged for him to have a kennel outside - that would teach him to be histrionic.

There were only five of us on the island: me and Annie and Benjamin as well as Manuelita and Victoria, and that suited me. I wanted peace to write. The town of Keswick was close by but far enough away over the water so it didn't bother us. There were lots of tourists in the Lake District, but they didn't get to come to our island, as there were big "Keep Out" and "Private" signs dotted all around the shore. It was so peaceful that we could have been miles away from civilization.

Sometimes the weather cut us off too. The winter still hung on and now and then the lake water was too rough for us to motor over in our little boat. I didn't mind, but Annie had a fear about the water and she always made sure she and Benji had life jackets on.

To begin with, I was very happy there.

The first disturbances came from Manuelita who claimed the

place was haunted. Over breakfast one morning, she started going on about the ghost.

"But you haven't seen anything?" I said. "That's right, isn't it?" I gave her a hard time, and I regretted it afterwards.

Manuelita said, "No, I haven't seen anything, Mr. Dougan. But I feel it all the time. It is all around this house."

I shook my head. "It's psychology, Manuelita; it's an old house. No one can come and rescue us easily on the island - not that they need to - but that's why you are feeling uneasy. You'll settle."

She gave an exasperated Hispanic shrug and walked off. Victoria had come up behind her and she smiled and made a screwy gesture at her temple. "She's loca, Mr. Dougan. My grandmother - her mother - has, how do you say, the second sight?' Victoria shrugged. 'But I don't believe any of it."

I frowned. "It's important that Benji doesn't get frightened. I don't want her repeating these things to him."

"Sure," said Victoria, "I'll talk to her."

Annie was late rising that morning. Victoria had taken her breakfast in bed after I got up. I came across her in the conservatory that was at the front of the house. She was sitting there reading among the orange trees in their pots with a blanket over her knees.

"Hello you," I said, bending down to kiss her.

She reached up and kissed me back. We have a good relationship. We're best friends as well as being husband and wife. She's supported me all the way through my sometimes difficult career. I told her about Manuelita.

She shuddered. "I don't want her talking like that in front of Benji."

"I've emphasized that to Victoria. She's going to speak to her."

"You know I have a thing about ghosts," said Annie. "The very idea of them terrifies me."

It surprised me. In all the years we'd been married, I don't think she'd ever mentioned her fear of ghosts. But then I didn't recall the subject coming up.

I had taken Benji out on the lake that day - me and him and Spot.

He wanted to take Cap'n Flint too and pretend we were pirates, but I said the parrot would just fly off. He was a mean-tempered bird too; he'd probably savage the ducks.

This day it was a Saturday. Benji went to the local school every week morning by boat; either me or Victoria would take him over. But at the weekends we had him all to ourselves. Instead of the motorboat, I took one of the rowing boats from the boathouse that belonged to our island. Annie hadn't wanted to let Benji go on the lake when we first arrived because he couldn't swim. I arranged for him to have lessons at the local pool in town to put her mind at rest. Rowing was good exercise for me and though Benji pleaded with me to let him have a go, I wouldn't let him - he just wasn't strong enough.

We rowed over to the small, rocky islands that dotted the lake here and there. Spot went crazy barking at the gulls that nested on some of the islands. I think he was enjoying being away from the house. Above us rose the mountains. The wind wasn't too strong, just a few little waves to made the boat bob. Benji loved it when the little boat lifted her bow to crest the waves.

For the time of the year, the weather wasn't too bad; there was the hint of spring in the air - but not enough so we could take our coats off. We moored at an island, slightly bigger than the rest that had a clump of trees and friendly ducks that came quacking round, looking for morsels. I had to tie Spot up, so he didn't eat the crumbs we threw for the ducks.

The exercise tired me out. I guess Benji was tired too because he didn't protest about going to bed and was soon slumbering. After reading my book about Cryptocurrencies, I must have fallen asleep about ten thirty. Annie was beside me, reading her novel. I dozed off before she did.

I woke when she screamed. I almost jumped out of my skin. It was the middle of the night and pitch black. I snapped the bedside light on. She was lying there, her eyes wide, rigid and trembling. I said, "What the hell is the matter?"

She shuddered. "I had a horrible dream. I dreamt that there was someone in the house — someone who didn't belong here."

She was beautiful. And fragile. I stroked her hair. "It's just a nightmare, Annie. That's all."

"No, it was something evil. It wanted to take Benji, and I was fighting it."

I made soothing noises. She took my hand and smiled hesitantly. "I'm so silly, I know. But it felt real — as if something really was here in the house."

"You've been listening to Manuelita too much."

She shook her head. "I know you said she'd spoken to you, but she's never mentioned anything to me."

"Good. That must be Victoria putting her straight," I said.

But Annie still looked uneasy. "Will you check on Benji?"

"Of course," I said, wondering why she didn't go herself. Not that I minded, but she was usually so protective of him - overprotective sometimes. And then I realized she was frightened to walk through the house on her own.

I got up out of bed and pulled on a t-shirt and jogging bottoms. Then I made my way along the corridor. The house was big — far bigger than we needed. The floor we slept on had six bedrooms though we only occupied two — me and Annie in one, and two doors away —Benji's. We'd put him in this room because it had a lovely view of the lake and just felt nicer.

Victoria and Manuelita had their bedrooms on the floor above. The very top floor was the attic, but we had hardly even visited it.

As I got to Benji's door, I stopped and turned. I had the strong feeling someone was there. I spun round. "Hello?" I said.

"Hello," replied Victoria in her distinctive Spanish accent. "I heard Mrs. Dougan scream. I just wondered if everything was ok." She was standing at the bottom of the stairs up in just her nightie. Her hair was tousled, and it looked like she'd just woken.

I laughed. "Yeah, just Annie having a nightmare. Don't worry. I just came to check it didn't wake Benji."

I looked into Benji's room. He was sleeping soundly.

Victoria lingered there. She seemed on edge.

"What's up?" I said.

"It's Manuelita — she's got me scared now."

I smiled indulgently. "How come?"

"She says there's a thing in this house. When I heard Mrs. Dougan cry out, it made me think maybe she'd seen it too."

'Who — Annie?'

She nodded.

I shook my head. "No, she hasn't seen anything. There's nothing to see." I tried to reassure her. "Listen, it's the middle of the night. Things will feel fine in the morning. Is Manuelita awake now?"

Victoria nodded. "She's sitting up in bed with her rosaries, calling on Mary and Jesus and all the saints to protect her." She stifled a sudden giggle. At least we'd broken the lingering heavy atmosphere.

"Ok," I said, "sleep tight, and remember, there are no such things as ghosts."

THEN THINGS WERE ok for a couple of days. The next time, a commotion above our bedroom woke me. It woke Annie too. "What's that?" she said with a tremor in her voice. "That banging."

"I don't know," I said, getting up and once again dressing. It was weird, but I was convinced there was a normal explanation for the sound.

Annie said, "Make sure Benji's safe."

The way she said it was like a command. I nearly told her to check him herself but I could see she was frightened, so I just went. I scooped Benji up and took him to his mother. He was sleepy and grumpy with his hair all mussed up but she took him and then there was another bang and a sound of furniture being moved above.

"For God's sake!" I muttered. I hurried out of the room and jogged up the stairs, flicking the lights on as I went. Victoria's door was open but Manuelita's was closed. I knocked on Victoria's room but there was no answer. She didn't seem to be in there. Then I knocked on Manuelita's door. A frightened voice said something in Spanish.

"Manuelita it's Howard! Are you ok?"

There was a shuffling and the sound of someone getting out of bed and then the scraping of furniture being moved just behind the door. It opened and there stood Manuelita in her nightdress. She had barricaded the door with the chest of drawers. To my greater surprise, there also was Victoria, huddled in Manuelita's bed with a look of fear on her face.

"Please tell me what's happening here?" I asked stonily.

Manuelita said, "Victoria heard it; she heard it outside on the landing."

I looked to Victoria for confirmation. She was obviously terrified. "Victoria, what's going on?"

I could see her eyes were filled with tears. She said, "I woke up. I don't know why, Mr. Dougan, but I was very frightened. There was an atmosphere in my room, but there was nothing there. Nothing I could see. Then I heard something outside. For a minute I thought it might be Benji sleepwalking. So I went to the door."

"Hang on a minute - Benji sleepwalking? Benji doesn't sleepwalk."

Both the women nodded. "Yes, he does. Not every night, but he comes up here, and he is asleep. We just take him back to his room."

I was astounded. "You've both done this?"

They said they both had.

"Why didn't you tell me?"

Manuelita shrugged. "Mrs. Dougan is very nervous and protective. We thought he would grow out of it so no need to tell you."

My brow furrowed. "Ok, I'm not happy about this, but why the hell have you barricaded yourselves in the room?"

Victoria continued. "So I went to look outside, in case it was Benji walking."

"But?"

Manuelita said, "She saw it - the thing. I have felt it, but she saw it."

"God give me strength." I turned to Victoria. "What did you see?"

She shuddered. Then she said, "It was like a black shape. It was moving outside. The temperature was very cold and the feeling very bad. Very evil."

"It was a fantasma - a demonio," said Manuelita.

"You expect me to believe this?" I said. I was angry but I could see that they certainly thought it was true. They were nervous as hell.

"Ok, I said. It's late. We can talk about it again in the morning."

I turned away and Manuelita closed the door and I heard her move the chest of drawers in front of it again. I shook my head in disbelief at their stupid superstitions and credulity.

But as I walked down the stairs, something caught my attention. I couldn't say what, but I spun round. There was nothing there of course. But a strange feeling of anxiety came over me, as if there was some threat in the house I wasn't aware of. Then I dismissed the weird feeling and went back to Annie.

In the morning, Manuelita told me she couldn't stay in the house anymore.

"You are a good man, Mr. Dougan, but this is una casa poseída - there is something wicked that lives here."

"So where will you go?" I said. I was mortified at the idea of losing Manuelita.

"I can get a lodging in the town. I will come every day, but I will not sleep here. And you should not also. Not with that little boy."

"Leave Benji out of this," I snapped, suddenly angry at her for bringing him into her stupid fears. Instead of being upset at my tone, Manuelita came and held my hands in a gesture of comfort. "Please, think on what I say. Leave and we will all be safe."

I turned to Victoria and said coldly, "And what about you?"

Victoria looked sheepish. She looked first at me and then at Manuelita. She said, "I will stay."

Manuelita exploded in a torrent of angry Spanish. I guessed she was telling the girl not to be so stupid, that she was putting herself at great danger and all of that baloney. With lots of hand gestures, Victoria explained herself right back. I was glad that she was staying.

And then I had to explain to Annie why Manuelita was going. We sat in the library and drank coffee that Victoria had brought us. Benji was at school. Behind us Cap'n Flint squawked his usual inanities about 'Pretty Polly' and 'Pieces of Eight' that Benji had taught him.

"I don't understand," said Annie when I told her; "I thought she liked us."

"She does," I said soothingly. "She's just a crazy middle-aged woman."

"So why is she going?"

I sighed. "She thinks the house is haunted. She thinks she saw something. Or rather that Victoria saw something. I mean, she didn't even see it herself!"

"Where did she see it?"

"Does it matter? Up on their floor. But there was nothing there, really."

A cloud passed over Annie's face. "I've thought I've seen something here in this house," she said finally.

I was exasperated - Annie too now. I exhaled. "It's nothing. We're all getting a little crazy. It's an old house. It creaks. It's big, it makes noises. The wind and rain make you think you hear things, but you don't."

She nodded. "I know. It's irrational. You're right."

"Thank you," I said. I loved that house on the lake and I didn't want my year of bliss to get spoiled by the crazy imaginings of a Spanish maid.

"But you know, I am scared of ghosts," said Annie.

"Yeah, you told me."

"Do you know why?"

"Nope," I said, taking a sip of coffee.

She laughed, but it wasn't a convincing laugh - almost as if she was trying to make herself feel better about something. She began, "Did I ever tell you about my twin - Amy?"

I nodded. "I knew you had a twin who died."

"That's right. We were about Benji's age. She drowned."

"I think I knew that." Feeling I'd been a bit of a dick and insensitive, I squeezed her hand.

"I still miss her. After all these years. Odd isn't it? But twins are close. It felt like a part of me had died. And I still think there's a hole in me where she should be." She started to cry softly.

I stroked her hand. "Yeah, but that's nothing to do with ghosts. There's no connection with this house."

"Well, it wasn't a ghost, really. It started off that she began to sleepwalk."

My heart froze. I hadn't told her about Benji. I certainly wouldn't now.

"My mum and dad would find Amy wandering all over the house. But mostly she went upstairs. She appeared very disturbed by it. She couldn't remember afterwards but she kept talking about 'grandfather'."

"Grandfather?"

Annie nodded. "When we were little, my dad's dad was still alive. He was a lovely man. But my mother's father was dead. Naturally my parents asked Amy to describe this grandfather she claimed to see around the house. Her description matched with my mum's dad."

"But surely her grandfather wouldn't want to hurt her? Surely if it was a ghost, he'd want to protect her."

Annie smiled thinly. "My maternal grandfather was a nasty man. He beat his wife and..."

She paused as if finding something difficult to say.

"And what?"

Her mouth wrinkled in distaste. "She said he was into black magic. That he had some kind of occult room in the basement. They lived in the marshlands in East Anglia. The basement was often flooded so that was his excuse why he wouldn't let people in there. But they say he spoke to the Devil. He drowned himself in the marsh in the end. Just when the police were closing in on him."

"What a freak," I said.

Annie nodded. "He was a disgusting man. Kids went missing in the neighbourhood. They never proved anything against him because he died, but people thought he'd taken them."

I felt suddenly sick. "But how is this related to Amy?"

"The sleepwalking got worse. My parents would find her upstairs in the attic. She said that Grandfather had told her to go there — that he wanted to play with her."

"He was already dead at this time?"

She nodded.

"Amy sleepwalking — how long was this before she died?" I felt awful asking her the question.

"About a month. They tried locking our bedroom door to keep her in. I would usually sleep through it, but sometimes I would wake up and see Amy standing in the room. I tried to talk to her, but she was asleep."

"Did you never see anything yourself?"

She shook her head.

"Then why didn't he come for you too?"

She laughed again. "You make it sound like you believe he really did come back from beyond the grave."

"Of course I don't."

"And then one night, I woke, and Amy was gone. The door — which my parents had locked — was open. I got up and saw that the front door was open too — our house wasn't very big. I woke my dad up. He was frantic — beside himself, as was my mum. They both went outside with torches and shouted for her. The neighbours helped them search, but they didn't find her."

She went quiet.

I said, "So who found her?"

"The Police the next day. She'd gone to the river. She was dead."

Annie broke down in sobs. I went to comfort her. "Don't worry, my love — that was then. This is now. Nothing bad is going to happen to my family. I won't let it."

I didn't like to admit it but I was unnerved myself. The whole atmosphere of the place changed - from being my getaway dream — it started to feel like a heavy, sullen place. Spot still wouldn't come in the house, and I wondered if he had always sensed something there.

I brought Benji's bed into our bedroom so I could monitor his sleepwalking. I didn't tell Annie why I'd done it.

. . .

ONE SUNDAY, Benji wasn't at school and he'd been talking to Cap'n Flint in the library trying to teach him new words. Manuelita had come over, even though Sunday was normally her day off because she and Victoria were planning to go back to London in the week for a break.

Annie was watching Breaking Bad on Netflix — at least our Internet connection was fast — and telling Benji off when he was trying to teach the parrot to say 'bum' and 'wee'.

I was half aware from the radio that played in my study, that there was a storm brewing. When it hit, it came suddenly blowing up the lake and the treetops round the house thrashed around. The grey waves started to break against the rocky shore of the island. I heard the wind push against the window in wild gusts and it started to rain heavily.

One of the windows in the library hadn't been fastened properly, and it blew open with a huge rush of air, scattering papers and making the parrot shriek. When I heard, I ran through from my study to see Annie trying to pick up the newspaper she'd read earlier. Benji was clapping his hands in delight at the parrot's terror. The rain was coming in. I closed the window creating a sudden calm inside even while the tempest blew outside.

"What an awful wind," said Annie. "Where did that come from?"

"It was forecast," I said. "I heard it on the radio. Still, we've got everything we need."

Annie said, "But Manuelita won't be happy. We won't be able to take her back to the town jetty — not with these waves."

"Well, she'll just have to stay here. You never know, she might have got over her silliness by now."

"Will the dog be okay outside?" asked Annie

"I guess he'll just hunker down in his kennel till the wind stops."

"I hope he's not scared."

"I'll go out and see him," I said.

I put on my coat and got a handful of dog biscuits as a treat. I pulled up my collar against the rain and I went over to the kennel.

Spot didn't like bad weather, and he was a bit of a coward, so I'd fully expected to find him cowering in his kennel. But he wasn't.

"Hmm - a mystery," I said to myself. I knew he couldn't get far on the island and I certainly not in this rain.

When I got back Annie asked if Spot was all right.

"Couldn't find him," I said.

"What?" she said, sounding concerned.

"It's an island. He'll be somewhere close by sheltering."

"I hope he hasn't gone in the lake."

"Spot's not exactly clever," I said, "but he's not stupid either."

THE WEATHER DIDN'T IMPROVE. The day was so dark and heavy that soon we had to put the lights on. As predicted Manuelita was very unhappy about having to stay in the house.

"I do not want to stay!" she said.

"I can't take you over in the boat in this weather," I said. "It's not safe."

"I'll take my chances," she said.

"But I won't Manuelita. That's the end of it. Sleep in Victoria's room."

Victoria came and put her arms round her aunt, cooing to her comfortingly in Spanish.

"It's ok, Mr. Dougan," said Victoria. "I will make sure she is ok."

"Of course she'll be ok!" I said. "What do you think could happen to her?"

Victoria shrugged and the two of them went back to the kitchen.

Benji was now watching TV with his mother in the library. We got our signal from a satellite, but the rain was so heavy that the picture kept breaking up. Giving up on that, we put on a DVD of the Disney hit - Frozen. That kept him quiet. He and Annie watched it while I was looking up stock prices on the Internet. Old habits die hard I guess. Even Cap'n Flint was quiet for a change.

It was about 8 pm and very dark outside when the next thing happened.

I heard Spot barking outside. "What is that bloody dog doing?" I said.

"Go and get him in Howard. It's horrible out there," said Annie.

I got up. "Silly bloody animal, if he'll come in."

I went to the front door. Manuelita was already there staring out into the dark. The rain was running down the glass panel. I could still hear Spot but couldn't see him. I opened the door and the wildness of the wind hit me. I strained to hold the door from being blown back.

"Spot!" I shouted. "Spot!" but I couldn't see him.

He sounded like he was barking at something.

"There's a man out there Mr. Dougan," said Manuelita from behind me.

"A man?"

"An evil man," she said.

I shook my head in disbelief then I ignored her terrified eyes and shouted for the dog louder this time. I thought about going out looking for him but the rain was horizontal and it was dark. I wouldn't see him. If he wanted to stay outside and play silly buggers that was up to him. I closed the door.

"I feel frightened for the dog," said Manuelita.

I just looked at her then walked past and went to hang up my dripping coat.

Frozen was nearly finished. "It's time for Benji's bed," I said.

Annie nodded. "I'll put him in the bath first." She got up. Manuelita, who had been sitting watching the movie, said she would go with her.

"Where's Victoria?" I asked.

"She's in the kitchen baking," said Manuelita. Then they all went out leaving me and the parrot. I swear Cap'n Flint was skittish too. He kept running up and down the wooden pole in his cage and clashing his beak against the metal bars.

"Can you pack that in?" I shouted at him, but he just kept running up and down. In the end, I put his cover over the cage to make him think it was night. But even then I could hear his sad squawking from inside it.

I got up and poured myself a whisky. What a night. The weather was making everyone crazy.

And then the generator failed.

The whole house was suddenly plunged into darkness. I pulled out my phone and used the flashlight function to light my way to the kitchen. Victoria was standing there, fumbling around to find the candles. She looked terrified.

"It's only the generator. Get the candles and then when I make sure everyone is ok, I'll go and see what the problem is."

We found some candles and there were plenty of candlesticks. I guessed that power outages were pretty common on the island.

"Don't leave me here," said Victoria.

I sighed. "Come on."

By the light of the candles we made our way upstairs. I could see the light of a torch and Manuelita flashed it in my face as I came upstairs, "Nombre de Dios!" she said.

"Silence, auntie," said Victoria in English. "It's only us."

Benji was sitting in the bath being soaped by his mum. He was enjoying being bathed by electric torchlight. He liked the candles too.

"Ok," I said, "I'm going to fix the generator."

"Ok," said Annie.

As I was going out onto the landing, Manuelita grabbed my arm and came part way with me.

"What?" I said tetchily.

"He has been here," she said.

That was the last thing I needed. "For the love of God, Manuelita, can you please keep all this shit to yourself?"

But she looked scared. Her eyes were wide. "I saw him. On the landing, just before the lights went out."

I shook my arm free. "I'm going to fix the generator," I said.

I WENT DOWNSTAIRS and back into the kitchen. There was a heavy-duty flashlight in a drawer there that would give me enough light to work. I wasn't relishing going out into the weather, but it had to be done. There were tools in the hut behind the house that housed the generator.

The wind howled, and the rain poured down as I went out of the door. At least the dog was quiet, I thought. I took a look at the kennel as I went past. Spot still wasn't there. If he had any sense, he'd found somewhere to shelter.

I made my way round to the hut. The door was banging in the wind. I shone the flashlight on it. It wasn't broken, just loose. Then I went in. The generator was dead. I checked the fuel. There was plenty. I tried to restart it but it nothing happened. I cursed. I kicked it. I had a basic understanding of how it was supposed to work, but that was it. I would need someone who actually knew what they were doing. It looked like tonight we'd have to make do with candles.

And so I turned back into the wind, bending almost double to make my way. Just to the side of the house, I stumbled over something. At first I thought it was a log, half hidden in the grass, but it was softer than that. I shone the light on it. It was Spot.

I knew at once that he was dead. A great rip of grief tore through me - my poor little dog. I leaned down and picked him up. He was heavy in my arms and he was still warm. He wasn't bleeding. In fact, I couldn't see how he could have died. He hadn't been struck by anything. There wasn't a mark on his body.

I hugged him to me and took him to his kennel. I placed him in it and wrapped his blanket around him, as if he needed it. I wished he would just have come and lived in the house then none of this would have happened. But he wouldn't — there was something about the house that scared him but it was outside that he'd died. I stood by the kennel. There were tears in my eyes as I said goodnight to my little buddy, and I promised I would come back for him soon.

I went back in by the front door. Everyone must still be upstairs, I thought. I took off my coat and with the torch still on; I mounted the stairs to the bathroom. They had obviously finished in there as it was empty. I turned and saw my own bedroom door was closed. That was weird.

I pushed it open and saw the three women standing there, wide eyed, and shaking with terror.

"What?" I said angrily.

"There was someone there," said Annie.

I would have expected this of Manuelita, but not Annie.

Victoria said, "We all saw it. A shape on the landing outside."

"Honestly, Howard. I'm really frightened," said Annie.

Manuelita was beside herself. I could see they really thought they'd seen something.

I tried to comfort them. "Listen, it's just the storm," I said.

Then Benji piped up, sitting there in his pyjamas; "It was Grandfather," he said.

Annie spun round. She was trembling so much I thought she was going to break down. "What did you say?" she said.

He smiled. "Grandfather. He lives in this house."

She grabbed him and put her hand over his mouth. "Don't say that my love. Please."

"Annie, this can't be what you think," I said. If I could only keep everyone together until morning, then we'd leave. If that's what they all wanted, we'd leave.

I closed the door behind me. And locked it.

"There," I said. "It's locked now. Let's just wait until daylight."

This seemed to calm them a little - as did me being there. The one thing I wasn't going to tell them about was Spot.

They decided that the three women would sleep in the double bed. Benji had his single bed, and they found me an extra blanket to cover me while I sat in the chair. They wanted to keep the candles burning, but I put all of them out except one, so we didn't run out of light. I also had the flashlight beside me.

As we sat there in a nervous silence, Victoria and Manuelita holding hands for comfort, the storm raged outside. At times, the wind was so wild that I feared the window would come in. Time went on. I saw that Benji had dropped off and also Annie. Manuelita was the last to fall asleep, she kept staring up at me with her eyes wide as a spooked horse, but eventually these too grew heavy and closed.

It was all too crazy, but it was late and I was emotionally exhausted. My head too began loll. I don't remember falling asleep but I must have. When I snapped awake, the candle was nearly dead. It was just a flickering yellow flame in a pool of wax on the saucer I'd stuck it to. The three women breathed rhythmically from the bed, Manuelita's breathing deepening to a slight snoring. I lifted my head up and looked for Benji.

His bed was empty. Where I'd expected to see him, there was only an indentation and disturbed bedclothes. I jumped up. Annie stirred at my movement.

The door was open. I hoped to God he hadn't gone sleepwalking.

All the women woke suddenly and looked around them.

"Benji's gone," I said. I could hear the panic in my voice.

Victoria said, still half asleep, "He's probably sleepwalking again."

Annie turned on her. "Sleepwalking? Since when does he sleepwalk?"

Victoria was quiet.

"Apparently he does," I said. "I'll go find him."

But memory had jumped up and snared Annie. "No!" she shrieked. "It's happening again."

I had to focus on Benji. I could comfort Annie later.

"I'll come too to look for Benji," said Manuelita.

"You don't have to," I said, but I was glad of any company. Victoria sat up in bed and swung her legs out. She bent over Annie who was sitting hugging her knees and rocking. The tears were running down her face.

"Victoria," I said. "You look after Annie,"

"Vale", she said. "Sure."

Manuelita and I made our way out of the bedroom onto the landing. She held onto my arm for dear life.

"Upstairs," she said. "He always tries to go upstairs."

So we went up the stairs to the floor where Victoria's bedroom was. There was no sign of Benji. Then I saw that the door to the attic was open.

Manuelita saw it too, and I thought her grip was going to break my arm. We went to the bottom of the stairs and I heard voices. I could hear Benji's voice. He was talking to a man. It was definitely a man's voice. I felt my stomach turn over.

Manuelita suddenly sobbed and started reciting the Lord's Prayer in Spanish. I was shaking, but I had to go up. I heard the sound of someone running upstairs from below. I turned and saw it was Victoria. "I heard my aunt," she said. "I thought something was wrong."

And then she too heard the voice of the man upstairs. Her face froze. Manuelita thrust her crucifix into Victoria's hand and then she fell down on her knees and began to pray fervently.

I took a step up.

"Don't go, Mr. Dougan," said Victoria. "That thing up there is from Hell."

"I've got to go," I said. "My son is up there."

I could still hear Benji's voice and the voice of Grandfather talking back to him. I mounted the stairs slowly. Each tread was an act of will, my body shrieking against where I was sending it. But I had to go to my son. To her credit, Victoria came up behind me. And as we reached the top, I saw that Benji was sitting there in the middle of the attic, sitting on the knee of a sinister old man. They both turned to me.

"Get off my son!" I screamed.

I could see Grandfather's teeth were filed to sharp points, and his eyes were black. He looked like the burned soul of a warlock when all the human flesh is stripped off. And the strange thing was that Grandfather was soaked; water ran off his drenched clothes.

"Get the hell off my son!" I roared, but I still couldn't force myself to step forward. And as Grandfather met my eyes. He was pure evil.

Benji didn't even look at me. He was playing with a toy train that Grandfather had given him.

And then Victoria screamed at that wicked thing. Whether she was cursing him with the most foul words she knew, or whether she was calling holy names to drive him away, I couldn't tell.

I ran forward and covered the ground between me and Benji. Victoria was holding up the crucifix like a weapon.

I grabbed my son, and I held him in my arms. When I looked up, the thing was standing in the corner of the attic, and, with its foul mouth, it smiled at me — then it vanished.

Victoria came to me and stroked Benji's head, muttering and crying. I held him as tight as I could. I thought I'd never let him go. Slowly and carefully I made my way down the steep attic stairs, Victoria behind me. Manuelita was there at the bottom. When she saw Benji was safe, she wept and thanked God and the angels for his deliverance.

We all stood there feeling such relief — such a sense of liberation.

Then I said, "Where's Annie?"

In our rush upstairs we'd forgotten that Annie was still in the bedroom.

I handed Benji to Victoria, and ran downstairs. When I got to our bedroom, Annie wasn't there. I was in a blind panic. I started shouting out her name. Manuelita and Victoria followed me down, still with Benji.

Benji said, "I know where mummy is."

I turned to him. "Tell me where she is Benji."

He nodded wisely and said, "She's with Grandfather."

I felt terror like I'd never know. I ran downstairs. The front door was banging in the wind. The rain had come in. I looked out into the howling night. Without putting on my coat I ran out the front of the house. I needed to find my Annie.

And I did find her.

I found her face down in the frigid water of the lake. She was soaked and her hair streamed out on the turbulent waves. I went into the water, up to my waist and I pulled her out. The water drained from her mouth and lungs, but she was already cold. There was no hope — she was dead.

And then I understood. Finally, after all these years, 'Grandfather' had come back to take the second twin.

16

THE MALLERSTANG BOGGLE

I'm nearing old age now and no longer live in Cumbria, but I remember the hot summer of 1976 with its drought and swarms of ladybirds. A funny thing happened to me that year.

Before that, I suppose I thought all spirits were ghosts, and that ghosts were the remnants of dead people, if I thought about it at all. But I'll get to that.

Let me begin at somewhere near the beginning. My name is Malcolm Ellwood. I now live in Newcastle upon Tyne, but I was born and brought up in Kendal, which at that time was in Westmorland. In 1974, just before this story they merged us with Cumberland and parts of Lancashire and Yorkshire to become the new county of Cumbria, named after the ancient kingdom.

My father and mother had a caravan in Mallerstang, and I hope I don't offend the (few) residents by describing Mallerstang as a bleak and remote valley that leads from Cumbria into the Yorkshire Dales. But my old mum and dad loved it, mainly my dad really — my mum wanted to go to Spain. But he never listened to her, and we went every year to that caravan which was parked on what was in essence a farmer's field with basic amenities. We stayed every summer for six weeks and if Easter wasn't bad, we'd go there for two weeks then as well..

I was about 12 then and still happy with fishing with nets in the becks and wandering over the fells and camping up there with the old tent my dad got from the Scouts. It was so hot that year; we swam a lot in the Eden too.

My friends were Alan Tremble from Penrith and John Mossop from Kirkby Stephen. Their parents had caravans there as well and the grown-ups spent the evenings drinking gin and tonic and playing card games while we went on our bikes and made dens.

Pendragon Castle lies in the valley. They say that it was the castle of Uther Pendragon, father of King Arthur, though the ruins of the existing castle only date from Norman times. Who knows, maybe King Arthur's dad lived there before that.

One night, we camped in the ruin because Alan thought it would be spooky. We pitched our four-man canvas tent with rope guys and wooden pegs that you had to hammer in with a mallet. I remember the ground was rock hard because of the drought and the mallet hurt my hand.

We set a fire and sat round sizzling pork sausages on forks tied to bamboo sticks with string. Often the string would burn through and the fork would drop with the sausage into the flaming wood and we'd have to pick it out with fingers or sticks. Gritty sausages caked in red-hot cinders never did me any harm.

Alan told ghost stories while me and John Mossop laughed at him. Then we grew tired and simply sat. The shadows grew long around the castle ruins. Cows grazed not far away among the reeds by the river and owls hooted from the trees. It was still warm.

I wasn't sure I believed in ghosts. If you'd asked me, I would have said I didn't, but that airless night, sitting by the dying fire, my actions might not have matched my words. I wasn't scared exactly, but I wasn't happy either. Alan had been telling a story about a drowned woman's spirit coming from the dead. I didn't believe him, but I kept looking towards the river.

Then we went to bed and crawled into our sleeping bags. They slept. I didn't. I just had that image of a woman coming out of the river. I heard Alan and John's breathing. The night was so hot; I climbed out of my sleeping bag. Owls called across the valley: kwik kwik went the males, and the females answered: hoo hoo.

But there was something else out there too. Something moved among the trees. At first I thought I was imagining it. I held my breath so I could hear better, but it didn't help that there were two people breathing loudly in the tent with me. Whatever it was, it was close. My heart started beating fast. I had images of this woman coming from the river for me — that she would snatch me from the tent, while the others slept. I was on the left-hand side, by the tent wall. She could just reach under the fly-sheet and drag me out. I shuffled closer in, but I couldn't get away because John was there. He muttered as I moved into him but didn't wake.

Something was moving around the ruins. It wasn't a bird in the trees; it was something on the ground. Something heavy footed.

I froze with fear. It was close now. Maybe it was a cow. Maybe it was a badger, but there was no snuffling noise, it was more like a pecking — like something pecking the ground. That was weird. More than weird, unnervingly scary. It came closer, pecking, pecking, pecking. What the heck pecked?

Then something took hold of the tent, like grabbed it. It ripped the canvas up, like a knife, waking Alan and John instantly who cried out in sleepy terror.

"Jesus, what the hell?" Alan said.

John rolled away. The tent was cut open and more than that, lifted up and thrown away. There was no moon, but the stars sparkled like thrown diamonds in the sky above. And against them was a huge black shape. It was no woman; it wasn't even human.

I jumped up and ran. I fled out of the ruins, across the fields. I crossed a fence. I don't even remember crossing it but I must have. I didn't look back for the others; I was so terrified. I got to the farm and the three caravans. There were no lights on anywhere, and only now, with no one after me and my heart finally slowing, I turned to look back for my friends.

"What the hell was that?" John said. He was first back. Alan appeared as a shadow before I answered. Not that I had an answer. "I don't know," I said.

I knocked sheepishly on the door of the caravan and my tousled mother answered. I gave some excuse about the tent ripping which she looked puzzled about but didn't question. My dad did though the next day. We salvaged the tent from the castle ruins and he ended up stitching it back together. He presumed we'd been messing about with knives because something had sliced the canvas open. He wouldn't have believed the true explanation, so I didn't tell him.

"It must have been a lunatic with a knife," John said.

"Or a sword, maybe?" Alan said.

"A machete,' John nodded. "That's it."

I shook my head. "Did you see the size of it?"

They both went quiet.

"What was it then?" John asked.

"I don't know," I said.

"I'm not camping there again," Alan said. "I'll stay in the caravan."

I said, "With a blade like that it could cut through the caravan, anyway."

News of us ripping the tent apparently spread because we were on our bikes up by The Thrang two days later when we came across Billy Boustead. Billy was a labourer on one of the farms by Shoregill. I have no idea how old he was then. He'll be long dead by now though. Billy was cutting down ragwort in the fields. He was simple and the farmers just gave him little jobs and paid him pocket money so he could buy beer and fags. He knew us well from all the summers we'd spent there. We stopped to drink some bottles of Coke we'd brought with us.

"Tent got cut, eh?"

Alan and John ignored him and kept drinking. I could never ignore him. He was a nice enough bloke. There was no harm in him.

"Aye," I said.

"In the middle of the night, down by the castle?"

"Aye, that's it." I thought he would say something about us messing round with knives again, but he didn't.

"That'll be the boggle," he said. "Did you see it?"

Alan and John looked round. "Let's go. He's an idiot," Alan said.

I was interested though. "What do you mean, the boggle?"

Billy laughed like it was us who was slow. "The boggle. The boggle that haunts the ruins."

John said, "I thought a boggle was something up your nose."

"What do you mean, a boggle?" I called to Billy.

He laughed again. "You don't know what a boggle is?"

I shrugged. "No."

"Well, it's a spirit."

"Like a ghost?" Alan said.

"No." Billy grimaced like Alan was really thick. "It's like a big thing. It's always been there."

"What are you talking about, Billy?" John said.

"The boggle that haunts the ruins," Billy said.

"You already said that," Alan said. "Come on, let's go." He got his bike ready to go, one foot up on the pedal ready to push off.

"It's a big black hen," Billy said.

"What?" Alan and John were laughing. "That's not scary!" John said.

But I remembered the pecking. A huge sharp beak could rip open a tent as easily as a knife. And the shape against the stars wasn't human at all. Just huge: huge and black.

I said, "A big black hen haunts the ruins? Why?"

Billy said, "It's not a hen, it's a boggle. It just takes on the shape of a hen. It could take on any shape it liked: a pig, or a column of sparks, or a big slithering blob."

"Come on, I've heard enough," Alan said, and started pedalling. John followed him, but I held back.

"What's it doing there, Billy?"

Billy tapped his nose. "You'd better get on after your friends."

"Tell me?" I said.

He narrowed his eyes, "It's guarding King Arthur's treasure. But don't tell anyone I said that. I don't want the Boggle coming after me."

"Will it come after you?" I said.

"Oh, aye. If the boggle thinks you're after the treasure, it'll come and kill you."

I gave him a long hard stare. He believed what he was saying, and I almost did too. Then he went quiet.

It didn't look like Billy was going to tell me any more. He probably didn't know any more to be fair, so I got on my bike and pedalled hard to catch up with Alan and John.

MY DAD HAD FIXED the tent. He used to have a boat on Windermere and had to repair sails, so he liked to show off his canvas repairing skills. He'd pitched it on the farmer's field within sight of the parents' three caravans. "Just to keep an eye on you," he said.

The three of us lads were outside the tent. John and Alan sitting and me throwing my sheath knife into a stump of wood. I told them about the treasure.

"He must mean King Arthur's dad's treasure," I said. "It was Uther's castle, not Arthur's."

"He doesn't mean anything," Alan said. "He's daft."

"I mean a huge black hen!" John laughed. "Come on."

"But what if there is treasure there?" I asked. I had just got hold of a copy of the Dungeons & Dragons rules and had been dungeon mastering it with some friends in Kendal. I liked the idea of finding treasure in a ruined castle, as unrealistic as it was. And I was a twelve-year-old boy of course.

"There's no treasure there," John said. "Someone would have found it already."

"Would they really?" I said. "What it it's been undiscovered all these years? What if we found it?"

Alan pooh-poohed the idea. John looked more receptive. "Well, we'd have to give half to the British Museum, but we could keep half as treasure trove."

I wasn't sure about the law but it sounded reasonable.

"You can't just go digging in a farmer's field," Alan said.

"Besides," John said. "It's a scheduled ancient monument. If anybody saw you digging, you'd get the police on you."

"And then you wouldn't get to keep the treasure," Alan said.

I pointed a victorious finger. "So you admit there could be treasure."

"I admit no such thing."

BUT WE WERE BOYS, and it was the summer holidays and we were in the business of adventures, whether it was wading in the beck among the duckweed looking for sticklebacks and frogs with our nets, or pretending we were Commandoes on a mountain warfare exercise.

I asked my dad for a spade.

"No," he said without thinking. Then he said, "Why do you want a spade?"

"Just do. For digging."

"Digging what?"

"Tunnels." It was the first thing I could think of.

My mother stuck her head round the caravan door from where she was cooking Chicken Fricassee. "You're not digging tunnels. They could collapse on you and you'd die."

"So, no," my dad said. "No spade."

BUT WE DIDN'T GIVE up. "There's some in the farmer's barn," John said. "I saw them."

"We can't steal them," I said.

"We wouldn't be stealing them," John said. "We'd give them back when we were done with them."

Alan nodded. "Exactly!"

So we stole the spades. There were two and a trowel. I got the trowel.

We stowed them in our tent under the sleeping bags while we drew up detailed plans for the treasure hunt.

It was midafternoon, and the sun was hot. We had more coke and mum provided three choc ices from the fridge in the van. When she was gone, we got down to business.

"I'm not camping there again," John said.

I thought of the huge shape and the cutting of the tent.

Alan looked scornfully at him. "Scared of the big black hen?"

"No!" John stared back.

"There was no hen," Alan said. "Don't believe anything Billy Boustead tells you."

"Then what cut the tent?" I asked.

Alan shrugged. "A branch. A broken branch that caught it in the wind."

"There was no wind," I said.

John nodded. "No. There wasn't any wind."

"There wasn't a big bloody hen either," Alan snorted.

I grunted. Alan pointed at me. "He thinks it was a big hen!"

John laughed too.

"No, I don't," I said, "But it wasn't a branch either."

WE WENT BY NIGHT. Worried about being caught digging for treasure in a scheduled ancient monument, either by the police or the farmer, we'd elected for darkness to cover our misdeeds. Mr Eilbeck who owned the land was a bad tempered old devil and if he caught us he'd beat us with his stick. Strangers could do that to kids then.

I was nervous.

"There's no hen," Alan said, as we set off, leaving the lights of the caravans behind and the grown ups playing Canasta and drinking gin.

I said nothing.

"There's no hen, Malcolm," he said again.

"Yeah, whatever you say."

He nudged me. "It was a stick. A sharp broken stick."

I said nothing but watched the shadows.

I had the foresight this time to fetch my father's big black rubber torch. I didn't switch on the beam yet. We were too close to the parents for comfort; them and farmers and policemen who might be lurking in the dark. Not to mention huge black hens.

We sidled our way closer to the broken walls of Pendragon Castle.

"Where do you think the treasure will be?" said John loudly.

"Whisht, man," Alan hissed. "Radio silence."

The walls loomed higher above us. The moon had come up which turned them white-grey and black. The shadows were thicker than India ink. The old limestone walls had a faint sparkle to them.

I gestured so we would walk round the wall. There was an entrance way still roofed that we could stoop down into and get through to the inner courtyard. The courtyard was grassed over now. I'd been many times before. But in daylight.

"Do you think it was a branch?" John asked.

"Of course it was a branch," Alan said. "What else could it be?"

We stood there hesitating before the dark mouth of the entranceway.

"Put the torch on, Malcolm" Alan said. "So we don't bang our heads."

"What about policemen?" John said.

"There's nobody here," Alan said.

And I listened. I could hear the River Eden gurgling by about fifty yards away. A slight breeze shifted the trees which rustled still in full summer leaf. Away to our right a sheep bleated, but that was that: no traffic noise, no aeroplanes, no sound of humanity at all.

I pressed the stiff button with my thumb and the torch light came on, its yellow beam sickly and weak but good enough to illuminate the rough entrance to the tunnel that would take us to the inner courtyard of the castle.

"Needs new batteries," John said.

"I know," I said. And I hesitated.

After a minute of me just standing listening for I don't know what: pecking, maybe? John said, "What we waiting for?"

Alan said, "He's waiting for the big hen."

"No, I'm not," I said.

"Then go on."

"Why do I have to go first?"

"Because you've got the torch." Alan's logic was as impeccable as it was irritating.

"Okay," I said, but I didn't.

"Go on!" Alan hissed.

I sighed, gathered my courage and stepped forward. I had to stoop to avoid banging my head on the uneven stones that roofed the passage. I guess this had been some kind of kitchen passage when the castle was functioning. It was pretty tumbledown now though.

I emerged first into the courtyard. There was nothing there, just stone and grass. I disturbed roosting crows who flapped into the air scaring Alan and John as they stepped out behind me. That made me happy.

Sickly moonlight bathed the courtyard. I had a trowel; they had spades.

"Dig here?" John asked.

"Aye, I think so," I said. "Start in the middle?"

The truth be told, I had no real idea of where we should dig and we could dig all night and find nothing, our plan was so harebrained. But I felt a thrill of excitement as I watched John turn the first sod. After a few shovelfuls he was breathing heavily. Alan stood with his spade idle, but I wanted a go.

"My turn," I said.

John handed me the spade, and I handed him the trowel. The trowel would be for when we found the treasure, to do the fine work of excavation.

I was digging heartily, when John said, "What's that?"

I stopped instantly. The moon still shone. All I heard was a vixen barking way off. "What?" I said.

"No, I heard it too," Alan said. "You were digging."

I had my hand on the spade. I'd managed to shovel a lot of dry earth. I hadn't heard anything. I wanted to dig more. I started again.

The moon went behind a cloud and I went to pick up the rubber torch I'd put down when I started digging.

Alan put his hand on my arm. "Listen."

I listened. I said, "I still can't—" but then I heard it.

"It's outside," John said. He meant outside the courtyard, through the tunnel. But something big enough could come over the walls too.

It was the pecking sound, I'd heard in the tent.

"What the hell's that noise?" Alan said.

"Pecking," John said. "Like there's something pecking at the ground."

Then the moon appeared again from behind the cloud. By the light I saw something metallic in the hole, at the bottom, covered by dirt. I said, "There's something in there."

"Stop," Alan said, "We've got to get out of here."

"We're safer in here," John said.

"What if it can get through the tunnel?" Alan said.

I picked up the torch and shone it. Something gleamed gold in the hole I'd dug. I knelt down and touched warm smooth metal. There was a golden plate, half buried, and coins. "Uther Pendragon's treasure," I said.

Then the boggle leapt the walls and landed in front of us. John screamed, Alan bolted for the tunnel out. I stood there petrified and shining the torch on the apparition in front of me.

It was a huge black hen the height of a giraffe but much wider. It had black shiny feathers and a red cockscomb that fell over itself. It had bright beady eyes and a yellow beak — a beak sharp enough to slice canvas, or my skin.

The hen lunged at me with its beak, but I darted sideways and then stooped and ran at the tunnel. More by luck than judgement I didn't brain myself on the stones. Panting, and wheezing with effort and fright, I shot out of the far side of the tunnel and ran from the castle, avoiding a low wall and jumping to land on soft grass. I turned and saw the huge shape of the hen clucking after me. I sprinted across the grass, hoping I wouldn't trip and got away from the castle. The hen was after me, then I jumped the narrow beck, mostly dried up by the long summer's heat.

And I fell. I was sure it would kill me, butcher me with its knife-like beak. But it didn't. I lay there cowering, my head down, waiting for my death. But when I didn't die, I turned. I rolled and saw the black hen with its black eyes watching me from the other side of the beck. I remembered something from old wives stories that spirits couldn't cross running water. That must be it.

As the black hen watched me, I stood up, spun round and fled. I didn't look back until I got back to our tent in the farmer's field. John and Alan were both there already.

Alan said, "We left the spades."

"And the trowel," John said. "Unless you brought it, Malcolm?"

I shook my head. "Did you see that?" I asked.

Both John and Alan remained silent.

"The boggle. The black hen."

"I don't want to talk about it," Alan said.

Whether it was for fear of ridicule or pure terror that such a thing could exist, we never spoke about it again. I went in the daylight to get the spades and trowels. They wouldn't come with me. There was no black hen. There was a hole where I'd dug, but in the clear light of the sun, there was no gold or treasure at the bottom of it.

And that was that.

Alan went to Australia and John died young of a brain haemorrhage. I never really saw either of them after that, because I got interested in girls and rock music so I stopped going to the caravan and stayed in Kendal with my school friends. Then I grew up and moved away.

. . .

I've been back to Pendragon a few times over the intervening years, but I never saw the boggle again. I'm not sure I'll return there now. Why would I?

But Pendragon Castle; that's where we used to meet — me and John and Alan — going on our bikes and fishing with nets and roaming the fells when we were young, at Mallerstang in the long hot summer of 1976.

ALSO BY TONY WALKER

Christmas Ghost Stories

More Cumbrian Ghost Stories

Further Ghost Stories

Haunted Castles

London Horror Stories

Horror Stories For Halloween